OMEGA SEED

ROSS RICHDALE

The search of a millennium is over. Computers aboard Inter-galactic Starship Omega find a planet with water and oxygen in usable quantities to sustain humanoid life. It is over populated, polluted and has one social problem; forty eight percent of the human population are males, well beyond the one in a thousand necessary on Planet Delta to maintain the sperm banks.

However, the humanoids aboard cannot be kept alive for the estimated two hundred years required to find another solar system so the journey must end. Minor alterations are needed in the humanoids' metabolism. The women need to understand English for a landing in Australia, the most unpolluted continent the computers can find. Sensations and emotions are changed back to natural; after all, a bearer needs emotions more than the neuter that these females were on the home planet.

It is time to arouse Pazz and prepare her for life on Earth while cloned younger sister Kylina, now 22 not 12 as remembered by Pazz, can be kept in reserve. There is also Lunol, from a primitive preindustrial planet and Kylina's partner but he is male and doesn't count.

Alone, with only an armlet computer for company, Pazz lands in the West Australian desert. She catches the Indian Pacific Express for Sydney, three days journey away but catches the flu virus. With no immunity she becomes seriously ill and is taken off the train at Adelaide. Doctor Duncan Bourne a linguist from The University Of Adelaide is contacted when nobody can understand her delirious speech. Duncan finds her speaking an ancient dead Greek language that he can understand. After she recovers, they become friends. Pazz adapts to life on Earth and, by having her qualifications entered into Earth computers, becomes Doctor Pazz D'rose, a mathematician and biochemist.

How does this affect Pazz, Kylina and her partner? Is Lunol rescued and how do the military on Earth react to having the alien humans in their midst?

National Library of New Zealand Cataloguing-in-Publication Data

Richdale, Ross, 1941-
Omega Seed / Ross Richdale.
ISBN 978-1-877438-18-9
I. Title.
NZ823.3—dc 22

Cover design by Ross Richdale

Published by
Purrbooks
Palmerston North
New Zealand

PROLOGUE

Except in size, Omega could have been a 1960s vintage NASA probe placed in an orbit around the planet below. The spherical intergalactic starship, though, was too large, being four hundred meters in diameter, too old and too advanced to have been manufactured on Earth.

The journey from the outer solar system to Earth took one week; this comparatively slow pace caused by rapid deceleration from ninety nine percent of light speed that had brought the craft across the galaxy. Computers board Omega homed in on what it had been searching for over the past millennium, a planet with water and oxygen in usable quantities to sustain life.

Cloaking devices made the craft's approach undetected as the vehicle swung into an orbit. The world below was penetrated with sophisticated data gathering probes, a hundred, three centimeter flying craft released into the stratosphere. These mechanical bugs plummeted into the planet's dense lower atmosphere until they reached a thousand meters altitude. At that point, tiny moving wings swung out like those of a dragonfly and minute motors propelled the craft towards predetermined targets.

The aim though was not to destroy but to observe and study everything about the planet, from its chemical makeup to signs of civilization. Languages were recorded and television monitored, photographs taken and the inhabitants studied. Within three days, ten million pieces of data were transmitted back to the mothership's three onboard computers before a signal pulsed out and the mechanical bugs self-destructed into nothingness. During the whole process, nobody below realized that their planet had been scrutinized by an alien life force, or that the spacecraft was still in orbit above. Everything worked as it was designed a thousand years before.

*

Computer Beta analyzed the data against the categories retained in memory banks. The planet was over populated, polluted but could sustain life quite comfortably in the less populated temperate zones; all the large land masses in the northern hemisphere were to be avoided but several to the south showed promise.

The humanoid population was similar to their own; in fact data gathered showed it was a home seeded planet from a previous visit, three thousand years before. Even a variation of the home alphabet was still in use in what was the cradle of civilization at the time, but Greek culture had long been superseded throughout the next three millennia. After being helped to climb the first step of a collective civilization by interbreeding with the local inhabitants; humans, for a reason lost in antiquity, were left to develop on their own.

There, however, was one problem that made Computer Beta reject the planet below. Roughly forty eight percent of the human population was seeders, or males as the dominant Earth language called them. This was completely outside the guidelines of no more than five percent seeders and well beyond the one in a thousand permitted at home. Furthermore, it appeared that none of the females of adult age were neuters so all were capable of bearing offspring, once again well beyond the guidelines of ten percent females necessary to maintain population size.

To balance this to some extent, was the knowledge that the inhabitants had not yet learnt to control DNA aging mechanisms, so the inhabitants had a limited lifespan, something like eighty years, less than one fourth that of humanoid's lifespan at home. All the data on human development led Computer Beta to recommend that this planet be bypassed.

However, Computer Gamma provided data that the humanoid aboard could not be kept alive for the estimated two hundred years required to find another solar system containing a planet harboring life, as they knew it. A vote was taken and Computer Alpha sided with Gamma to outvote Beta so the decision was made to arouse the humanoid.

There one was a perfect specimen, short at a meter seventy-eight with fair skin and blonde hair that floated in the vacuum to encircle the woman's body like a natural cloak. A life sustaining umbilical cord connected to her navel. In many ways she appeared like a fetus with the body of a twenty-year-old, her natural age being a dozen years beyond that.

Once the decision to end the journey was made, minor alterations were needed and Computer Gamma set about performing them. The woman had her brain patterns transformed to understand English, the main Earth language in the territory designated for landing. All other memories and abilities remained unchanged. Computer Gamma, though, persuaded the others that the humanoid's sensations and emotions should be changed back to natural, rather than being suppressed fifty percent as was the unwritten rule back home. After all, a bearer needed emotions more than the neuter that this female used to be.

4

Now was the time to arouse the woman so she could prepare herself for landing and her future life ahead. It was a crude hostile planet, not a great deal superior to their first choice that had been such a disappointment nor the others unanimously rejected, but it would have to do. They could not return and this was one small chance to continue the species. Communication with Delta had been lost over a century before so perhaps their humanoids were the last of their species.

*

CHAPTER ONE

The woman floated in the shower of warm compressed air as it blew away the last of the jelly substance that had protected her skin. She used electronic scissors to clip her hair to a manageable shoulder length, let the two-meter hair strands be sucked away, turned the machine to fluff and relished as puffs of warm air engulfed her. Finally, she glided out of the cleansing chamber and wriggled into a protective one-piece coverall ready for a bank of medical tests.

'You must speak orally in your new language, Pazz,' Gamma's voice in English filled the small outer room.

'I know,' she mumbled. 'You've been through this at least three times.' Her blue eyes rolled. 'Why do I feel so lousy?'

'Your emotions are not now artificially suppressed, Pazz. It's a combination of nervous anticipation and the vibrations of your stomach caused by the pitch and twenty percent roll of this space capsule and is further aggravated by...'

'Okay,' the woman interrupted. 'I understand.' She stared out the circular window at the blue and white planet below and sighed. 'Except for the continental shapes, it could be home.'

'But it isn't, Pazz,' cautioned Gamma. 'It's a primitive planet still controlled by males who make up half the population. I would advise you to research the history chips about our own gender wars. These have yet to happen on Earth.'

'Perhaps never will,' Pazz said. 'Anyhow, isn't that my reason for being here; to replenish our stock of seeders and return home.'

Gamma's neutral voice almost showed emotion as she spoke. 'That is not now possible, Pazz. You cannot return, either by yourself or with a cargo of seeders.'

'Why? 'Of course I can return home.'

'The journey took one thousand, three hundred and eighty six years, Pazz, not three.'

'What!' Pazz's face drained of color as she stared at the tiny silver speaker on the wall. 'I was sentenced to do this job instead of the equivalent seven years incarceration.'

'You were considered a problem, Pazz; too independent. Your push for individual rights and an increase in the seeder's population did not go down well at your trial. The proctors, barred by the constitution from sentencing you to death invoked Choice 23, Sub clause 6.'

'Banishment!' Pazz hissed.

'The controls of Omega were set to infinity with only Computer Alpha and life support systems active. Beta and myself were reactivated three hundred and eighty two years ago.'

'Why?'

'At that stage, Alpha had put us in orbit around a planet. She needed our assistance to analyze it. The place was unsuitable so we moved on. Since then three other water planets were deemed unsuitable, as was this one.'

'So why am I awake?' The young woman's eyebrows contracted in anxiety.

'Your body could not be maintained for the time needed to find another suitable planet. We voted two to one to place you down here.'

'So what happens?' Pazz gasped and realized for the first time in her thirty-two years of natural life, she was trembling with emotion and her eyes blinked tears. 'I am alone. Even if I went back, twenty generations would have past. Wouldn't it have been kinder to just shut down life support systems?'

'Choice 1, Sub clause 16 will not allow females to be terminated unless it is at their own request and they are over one hundred and twenty years of age. This cannot apply to you. Only males can be disposed of if they fail in their basic function of seeding the community.'

Pazz glared. 'That was a millennium ago. Our planet may not even exist any more, let alone still have the constitution.'

'It is in my program.'

'Yes, I forgot you're just a machine,' Pazz retorted and another suppressed emotion rose inside her. The feeling of loneliness. She thought back to her one sister, only twelve when she left, and her mother both smiling and relieved after her trial and light sentence. When the average lifespan was two hundred and forty years, seven was only a minor sentence. A far more severe charge would have been denial of access to anti-aging DNA leading to a life span of less than a century.

Pazz grimaced and switched her thoughts into the native language; English didn't have the vocabulary to represent the memories she had in her mind.

'One other item,' interrupted the computer. ' You are a bearer now, like your mother. Our collective decision was to make you one so you'd fit into Earth society. There are no neuters on Earth. For better or for worse, that is also the reason your emotions were fully restored'

'Thank you,' Pazz said. 'That is an honor I would never have reached back home; not with my sentence.'

'You are now one of billions of Earth women, the same in every way except you will have access to anti-aging procedures.

Pazz nodded. 'Not that that matters now, anyway. Is there anything else you failed to tell me?'

'Food and energy resources held within you would last fifteen Earth days after your arrival. When they are depleted, you will have to eat, breathe and exercise normally to maintain your body.'

Pazz smiled for the first time. 'That's a relief,' she added. 'I never liked the artificial food and muscle energizers anyway.'

' According to…'

'I know! I know! The constitution did not allow these to be withheld from me.'

'One last item. Males have equal rights on Earth, are stronger than the female and, in many cases are predatory creatures. Beware when you meet them.'

'I know,' Pazz retorted.

'You have never met one in real life,' the computer warned. 'Just be warned. They are not the docile creatures you learned about at home. They can be recognized by their facial hair though in most cases this is shaved off and deep voices. Clothes always cover their bodies. Unlike bearers at home, who were genetically selected to be of small stature, they are powerfully built. Most of them will be taller and heavier than yourself while the females will tend to be shorter than you are.'

The girl grimaced and once again stared out at the planet below. 'When do I land?' she asked.

'The site is selected and the landing will be during the night hours in three Earth days time, three point zero six Planet Delta days. The landing pod will put down in a lightly populated area so the chance of the landing being seen is minimal. It is a risk we have to take.'

'I have to take,' Pazz corrected. 'It is my life.'

'Yes,' Gamma replied. 'Sorry for the mistake.'

*

It was two in the morning when the 4X4 Landcruiser screeched to a stop in a cloud of red dust off the highway that was really just a strip of bitumen through rolling desert in the driest continent in the world; Australia.

'Oh Hell!' gasped Greg Blackburn and dug his sleeping companion in the ribs.

Stan Saunders woke up, grunted and stared out over the salt bushes reflected in the car's headlights. A silver cylinder was flying about twenty meters above the highway. That was it! There were no wings or tail, just this object like a drainage pipe with closed ends. Under it, two rows of small blue flames showed. As the men watched, three tiny landing skids unfolded from the craft, it wobbled to a hover before landing in a cloud of red dust a few meters to the side of the road.

'Kill your lights,' Stan gasped and reached over to where a hunter's rifle lay across the back seat. With shaking hands he fumbled in the glove box, found a carton of bullets and loaded the weapon.

'What is it?' Greg stuttered.

'How the hell would I know?'

Greg wound down the window and clapped hands over his ears. A high-pitched scream hit his eardrums with such velocity that his head rung, air swished around him and the vehicle shook. The craft was on the ground in swirling dust that pelted the Landcruiser like a dust storm. The blue flamed engines cut and the screaming whine groaned to a stop. Silence descended on the lonely highway as the swirling dust settled.

The man stared, wide eyed at his companion, nodded and slid outside. With Stan panting beside him, he bent low and ran along the roadside toward a small cutting. He flung himself down and crawled up the bank, parted the brush and fixed his eyes on the strange craft that now stood silently on tripod legs.

'That's no aircraft,' Stan whispered.

'No, it looks like an emergency escape vehicle. Perhaps it's something from that secret military base over in South Australia.'

The men studied the object in question. Except for protruding landing skids it was a perfect cylinder with no outward signs of windows or doors. It glistened in the dull moonlight like stainless steel but had a sort of intrinsic glow radiating out, like those cats' eyes that mark the center of the road. For several moments the men lay and stared. Stan gripped the rifle and aimed it up at the craft.

'And a lot of bloody good that'll do you,' snapped Greg. 'Keep your head out of sight, will you?'

'So what do you suggest?' Stan argued.

'Just watch!'

The men riveted their eyes on the craft and gasped in surprise as a hatch on the top lifted like on a jet fighter and a small ladder unfolded out over the fuselage to hinge down to the ground.

'Oh hell!' muttered Greg for a second time. 'Look!'

A light flickered on in the emergency escape jet, or whatever it was, and a girl rose behind the hatchway. She was, though, not dressed in flying clothes or wore a helmet, as one would expect. Instead, she was dressed in a suede jacket, tank top, jeans and brown calf length boots. A backpack was slung across her shoulders. For a second she stood and gazed around before stepping onto the ladder and descending to the ground. The men goggled in the darkness as her silhouette turned and she walked towards the road where the Landcruiser was parked.

When she reached the bitumen, the girl turned and stood with her hands by her side and watched the craft she'd just left. The ladder retracted, hatch closed and there was a whine as the engines started. The noise increased to the ear-shattering howl that had both men clamping hands over their ears again. The scream became louder and louder but the girl, seemly unaffected by the noise, just stood watching.

The skids folded up to be replaced by spurts of blue flames from beneath the craft. It lifted straight up like a helicopter, hovered for a few seconds, the screaming motors reached a still higher pitch, there was a slight clunk, a whoosh and it accelerated away faster than a skyrocket.

'Oh, my God!' gasped Stan.

One minute it was hovering above them, seconds later the aircraft was smaller than a white glowing tennis ball hundreds of meters up before the scream became a clap of thunder and it disappeared amongst the million stars overhead.

During the whole ascent, the only movement from the girl was her blonde hair wavering in the downdraft. Finally she turned and stared directly at the two hidden men behind the bank.

'I know you're there so you might as well come out,' she called in an unaccented Australian voice.

A flashlight flickered on and she bathed the area in light. Both men stood sheepishly up and Stan clicked a bullet up into rifle's barrel ready to fire.

The girl's eyes flickered for a moment when she saw the weapon. 'That rifle is hardly needed,' she said, 'I need a ride. Can you help?'

Greg grinned. She was a local girl, bloody good looker too. Probably that was some secret machine and she was an air force woman on maneuvers. He'd heard of them. They had twenty-four hours to get back to camp without being caught or spending any money.

'Put the rifle away, Stan,' he snapped. 'Come on. The poor girl needs a ride. That's why she landed near us. Let's go.' He gave Stan a knowing glance. 'You drive. Okay!'

'Sure!' Stan said.

*

Pazz swallowed bile as the new emotions surged through her body; fear, terror, loneliness, feelings akin to those she'd only felt before her trial back home. The landing craft lifted, slowly at first then accelerated into night air to self-destruct twenty thousand meters up. But the alien visitor wasn't completely alone. She fingered the gold armlet through the thin jacket and immediately Epsilon, the mobile computer responded.

'We are not alone,' the thoughts flashed into Pazz's mind in her home language. 'My sensors register two humans watching us from beyond that bank, not in that wheeled vehicle.'

Pazz stared out in to the darkness and focused her eyes. The darkness shimmered as her infrared eyesight activated and she could see the lighter shimmer of body heat behind the bushes.

'I know you're there,' she called in her new language and turned the flashlight on. 'So you might as well come out.'

'Caution,' warned Epsilon in her mind. 'They are seeders. '

'So what?' Pazz thought while she spoke orally about the rifle.

'We do not know if they can be trusted. That's all,' Epsilon replied. 'On this planet males are the stronger gender; they were on ours too before we won the gender wars.'

By now Pazz had reached the Landcruiser, a strange craft that still used wheels to propel it along. She'd seen one in a museum at home.

'What say we sit in the back while Stan drives,' Greg stated in a soft voice. He held the rear door open.

'No thank you!' Pazz replied. 'The front will do.' She opened the door herself and slid into the dark interior that stunk of a strange smoke and liquid. Greg shrugged and squeezed beside her.

'Take her away, Stan,' he grunted and the girl beside him noticed his sideways glance as the Landcruiser headed towards the settlement an hour's drive ahead.

'In the air force are you?' he asked casually enough. Pazz could sense his primitive emotions but jumped when a hand squeezed her leg.

'Epsilon,' she thought. 'I'm scared.'

*

'No,' said a strangely metallic voice and Greg's wandering hand was gripped and squeezed so hard in return he let out a stifled gasp of agony as it was thrust away.

'Who are you?' he grumbled in embarrassment as Pazz glared at him.

'I am Epsilon,' replied the same metallic voice. 'You do not touch Pazz.'

The girl suddenly blinked and the stare softened. 'Thank you. I'm okay now,' she said as if talking to herself.

'Who's Pazz?' the man grumbled but he was not physically touching her leg any more.

'I am,' Pazz said. 'Epsilon is my guardian angel, I guess you'd call her in English.' She kept her voice hard. 'There is a railway settlement a hundred kilometers or so ahead, I believe. Are you heading that far?'

'Yeah,' Stan replied. 'We can take you all the way. The cattle station where we work is further on, still.'

'Thanks,' Pazz replied and began to chatter away as if nothing had happened. Greg frowned for a moment before shrugging and joining in the conversation.

'Have you any money cards?' Pazz asked a few moments later and shrugged. 'Credit cards, I mean.'

'Sure,' muttered Glen, 'but why?'

' Could I borrow one for a moment. I'll give it back'

'Yes, sure,' Glen stuttered and reached in his pocket. He fumbled with his wallet for a moment and extracted a couple of cards.

*

'Thanks,' Pazz said when Greg handed the two cards to her and, in the darkness of the vehicle, discretely brought them up to touch the armlet.

'Got it,' Epsilon replied. "They should not be hard to duplicate but you'll have to bring them with you when we leave.'

Pazz pretended to study the name on the cards and handed them back. 'Thanks Greg,' she said and sat back to relax.

The journey was completed in fifty minutes. When the Landcruiser pulled in beside a motel lit by a neon light almost bigger than the building itself, Stan glanced at a sleeping Greg.

'This is the railway settlement. I'm not sure when the train comes through,' he said. 'I guess you know where you're going. I'll let you out my side. Old Greg there is sleeping like a baby.'

'Thanks' Pazz replied, slid across behind the steering wheel, smiled and watched as Stan waved, clunked the 4X4 into gear and accelerated off with wheels screaming in the dust. She felt like a thief as she poked the wallet she'd extracted from Greg's pocket into her backpack.

'You're too honest, Pazz,' replied Epsilon. 'You can always return it to the man later. '

'Yes, I guess.' She glanced around and, because to her English implant, could read the sign on the door. *Open 24 Hours. Please ring and enter.*

'Here goes,' Pazz whispered and walked into the motel.

Five minutes later she was in her very first Earth living quarters, a pleasant motel room with beds similar to at home except they were designed for two, running water and a hygienic toilet that used water to flush. For the first time in a millennium, the young woman had a drink of milk from the refrigerator and began to feel human.

'Pazz, ' communicated Epsilon as she lay under the sheet on the bed. It was too hot for blankets. 'Alpha, Beta and Gamma changed their mind.'

'How?' Pazz said as sleep almost overtook her.

' I can stay with you as long as you wish, not just two weeks. When I remain on your arm I can help you. Just keep me uncovered at times so the sun can recharge my batteries.'

'I'm glad,' Pazz said. 'Thanks for taking over and stopping that man.' she sighed. 'He made me quite scared for a moment.'

'You're a bearer now, Pazz, a woman. My memory banks tell me bearers back home often mated naturally with seeders.'

'It was illegal!' Pazz gasped out loud.

'I know but that's how you were conceived.'

'You mean my mother…' Pazz gasped.

'Yes. I was her computer too, remember.'

Pazz stared into the darkness. She never really knew Zandra, her mother. Affection between bearers and their offspring was seen as a weakness back home. Female babies were raised in community buildings, the closest English word would be an orphanage and the one in a thousand male child was immediately sent to offshore islands where seeders were allowed to live until they were required to replenish the sperm banks. Thinking back, Pazz realized it was only through her mother's determination that they had been allowed to live and grow up as a family; another Earth word that really had no corresponding one in their native tongue.

'I liked how the lady wrote your name on the register,' Epsilon interrupted and Pazz switched her thoughts back to her present situation.

Pazz picked up the invoice and grinned. 'I could hardly say my real name,' she said. 'It's unpronounceable in English and the literal translation of Fourth Flower would hardly fit so I picked an Earth flower and the fourth letter in the English alphabet. I worked it all out back on Omega.'

She read the woman's spelling, which came out as D'rose.

'Pazz D'rose has a nice ring to it,' she said. 'I think I'll keep it that way.'

'One other thing,' Epsilon transmitted. 'They call women Mrs., Miss or Ms and males just Mr. on Earth but don't ask me why.'

Pazz sighed. She had so much to learn but guessed her first encounter with humans hadn't come out too badly. With one hand touching the golden armlet, she drifted asleep and dreamed of home. It seemed like only the week before she was in that courtroom, not a millennium ago. The intervening time period was just too much to grasp.

*

CHAPTER TWO

It was after nine o'clock the following morning and the sun blazed in a cloudless sky when Pazz walked into the motel office with Greg's wallet in her hand. She assumed there was something that had to be done to pay for the use of the bedroom.

'Do you want to pay by direct credit?' the woman behind the counter asked in a casual voice.

'That plastic card in the wallet is a crude device similar to ours at home,' Epsilon's thoughts commented in Pazz's mind. 'Say yes but make sure you touch me against the instrument.'

'Yes, please,' Pazz replied, took a credit card from Glenn's wallet and handed it to the woman. Afterwards she casually removed the armlet and held it between her fingers so it touched the swipe machine.

The proprietress smiled, swiped the card and glanced at Pazz. 'Your pin, please.' she said.

Pazz frowned. Pin? Why would the woman want that small metal thing like a needle? She frowned and placed the armlet back on her arm so communication with Epsilon could be reestablished.

'Take the instrument and press in the numbers 5, 9, 0, 7, then "Enter",' the computer advised.

Pazz felt her face grow hot in embarrassment; another new emotion, but the card was accepted, the woman chatted away about nothing in particular and handed it back.

'I gave you a bank account,' Epsilon explained. 'The number I gave you is called a pin number so remember it. Hold the card against me.'

Pazz did so and grinned when she looked at the card again. The signature on it now read "Pazz D'rose" in her own handwriting.

'That's the best I could do,' Epsilon apologized. 'You'll have to practice writing it that way. It's a signature, a crude identification device. You're lucky there are no automatic eye identification computers on Earth. I've given you ten thousand dollars in your bank account. It should do for now.'

'Isn't that dishonest?' Pazz complained.

'Yes but would you prefer being destitute? Our credits from home are useless here.'

'I guess you're right,' Pazz replied but her conscience made her feel this was wrong.

'Remember, too, your inbuilt reserves run out soon? Everything on this planet costs money, even food,' Epsilon continued. 'According to a sign at that gas station outside air is free so I guess that is something.'

'So what now?' Pazz asked.

'Keep the money and card but dispose of that wallet. Buy a train ticket for a place called Sydney,' Epsilon replied. 'It takes several days by these slow vehicles but you can relax and watch the scenery.'

'Okay.' Pazz turned back to the woman.

'Could you tell me when the train is due?' she asked.

'East or west?' the woman replied.

'Sydney,' Pazz answered.

'That means you'll have to stay another night,' the motel proprietor said. 'Look, since you arrived so late and the sheets haven't been changed yet, I won't charge you an extra day. The Indian Pacific pulls in at quarter past four in the morning. If you like, we can wake you at three. We often do this for our guests. I also sell tickets if you wish to buy one.'

' Thank you for letting me keep the room,' Pazz said.' I would like a ticket. Can I pay with my card again?'

'Sure,' came the reply as the woman typed into her computer terminal. She glanced up. 'There's a holiday class twinette sleeper available. It's slightly dearer but well worthwhile if you want to sleep properly. You'll be sharing with one other woman who is getting on from here, too.'

'I'll take it,' Pazz replied and thought this Earth woman could easily be from home.

She walked into the small restaurant attached to the motel and was engulfed by the smell of food. Though her inbuilt supply still had days to run the scrumptious smell made her stomach growl, another new experience.

'Well, order something,' Epsilon suggested. 'If you eat food now, your reserves are just kept until later. I have a feeling you're going to like Earth food.'

'I'll use the proper money this time,' Pazz answered and took delight in having her first cooked meal on Earth followed by steaming coffee, a drink not unlike hot herbal drinks at home.

Afterwards, she walked up the street of the town. At over thirty degrees, it was hotter than at home but still quite bearable. The whole settlement consisted of the motel, gas station and general store, the railway station and an old wooden building with a row of vehicles parked in front and seemed to be filled with laughing male voices inside.

'Stay out of there,' warned Epsilon. 'My sensors pick up the same stench as in that vehicle you were in. I think it serves as a drug to lubricate a male's stomach.'

Pazz crossed the road and tried not to stare at the locals. Most of the few people around were males of all description; young, old, tall, fat, thin and there were even male children. They were all dressed for the hot weather with large hats to shade their eyes and seemed quite friendly. Several even caught her eye and nodded or commented about the weather. Of course, there were women around too, but not as many. Most were like her and could have easily been from home but others had dark skin. Once again it appeared as if Earth had not learned the art of changing color pigmentation so everyone was the same.

With the two genders and races all mixing together, this was a strange planet but Pazz felt an unusual excitement tingle inside her. Though primitive, Earth could be an interesting place.

'Buy yourself a watch,' Epsilon interrupted her thoughts. 'It tells you the time. You'll need it in the morning. Their method of measuring time is not difficult to follow.'

'Right,' Pazz said out loud, walked in the general store and was fascinated by the interior. She bought a watch with digital numbers and placed it on her wrist then noticed a clothing section with blouses and skirts, a garment unfamiliar to her but one she'd seen several woman wearing. In the hot weather it seemed a sensible alternative to the clothes she had on.

The woman serving her smiled and clucked around with suggestions and letting her try items on. Pazz ended up buying three colorful blouses, two skirts, a summer dress, underwear and two nighties. She guessed she would not have enough money so used her bankcard again. It worked perfectly but she still felt guilty.

'Don't worry,' chided Epsilon. 'Nothing has come out of Greg's account. I've taken thousandths of a cent off hundreds of accounts to create yours. Nobody will suffer. People speculate with money here all the time and many make millions by buying and selling money.'

'You mean they use other people's money to get rich?' Pazz asked. 'That's immoral.'

'At home, maybe, but not here,' Epsilon explained. 'Once you get settled and help these people you'll more than pay this amount back, anyway.'

'I guess,' Pazz muttered.

She walked along to a small building women were walking in and out of. A sign said *Women's Rest Room* and apparently men stayed out. Pazz went in and found a toilet and other small rooms. Another female was there changing a baby. Pazz smiled shyly when the woman began to chat. She would be in her mid-twenties, it was difficult to estimate Earth people's ages, was a little chubby, had short dark hair and warm eyes.

Pazz switched her eyes to the infant and suppressed a gasp. Something was wrong with her but straight away she realized the mistake. The deformity between the baby's legs was not that at all but male organs. The baby was a little boy.

'Lovely little boy,' she said and hoped the woman didn't notice her flushed face.

'Thank you. Jason's six weeks old now, aren't you, Sweetheart?' The woman grinned and held out her hand. 'My name's Lynn Kilmore. I guess you're waiting for the train, too.'

'Shake her hand, look into her eyes and smile,' Epsilon instructed. 'It's a sign of friendliness, here.'

'Pazz D'rose,' she introduced herself and followed the computer's instructions. 'Yes, I am going on the train.'

Lynn talked a while, said she might see Pazz later and departed. Pazz grinned and realized that the Earth people seemed friendly; even the males. She slipped into the toilet and afterwards headed back to the motel.

A feeling of excitement filled her body as she changed into new clothes. Soft material touched her skin and felt so smooth. She used a comb and brush, surprisingly similar to those at home, to comb out her hair. Finally, she replaced her hot boots with lightweight shoes she'd also purchased and packed everything else in the backpack. The computers had done a great job. This backpack looked identical to one she had seen in the shop.

'You look a beautiful Earthling; the clothes fit you well but you could do with a little make up,' Epsilon congratulated.

Pazz studied her reflection in the mirror. She knew the computer could pick up the images she was seeing, 'What's that?' she thought.

'Didn't you see Lynn paint her lips with that red tube? It's called lipstick.'

'Is it a skin protection?'

'No,' replied the computer. 'The woman brightens their lips and skin to look more attractive. They also wear little ornaments attached their ear lobes.'

'Well,' Pazz said as she walked into the tiny kitchen to put the kettle on. 'We'd better buy some hadn't we? I'm going to be on this planet for quite a while so might as well begin to look like an Earth woman.'

*

When the Indian Pacific Express glided into the station with it's front light cutting a searchlight through the hot darkness, Pazz felt nervous in anticipation. She watched the green and yellow diesel engine sweep by with a rush of wind followed by carriage after carriage, most in darkness but a few with lights shining inside. After the eighth carriage, Pazz stopped counting but instead concentrated on the letters showing. She was in carriage "J", Berth 6, which she had been told was near the center of the train.

Finally the massive mechanical monster stopped and a conductor stepped down from the carriage immediately in front of Pazz and smiled at her.

'Welcome aboard the Indian Pacific, Madam,' he said and examined her ticket. 'Please follow me.'

He picked Pazz's backpack up and waited for her to step aboard. She found herself in a long narrow, pleasantly lit and surprisingly cool corridor with a painting of a massive bird along the interior wall.

'That's the Wedge-Tailed eagle, the symbol of our train,' the conductor explained. 'Tomorrow morning just after daylight you may see one soaring over the desert.' He stopped and held a door open. 'I took the liberty in lowering the sleeping birth ready for you. Can I get you a coffee before you settle in?'

Pazz smiled, walked in and inspected the tiny compartment. It reminded her of one in a starship. She sat on the bottom bunk just as the train started again and the lights of the tiny settlement disappeared in the darkness. A moment later the conductor reappeared with another passenger.

'Hello again!' It was Lynn, the woman Pazz had met at the rest room. 'We are sharing. I hope you don't mind Jason. He's asleep at the moment.' She hoisted the carrycot onto the bed and glanced at her ticket. 'Blast, I've got the top bunk. That'll be a bit hard with Bubs here.'

'Well, swap,' Pazz said and stood up. 'I don't mind the top bunk.'

She felt quite pleased to have someone she'd met before, no matter how briefly. Lynn chatted away and by the time the conductor returned with two mugs of coffee they were like old friends.

'I once shared with a grouchy old bag who moaned all day and snored all night,' Lynn laughed after they'd both settled into their bunks and the lights were turned off. 'I'm glad I have someone like yourself.'

'Me too,' Pazz smiled into the darkness and gazed out the windows at the stars. Somewhere up there, Omega was orbiting around and further away still but probably too small to see, was her home star, just called *The Light* in English. Her planet, the fourth one out was named Delta, the fourth letter of their alphabet and strangely enough one still used, according to Epsilon, by a few Earth inhabitants. Pazz wondered how many other home items survived on Earth after three thousand years.

'Are you a long way from home?' Lynn's voice made Pazz jump in fright.

'Yes,' she said. 'A long way.'

'I'm returning to Sydney after four years in Perth...' she rattled on until they both women grew tired and Pazz lapsed into sleep.

She dreamed of her family and sister and woke disorientated. The light below her was on and she glanced down to see Lynn breast-feeding the baby. The sight made her feel all warm inside; these new emotions she was now exposed to came and went all the time. It was as if she was alive and living for the first time. Thoughts of meeting males switched to the thrill of feeling soft new clothes against her skin, the excitement when the train arrived and now this young Earth woman feeding a male child.

'I hope Jason didn't awaken you. He howled a bit.' Lynn said when she realized Pazz was gazing at her.

'No, not at all,' Pazz replied. 'Do all the woman here breast feed their infants?'

Lynn smiled. 'Half in half. I'm sort of weaning Bubs but will keep feeding him for a while yet. Why do you ask? You're Australian aren't you? You sound like one.'

Pazz flushed in embarrassment. What a stupid question she had asked!

'Tell her you're from Auckland, New Zealand. It's a country nearby and their accent is quite similar.' Epsilon helped.

'Auckland, New Zealand,' Pazz stuttered.

'Fair enough,' Lynn replied. 'Nice place.'

Pazz grinned. With her computer's help she was managing to fit into her new environment quite well. She chattered awhile and drifted back to sleep. The sun rose flooded the Indian Pacific Express with daylight when Pazz awoke.

'I thought you'd never wake up,' Lynn smiled at her. 'I brought you some breakfast. The dining car closed at nine.'

'Nine,' muttered a sleepy Pazz and glanced at her new watch that said nine thirty. 'I'm sorry. I guess I didn't realize how sleepy I was.'

'It doesn't matter,' laughed Lynn. 'There's not a lot else to do.'

Pazz glanced at the breakfast on a little tray Lynn was holding. It smelt appetizing and she realized she was hungry again.

'How do you do it?' Lynn asked a few moments later as Pazz finished munching her third piece of toast, poured out a second cup of coffee and added sugar and cream.

'Do what, Lynn?'

'Eat! You eat twice the amount I do and look at you; slim as a film star. If I ate like you I'd be as chubby as an elephant.'

Pazz flushed. She enjoyed the food but never really thought of it affecting her weight. Back home, food was automatically impregnated with additives to prevent one becoming overweight. Pazz frowned. That was how women were kept as neuters, too. Additives in the water supply suppressed female hormones and it was only by providing a neutralizer that women could become bearers and later have offspring after being artificially fertilized. Of course they had to be genetically pure and of good moral character to be allowed to breed. Everything was controlled.

That was why she was arrested in the first place. Even in her lifetime, individual freedoms were becoming more and more suppressed. She had been foolish enough to speak up at a university seminar, someone had reported her to the constabulary, and she was arrested for fanning flames of hatred against the common good, as the charge sheet read.

'You're deep in thought,' Lynn stared at Pazz. 'Is there something I can help you with?'

'No,' Pazz said and smiled faintly. 'Just family matters.'

'Yeah I know,' Lynn replied and her face turned serious, too. She stared out the window. 'That's why I was in that little town. I sneaked off the train there three days ago in an attempt to escape from James.'

Pazz waited, as it seemed Lynn wanted to talk.

'My husband and Jason's father...' She screwed her nose up. 'I just couldn't stick it any longer so took Jason and cleared out. I was sure he knew I was on the train last Tuesday and I reckoned he'd fly across to Sydney and find me when the train arrived. My parents are in Sydney but they don't really understand.' She shrugged. 'There's really only Jason and myself.' She grinned and glanced out the window at the desert flashing by. 'But you don't want to hear my moans, do you?'

'Why not?' Pazz replied. 'We can't keep everything in our body, can we?'

Lynn smiled. 'No, I guess not. You say the funniest things at times, Pazz but I know what you mean.' She turned and gazed outside again. 'Look!' she gasped and pointed.

Pazz followed her glance and saw a massive black and white bird soaring high above the desert. 'The largest eagle in the world,' explained Lynn. 'The Wedge-Tail Eagle like the painting in the corridor.' She sighed. 'Oh, to be free like him.'

'Yes,' Pazz replied. They had birds at home, too but she'd never really related them to freedom. She glanced at her companion but the mood was broken when the baby woke up crying. Lynn lifted him in her arms. 'He's got a rash, poor wee thing,' she said.

'Can I hold him?' Pazz asked.

'Sure, but I'll change his napkins first.'

Pazz watched while the job was completed and, moments later cuddled the little boy in her arms. He was so perfect and dependent upon his mother. She found tears in her eyes as she kissed the soft cheek and handed him back. Lynn looked at her intently, smiled but said nothing.

'God, we're getting melancholy,' Lynn laughed. 'Come on let's go for a walk along to the lounge car. I know you've just had breakfast but I'm ready for morning tea.'

Pazz laughed too. 'Sure,' she replied. 'That's a grand idea.'

*

The pair were sitting in the lounge car when a conductor came to their table with a telephone in his hand. 'Mrs. Lynn Kilmore?' he inquired.

'Yes,' answered Lynn and her face drained of color.

'There is a telephone call from Sydney for you, Mrs. Kilmore.' He handed Lynn the instrument. 'Just press three to receive your call. I'll return to get the telephone later.' He gave a slight bow and walked away. 'It'll be my husband,' Lynn whispered in a distressed voice. 'I know he's flown across to Sydney. I don't want to talk to him.'

'Are you sure?' Pazz asked and Lynn nodded miserably. 'Okay, give it to me.'

Pazz picked up the unfamiliar instrument, pressed the three and put it to her ear. 'Good morning. This is the senior administrative officer on the Indian Pacific Express. Can I be of assistance?'

'My name is James Kilmore and I was informed my wife, Lynn is a passenger on your train. Could I speak to her please,' came the reply

Pazz nodded at Lynn. 'I am sorry Mr. Kilmore but Mrs. Lynn Kilmore cannot be located at the moment. She is not in her apartment nor the dining car.' Her eyes met Lynn's who indicated with her fingers she was doing the correct thing.

'Wait one moment,' Pazz continued. 'I have a message coming up on my computer.' She paused. 'Yes, here it is. Apparently Mrs. Kilmore decided to break her journey and left the train in the township of Cook. I believe she will be continuing on the next train through.'

'Damn!' the male voice continued. 'Have you a forwarding address? It is rather urgent.'

'There was no address, Mr. Kilmore but Cook is only a small town. Perhaps if you give me your message, I'll send it to Cook Railway Station and they may find her.'

'Thank you. Just say James is trying to contact her and she should ring her parents in Sydney.'

Pazz repeated the message with her eyes on Lynn who nodded. 'I shall forward your message through to Cook straight away, Mr. Kilmore. Thank you for your call.'

She handed the telephone to Lynn who pressed the disconnect button and gave a tiny smile. 'You're a wonder, Pazz,' she said. 'Thank you. My God, how did he trace me here?'

'I guess that wasn't too hard,' Pazz responded .She glanced at Lynn's apprehensive face. 'Why are you staying away from him?' she asked.

Lynn picked Jason up from the carrycot he was lying in and cuddled him. 'He's ten years older than I am, a prosperous businessman.' She bit on her bottom lip. 'About three months after we were married he began beating me. That's three and a half years now. Even when I was pregnant he would beat me over the slightest pretence. He gets insanely jealous and accuses me of flirting at anyone who comes near but it is all in his mind. Finally, I could stand it no longer. 'Look!'

She pulled back the sleeve of her blouse to show several dark bruises on her arm. 'There's more,' she whispered. 'Oh, he was crafty and never hit me on the face. Afterwards he always apologized and said he would never do it again. For a while I believed him but the beatings became worse.' Her eyes watered as she looked at Pazz. 'I must say he has never hurt Jason. I guess that 's something.'

'So what are you going to do, Lynn?'

Lynn shrugged. 'I was going home but my parents are so old fashioned they think I should stay in the marriage.' She shrugged. 'Mind you, if Dad knew of all the beatings he'd stick up for me. I've got money so that's no problem. I think I'll just try to disappear once I arrive in Sydney. It's a pretty big city, as you know.'

Pazz didn't but smiled and considered her reply. 'Would you like to stay with me? I have no attachments at the moment. I was just going to the big city to look for a job. I spent a few months working on a cattle station,' she lied and hoped her face didn't look guilty.

Lynn though seemed too worried about her own affairs to notice the slight quiver in Pazz's voice. 'I'd like that Pazz,' she said. 'Even if it's just for a while until I can get settled. What about Jason? Won't he be a nuisance?'

'Not at all,' said Pazz. 'I love babies.'

'You're doing well, Pazz.' Epsilon's voice entered her mind. 'By her facial expressions and voice tone, I would say Lynn is quite genuine. You sure heated up when you told those lies, though. Don't be so self-conscious.'

'Hush up!' Pazz snapped back in her mind and smiled at Lynn. 'Good, we stick together then. Agreed!'

'Agreed,' Lynn said and reached across to take Pazz's hands in hers.

'I notice you have a bottle for Jason,' she said. 'Can I feed him when it's time?'

'Sure,' said Lynn. 'Anytime. Change his napkins, too if you wish.'

'I might just do that,' Pazz replied and smiled into the baby's round eyes. 'You'll have to show me how, though.'

*

CHAPTER THREE

Pazz would have been horrified had she known that in a different part of Omega, separated by half a dozen airlocks, a young man was unintentionally brought out of suspended animation, too. He was a human, every bit as much as Pazz was but came from another world, known only on intergalactic records as Planet 38675.6, a place perfectly suited for human life but inhabited by a pre-industrial civilization.

Lunol Pendlf had managed to care for him reasonably well, considering he had no knowledge of the computer's language or how to operate electronic equipment. Now, clean, with his hair cut short in the style he was used to on Custronomus, his home kingdom, he was still self-conscious about the strange clothes he'd been left to wear.

Worse, though, he was worried about Kagit, his woman companion who had brought him to the sky ship. In a world of sailing ships the idea of a space ship was almost beyond his comprehension.

'Oh Kagit, My Love. Where are you?' he muttered in Custron, his native language as he walked down yet another semicircular corridor and ignored the computer voices. He couldn't understand their language anyhow. He glanced around. This corridor was identical to the others except for one thing. It was painted a pale orange, not light blue. Good, at lease he wasn't walking in circles like the last time. He did not know but he was on the spinning layer of Omega just below the outer skin so an artificial gravity made it just like home.

He came to an airlock and opened the tiny notebook Kagit had left him. She had tried to explain what to do when he awoke and had listed all the possibilities in her neat handwriting. For really the first time, Lunol appreciated learning how to read as he thumbed through the notes.

"The computers will not understand you," she had written but had included a few basic commands in her language, "but most equipment has a manual over ride." Lunol searched further down her list until he came for directions for opening this steel door; an airlock Kagit had called it. He read the details and glanced at the door. Yes there was a row of buttons. Now, he had to push the red and blue ones together.

'Okay,' he muttered and pushed them. The computer's voice droned out an incomprehensible command but the door slid back.

Lunol smiled when he recognized the interior. This was one of the control rooms he'd been shown when they had arrived on board. He stared up and gasped. Across from him, a gigantic television screen was playing. From his friend's earlier description he knew this moving picture showed something happening somewhere else on or outside the ship.

At the moment it showed a massive planet just like his own with blue water, various colored landmasses and white polar sections. He consulted his notebook, walked up to a console and pressed another manual override button. The scene immediately changed to the interior of Omega; the room he was in, actually. He could see himself at the control panel. He pressed other buttons and different scenes appeared on the screen. Good, now he could try to find Kagit.

For twenty minutes he flicked through the images of electronic machinery, corridors, rooms, storage bays and more closed pods like the one he'd awoken in. There were also voice comments in Kagit's language and written information, once again in an alphabet that he could not comprehend.

Suddenly he saw her!

'Kagit!' he called. She was in a huge barn type room climbing into a small rescue pod. He could see her brown hair and when she looked up, he was sure her eyes looked directly into his.

He watched, fascinated but was also very worried as mechanical arms closed the pod and two massive doors slid open to show black sky and thousands of stars outside. The tiny craft floated in the chamber for a moment, flames burned and the craft accelerated away. A shiver of apprehension went though his body. She had gone and left him behind! Why would she do this?

He just sat staring at the scene that, without being touched, had switched to show a view of the Earth coming closer and closer. Of course, he was now seeing the view from the rescue pod. For almost an hour he watched, fascinated, until he saw darkness on the screen, there was a slight vibration and rocks and sand could be seen in shimmering red light. Suddenly she was walking in front of the craft, turned, sort of smiled and the view vanished. Kagit was safe somewhere on the world below but Lunol still did not understand why she had not waited for him.

'Damn!' he cried out loud. This was not like her. She would not just abandon him; not after everything they'd gone through. Perhaps she wanted to explore the place first and would come back. He decided to wait a few days before making any decision about what to do and shrugged. There was not much that could be done, anyway. This ship was far beyond his understanding.

*

On the morning of the third day, once again the artificially created days and nights were beyond Lunol's understanding; the computer spoke to him.

'Good morning, Lunol,' said a female voice. 'I am computer Alpha. We have been recording your voice and have developed a rudimentary knowledge of your language over the last three Earth days. You seemed distracted and distressed. Can I be of assistance?'

'It's Kagit,' Lunol replied. 'She's landed on that world below but has not returned. I'm worried about her.'

'I know of no name Kagit,' the computer replied. 'Perhaps in our language she has a different name.'

'I saw her on the moving picture screen.'

'That would be Pazz,' the computer replied. 'She is safe but will not return to Omega.'

Omega, Lunol knew, was the name of the ship.

'But why?' he gasped.

'She did not know you were aboard,' Alpha replied. 'She thought she was alone on Omega.'

'I see,' Lunol nodded and stared around the bunkroom he'd been using. Of course, if she thought he was dead that could explain everything.

'Can I follow her?' he asked.

'It will be difficult. You lack much of our scientific knowledge and may not survive the journey to Earth. Even if you do, we can not protect you there in the way our human is protected.'

'Why not?'

'You have not had the transplants necessary.' Lunol blinked. He did not understand what Alpha meant. 'We can however, provide you with clothing, food and water as well as a tracking device which could lead you to our human. Beware though, the distances are great and the temperatures far higher than in your country. Wouldn't it be better to stay on Omega? We could contact our human and tell her of your safe condition.'

Lunol, though, shook his head. 'I can't stay here for ever,' he said. 'No, I'd like to follow her.'

'Very well,' replied Alpha. 'We shall prepare a landing pod. The journey down should be safe but we'll give you some basic training in case anything goes wrong.'

'Thank you.' Lunol replied.

'Now we understand each other you only need to speak anywhere in Omega, we will hear your instructions and help if we can.'

'Good,' Lunol replied. 'Give me time to get dressed and have

breakfast then you can show
'That sounds a good idea, Lunol,' the computer commented and went silent.

*

Over the next week the impatient Lunol was given intensive training by the computers on safety procedures with the landing pod, basic knowledge of the English language and desert survival techniques.

It was decided, for various technical and cultural reasons not to provide him with a powerful computer armlet. After all, he was a male and therefore could not be completely trusted nor considered intelligent enough to handle such sophisticated electronics. Instead, Alpha downloaded a more basic computer named Sigma from her archives. Sigma could communicate orally rather than by direct thought waves. She could convert oral and written language and had been programmed with a basic moral code and empathy towards her owner. Also, a homing device linked with Epsilon was included.

As an extra precaution, Sigma was programmed to obey their own electronic commands or Lunol's voice patterns and had other self-preservation programs. The computer was given a female voice and had the ability to initiate speech if it was considered necessary and could respond with Earthlings who spoke to it. Though antiquated by Delta standards, Sigma was still many generations superior to computers monitored from Earth.

After studying Earth television broadcasts, Alpha's mechanical arms made Sigma into the shape of a four centimeter high stylized koala bear which could hang around Lunol's neck with an authentic looking leather cord. The workshop also produced a realistic backpack that contained extra clothing, first aid, high-energy food pellets, and a jerrican containing several liters of water. Though looking authentic by Earth standards, this was another advanced piece of equipment that could convert the driest of atmospheres into water droplets. With care, therefore, his water supply would be constantly replenished.

On Lunol's last night aboard, Alpha, Beta and Gamma had another electronic conference about their charge. The fact that he was a seeder, a male, from a primitive planet was a concern. Their memory banks showed that Pazz had made no reference to this man. In fact all the time Omega was orbiting his home planet she was in suspended animation.

'We should research the other humans still asleep on board,'

Gamma suggested. 'They may provide information.'

'We have only one back up human left,' Beta noted 'She is required if this planet is unsuitable and Omega has to continue her search elsewhere. Human Pazz is our prime objective for our protection. What if this seeder attempts to harm her? She still needs many weeks to adjust to Earth society.'

'We could put this man back into suspended animation,' Gamma added, 'but I would prefer not to keep him aboard.'

'Australia is a large continent.' Alpha added. 'I suggest we land him in a remote place so it takes him many weeks to find her. It will show his intentions, too. If he is genuine in his effort to seek her out, and I believe he is, this will be a true test. If not, he can just blend into the Earth society and will be no different from the other millions of males on the planet. '

The vote on Alpha's suggestion was unanimous and a spot many kilometers from Adelaide but not so remote that the man would not survive, was selected .The landing pod would arrive an area away from but within walking distance of inhabitation. In line with all inter-computer decisions, Lunol was not informed of his fate but only told the journey to Earth would take place the next day.

Lunol grinned that evening when he was shown the equipment manufactured for his use. He slung the necklace on and jumped in fright when the computer began speaking in his own language.

'Hello Lunol,' it said. 'I am Sigma, your companion down on Earth. To communicate, just speak to me. Okay?'

'Sure!' the man answered and wondered what to ask. 'When will we land?'

'5.45 a.m., Central Standard Time, in the cooler hours of the morning,' Sigma replied in a slightly metallic voice. 'I would advise six hours sleep before you leave so you are in peak physical condition for the descent. We leave Omega at 5.00 a.m. and the journey will last forty five Earth minutes which is equivalent to 27.1 of your own minor time units in the Kingdom of Custronomus, your homeland.'

'You are precise.' Lunol smiled and gazed in excitement and some apprehension out the viewing port at Earth that now only showed as a black gap in the star strewn space. A small crescent of red and yellow showed where the sun was hidden as Australia was in darkness.

*

During its traverse of the galaxy, Starship Omega had been struck several times by rogue meteorites, ranging in size from that of a pea to one spinning chunk of rock as large as a golf ball. The self-sealing hull, though damaged, defected the meteorite and a sticky white paste squeezed through the outer hull puncture and solidified. However, one tiny slither broke off the rock, became embedded in the fracture and lay there for centuries doing no harm. However, the final firing of engines to slow Omega into its Earth orbit vibrated this fragment loose. Interior air pressure pushed it out and, without a sound, for there is no sound in the vacuum of space, a cloud of life sustaining air began to escape and instantly vaporize like a long thin cloud of white beside Omega.

'We have a fracture,' Beta electronically reported mere hours after Lunol's departure. 'Air is escaping at a faster rate than it can be replenished. Unless stopped, all human and plant life aboard will cease to exist in a time span still to be determined.'

Pazz was safe on Earth but unknown to her, after she had be put in suspended animation above Planet Delta, one other person had sneaked boarded Omega and persuaded the computers to allow her to go on the journey. Unlike Pazz she was awakened above Planet 38675.6 and spent many years there before Omega continued the journey through the galaxy. This time, Pazz and Lunol were both brought back from suspended animation and were now both on Earth. This third human, in the computer logic of being kept as a backup; even in suspended animation, needed air to stay alive. Computer Beta diverted her resources to resuscitate this last human, Alpha attempted to repair the hull and Gamma used the dwindling resources to increase the air supply. Whether Omega's computers could repair the fault before all life aboard ceased was possible but the mathematical probability was low; too low unless someone else could help.

*

Hundreds of kilometers north east of Adelaide, a young man lay exhausted and dehydrated under a small mound of rock while insects ran over his blistered swollen skin as if to add the last insult in his effort to stay alive. It was almost three weeks since Lunol had landed and in all that time he'd met nobody.

'Wake up, Lunol,' Sigma the talking computer urged. 'It's late afternoon. You have survived another day and another liter of water has been replenished in your jerrican. You can take a few more mouthfuls of drink.'

Lunol squinted in the harsh glare. His eyelids felt like course sand

and the fire in his throat was every bit as bad as when he had the plague back home. At least he could breathe. He grunted, thrust flies away from his face and threw sand over his legs at the hundreds of small creatures that seemed to be everywhere. Finally, he unscrewed the top of the jerrican and took two sips of water and swished the precious liquid around his mouth before swallowing. His tortured body screamed for more but he methodically screwed the top back on and wiped his sore eyes.

The Earth had no sign of humans but it did have life; insects. Sigma said the word in English. There were some birds in the mornings and evenings and slithery reptiles that looked highly poisonous. The land was red and covered in thorny bushes, the sky cloudless with a yellow sun and blistering heat, worse than any he had experienced. He staggered to his feet and attempted to walk, grimaced in pain, as needles seemed to shoot up his legs and muscles knotted. He collapsed back into a sitting position again.

'I think you have to reconsider your previous decision, Lunol,' Sigma spoke out.

'What now!' retorted the man but gave a mental grin. Without the computer's continuous talking and advice he would not have lasted into the week.

'Take off your boots and socks.'

'I'll never get them on again,' he argued. 'With bare feet I wouldn't last another day.'

'The medicinal ointment in your backpack is designed to replenish blistered skin. Apply some and rest until evening. It's only 2.3 hours until sunset.'

Lunol sighed but reached forward and undid the laces of his boots. With a grunt of pain, he removed one and then the other. The socks beneath stunk of perspiration and filth but with infinite care he rolled them off and examined his feet for the first time in three days. The heels were red and swollen but the skin unbroken. However, the underside consisted of several wide watery blisters and his toes were swollen and bruised with blood blisters under the nails.

'I need some of the herbal cures from home,' he muttered as he stretched and relaxed his toes in an attempt to restore circulation.

'Use the tube with the red label,' Sigma advised.

'Okay, you little know it all,' Lunol grunted, pulled his hat down lower, bent forward and squeezed the white antibiotic out. It was also an anesthetic and the pain began to subside. When he had finished he wiped his hands, arms and neck with the cooling paste and felt better.

'Time for dinner,' he joked, swallowed the third to last energy capsule and washed it down with one more mouthful of water. The stuff was tasteless but at least it was liquid.

'Now bind your feet with bandages before insects are attracted to it and put clean socks on,' Sigma said. 'Rest up a couple of hours and at sunset we'll be on our way.'

'We,' retorted Lunol. 'Why couldn't you grow legs and carry me?'

'I am not programmed to do that but assure you my additional weight does not sufficiently handicap your effort to walk.'

'Yeah, I know,' Lunol grinned and began wrapping a bandage around his right foot. 'Damn fool of a computer.'

'I perceive that's a joke, Lunol,' Sigma replied.

'Yeah, you're learning my little friend,' he sighed, swished flies away from his face and continued doctoring his feet.

*

CHAPTER FOUR

With the air supply depleted, the battle for life aboard Omega was being lost. All plant life had expired but the human, still in suspended animation, was clinging to life in a landing pod with its own separate air supply. By diverting air from the remaining pods there was enough for sixteen Earth days, five if the human was aroused and active. However, with no air there wasn't any heat. All liquid froze and with it, the back up electricity supplies. The computers now relied on solar energy but this was only available when Omega was in daylight, only half the time.

Calculations were made. There was enough energy to awaken the human and provide her with life support or to safely control the landing pod on its trip to Earth, but not both! Outside help was required but this could only come from the unsuspecting population below.

The human would be kept asleep as long as possible and the planet contacted. There was Pazz, or even Lunol, but an approach to them was rejected as they had no resources and knowledge of the plight aboard would hinder their own welfare.

Earth's electronic resources were monitored. One nation alone, the United States had the capacity to help but would they? Evidence showed males ruled the nation and therefore suspect, but perhaps a little subterfuge would be successful. It was a gamble but mathematically possible.

A decision was made and acted upon. For five seconds Gamma switched off the cloaking device, time to be seen but not for their presence to be confirmed. If the Earthling's curiosity was raised they just might come up and check.

*

Throughout the day and into the evening the *Indian Pacific* continued along one of the world's longest railway journeys, past occasional settlements, many named after Australian politicians, but mainly through empty desert. During Pazz and Lynn's evening meal they passed through Pimba where one of the train directors commented that the Indian Pacific was traveling near to Magaroona, a top secret military installation which was part of the United States Air force Early Warning System.

'Are they looking for visitors from space?' Pazz asked Lynn in a hushed voice.

Lynn was about to laugh when she saw her friend's serious face. 'They trace Russian and Chinese satellites, but nothing from other worlds, if that's what you mean. I remember reading about a giant radio observatory in America that is trying to find signs of life in outer space. They haven't found any yet.' She shrugged. 'I guess they wouldn't tell us if they did.'

'Pazz,' Epsilon interrupted. 'I don't think our landing was traced, if that's what you're worried about. The Earth tracking devices are quite crude and, even if they saw us, we would have only been recognized as a meteorite. However, I'll probe the atmosphere for any signals if you wish.'

'Only receive,' Pazz warned. 'Don't transmit anything to Omega. We don't really know their capabilities.'

'Will do,' answered the computer and went silent.

Lynn watched Pazz. 'You're deep in thought again,' she said. ' Are you having an argument with yourself?'

'No,' Pazz said. Lynn was quite observant. This was the second time she'd noticed her communicate with the computer. 'Just curious about things, that's all. It's so huge and empty out there.'

They finished their meal, put their watches forward an hour and a half to the new time zone and retreated to their compartment to chat and relax before their bunks were pulled down for a second night ahead.

It was dark when Pazz woke up feeling terrible; her head and whole body ached, throat aflame and her new nightgown was soaked in perspiration.

She was hesitant about switching on her bed light, as Lynn and the baby were both asleep so used her infrared capabilities to see in the darkness. Suddenly her heaving stomach could hold back no longer. She was about to vomit. Luckily, she made it across the small compartment to the tiny corner sink before she heaved and spewed up the evening's meal. She turned the tap on, washed the vomit away and was about to drink a small tumbler of water to clean the taste out of her mouth when the room began to spin.

The feeling was quite terrifying as viral and bacterial diseases had long been conquered at home and Pazz had never been ill in her life before. She grabbed the sink top to steady herself and retched into the sink again but felt no better. Even with her eyes shut the world spun and purple blotches appeared in the blackness.

'Lynn!' she gasped. 'I don't feel too well.'

'I can't help,' Epsilon's thoughts came through. 'It's no known disease.'

But Pazz never heard. She tried to step across to reach Lynn but failed and collapsed unconscious to the floor.

*

Lynn woke from a deep sleep and could smell the vomit. Thinking it was her baby she immediately switched on her bedside light but saw he was in a peaceful sleep. Seconds later, she found Pazz lying on the floor with blood pouring down her floral nightgown.

'Pazz!' Lynn cried in alarm, leaped out of her bunk and bent down by her companion. Pazz had obviously vomited but the blood came from a cut chin. She grabbed a towel, wet it and wiped the other woman's face but, except for a low moan, there was no response.

'Oh My God!' Lynn wailed as she continued to wipe the damp towel over her friend's forehead. She realized help was needed and pressed the emergency summons button.

'My friend is ill,' she explained to the conductor who arrived a couple of moments later. 'She vomited and collapsed but I can't wake her up.'

'Right,' the conductor replied and talked on his mobile phone before turning on the main compartment lights and bending down to examine the passenger. He grunted and pulled a blanket off the top bunk to wrap around her 'A doctor will be here soon,' he said in a professional but kind voice.

'Thank God,' Lynn replied. 'She was fine last night.'

Another man in a dressing gown and the inevitable leather bag appeared. 'I'm Doctor Alan Meehan,' he introduced himself, knelt down beside Pazz and immediately began an examination. 'We'll need to take her to the infirmary,' he said. 'She has a high temperature, racing heart and cannot breath properly.'

Lynn wiped a hand down her nose in frustration. Already Pazz had turned purple and her whole body was shaking almost in convulsions. The doctor strapped a small oxygen mask around the patient's face and injected a sedative in her arm.

'You were correct to call me,' he said. 'The injection should slow her racing heartbeat while the oxygen helps her breath.' He frowned. 'It's almost as if she is suffering from altitude sickness but that's impossible. We're almost at sea level.'

He glanced at the conductor. 'Have you a stretcher?'

'Yes, it's already on its way,' the other man answered.

When Pazz was wheeled along through to the train's mini hospital, three carriages away, Lynn gathered up Jason, grabbed a dressing gown and followed.

Dawn was breaking by the time Pazz opened her eyes and focused on a worried Lynn. She still felt terrible but at least the room wasn't spinning.

'You've had a bad turn and are in the infirmary, Pazz,' Lynn explained. 'The train will be arriving in Adelaide at six and an ambulance will take you to hospital. A doctor on board the train has been helping. He's talking on the phone to an Adelaide hospital at the moment.'

Pazz attempted to smile but felt violently ill again and vomited in a basin Lynn held under her mouth. 'I'm sorry, Lynn,' she said. 'This has never happened to me before.'

'It's not your fault,' Lynn answered and stood back when Doctor Meehan returned, gave Pazz another injection and clamped back the oxygen mask.

'Just relax, Pazz,' he said kindly and held a hand under her head. 'I think the worse is over.'

'Thank you, Doctor,' Pazz replied. She gave a tiny cough and slipped into unconsciousness.

*

For two weeks, Pazz lapsed in and out of a semi-consciousness state. She noticed pale blue walls, tubes in her arms and nose and could hear her own racing heart. At other times, Epsilon communicated and encouraged her. She saw strangers in white coats and Lynn, always Lynn talking to her, reading to her. Sometimes Jason was on the bed too while, at other times, her friend was by herself. Perhaps it was a hallucination. She knew she was in a hospital and Lynn would be on the train traveling to Sydney so how could she still be with her?

Finally in the dark early hours of one morning she awoke and used infrared vision to see a man sitting in a chair by her bed. She reached across, clicked on a light and noticed his deep gaze. Pazz trembled and clutched at the bed blankets.

'Hello, you are awake, Pazz? I did not realize' said the man in a soft voice. 'You're in the Royal Adelaide Hospital and I'm Doctor Duncan Bourne. I'm an associate professor of languages from the university, not a medical doctor. Your condition has been brought to my attention.'

'It's stupid having the same title for two completely different occupations,' Pazz replied. 'We don't.' She flushed and immediately regretted her words but Duncan Bourne did not seem to have noticed.

'It appears from all the tests given to you, the virus you caught was a strain of flu that is quite common in Australia at the moment.' he said and picked up a clipboard from the end of the bed. 'Are you well enough to talk or would you rather I left you to relax.'

'Where's Lynn? I know she was here.' Pazz asked.

'We sent her home at midnight. I believe she is staying in a motel near the hospital,' the man replied. 'She's a good friend; old school mate, is she?' He raised an eyebrow.

'Sort of.' Pazz realized she was safe and wiggled into a sitting position. She felt hungry but otherwise quite normal.

'What brought me into your case was not your reaction to this virus, which was interesting in its own right.' continued Doctor Bourne. 'Normally, after a couple of days, a person's natural immune system would control the virus and the patient begins to get well. In your case, your bloodstream became flooded with antibodies but none of them had any affect. You just became more ill.'

He gave a frown. 'We almost lost you and would have if it wasn't for a powerful drug still being researched.' His eyes gripped Pazz. 'You speak English without an accent yet you're not originally from Australia, are you?'

'How do you know?' Pazz whispered.

'In your semi conscious state you called out and talked in a foreign language. One of my colleagues recorded your voice and sent me a copy. The language you were speaking fluently is what is known as a dead language.'

'That's impossible,' snapped Pazz.

'Steady,' warned Epsilon. 'Think before you talk, Pazz.'

'Sorry,' Pazz replied out loud and flushed when she realized the university professor thought she had spoken to him.

'That's fine,' he replied. 'Sure you don't want to rest?'

'No,' Pazz said. 'I'm interested.'

"The language you spoke was traced back to the Aegean area and is believed to be a subgroup of Classic Greek. Nobody has spoken it for a couple of thousand years. I doubt if more than fifty people worldwide can understand it.'

'But you can,' Pazz replied.

'Not really,' said the man. 'I've studied some of the ancient written text but cannot speak it. From my research, it appears to have influenced Classic Greek, rather than the other way around.'

'I think you are mistaken, Doctor,' Pazz replied. 'I come from

Auckland, New Zealand. I know a little Japanese and German but that's my limit of foreign language knowledge.'

'I see,' said the man, 'Can you explain therefore, why your lungs were smaller in size than a comparable woman of your age?' He shut one eye and frowned. 'You're in your late twenties, I'd guess. Part of the reason you were so ill was that you were suffering from a diminished oxygen intake. It was as if you were visiting a high altitude country such as Peru in South America but we're at sea level. Furthermore, during the last week, your lungs actually expanded to be normal size. This has never happened before.'

'I did that for you,' Epsilon interrupted in her mind. 'You were suffocating.'

Pazz ignored her computer, as she was more concerned with the man's conversation. 'I have nothing to say,' she gasped in fright. 'You cannot force me. I know my rights. Australia is one of the most democratic countries on Earth.'

'Is that why you chose it?' Duncan said in a soft voice.

Suddenly, tears built in Pazz's eyes and she turned away. 'I'm a threat to nobody,' she whispered.

'I guessed that,' Duncan replied. 'That is why I have kept my research into your language confidential. I told everyone it was your Greek ancestry. We have many Greeks in Australia,' He smiled. 'Though I must admit there are not many with blonde hair and blue eyes. Perhaps I should have said you were from Sweden.'

'Why bother?' Pazz retorted.

'Shall I go?' the man asked. 'It is three in the morning.'

Pazz blew her nose and almost smiled. 'No, I can sense you're genuine,' Epsilon had just suggested it to her but she could not admit that. 'Please stay. I would like a cold drink if it is at all possible, though.'

'Sure,' he replied and reached over to a jug of lemon juice on a side cabinet, filled a tumbler and handed it to Pazz.

'Do you want to hear more?' he continued.

'Yes,' replied Pazz. She sipped the lemon juice and studied the man. He looked about her own age, had a scruffy hair growing on his face, was tanned and not what she would imagine an academic to be like at all. Actually, she really had no idea what a male academic should look like.

'We received some top-secret information from the local air force headquarters. An unidentified flying object was traced to that town where you boarded the *Indian Pacific*. A local jackaroo admitted giving a woman a ride to the town. He muttered away about an alien woman landing in the desert, hitching a ride and stealing all his money. His friend denied this and said they'd only given a Royal Australian Air Force officer a lift to the railway.' He searched Pazz with his eyes. 'However, the air force said there were no maneuvers in the area at that time and reported no missing personnel.' He leaned forward. 'One of them was lying,' he added almost as an afterthought.

Pazz nodded. 'And you think the woman was me?'

'I have an open mind, Pazz,' Duncan replied. He coughed and changed the topic. 'Tell me, what academic qualifications do you have?'

'None that would be recognized,' Pazz replied and again regretted her reply.

'Equivalent to what, then?'

'About yours,' admitted Pazz after a moment so Epsilon could advise her on what to say. 'Physics, biochemistry and quantum mathematics actually. I did an eight-year degree that you'd call a Ph.D. but I'm saying no more.'

'Would you like a job?' Duncan abruptly added.

Pazz frowned. 'What?' she asked.

'It would only be an assistant's job at the university but the pay is quite good. Later, we could possibly credit you for your knowledge, though I imagine you are far ahead of us in that aspect. If you walk to the other side of the hospital, the buildings you see across the road are part of the University of Adelaide where I work.'

'Careful,' warned Epsilon. 'He seems to have worked out you're not from Earth.'

'Just on your hunch?' Pazz said to Doctor Bourne.

'Everything I said is confidential between us, Pazz. If you wish to tell me nothing, so be it. I'll respect your confidence. That's a promise.'

'Can I think about it?'

'Certainly. If you don't mind I'd like to visit you tomorrow,' he said and glanced at his watch. 'Well, later today, actually.'

'For a male you're okay,' Pazz said. 'I would enjoy another visit. Thank you, Duncan. Can I call you that?'

'Please do,' Duncan said. He seemed to think about her comment for a moment and repeated it 'For a male,' he mumbled and scratched his hairy chin. 'Interesting! I'll take that as a compliment. Take care. See you later,' He gave her shoulder a slight squeeze and walked out.

Pazz stared after him with mixed emotions but found she liked the man. He seemed honest and considerate.

'Yes, I think so, too,' muttered Epsilon. 'However, if you don't object, I'd like to stay around a bit longer.'

'And I couldn't do without you,' Pazz said. She fluffed up her pillow, lay back and let her mind think of Earth, her new home. The place had possibilities.

*

It was eight in the morning when Lynn appeared with Jason on her hip.

'Pazz, ' she cried in excitement. 'Nobody told me you were awake!' She rushed up, placed Jason on the bed and hugged Pazz. 'It's been three weeks. I thought you'd die. My God, I prayed for you. The doctors gave up and said it was in his hands.'

'And how are you, Lynn?' Pazz asked.

'I'm okay. James hasn't been able to trace me.'

'But why are you here?' Pazz pushed.

Lynn grinned. 'Well someone had to look after your backpack, didn't they? Adelaide's a pretty nice place and I got sick of the train.'

'Thanks, Lynn,' Pazz said. 'The doctor examined me this morning and said I made an amazing recovery; the flu has gone and my lungs are clear. Apparently when the flu got into them they caused all the trouble.'

The other woman stared at her. 'Don't lie, Pazz,' she said. 'It was far worse than that. My God, there were doctors everywhere and that guy from the university, too.'

'Duncan, you mean?'

'Yes,' Lynn replied. 'Seems a pleasant enough chap.'

'He offered me a job at the university,' Pazz volunteered.

'Did he?' Lynn said. 'I wondered why he was hanging around. You got a degree?'

'A bit of one,' confessed Pazz. 'Enough to get an assistant's job, I guess.'

Lynn frowned. 'There's something strange about you, Pazz,' she said. 'God, I was frightened when you were babbling in a foreign language.'

'My grandfather was Greek,' Pazz lied. 'He taught me the language. We always spoke it at his place. I guess I must have been dreaming about him. He only died last year.'

'Yeah sure,' Lynn replied with her eyes on Pazz. 'So this professor of ancient languages sits here for hours listening to you talking Greek that he could hear at a restaurant anytime downtown.'

'Oh Lynn, bare with me a little longer,' Pazz whispered. 'You're my only friend, you know. I have nobody else.'

'Okay,' Lynn said. 'But if you want to talk, it will go no further. Anyhow, do you want to hear my news?'

'What news?'

'I bought a house in the suburbs and I want you to move in with Jason and myself.'

'Are you sure?'

'Yes. I told you I had a bit of money. It came from my grandfather.' She laughed. 'He wasn't even Greek. If I don't spend some, my scheming husband will only get his hands on it.'

'But you hardly know me.'

'No I don't but the part I do know, I like. Anyhow, if you have a job, we can share living costs, unless of course, you want to keep going to Sydney.'

'No,' laughed Pazz. 'I don't know anything about Adelaide but I don't know Sydney either.'

' ...Or Auckland, New Zealand,' Lynn added.

Pazz felt her face burn. 'No, I've never been there either. I lied about that.'

'Who cares. You know, Jason's eating solid food now, just a little.'

'He's grown.' Pazz said and reached out to cuddle the baby gazing at her. 'I'm sure he recognizes me. How are you, Sweetheart?'

Jason gooed and gave a wee cackle when Pazz swung him up in her arms. She felt strangely happy when she glanced at the baby and on to her friend. It seemed as if she'd known them for ever, not just a few weeks; days really if she took off her time in hospital.

*

During Pazz's extra week's stay in hospital she experienced a huge range of emotions that fluctuated from hour to hour. When Lynn visited with the baby, Pazz felt relaxed and contented; the friendliness of her human friend seemed to rebound inside her. Afterwards, though, she felt lost and lonely; thoughts retreated back to home and her mother without reason it seemed she'd find herself in tears. Depression, common in the hospital began to grip.

'It's quite natural,' Jenny, one of the night nurses said late the next night. 'You've been through quite an ordeal, Pazz. Often a patient recovers physically far quicker than their emotions do. I'll get a sedative for you.'

'No,' Pazz replied. 'I want nothing artificial. I'll cope.'

Jenny must have noticed Pazz's determined expression for she smiled. 'Okay,' she replied. 'Look, it's late. I've finished my rounds and aren't due to go off duty for an hour so how would you like to just talk.'

'I'd like that,' Pazz said. 'Tell me about Adelaide. The view out the window is so beautiful but I don't know the city at all.'

Jenny sat on the bed began to chat about her city, a place she seemed very proud of, while Pazz relaxed again. Her eyelids grew heavy and she fell asleep.

Duncan visited daily and Pazz found her feelings towards this male was different from that towards Lynn or Jenny. She could not explain it but her first fears and defensive stance turned to an eager anticipation of his late morning or early evening visits.

'It's because he's a male,' Epsilon diagnosed when they were alone. 'Think of a magnet. Opposite poles attract. It's the same when humans live together naturally. Our planet was like this six millenniums ago, about the time of the great space discoveries when our ancestors visited Earth. It was only after hundreds of years that the conflicts started, then the overthrow of dominant males and finally the gender wars. I think Earth is taking a better track.'

'And that is?'

'Equality. On Earth now, most women can control their lives and are considered equal to men. On Delta, perhaps we went too far.'

'But we were told males are barbarians,' Paz argued.

'Is Duncan or even those young men who gave you a lift barbarians?' the computer asked.

'No,' Pazz whispered. 'They were okay and Duncan is like Lynn. I'd call him a friend.'

'So your heart beat races when he walks in the room?'

'Hell, I don't know,' snapped Pazz. 'Switch off!'

Like calling the computer's name in an emergency, this command worked like the power switch on an Earth computer. Epsilon's presence immediately died and Pazz was by herself again to just think.

'Hello,' said a well-known voice and Pazz swung around to see Duncan standing there with a bunch of roses. 'I thought you'd like some flowers.'

The fragrance reached Pazz's nose and her eyes lit up at the wonderful Earth flowers. 'Duncan, they're wonderful. Thank you.' Her eyes met his. 'Nobody has ever bought me flowers before.'

'Nobody?' Duncan replied quietly. 'I find that hard to believe. Don't they have flowers in your homeland?'

'Duncan,' Pazz answered. 'You're slipping in a question again. We agreed you wouldn't.'

She reached for the flowers and her fingers touched his. For a second an emotion shot through her, she felt a tingle inside and pulled back in alarm.

'What's wrong, Pazz?' Duncan reacted. 'Shall I call a nurse?'

'No,' Pazz said and reached over to the adjacent sink to fill a vase with water. 'Just a spasm, that's all.'

'Here let me do that,' Duncan replied. He took the vase from her, filled it and arranged the roses. 'I'll put them on your cabinet,' he said.

'Yes,' whispered Pazz. Her lips continued to tingle. She smiled.

Suddenly Duncan did the strangest thing. Without even saying a word he bent forward and kissed her lightly on the lips. It was so sudden, Pazz's face flushed a bright red but she seemed to know what to do.

Duncan stood up and Pazz noticed his face was also flushed. 'I'm sorry,' he apologized. 'I shouldn't have kissed you. Forgive me.'

'For being human,' Pazz answered. She reached out and found his hand to squeeze. 'I am honored.'

'Yes!' Duncan became all formal. 'The intimate moment had gone. 'I have a small math problem one of my students gave me. Can you help?'

'Let me see,' Pazz said and glanced at the page of mathematical symbols Duncan produced. Within seconds she read the equation and pointed to a section near the end of the page. 'There's the error,' she said and explained what was wrong. 'Have you a pen?'

'Sure,' Duncan replied and watched, fascinated as Pazz crossed out and changed symbols. She turned the page over and, totally absorbed, proceeded to write so quickly she never noticed his eyes glued on her writing. Finally she glanced up and smiled. 'I did this in my third year,' she commented.

'He tricked you,' Epsilon warned.

'Oh hell,' Pazz swore and glowered at Duncan. 'This is not student's work is it?'

Duncan flushed for a second time. 'No,' he admitted.' The equation was not from a student at all but a highly technical problem in quantum physics a research doctor gave me. I can't understand your work but am confident that you have solved a problem my colleague back at the university has been working on for five months. Everyone believes his theories cannot be proved.'

Pazz bit on her lip and didn't know whether to laugh or cry. She diverted her eyes and gazed out the window at the green lawns and gardens far below.

'Pazz, I'm sorry,' Duncan said in a soft voice.

Pazz swung around with her eyes filled with tears. 'Are you Duncan?' she retorted and flung the papers at him. 'Tell your friend if he reads my summary, he'll find he was on the right track.' She stared into his eyes. 'Tell him that is just elementary theory where I came from. 'She glowered. 'If you try another nasty move like that again you can take your bloody job and stuff it.' Her command of Australian English expletives was by now, quite full. 'I thought we had an understanding,' she continued as she managed to control her voice. 'Please go!'

'Pazz, I…' Duncan attempted to explain.

'Go!' screamed Pazz and flung herself over so she was facing away from him. Why did she now feel so lousy?

Duncan stood, gathered up the paper and quietly walked out. As he walked out the ward door he very methodically ripped the paper into eight sections and tossed it in the rubbish bin.

'Duncan,' Pazz had turned back and watched his actions. 'Tell your colleague I'll help him if he wishes. Come back tomorrow.'

Duncan looked back at her. 'Tonight, if you like?' he answered in such a quiet voice she hardly heard him.

'Yes,' Pazz answered and brushed away the tears still on her cheeks, 'Just you. No work. Understand?'

'I think I do.' Duncan smiled and left the room.

*

CHAPTER FIVE

'Colonel look at this,' Master Sergeant Colin Fields, the tall black professional, said in a precise voice as he sat in the darkened room with eyes firmly fixed on the green revolving light on a screen.

However, by the time Colonel Ira Pope had walked across the Magaroona Radio Telescope control center room, warning bells were ringing and colored lights lit up everywhere.

'It's gone,' muttered Fields. The screen had reverted to its normal pattern.

'What was it, Sergeant?' Pope retorted.

'I don't rightly know, Sir. For a few seconds the line jumped off the scale.' He reached across to where the continuous radar reading was recorded on paper. The fluctuating ink line had leaped literally off the top and bottom of the paper for precisely five seconds before reverting to normal.

Throughout the massive room thirty meters beneath the ground, sixteen other United States Air Force personnel reported the same fluctuation. Computers began turning out data and every radio telescope in the Pacific and Indian Oceans, as well as California, Alaska and two South American sites reported the massive disturbance.

'Keep an eye on it, Sergeant,' Fields ordered and stalked into another room where one of the world's most advanced computers was analyzing the data.

'We have a visual,' an officer reported. 'Satellite H 67 was in the area and its transmission is coming through now.' He pressed a button and a gigantic five-meter high screen lit up at the end of the room. Slowly, one line at a time, a full colored photograph appeared. Throughout the building everyone not directly monitoring other equipment, stared enraptured as the scene unfolded. In front of the Earth with its blue ocean, white clouds and a brown South Australian land mass, a massive spherical object came onto view. It shone in the sunlight like silver and appeared to be made of thousands of overlapping tiles. As more became uncovered, a slight jagged section, less than thirty centimeters in diameter, was shown near the top. White condensation was streaming out from it in a long thin cloud that vanished out of sight off the edge of the screen.

'Shit!' someone gasped as the picture lines, now three-quarters up the screen continued to light up. An opening about the size of a garage door near the top, in what could be described as the North Pole, appeared with something inside.

The computer-enhanced picture was complete and was immediately being replaced by a second that just showed Earth and space. The spacecraft, or whatever it was, had disappeared.

'Bring back Screen One,' barked the colonel and stared as the original photograph reappeared. 'Focus on the opening and magnify!' he ordered.

Gasps filled the room as the magnification filled the screen. Inside the spacecraft was a cylindrical craft anchored by two metal arms to a floating platform.

'It was directly above South Australia when this photograph was taken,' Pope reported from his monitoring screen. 'I confirm the vision lasted exactly five seconds; but we have video,' he added as another bank of lights lit up.

A grim Colonel Pope nodded. 'Play it.'

'Everyone expected a cackle of intergalactic space but instead a voice filled the room in Australian accented English.

'We need your help, Houston. Life support systems have gone!'

'Who switched that in?' roared the Colonel.' By God, I'll have his job for this.'

'That was the message that came through in those five seconds, sir,' Fields reported.

The Colonel ran a tongue over thin lips and his eyes riveted to the screen in front of Fields before he spoke. 'Red Priority Call through to the Pentagon, Sergeant Fields.'

'Yes sir,' the man paled and reached for a glass-encased button. The sign above read. *Warning- Direct line. Top Priority. For Emergency Communication Only.* He had never used this equipment before.

*

After Duncan had left, Pazz slipped out of bed and recovered the notes he'd ripped up from the rubbish bin, asked a nurse for some paper and spent two hours scribbling figures down in her neat clipped writing. Whether it was the English implant in her mind, she did not know but the mathematical symbols were completely familiar except that some of the more advanced ones were missing. She had a break for lunch and another when Lynn visited with Jason but by early evening, fifteen pages with mathematical symbols and explanatory notes had been completed.

'Don't get too advanced or you won't be understood,' Epsilon warned. 'This is only third year quantum physics you did up to Year Eight. We would at least five hundred years in advance of their knowledge.'

'I know,' Pazz snapped and continued with her notes.

Just after five, Duncan arrived with another little present and watched as she opened it. 'Oh Duncan, perfume. Thank you.'

Once again she flushed as she felt her body reacting to his presence. Strange things were happening inside which she only partly understood. 'Duncan,' she said in a shy voice. 'Can you kiss me?'

He nodded and appeared speechless himself but bent over and their lips touched. His arms encircled Pazz and the soft embrace from the morning became more frantic as they held on to each other and he kissed her cheeks, neck and even hair before returning to her lips. Finally they stopped and Duncan sat on the bed with his arm around her while she tucked her head in the nap of his neck. Nothing was said for a moment before Duncan spoke.

'I got a bit carried away, Pazz,' he apologized.

'I don't mind,' she answered and flushed in embarrassment. She bent over and opened the tiny drawer of the cabinet next to the bed. 'I reconsidered,' she said modestly. 'Give this to your friend. Tell him if he wants help, it'll cost him. I think I'll be a business woman.'

Duncan began to read the equations, turned to the next page and continued. 'You did this today?' he gasped.

Pazz nodded. 'I got interested.' She shrugged. 'He had two basic flaws in his hypothesis and would have come to, what do you call it, a dead end? Basically, though, he was on the right track.'

'Can I show him these?' Duncan asked.

'Yes, but we need a cover story, don't we?' Pazz said.

Duncan stayed for two more hours and promised to get back the next day. He became so engrossed; the attraction between them from earlier in the evening was almost forgotten. Almost, but not completely!

After he left Epsilon burst into her mind. 'You had better ask the nurse for some tampons, Pazz. You're a bearer now remember. I think your first period is due.'

'I remember my mother,' Pazz replied with a slight tinge of excitement. 'She said it was the necessary curse of motherhood.'

'No, it's just being a woman, Pazz,' corrected the computer. 'You're just a little later than Earth woman, that is all.'

'And my reaction when Duncan kissed me?'

'They call it love on Earth, Pazz,' the computer added. 'I'm not too sure on the processes either. We're both on a learning curve here; how about that for a quaint English saying?'

'You're going well, Epsilon,' Pazz laughed and lay back against her pillow. The nurse said she could be discharged the next day but it depended on the doctor when he did his morning rounds.

Outside a whole new world waited.

*

'Look at this, Matthew,' Duncan said the next morning as he placed Pazz's calculations in front of Doctor Matthew McHardy's computer. 'My associate corrected your errors.'

'Don't be ridiculous,' scoffed the man. He picked up the notes and tossed them in a plastic tray.

'Read them, Matthew,' Duncan said. 'Doctor D'rose said you were on the right track but there were two basic flaws in your hypothesis. She's written it all out for you.'

'Ha! Ha! Big joke,' the mathematician and physics expert retorted. He was usually quite a pleasant guy but was prone to be abrupt if he was interrupted while deep in thought.

'It's no joke,' Duncan stressed. 'I'll be back in an hour for your comment.'

True to his word, he returned to McHardy's office an hour latter to find the man up to page ten of Pazz's notes and his computer filled with a copy of her mathematical equations.

'You were right,' the mathematician commented with a new respect in his eyes. 'I never knew another research project was so far advanced. It's brilliant.' He grinned like a schoolboy. 'Look at this.' He tapped the computer screen. 'I've been trying to sort that one out for months. How long did this take her?'

Duncan didn't dare say one afternoon so switched to the story Pazz and himself had worked out together. 'She was working for an industrial firm in The States; the name of it is confidential, but when her grant came up for renewal they stated her research was not practical enough and cancelled her contract. However, she kept all the rights to her own research and is looking for another sponsor.'

'The fools!' McHardy interjected.

'Anyway, I heard Oxford in England has offered her a research grant but she is interested in staying in Australia. Apparently she likes our way of life and the outback,'

'What's her name again?' McHardy asked.

'Doctor Pazz D'rose; mother's Swedish and father's French. She actually grew up in Australia and returned to Europe in her early teens.' Duncan was beginning to enjoy himself. He had Matthew, hook, line and sinker. There were problems, of course, if his colleague wanted proof of Pazz's qualifications but with a little care, that could be overcome. 'She won't come cheap,' he added. 'At least a salary equivalent to an Associate Professor's.'

McHardy rubbed his chin and frowned. 'I'll need to interview her, of course. You say she's gone beyond what is included here?' He nodded at the notes.

'I think she's testing a new hypothesis, yes' Duncan. 'If you read her last page…'

'I did,' McHardy responded and just shook his head in amazement. 'With her on our team…' he said and stood up. 'When can I see her?'

'She's off to Melbourne for a few days but should be available early next week,' lied Duncan. 'Shall I tell her, you're interested?'

'I am,' Matthew replied and stared back at the computer screen. 'Very interested!'

*

'Oh my God!' screamed Pazz and Lynn manipulated the car she'd just purchased through yet another traffic light, indicated and crossed into another lane before driving onto the M2 expressway and accelerating along the central lane. 'The traffic. How do you do it?'

'Can you drive?' Lynn said, glanced back at Jason strapped in a back seat cot and accelerated to well over the speed limit.

'No!' gasped Pazz and never mentioned this was only her second trip in a road vehicle. 'The traffic. Oh my God, look at that truck?'

A tractor unit with over twenty wheels rumbled up beside them with diesel fumes belching out of its two vertical exhaust pipes. After another ten minutes Lynne took an off ramp and slowed down to sixty, the urban speed limit. Pazz now stared at street after street of single story urban houses, each with its little patch of lawn and gardens. Compared with the desert everything was so green.

Lynn turned off the busy through-road into a smaller suburban street, left into a cul-de-sac and up a driveway to a neat white house with a tile roof. 'Our Home, Pazz,' she said and pulled to a stop.

Since leaving hospital just before noon, everything Pazz saw stretched her imagination to the fullest; the roads, buildings, green belt of fields and gardens, vehicles, the rumble of jumbo jets overhead. It was so different than her home city of Quintrex she could hardly begin to compare. It was hot, too but the interior of the car's air conditioning blew cool air into her face on the trip out.

She stepped out onto the drive, gasped as a blast of heat hit her face and just stood looking wide eyed at the neat garden, lawn browned by the sun, and a garden of golden flowers. 'Oh Lynn,' she whispered. 'Is this yours?'

'Yes. Took it over a week back. It's a bit empty inside but I got beds, couch and TV, of course,' Lynn shrugged. 'It's hard starting from scratch. Come inside.'

'Your room,' Lynn smiled a few moments later and held a door open.

Pazz gasped at the bedroom with pastel colored walls, frilly curtains, a double bed and dressing table.

'Just me!' she said. 'At home this was almost the size of our whole apartment and that was on the thirty-sixth floor.'

Lynn stared at her but never commented. 'There's a swimming pool out the back. It's only tiny but will get you wet. Can you swim?'

'Yes,' laughed Pazz. 'We had an aquatic center in our building. I love swimming.'

Even the kitchen amazed Pazz as she examined everything. 'It's so big and bright,' she said with a laugh. 'Oh my God!'

'We'll cool down when the air conditioning is on for a while,' Lynn commented. 'Bring your gear in and I'll get us a drink.' She kissed Jason she'd been carrying around and sat him in a playpen already assembled in the corner of the living room. 'Play with your teddy, Sweetheart while I get Auntie Pazz a drink of coffee.' she said.

Pazz swung around and continued to stare at everything. She walked in the bathroom, out to the back yard and ran her hands in the swimming pool with its clear filtered water, almost skipped along the drive to gaze up the street then strolled back inside.

'My, you are excited, aren't you?' Lynn laughed. 'It's really just a small place, half the size to the one we had in Perth.' She frowned and looked sad for a moment. 'All flash but like a prison inside with my ex-husband; the old bastard.' She smiled again. 'We're about twenty kilometers from the university but there is a railway station only two blocks away and a shopping mall close by, too.'

'I love it, Lynn,' Pazz replied with her eyes still glowing. 'Thanks for inviting me to stay with you. I'll help with expenses and with Jason, too.'

'And I'll teach you to drive,' Lynn added. 'You really need to out here.'

'It's a deal,' Pazz replied. 'This is so amazing, Lynn I can't find the words to express my feelings.'

'Then don't,' Lynn replied. 'Have your coffee. Later you can help cook our dinner. I invited Duncan for a meal. He'll be here after work.'

Pazz stared at her. 'Why?' she asked.

Lynn screwed her nose up. 'I thought you'd like his company. Did I do wrong?'

'No,' Pazz replied in a hushed voice. 'I'm nervous, that's all.'

'Then don't be. He's a real hulk and I know he's got the hots for you.'

'What?' Pazz laughed 'What does that mean?'

'You'll see.' Lynn said and gave her friend a playful slap on the back. 'You'll see.'

That evening Duncan arrived, dressed in casual clothes and carrying yet another gift, a bottle of wine for them all. Pazz met him at the door and it only seemed natural when he held her waist and kissed her on the lips. Once again, she felt so strange inside, not nervous now he was here but just strange.

'I like your place,' he said. 'I've just got a small inner city apartment near the university, handy but sterile.'

Lynn was a perfect host and their conversation covered everything, except perhaps their personal lives. They ate and sipped wine, giggled and, after all helped with the dishes, retreated to the living room and a game of cards Lynn knew. Pazz gasped at the cards. Though not exactly the same, they were so close to cards at home, it was uncanny. Even the lighthearted game of *Rage* was similar to a game she played as a child.

Supper came and Duncan mentioned the visit to Matthew McHardy for the first time when Lynn had slipped out to get something. 'No, I don't mind you telling Lynn.' she said in answer to his query and gave him a strange look. 'She's my friend, just like you. I trust you both now.'

Duncan nodded and looked her in the eye. 'Pazz,' he said quietly. 'I'm glad you do and I promise I'll never let you down. You see...' he glanced up as Lynn returned with a plate of sandwiches and retreated into a grin but reached across and squeezed Pazz's hand.

'I know,' Pazz replied but didn't really.

'Go with the flow, Pazz,' Epsilon advised. 'I like these English sayings. There's hundreds of them, you know.'

'I do,' Pazz though and wondered about her body. Her period had arrived and she still reacted when Duncan was near. It was unnerving but so exciting, too. Duncan's hand was still in hers so she squeezed it and smiled into his eyes. 'You were telling me about Doctor McHardie,' she said.

'Act standoffish,' Duncan advised when he had both woman laughing when he explained what had happened. 'Tell him you'll need to consider it and another Adelaide university has approached you. That'll make him panic a little.'

'You're a bit of a rogue,' Lynne laughed. 'I almost feel sorry for the man.'

'He's not a bad sort and we're quite good mates. He can get pompous at times in his own field. I said you'd only accept an Associate Professor's salary.'

Pazz smiled but turned serious. 'But my qualifications, Duncan?'

'Have you got them with you.' he asked.

'Stored on computer files but they aren't in English.'

Duncan stare glanced at Lynn but she just shrugged. 'Can they be converted?' he asked.

'Easily but.'

'Then do it. We'll print it out and then see how it compares with our documents. Are they a lot different.'

'I don't know,' Pazz answered. 'I've never seen your documents.'

'Pazz,' warned Epsilon. 'Careful.'

'They're friends,' Pazz thought back. 'I can't keep everything a secret forever, can I? They both guess I'm from somewhere out of this world, anyway.'

'Just wait a while,' Epsilon advised. 'There's no hurry. Do it in parts, a bit at a time.'

'Okay.' Pazz almost sighed out loud.

'...Don't you think,' Duncan was saying

Pazz jerked her mind back. 'Yes, sure,' she said but didn't really know what he'd said.

'Good,' Duncan said. 'We'll do it tomorrow.'

Pazz glanced at Lynn and raised an eyebrow.

'Duncan suggested you photocopy your documents out so they can be compared with his,' Lynn said and gave Pazz a wink as if she knew about Epsilon.

'It's possible as long as I can touch their machine,' Epsilon stated.

'That's a great idea,' Pazz said when she found Duncan looking intently at her. 'We can do it tomorrow.'

It was close to midnight when Duncan reluctantly left. Pazz walked out into the drive to see him off and once more they just sort of ended up in each others arms in a tight embrace; kissing frantically. Their bodies rubbed into each other almost as if they were one. He was so strong but gentle so, Pazz searched for the word in her mind; masculine, that was it.

'See you tomorrow, Duncan,' she whispered when she finally stepped back so their eyes met. 'Thanks for everything.'

'Pazz,' Duncan whispered.

'Yes.'

Duncan placed a thumb under her chin and kissed her again. 'Bye,' he said, climbed into his car, reversed onto the street, waved and drove away.

'A real hulk,' Lynn's voice came across from the veranda and Pazz jumped in fright.

'You were watching,' she retorted and swung around.

'Not really,' Lynn said. 'Just caught the last bit, that's all. Don't worry, he's a perfect gentleman.'

'Yes, isn't he?' Pazz replied and almost wished he wasn't.

*

Duncan's office in the University of Adelaide was typical of that of many academics. It was untidy with books and papers everywhere. He slid a pile of books off a chair in front of the computer terminal and coughed in embarrassment as he turned the set on.

'Go to it,' he said and watched but did not recognize anything different when Pazz casually withdrew her armlet and placed it by the mouse.

'Go for a walk for an hour,' Epsilon communicated after her fingers touched the armlet. 'This is like working in a museum but I can already see the possibilities.'

Pazz grinned out the window, 'Could you give me a brief look around, Duncan?' she asked.

'Yes, sure,' he replied. 'See out there. That's the road where we came in. This is just one campus. There are others at…' His voice continued on as he escorted her around.

Dressed in lightweight summer clothes and a large brimmed hat to shade her eyes, Pazz looked identical to the hundreds of students, walking with determined looks to and from the myriad of squat buildings. To Pazz, used to hundred floor skyscrapers, linked by air corridors and driverless archers pulling into vacuum stations, it was all quite quaint. What impressed her more than the buildings were the grounds with trees, lawns and gardens. Colorful birds cackled and flew around and even an occasional animal darted across in front of students walking everywhere.

For an hour she played the part of a tourist before, almost abruptly suggested they should return to Duncan's office.

'Okay,' he replied and gazed fondly at his companion. For once his mind was not on the work waiting for him.

'Well, how'd you like to start?' he asked as Pazz slipped the glistening golden armlet back on.

'You are now officially Doctor D'rose,' Epsilon's voice flooded in, 'A graduate of Auckland University in New Zealand with M.A. and Honors and a Ph.D. from Oregon University in United States. I tossed in a couple of other qualifications equivalent to those you earned at home, too. Their computers have your full academic record. Ninety one percent was a direct cross reference from your home records and a minor part converted into subjects which people here can understand.'

'Thank you,' Pazz nodded and grinned at Duncan.

'I also had your birth recorded in Perth Australia but made you five years younger than your Home Awake Age. That makes you twenty-eight. You have another bank account with twenty thousand dollars in it with the Westpac Bank. Your Australian passport is approved and will be dispatched. I even sent them one of your identification photographs. All other official records are in the memory banks of government computers and, oh yes, your driver's license is in the mail.'

'But I can't drive.' Pazz exclaimed out loud and squeezed Duncan's hand when he stared at her in a strange fashion.

'All the university information is being printed out in the administration block.' Epsilon's voice almost sounded excited. 'Ask Duncan to take you there.'

Duncan continued to stare at Pazz. 'How do you communicate?' he asked. 'And don't tell me you don't. Your eyes sort of glaze over and you look a thousand kilometers away.'

'Just thinking,' Pazz whispered. 'Will you take me to the Administration's Office where the computer readouts are printed, Duncan?'

'Sure,' he frowned, 'but why?'

Pazz merely grinned, glanced out the open office door to see if the corridor was empty and stretched up to kiss Duncan on the lips. 'Someday, I'll tell you.'

After Pazz walked up and identified herself, the woman behind the long polished counter beamed.

'Doctor D'rose, welcome to The University of Adelaide,' she said and held out a hand 'Your appointment with Doctor McHardy is confirmed for Monday morning.' She pulled out a large white envelope. 'Here is a printed copy of your records from New Zealand and United

States. It was quite a coincident really but they both arrived through almost simultaneously.' The woman, who must have read the records, was almost gushing while Duncan stood back with a dumbfounded expression and stared wide eyed at Pazz.

'They're genuine,' Pazz said a few moments later in Duncan's office as he examined her academic record and gave a low whistle. 'Check through to the universities, if you wish.'

'No,' he replied. 'I'm sure they are perfect, in every way but how…' he frowned and his eyes caught hers. 'There wasn't time.' He broke into a grin.

'Don't ask!'

' I know one thing, though.'

'And that is?'

'That beautiful arm bracelet you slip off and on, oh so discretely, has something to do with it.'

Pazz flushed.

'Hand me to him,' Epsilon directed.

Pazz smiled faintly, slipped the armlet off and held it out. 'Put it on your arm, Duncan,' she said. 'You will find it fits.'

*

The Associate Professor nodded and, with a serious nod, slipped it over his massive hand and up a muscular arm where it expanded like elastic to grip him. No sooner was it in place than a voice almost screamed into his head.

'Hello Doctor Bourne, I am Epsilon, Pazz's personal computer and you could say Guardian Angel. There is a lot about her you do not know but I can vouch for her honesty and integrity…'

Duncan almost staggered and gripped the side of his desk. He stared in complete wonder at a faintly smiling Pazz as he listened to the voice in his mind. It was as if he was hearing it normally yet he knew that no sound had been made.

Epsilon continued. 'She is attracted to you Duncan in a way we do not really understand. My advice at the moment is that you should consider your relationship with her. If it is purely academic, leave her alone before she is deeply hurt. Just continue your life as before. If, however, it is more personal, be patient. I access you as a caring, honest individual but you are male, a gender we are not used to. That is all, my new friend.' The voice was gone.

Deep in thought, Duncan withdrew the armlet and handed it back to Pazz. His only acknowledgement of anything different was a slight tremble of his beard as he watched her slip the armlet back on. Afterwards he smiled, tucked his arms around her and just held her into him.

'I think I understand,' he finally said. 'Not everything, Pazz but enough to know how alone you really are. Tell Epsilon it is more than just an academic interest and I'm moving into new territory, too. All my life I've been committed to my studies and,' he shrugged,' I guess I've never really thought about women and families.'

*

'She knows,' Pazz replied and fixed her eyes on his. They grabbed hands and, once again kissed, not as friends but as lovers attracted to each other. Suppressed emotions through eight generations could not stop the surge of sheer joy passing through the young woman's mind at that moment. Kisses became more and more intense and tongues lashed between opened mouths. She did not want to stop but managed to do so through sheer will power.

'I must be going,' Pazz whispered and felt her face heat up when Duncan kissed her lightly again. 'Lynn offered to pick me up by Gate 6 at eleven. It's almost that now.'

'Can I see you tonight?' Duncan asked. 'It is Friday and there's a weekend ahead.'

'You know where I live,' Pazz said and wriggled out of his arms. 'I'm glad I yelled out in my sleep in the hospital.'

'Yes, me too. I'll show you where the gate is.'

Even Lynn noticed their smiles when Pazz and sat in the car and waved goodbye.

'Everything worked out, I see,' she laughed. 'Want to go shopping? I'll shout you lunch.'

Yes, I'd love that.' Pazz said. 'I need to buy some more clothes, anyway.'

*

CHAPTER SIX

The seed had been sown but outcome unknown. Monitoring of Earth's electronics, though, showed a rapidly increased volume of physical activity at known space installations.

Activity aboard Omega could almost be described as frantic and the three onboard computers prepared their one remaining humanoid for a journey to Earth, if indeed, it took place. As with Pazz, brain waves were altered to implant knowledge of English but additional services were also performed. The patient's lungs were expanded to suit Earth conditions but nothing could be done to counteract the flu virus. The suspended animation chamber was drained of fluid and the humanoid attached to an armlet computer named Theta who immediately set about establishing continuous contact with Epsilon.

A breathing mask to the nose and fluid tubes in the arm replaced the umbilical cord. Mechanical arms moved the humanoid to the escape pod, trimmed her hair to shoulder length and dressed her in Earth clothes designed to Epsilon's specifications. Afterwards, an emergency spacesuit was sealed around her body.

*

'We have contact,' Master Sergeant Fields reported and, within seconds, Pope was beside him and the main screen activated.

For five seconds the monitor showed the sphere above the Earth before it vibrated into a new scene. Even the dour Pope gave a low whistle as the empty interior of a starship can into view, alive and moving. The interior camera zoomed in on a cylinder, almost like a coffin, held secure by mechanical arms.

A human girl lay, as if asleep on a soft mattress. She was dressed in a spacesuit but her head was covered with nothing except a breathing mask. Long blonde hair, looking combed and neat was gathered around a Caucasian face with fine features common to people from Northern Europe.

'This is Omega calling Magaroona Tracking Station. You are viewing our child who can harm nobody.' The voice filled the space center. 'We can do no more for her so ask for your help. Life support runs out in eleven Earth days. We can be at any co-ordinate you send us. Use any frequency. They are all monitored.'

'Wait, Omega!' Pope called into a microphone but the scene

shivered away and was replaced by a satellite view of the Earth.

' It was directly above us again, Sir,' Fields reported.

'I see,' Pope replied. 'Could the signal have been transmitted from Earth and bounced off a communications satellite?'

'Not on that frequency, Sir. The source was right where our computers predicted the unidentified space probe would be. That was classified information.'

'The transmission lasted thirty seconds to the microsecond, Sir,' another voice said. 'All trace of the craft has now gone.'

'I see,' Pope replied. 'Transmit a recording of this to Kennedy Space Center and...'

'We cannot, Sir. Everything has been wiped from our files.' Fields glanced up at Pope with wide eyes. 'It was as if it never happened.'

'Everything!' snapped Pope.

'Yes Sir,' confirmed another officer. 'The visual just shows the Earth and the voice, Oh My God,' he stuttered.

'What?' snapped Pope.

'It's playing Australia's National Anthem.'

'No other tracking stations received any signals, visual or sound, Sir,' another operator reported.

'Not even a blip on radar, Sir,' Fields added.

'Well, Son,' Pope placed a hand on the Master Sergeant's shoulder and almost grinned. 'You'd better patch me through to The White House.'

*

Friday afternoon was hot and sultry but Pazz did not mind the thirty-five degrees Celsius temperature. In fact it was one of the few things, which reminded her of Delta. After shopping for hours, they'd returned home and Lynn and Jason were now both sound asleep. She wrote a short note to her friend and slipped out for a walk around the deserted suburban streets to a nearby park.

In appearance, she looked a complete local in shorts, tiny bikini top, sun hat and thongs. Closer inspection showed, though, her bronzed skin was perfect even on shaded inside parts of her arms and the clothes showed no trace of perspiration. She hummed a little tune popular on the radio and paused every now and then to gaze at flowers or a bird flying around. By mid-afternoon she had walked several kilometers and had almost completed a circle so was now only a block from home.

She licked the last glob of an ice cream, turned into their cul-de-sac and noticed a large dark blue car in their driveway. With a tiny frown she slowed and wondered whether to wait a while but a sound hit her ears.

It was a stifled scream! Pazz increased her pace and walked inside to the sound of Jason crying and an angry male voice.

'You little bitch,' a man screamed. 'So you thought you could take Jason and just fade away with your lover boy.'

Pazz pushed the closed door open and gasped in alarm. Lynn was standing whimpering against the far wall with a blood soaked blouse ripped open. A monstrous male had his back to her and as she watched he bend forward and thrust at Lynn with a shining object. It was a knife!

Lynn screamed and flung her arms up in a valiant attempt to ward off the attack but the knife buried itself in her stomach. The screams turned to gurgling sobs of agony as the young woman buckled forward and staggered to her knees. Her eyes reflected the shock and terror of tortured suffering.

'Your pretty boy won't like you by the time I've finished, you slut,' the man snarled as he pulled the knife out and very purposely kicked his wounded wife so she rolled into a pool of blood.

'No, James!' she screamed in complete hysteria. 'For God's sake, my flat mate is a girl.'

'So you've gone all kinky,' he hissed and reached back to thrust the knife again while Lynn let out another scream and attempted to crawl away. James grabbed the petrified woman by the hair so her head was forced back. He grinned sadistically and turned the knife sideways to slash at her exposed throat.

'Epsilon, help!' a terrified Pass whispered.

Without any warning, Lynn's husband's wrist was grabbed in a grip of steel, the man grunted and swung around to find ice blue eyes staring at him.

'That will do James Kilmore,' said a melodious voice. Pazz reached across with her other hand and removed the knife from the clasped fingers. She stepped back and the man came too.

'What the hell!' he muttered and kicked out.

The kick hit Pazz's leg but she did not even flinch. Instead, it was the man who groaned out in agony and thrashed out with his one free arm. He was large and heavy but she dragged him across the room like a child. The arm was gripped so tightly the forearm turned anemic as blood supply was cut off. Lynn, now sobbing on the floor with a hand trying, without success to stop blood spurting from her stomach, opened her eyes and saw her holding James.

' Get away, Pazz!' she screamed hysterically as she tried to stand up.

'He'll kill you!'

'No he won't,' Pazz growled. 'Lynn is Pazz's friend. Her friends are my friends. You have committed a capital offence by attacking a bearer.'

'What you some sort of idiot?' James managed to splutter but the eyes staring into his were strangely calm. He shuddered and attempted to remove his arm. 'Let me go, you bitch. This is between my wife and myself.'

'Your widow,' replied Pazz. 'I am Epsilon. I repeat. Attacking a breeder is a capital offence. However, on this planet it appears the law is more lenient'

'Let me...' James Kilmore started but his voice built to a high-pitched whimper. His arm, the one held by the alien woman began to shake and turn black. The man's eyes bulged and the mouth opened. Saliva ran down a quivering face; in fact the whole body was quivering. 'No!' he groaned in agony, ' No!'

Pazz's face showed no expression but the grip intensified and the male continued to shake, the face turned white then gray. A gurgled came from the throat and the body went limp. The woman let go and James slumped to the floor.

'Your husband just had a heart attack, Lynn,' she explained almost like a doctor lecturing first year medical students. 'Ironical, isn't it?'

A terrified Lynn stared up. 'Who are you?' she gasped and trembled in shock as she looked down at her bloody hands and dark red liquid pouring from her abdomen. She staggered again, but the ordeal was too much and she sank, unconscious to the floor beside her lifeless husband.

Pazz blinked and stepped back with a hand to her mouth. 'What have you done, Epsilon?' she gasped. 'You can't kill the man.'

'He deserved it,' the computer replied. 'Listen to me. If we don't hurry Lynn will die. You must slip me on her arm.'

'Why?' whimpered a distressed Pazz.

'Do it!' commanded the computer.

Pazz nodded and bent down beside Lynn. There was more than one stab wound in her friend's body. Pazz could see at least four gashes across the stomach and breast but blood was everywhere and still pulsing out. It splashed on Pazz's arms and legs and soaked into her clothes but as she reached out, grabbed her friend's arms and slid the armlet on.

'Look after the baby,' Epsilon said as Pazz let the armlet go and communication was broken.

Pazz found tears streaming down her face but she nodded and walked across to the howling infant, picked him up to cuddle close. 'Mummy will be fine, sweetheart,' she cried and turned to watch.

Lynn had her eyes closed but already the blood had stopped flowing. The most recent wound, the one Pazz witnessed, began to close; all the wounds began to blend together and heal. Lynn's heartbeat slowed to normal and her ashen face became flushed and still the wounds knitted together. The deep jagged cuts began to be repaired from the inside out. Flesh joined, blood vessels reattached and the skin puckered, grew together and began to smooth. The ugly red welts began to shrink.

Still more was changed. Lynn's slightly chubby cheeks and body slimmed until her shorts were loose and still her body repaired itself. The wounds were now scars and, even as Pazz watched, these blended into nothingness as Lynn sighed and drifted out of unconsciousness into a gentle sleep.

By now, Pazz had found a bottle for Jason and was feeding him. She had seen this happen before, at home. The computer had really only stimulated the body to repair itself at ten thousand times it's normal speed. She ignored the man on the floor and slipped Epsilon back on her arm.

'What now?' she asked.

'The seeder is dead. Finish feeding Jason and put him down. Afterwards, run your hand over the blood on the carpet,' Epsilon requested. 'I'll absorb it in your skin pores.

Pazz did and within moments, the blood was gone but her hand was bloated and full. She stood and walked to the laundry sink, turned on the tap and released the blood. It poured out from under her fingernails but did not hurt. There was no sensation at all for once again Epsilon was in command. Pazz made three trips back to absorb blood before pulling the stained clothes off her friend and carrying her into the bedroom. Back as herself again, she washed her friend down with a warm face cloth and dressed her in clean clothes. Next she changed her own clothes and cleaned the few remaining signs of the attack in the kitchen.

Lynn awoke to see Pazz smiling at her. 'Let me explain,' Pazz said and gently slipped the armlet onto her friend.

Lynn's apprehensive face turned to wonder before a small smile appeared on her face and she went into a trance like condition. The armlet stayed with Lynn for five minutes before the eyes opened and she smiled at Pazz. She reached up and handed Epsilon back then grabbed her in a hug and burst into tears.

'Thank you,' she sobbed. 'Epsilon told me everything, Pazz. I knew you were different but never guessed how much.' She sniffed back a tear and stood up. 'Epsilon said the wounds are gone and she must be right for there's no pain. Nothing!'

She swung around in front of a mirror, stared at her reflection and burst into tears again. 'Pazz, you saved my life, you know. He just about killed me back in Perth and would have done it this time.'

'Epsilon saved you,' Pazz replied but she looked worried and bit on her lip. 'What about your husband?' she asked. 'We cleaned up but he is still lying there.'

Lynn glanced up. 'It's okay, Pazz, Epsilon told me what to do.'

She walked to the telephone and dialed the emergency number. 'Hello,' she sobbed into the instrument. 'My husband has just collapsed. I think he had a heart attack. Can you an ambulance straight away?'

*

An hour later a doctor walked into the waiting room of the hospital. 'Mrs. Kilmore,' he said, 'I regret to say your husband had a massive heart attack and was dead on arrival. All attempts to resuscitate him were unsuccessful.' He touched her arm. 'I am sorry. If it is any help, I doubt if he felt any pain so, in that way, he was fortunate.'

'Thank you doctor,' Lynn replied. Her eyes were dry but expression sad. 'I think I realized that when I called the hospital. It's just that it all happened so quickly.'

'I know,' said the doctor, 'Heart attacks can be unpredictable. A pathologist will need to make a report but it was just his time, I guess.'

'Yes,' Lynn replied and fixed emotionless eyes on Pazz.

Pazz reached out and touched her friend's hand, a touch of empathy and also to allow Epsilon to flow into her friend. A minute charge of electricity moved into Lynn's brain to calm and pacify her and to blunt the memories.

'Lynn will remember being attacked,' Epsilon explained as they drove home in a taxi.' However, she will not remember the stabbing or the severity of the assault. She will remember your arrival, a brief fight and her husband collapsing to the floor. Like everyone else, she will think it was a heart attack caused by natural events.'

'Yeah with your help,' Pazz thought. 'But will she remember you?'

'Oh yes,' the computer replied, 'and a little I told about you. This was more than Duncan knows but not everything. I'll leave that for you.' The computer went silent before adding, 'Wait a moment I have an incoming message.' The computer switched off; something she rarely did.

Pazz frowned but found Lynn was gazing at her.

'Epsilon talking?' she asked.

'Yes,' said Pazz. 'She wants to know how you feel.'

'Numb,' Lynn replied. 'I can't feel sad for James. He was a brute. You know if you did not return home then I'm sure he would have stabbed me.' She gazed at Pazz.' I know you helped Pazz but can't remember how.' She frowned.

'He knocked you unconscious, Lynn.'

'Yeah, and I don't even have a bruise on my body and find I lost ten kilograms.' Her eyes gazed through the darkened taxi at her friend. 'Thank you, Pazz. I have a feeling if you had not intervened a different member of the Kilmore family would be lying in the morgue right now.'

'But you're safe Lynn, and Jason still has his mother to love and look after him. That is what matters.'

'Jason!' gasped Lynn in a sudden state of panic. 'Where is he?'

'Don't worry,' Pazz said. 'When the ambulance arrived, Dorothy Bristow from next door insisted on looking after him.'

*

The next week affected Pazz more than Lynn as she was overwhelmed by one of humanity's most basic emotions, that of conscience and guilt. Everybody, including Lynn thought James Kilmore's dead was a natural result of a heart attack but Pazz realized her own hands had killed him.

Duncan did a marvelous job in helping both women. Without even asking he did nearly all the administrative work for James Kilmore's funeral so by Tuesday the body had been returned to Perth for a Thursday funeral.

He knew Pazz wasn't up her interview with Matthew McHardy so had it postponed for a week. In some ways this helped, as Doctor McHardy had read up Pazz's academic record and was keener than ever to have her join his research team.

'I shall be back,' Lynn told a somber Pazz at the airport on Wednesday afternoon. 'Adelaide is my home now. Even with James dead I have no wish to live in Perth.' She said. 'My in-laws there are a ripe pain in the butt, anyhow. I can't stand his sister and as for my mother-in-law…' She threw her hands up in fake horror, kissed Pazz and Duncan each on the on the cheek and walked out to her Qantas flight with Jason in her arms.

All that week Epsilon seemed to be distracted if a computer can be called that and for long periods was off line. When Pazz asked why, the computer replied that classified information was being monitored from Omega.

'Don't worry,' Epsilon added, 'I am merely downloading information to help us in the future. The collective computers have decided to place Omega in a stationary orbit over Earth and close her down. Only Alpha will remain on line to maintain the cloaking device and deal with any emergencies. It's your next step to independence, Pazz.'

Pazz knew the communicated correct information but she suspected that she had not heard the full story. She became more despondent as the week progressed as she felt everything that had happened since her arrival was based on deceit and dishonesty.

Her bank accounts and even her academic records were really fabricated by Epsilon and now she'd killed a man. What would happen in the future when things went wrong? Could she ever deal with it herself or would that band of electronics around her arm always a step in with ruthless consequences? True, she could close down Epsilon with one word or remove the armlet altogether but she was still psychologically dependent on the one link to her past live.

Towards the end of the week she was once again walking in the park near Elden Crescent when she burst into tears and realized what was also wrong. She missed her family, the family who had been dead for eight hundred years. She could think of Zandra, her mother and sister Kylina, so alive in her mind; it as seemed if she could visit them anytime but that was impossible now.

Also the death of Lynn's husband played on her mind. At home people died; there were accidents, still unconquered diseases, murders and suicides the same as on Earth but with a life span of hundreds of years it was, somehow so remote when you were young. Except for her great great grandmother's death when she was sixteen she had never personally experienced death yet now her own hands had killed someone.

'I thought I might find you here,' said a voice from behind the park bench where Pazz was sitting. She turned and saw a man standing in the sunshine smiling at her. 'Duncan!' she gasped. 'You should be at the university. Why are you here?'

'To see you, Dear.' He'd never called her that before. 'You are the most important thing in my life at the moment. I know you're hurting and I want you to know, I'm here whenever you need me.'

'Oh, Duncan,' Pazz responded.

She stood, stepped into his arms and burst into long sobbing tears. He just held on and moved her long hair aside to tenderly kiss the back of her neck. She did not realize but it was a grieving process she had encountered. She would soon come out the other side more secure and, yes, human than before.

On Saturday Lynn flew back and that night Pazz told them both everything about herself and what had happened since her arrival on Earth.

'You were stabbed Lynn,' she concluded as her two friends clung to every word. 'James had stabbed you at least four times when I arrived and was about to do it again. I was frantic and called on Epsilon to help.' Her eyes flooded with tears and chin quivered. 'Epsilon electrocuted James and stopped his heart beating. I killed him.'

'So what I thought was true,' Lynn replied in a whisper. 'You did save my life.' She glanced across their living room at Pazz. 'But you did not kill James, Pazz. He always had a weak heart. You may have given him a fright but he died of natural causes.'

Pazz fixed her eyes on Lynn. 'Is that true or are you just trying to help?'

'I can prove it if you wish,' Lynn replied. 'There are hospital records in Perth. He had a heart attack three years ago and barely survived. I guess that's why I stayed with him so long and also that could be the reason he grew more violent. He could not face his own mortality and took it out on me.'

'I see,' Pazz almost smiled then faced Duncan. 'That was why I spoke an ancient Aegean language. We brought it to this world over three millennia ago along with our alphabet. If you want nothing to do with this alien creature, I understand.'

Duncan frowned, reached out and pulled her onto his knees. 'Excuse me, Lynn,' he said and hugged Pazz so closely she could hardly breathe and kissed her on the lips.

'I love you, you silly little alien girl, ' he said. 'Lynn is my witness.'

'Sure am,' Lynn said, ' and Duncan is never going to forget what he just said. Okay?'

Pazz nodded as Lynn stood; placed her arms around them both and they all broke into smiles.

*

CHAPTER SEVEN

It took ten days to prepare Space Shuttle Discovery for flight but, finally, three astronauts blasted into orbit in a top-secret mission classified for the media as the routine maintenance of orbiting satellites. No communication at all had been made with the alien craft so Discovery was put into an orbit Earth computers predicted the visitor would be following. However, on the third orbit, Discovery and all communication with it abruptly disappeared. It was as if the space shuttle did not exist.

On board, Astronauts Colonel Tony Sneddon, Major Val Wikstrom and civilian physician Doctor Graeme McKerras grimaced at each other as, like a press of a button, all communication with Earth was cut off. Every other control and electronic equipment acted perfectly but they were alone above the Indian Ocean in an orbit that would arrive over Australia within a few moments.

'I would say we'll have contact shortly,' Tony observed.

Val nodded and ran a tongue over her dry lips. They were professionals and did not expect Discovery to be harmed but this sudden blackout of communication appeared ominous.

'Electronic contact,' she reported as an instrument lit up and a computer screen began filling up with incomprehensible data.

Data poured out for two minutes before English words appeared across the screen. *Thank you for your assistance*, they flashed, ribbon like from left to right. *You have been scanned and have no weapons harmful to us. Your journey appears genuine. On your next orbit, please change course to the following co-ordinates.* Very precise instructions followed before the screen blanked out. Five seconds later contact with Houston Control was established once again as if nothing was wrong.

'What the hell's happening up there?' General Jarvis appeared on a monitor. 'This was a military mission and I do not like losing control of events.'

'We have contact, Houston Control,' Sneddon replied. 'We anticipate loss of communication again. All systems are operating perfectly.'

'Like hell they are!' the general retorted. 'Not when every single monitoring device is cut on the whim of whoever is out there.'

'Request change of course, Houston Control. Data following.' Sneddon chose to ignore his superior. He was the commander of this mission and had the ultimate responsibility.

The general glowered out from the monitor but nodded sideways at the scientists and NASA officials in the room.

'Course change approved, Discovery. Do you want us to activate it?'

'No need,' cut in Sneddon. 'We shall… Oh damn,' he swore as the communications were blanked out again. He turned to Major Wikstrom. 'Well Val, change our course.'

'Yes, Sir.' The woman astronaut nodded and reached forward to the console.

*

Discovery was over Australia when, without warning, Omega appeared in front and, in relation to Earth, slightly above the space shuttle.

'Oh my God,' Graeme McKerras gasped. 'Look at it!'

The three astronauts fixed their eyes through the windshield at the gigantic ball in front of the shuttle. An opening in the top quadrant of the alien craft showed movement and, as they watched, a small cylinder attached to a cord, floated out. This was followed by a voice echoing through the shuttle.

'This is Computer Alpha from starship Omega communicating. We are from the planet Delta in the solar system of Light, which is unknown to your astronomers. For reasons to complex to itemize at this time, our society has little trust of the male of the species so we will only communicate with your Major Val Wikstrom.'

Val, who was responsible for communications anyway, grinned at her two colleagues and replied. 'I am receiving your transmission, Omega. This is Major Wikstrom speaking.'

'We are sending our human into your care. The rescue pod has only three hours life support left. It should be possible to use your recovery equipment to bring it aboard.

The human has not been awoken but will do so shortly. She will be healthy and capable of understanding English but will need immediate inoculation against the flu virus, strain 076 that we believe your scientists have it listed as. Also, the general inoculations you give to newly born infants would be appreciated for our human.'

'We can use our recovery equipment and shall do everything you ask, Omega,' Val replied while she still stared fascinated at the alien vessel. 'Can we be of further assistance?'

'Yes,' replied Alpha. 'You have, we believe an emergency landing port in Magaroona, Southern Australia. Could you please land your craft there? Our human has to go to the city of Adelaide.'

The astronaut frowned. 'That will be difficult, Omega,' she replied. 'We are programmed to land at Kennedy Space Center in Florida U.S.A. Our alternative is in Nevada, United States. Magaroona is only equipped for an extreme emergency.'

The space shuttle went silent for ten seconds as if the alien craft was considering Val Wisdom's reply.

'Computer Alpha answering. We have the technology to over ride your equipment and land your shuttle ourselves but would prefer you to voluntarily abide by our request. Voice communication with Houston Control will be reestablished for five Earth minutes then you will inform us whether you will land in Australia voluntarily or be forced to do so. Thank you.'

'That's telling us, isn't it?' Colonel Sneddon grunted.

The voice cut out and was immediately supplanted by a flow of data from Houston Control but all visual contact remained off line.

'We need to speak to the White House, Sir,' Tony Sneddon reported to a somewhat irate General Jarvis. 'There are only five minutes.'

'White House here. Secretary of State, David Somerville, speaking. We are monitoring your broadcast. What is your request, Discovery?'

Sneddon replayed Alpha's voice that to his surprise had not been erased. 'I believe they have the technology to override our controls, Mr. Secretary,' Doctor McKerras added.

There was a grunt and another voice came on, an easily recognizable voice, that of one of the most powerful people in the world. 'Permission granted, Discovery,' the United States President stated. 'And may God be with you all.'

Contact was again lost and Alpha's voice returned. 'Thank you, Discovery,' she said. 'We shall send our rescue pod over to you. Please use your mechanical arms to take it inside. Unless there is an emergency, this will be our last communication except to say thank you. Our choice of your planet may yet to prove to be the correct one. If treated well, our humans will be of great benefit to your society. Farewell.'

The voice cut off and the sphere shimmered into nothingness. Only the small rescue pod attached to a lone waving lifeline remained visible. As the astronauts watched, a tiny red flame shot from the small craft. It accelerated towards them before a retrograde rocket fired and the pod floated in a precise movement adjacent to their hull. A small metal arm telescoped out and everyone felt a small shudder as something attached to Discovery's hull.

'Okay,' Tony muttered and grinned as all instruments and

communication came on line. 'Bring her aboard.'

The maneuver was faultless and within minutes Discovery's hatches were closed, sealed and the interior pressurized. Val and Graeme floated through to find the canopy of the alien life pod already raised. They moved over to it and examined the visitor with fascination.

A young Caucasian woman who could have been one of millions of similar persons on Earth was lying on a soft mattress. She was clothed in a metallic type pressure suit, not unlike the astronauts' own, but with the headpiece tucked in a side pocket of the craft. A design shaped like a vertical curled loop was engraved on the left breast pocket.

'That's the uppercase letter Omega,' Val whispered in the hushed silence. 'The last letter in the Greek alphabet.'

Graeme nodded and reached in and touched the alien's neck, which felt warm and had a normal pulse rate. It was as if she was asleep with even rapid eye movement noticed behind closed lids.

'She seems healthy,' he reported and gently shook the girl. 'Hello,' he said but received quite a surprise when the eyelids jerked open and bright blue eyes stared into his, curious but not frightened.

'I was told you agreed to take me down to Earth,' she said with a broad Australian accent. 'I am afraid my craft had a malfunction and life support is almost gone.'

Graeme grimaced at Val and glanced at the girl as she sat up in the pod and examined the interior of Discovery with expressionless eyes.

'I am Doctor Graeme McKerras and this is Major Val Wikstrom, ' he began. 'You are on Space Shuttle Discovery...'

'I have been informed of all the details.' The girl gave a shy smile. 'I may be a little disorientated for a while and for that, I apologize. Thank you for the trouble and expense the United States Government has gone to for this rescue.' She accepted Graeme's hand, floated out of the life pod, turned and fixed her eyes on Val. 'Delta, my homeland, is a society of women,' she continued. 'My computers were pleased, therefore, that you are aboard, Major.'

'Call me Val,' the astronaut replied and seemed unsure about what to say next. After all, what does one say to a species from another galaxy?

The girl smiled and held out a hand, something else she'd been instructed to do by Theta, firmly in place around her arm. 'Hello Val,' she said. 'My name in English is Kylina Flower.' She turned and shook Graeme's hand. 'I was told many medical doctors are males,' she added.

Graeme coughed and also seemed somewhat self-conscious. This young woman, and she appeared to be about twenty, seemed to know everything about them while, in return, they were completely ignorant of her background, where she came from or even the reason the alien spacecraft was orbiting Earth.

Kylina fixed her eyes on Graeme. 'I know I am a stranger to be feared but let me assure you that if we had intended to harm the inhabitants on Earth, it would have been done weeks ago when we arrived and carried out a survey of your planet. I am, what shall I call it, a refugee three millennia from home.'

Val frowned. 'How long?' she asked in a hushed voice.

'Omega, my starship traveled for three thousand years to find a suitable planet that we could live on.'

'We?' queried Graeme. 'Are there more of you?'

Kylina grimaced. 'Only my sister now. My other friend did not survive the trip.'

She glanced up as Colonel Sneddon floated in and went through another quite formal introduction. Tony nodded and looked into the blue eyes. 'You said it took three thousand years to find a planet suitable for human life.' he said. 'Forgive me but you do appear human. In all that time were we the only suitable planet?'

Kylina frowned. 'No second,' she answered. 'There were problems with the first.'

'And your sister?' Val added. 'Where is she?'

Kylina glanced out the porthole at the massive blue and white sphere above them.

'There,' she said and pointed to the brown mass that filled most of the Earth they were orbiting over. 'Australia. I need to find her.' She grimaced and flushed. 'She had no immunity to your diseases and almost died. That is why I need protection; but I believe you've been instructed on this.'

'Yes,' Graeme replied. 'I don't have the inoculations here on board but you'll be kept isolated when we land and be given them before being exposed to our atmosphere. It should prevent you from catching any of the more common Earth diseases. I assume your anatomy is similar to ours.'

'Oh yes,' Kylina replied but could not suppress a smile. 'Your people are related to mine, Doctor McKerras. My ancestors have visited before. I am like a distant cousin returning to the family.'

The three astronauts studied the alien girl and each other. There was so much they had to learn.

*

Doctor Matthew McHardy stared at the young woman in front of him. He was told she was twenty-eight but she looked twenty. There was something wrong here. . For close to twenty years he had devoted his life to advance mathematics and quantum physics so how could this young upstart be so advanced and an authority in his field of knowledge.

'You seem to doubt my ability, Doctor McHardy,' Pazz stated bluntly. 'That is within your right so I shall take no more of your time.' She stood, brushed a hand down a brand new navy blue suit and stepped towards the door.

'No! Doctor D'rose,' McHardy blustered. 'It is only your age that is of concern to me.'

'Not my gender?' Pazz's eyes bored into him.

'Of course not,' McHardy continued. 'You may have the ability but when I agreed to interview you I imagined someone, well, in their late thirties. With all due respect, I doubt if you have had the time to develop the expertise in this very advanced research project I have the honor to lead.'

'I see,' Pazz replied and sat back in the chair she had just left, crossed her legs and pulled the skirt of her suit down a fraction, as Earth women seemed to do. 'Age discrimination is against state employment laws, I believe, Doctor McHardy. If you do not want my services because of my lack of experience or ability is within your right but blatant discrimination is something different. '

Matthew McHardy flushed. She might look like a twenty-year-old but this confident woman acted with maturity well beyond her years. 'I apologize, Doctor D'rose,' he continued and slid a sheet of paper across his desk. 'I read your notes from two weeks back and contacted the universities where you trained. They both returned excellent references, as did the firm you worked for…'

Pazz almost smiled. This was something she didn't know about. 'One of the top pharmaceutical companies,' Epsilon said. 'I picked one so large, nobody personally knows anyone.'

'Cheater,' she replied in her thoughts.

McHardy realized Pazz had stopped listening and gave a cough. 'As I was saying, can you tell me why the theory in front of you cannot work?'

Pazz sped read the equations and gave a tiny laugh. It was the basic trick question she'd had at university when she was doing the equivalent to her master's degree. 'Basically this is trying to prove infinity is finite and could be like saying one is equal to zero, Doctor,' she muttered, took a ballpoint pen from her pocket and scribbled three more lines of equations. 'Using the same theory, Doctor McHardy, one can prove time reversal so anyone reaching fifty can make forty nine their next birthday. She circled part of McHardy's equation and handed it back. 'The basic flaw is, of course, in the fifth line there. Fix that up and everything else falls apart.'

McHardy stared at Pazz's figures and shook his head. He had purposely spent hours finding an almost fool proof theory and she discovered the faulty thinking in seconds. He stood and reached out his hand. 'Shall we negotiate a contract and starting salary, Doctor D'rose?' he said.

'Call me Pazz,' she replied and saw why Duncan liked the man. His pride had been pricked a little, she guessed but she was glad she hadn't shown him a really advanced problem on the theory of the inverse of universal expansion. That would have really demoralized him.

Half an hour later she walked into Duncan's office and saw him standing with his head gazing out the window where hundreds of students were walking though the paths below. She shut the door sneaked up, placed her arms around under his and kissed his neck. Duncan jumped in fright and swung around to grab her. She was only a couple of centimeters shorter than him but much slimmer.

'Where's that shy young lady from just a few weeks back?' he laughed as she buried her head in his beard.

'I found out what I had been missing,' she said and kissed him passionately. 'Now we're colleagues I guess we shouldn't fraternize,' she teased and stepped away.

'I hope you weren't too tough on Matthew,' he said.

'Oh, he'll come around.' Pazz laughed. 'Thought I was too young, that's all.'

'I wonder why,' Duncan replied and stared at Pazz who was dressed in that suit, with a frilly cream blouse and had her hair combed out over her shoulders.

'Duncan,' she frowned. 'Stop staring at me like that. It unnerves me.'

'Sorry, Dear,' he flushed. 'Can I take you out for dinner to celebrate, then a visit to the theater.' He grinned. 'I managed to get some tickets for that musical you said you would like to see.'

'I think I'll like that, Duncan,' Pazz said and sat down to tell him about the how Matthew had tried to trick her. 'We did almost the same theory at home. It was a classic mistake in quantum physics."

'So I hope you didn't solve it too quickly,' Duncan added.

'No,' said Pazz. 'I didn't have a heart to point out some other basic flaws he had in his reasoning. That can wait.'

*

That evening, after a tremendous meal and delightful time at the theater, Duncan invited Pazz back to his flat for supper and, like two people in love the word over. It was how it should be, the climax of their love for each other.

'Lynn explained it all to me but I never realized...' she stuttered when they both woke up about six in the morning and found themselves wanting and made love a second time, She flushed grabbed her clothes and redressed while Duncan went and put the kettle on.

'We forgot our coffee,' he said when she walked into the kitchen with a towel around her head after a hot shower. 'Wasn't that what we came here for?'

'No,' she replied bluntly. 'We both knew what we wanted, Duncan. It makes us human, not machines.' Her voice seemed sad for a moment then she smiled, tucked her arms around Duncan again and just clung on. 'But I would like some breakfast now.' she added almost as an after thought.

*

Just after seven in the morning while Duncan drove Pazz home through the suburbs, hundreds of kilometers to the northwest, Discovery thundered down the runway at Magaroona. Three quarters way down the five kilometer runway, the Discovery was met by four gigantic tankers that sprayed the shuttle with high intensity foam capable of killing any organisms that survived the reentry into Earth's atmosphere. Afterwards, two equally large tractor units towed Discovery in through sliding doors to an elevator similar to those on an aircraft carrier.

Once inside, the doors closed and the huge interior hanger was sealed from the outside atmosphere. Discovery was again blasted with high-pressure steam and the condensation sucked away into underground chambers. From there, the whole craft was taken down five levels into the bowls of the Earth and pulled by two more tractors, these with electric motors, into another sealed chamber. Only then were the three astronauts and their alien visitor allowed to disembark.

Val and Kylina were directed by a public address system into a dressing chamber. They were asked to shower and change into new clothes that were waiting for them. Kylina was impressed by the precautions but managed to slip through the shower with Theta still attached to her arm. Afterwards, the two women met up with the male astronauts who had gone through a similar procedure and the four went through into another chamber where they were asked to put on breathing helmets while the air was replaced.

Finally, the inner chamber airlock that reminded Kylina of those on Omega, opened and they walked into a well-lit entrance foyer. All one wall had flowers and bushes growing in a garden while another had a massive tank of tropical fish swimming around. Carpet covered the floor and sofas and armchairs were arranged around two low kidney shaped tables. They certainly did not seem to be thirty meters underground.

A man in military uniform stood by one table with his eyes fixed on Kylina. He stepped forward and held out a hand. 'Please excuse the precautions, Ms Flower,' he said and gave her hand a firm handshake while warm eyes gazed into hers. 'I am Colonel Ira Pope, Commander of Magaroona Research Station.'

'Kylina Flower,' the alien girl replied and the three marines also in the room grinned at her Australian accent. 'Could you thank your superiors for permitting the Discovery to land me in Australia.'

'Err yes,' the colonel said. 'Your computer did not really give us much choice. You must be tired so I will not delay you any longer. My staff will show you to your quarters and afterwards a meal will be provided in the mess.'

Kylina nodded but was pleased when a woman in uniform came up and lead her away down a myriad of corridors to a small but tastefully furnished apartment with living room, kitchen, bedroom and en suite with the usual bathroom facilities. Once again Kylina felt almost at home with the furniture and equipment. The use of hot running water, lights and even the microwave oven were similar to those in Delta and far superior to the conditions she had used for ten years in Custronomus on Planet 38675.6. Though only two dimensional and not capable of transmitting the sense of smell, the television, which was broadcasting an Adelaide channel when she walked in, almost seemed like an old friend.

'I'll leave you to relax, Ma'am,' the woman marine said in a formal voice. 'Press that green button by the door if you need assistance. You will find a wardrobe of clothes your size in the bedroom. Major Wikstrom said she'd drop by to see you shortly.'

'Thank you,' Kylina replied and sighed as she was left alone for the first time since she'd awoken

Events had happened quickly. It only seemed the day before when she had almost drowned and was evacuated to Omega to avoid being arrested. They blasted off into space and she drifted into sleep in the suspended animation chamber; a sleep that lasted several centuries. Now she was on a new planet alone again. The computers had told her Lunol was gone. Tears rushed to her eyes. Lunol was dead! After everything they'd gone through.

'Lots has happened, Kylina,' Theta interrupted her thoughts.' Pazz woke up and is on the planet. You can go to her.'

'What!' the young woman gasped. 'Is Pazz alive after all those years of being kept in suspended animation?'

'The onboard computers managed to over ride the controls that were set to infinity,' Theta continued. 'With Pazz alive you will not be entirely alone like when you arrived on Planet 38675.6.'

'If they let me find her,' Kylina said. 'Poor Lunol. Why did he have to die?'

*

Theta never answered the question nor told Kylina that additional information that was being received.

'Welcome to Earth, Theta,' Epsilon transmitted. 'This is indeed a different and perhaps even better place for our charges but make sure your human is immunized against the local viruses. I almost lost mine.'

Their transmission was interrupted by a third voice. 'Alpha here. Beta and Gamma are deactivated and Omega is now in a stationary orbit above your continent. We have managed to fix the leak; the air supply is being replenished and plant life reseeded. Within three Earth months we will be able to support human life again. Meanwhile, I'll remain on duty to operate the cloaking device. I can be contacted on emergency frequencies. Look after our humans. That is all.'

'We have landed and I sense Kylina is quite excited,' Theta added. 'Keep in touch.'

'Will do,' Epsilon replied.

*

At Magaroona Research station three weeks slipped by. Kylina saw the reason for being placed in an isolation facility but became irritated when man after man came to examine and interview her and there seemed to be no hint of her being allowed to leave. Finally she asked to see Colonel Pope.

'I wish to complain, colonel,' she said after being invited to sit down. 'I have been poked and prodded, had x-rays taken of my anatomy and been constantly harassed by your subordinates. You are a military man and are under orders to extract as much information from me as you can, I guess but enough is enough.'

'But you are not very forthcoming, Young Lady,' Colonel stated quietly, 'You have succeeded in telling us nothing about yourself, your planet or why you are here.'

Kylina's eyes flashed. 'Don't be condescending, Colonel. It may be of interest that I am under orders, too but have been permitted to make a statement.'

'Who do receive your orders from, Ms Flower and how do you receive them?' the colonel interrupted.

Kylina's expression changed to a smile. 'That, Colonel Pope, is classified.'

The man grunted. 'That statement will do for now then, Kylina,' he said

'We wish to register a protest at how we are being held in this isolated military establishment and demand to see a representative of the Australian government on whose land we now stand.' Kylina said.

'You always speak in the plural,' the colonel asked. 'Why?'

Kylina flushed slightly and continued in the first person. 'I appreciate your government's help in saving my life but resent being treated like an enemy. I am not your enemy, Colonel Pope but a refugee from a distant world that may not even exist any more. I was placed in suspended animation for three thousand years for the journey here. Omega is the only starship to get this far out in the galaxy so you need not fear an invading army, or whatever, following There is none' Her eyes fixed on the colonel. 'And why did I speak in the plural, you ask. My only companions for my journey have been the starship's computers.' She shrugged and her eyes dropped. 'I guess they are my only friends. I have no more to say.'

She stood up and walked to the door where two marine guards stepped out to stop her.

'Theta,' Kylina thought and reached out with both hands to touch the men.

They both stared wide-eyed at her, gave a slight moan and collapsed, unconscious on the floor.

Kylina turned to Colonel Pope. 'They are unhurt, colonel.' Kylina said sweetly, 'However, I will not be treated like a prisoner or child. I would like transport to the city of Adelaide in the morning. Thank you.'

She shut the door, walked out along the corridor and back to her quarters.

*

Ira Pope stared, deep in thought at the two marines who awoke and staggered to their feet.

'When she touched me, it was as if I was hit by a bolt of electricity, Sir,' one of them gasped.

'And I heard a voice, Sir,' the second reported. 'It said, "Don't try to use force sergeant for our powers far exceed your own." then I found myself on the floor.'

Ira Pope nodded. 'I have no doubt they do, sergeant. There is more to that young woman than meets the eye. That's the difficulty.' He rubbed his chin. 'Neither of you are to say anything about your ... err slight blackout, and that is an order.'

'Yes, Sir!'

The two embarrassed marines saluted and took up their guard positions outside his door again while the Colonel reached for a phone, pressed a button to scramble his call and punched in a high priority number to Washington. D.C.

*

CHAPTER EIGHT

When Kylina reached the sleeping quarters her poise collapsed and she flung herself on the bed and wept long tears of frustration and loneliness as new emotions seized her. She did not want to be a specimen under a magnifying glass, all she wanted was to find Pazz in that strange sounding city called Adelaide. She sighed and stared at nothing in particular with her mind deep in thought for several moments before a tap sounded on the door.

'Can I come in,' said a female voice. It was Val Wikstrom.

'If you wish, 'Kylina replied, sat up and wiped her eyes.

'It's hard isn't it?' Val said and sat on the edge of the bed.

Kylina nodded. 'I've had little to do with modern men,' she sniffed. 'I guess that makes it hard.'

'Why men in particular,' Val asked. 'Sure we learnt a bit from your computers and yourself on the Discovery but...'

'Women ran our civilization without the need of males. Over hundreds of years, except for a few kept for reproductive purposes, men had been genetically removed from our society. There's was only one male for a thousand women and they were kept on an off shore island. Until the journey on Omega I had never met any.' Kylina glanced up. ' That changed on the planet where I really grew up.' She sighed.' But that was so different, too. I'm naive, I guess but I thought I could just go my own way once I arrived.'

'And where would you go, Kylina?' Val asked in a kind voice.

'Have you been sent by Colonel Pope?' the girl retorted. 'If so...'

'I haven't, Kylina. We both know your room here was bugged but you have jammed all transmissions somehow so nobody can overhear us. I promise that anything you say will be told to nobody else unless you want it. Okay?'

'My sister lives in Adelaide,' Kylina spouted out. 'She did not know I was on Omega. All I want to do is find her. There is nothing sinister or no great military reason for me being here, as Colonel Pope seems to believe. Earth was picked at random because it supported human life. Our civilization is far ahead of yours and we could help you in many ways but have to be trusted.' She stared at the woman astronaut. 'We trusted you by making the initial contact and appreciate what was done. I guess I'd be dead by now if Discovery hadn't rescued me.' Her eyes grew moist again. 'However, if I am going to be held prisoner I might as well be dead.'

'How old are you, Kylina,' Val asked quietly.

'Twenty two but Pazz only remembers me as a twelve year old.'

'How?' Val asked.

Kylina scratched her hair. 'It's a long story but basically Omega found a planet for us to settle on but Pazz could not be awoken from her suspended animation. I lived on the planet for almost ten years. It was a pre-industrial civilization with sailing ships and that. Anyhow, we managed quite well until a plague arrived. Alpha said you had a similar one on Earth several hundred years ago on the continent called Europe.'

'That's correct,' Val nodded. 'It was called the Black Plague.'

'A friend and myself managed to get rescued by a landing pod from our starship. Once on board there were medical facilities to cure us but we decided it was too risky to return to the planet. We went into suspended animation while Omega set off into deep space looking for another world. Alpha, that's one of the onboard computers, said that was about four hundred years ago. I woke up with an implant so I could understand English. I was told only my sister and I survived the journey and Pazz, that's her name, was already on Earth living in Adelaide. The computers had decided not to awaken me until Pazz became established.' She grimaced. 'There was a hull leak and our air supply ran out. That's when we contacted your government. We knew you had a crude spacecraft that could reach me. That's about it.'

'Why doesn't Pazz know you're here?' Val asked.

The girl shrugged. 'The computers didn't tell me so I guess, she hasn't been told about me. They wouldn't want her to worry.'

'You must have highly sophisticated computers if they consider emotions,' Val sad.

Kylina smiled. 'I guess,' she said as a warning came through from Theta not to say any more. 'But they're still only machines.'

Val nodded. 'Look. I'll see what I can do. You had all your inoculations and appear to be in perfect health. I don't believe you're a threat to anyone but we have to be cautious, you know.'

'I know,' Kylina replied, 'but it is twenty-three days. In that time I've only been to the surface twice. That's why I went to see Colonel Pope. My patience has gone.'

'And no doubt you could leave if you wanted to,' Val added.

'If necessary, but I'd then be considered an enemy and hunted down like one. They can't seem to understand, I want to hurt nobody. I am not a threat to anyone.' She shrugged. 'I told the colonel that but I don't think he believed me.'

'I think he did,' Val replied, 'and I know he is very impressed with you. Have a little patience and I'm sure things will happen in the next couple of days.'

She stayed with Kylina for another twenty minutes with stories of her own life and other facts about Earth before finally leaving and returning to her own quarters. Kylina appreciated the visit but suspected that everything was being manipulated from higher up the government hierarchy.

"That's true," Theta said. "Even Colonel Pope is acting under orders."

*

Kylina, now used to Earth time, glanced at the small bedside clock that showed seven a.m., time to get up. She slipped into a dressing gown, grabbed a towel and toilet bag and headed out the door.

'Good morning, Steve' she said to the young marine guard standing, as usual outside the door. After all the years of living in Custronomus on Planet 38675.6 she was used to men and was actually quite flattered by the attention they paid to her.

'Hi, Kylina,' the thin tall marine grinned. 'Right on time, as usual. You should join the marines.'

'Yeah.' She laughed. 'I doubt if they'll have me.'

It was two days after her talk with Val who had become quite a friend had brought her new clothes and other supplies. After wearing long dresses since she was twelve, in what Theta told her was a society equivalent to seventeenth century Earth, it was a pleasure to dress in modern clothes. She walked into the women's ablution block, ran a bath and enjoyed a morning soak. She had just dressed and was combing her hair when there was a tiny tap on the bathroom door.

'This room's in use,' she called out but instead of the person going away a voice replied.

'Kylina, it's Val. We need to talk in private. Can I come in?'

'Sure,' she replied and pulled the tiny latch back and the astronaut slipped in the steamy room. Her usually smiling face was grim.

'Listen Kylina,' she said. 'There isn't much time and I've been told to stay away from you.'

'Why?'

Val tilted her head as if to say "wait" and went and turned the shower on full speed so there was a hiss of falling water before she turned and faced the alien girl.

'After breakfast, Colonel Pope is going to speak to you. He will say they have agreed to take you to Adelaide and you'll be flown there this morning. It's about an hour's flight.'

'Isn't that good news?' Kylina interrupted but could tell something was wrong.

'No,' replied Val. 'The plane looks Australian but is one of ours. Once you're in the air it is going to fly directly out across the Pacific to United States and another military airport in Nevada. They won't hurt you but are not prepared to let you go either. Once in my homeland, they won't have to deal with a foreign government like Australia and I'm afraid the chance of ever finding your sister would be almost nil.'

'Do they know about Pazz?' Kylina gasped.

'I told nobody about your sister so don't worry about that.' Val shrugged. 'I wish I could have done more. I know Ira Pope tried to get you turned over to Australian authorities but was overruled.'

'I see,' Kylina gave a thin smile and touched Val's shoulder affectionately. 'Thanks for the warning. I'll be okay.'

Val handed her a small card. 'My American address,' she said. 'Ring me if you need any help. I'll do everything I can to help trace your sister.' She turned off the shower gave a nod and slipped out.

'Can you help, Theta?' Kylina asked.

'Sure,' the computer replied. 'Just say when. I would advise though…' The words rang through Kylina's determined mind.

'Why not?' she said out loud. 'We'll do it.'

*

When Kylina walked out of the elevator, the forty-degree Celsius temperature made her gasp. It was like the Restricted Zone she remembered visiting as a child back on Delta.

'Climb aboard,' Ira Pope said as a jeep pulled in beside the building.

The girl stared at two jets lined up beside a long runway she last saw when Discovery had landed. The shuttle was now sitting piggyback style on the top of a monstrous four-engine jet.

'The 747 is flying the Discovery back to United States for refitting,' the colonel explained. 'I guess it is quite primitive to you.'

'Yes, archaic,' Kylina grunted and, though warned by Theta to act normally, cast cold eyes at the man.

'Your plane is the Qantas 777 next to it,' he continued as his eyes studied the girl with an intense look. 'That's the Australian airline that will fly you to Adelaide.'

'That's nice,' Kylina responded without emotion as she attempted to hide her apprehension. 'I like the big red pattern on the tail.'

'A stylized kangaroo,' Pope explained. 'That's a native animal. Well, it's not a mammal...'

'I know,' cut in the girl. 'I've studied everything I could find about my new home.' Her blue eyes bore in the man.

'Yes, well.' He coughed. 'We leave straight away.'

'Will you be on board, Colonel?' Kylina asked in a more congenial voice.

'No,' he answered. 'I have to remain on base, here.'

'I see,' she replied, 'then I'd like to thank you, Colonel Pope for your help. I realize you only had to follow orders.' She shook hands, that strange Earth custom, grabbed the small handbag she'd been given and walked towards the aircraft without turning back.

The colonel watched as the plane started it's two massive engines and began to roll out onto the runway. He frowned and nodded to his companion. 'I have a strange feeling lieutenant,' he muttered to his driver.

'What about, Sir?'

'I think that if our young alien friend doesn't want to be flown to United States, she won't be.'

'But how can she stop us, Sir? It's a non-stop flight.'

'With a civilization five hundred years in advance of us lieutenant, anything is possible.' He watched the Boeing lift into the air and pulled himself into the front seat of the jeep. 'Head for the control tower, Lieutenant. I want to keep an eye on that 777.'

*

Kylina settled back and pretended to watch the desert below but, in fact was sizing up the people aboard. There were half a dozen passengers, all men dressed in civilian clothes but she recognized them as marines. Two airhostesses hovered around, dressed in attractive Qantas uniforms and that was it. A hostess had told her there was a flight crew of two in the cockpit but nobody was permitted up there.

'Okay Theta,' she whispered. 'Over to you.'

With a slightly glazed expression she stood and walked down the aisle to the tiny toilet out of sight from the main cabin. She smiled at an airhostess and touched her arm. The woman swung around, stared out with terrified eyes, gave a slight gurgle and collapsed on the floor. Theta, now using Kylina's body, grabbed the woman and dragged her into the toilet. Within seconds, she stripped the uniform off and slipped it on herself. Next, she stepped out and headed forward, through the empty first class section and reached the door to the cockpit. Her armband was removed and she touched the electronic door that sprung open.

One of the pilots who, unusual for a civilian jet, was dressed in military uniform, swung around and smiled at the airhostess.

'Hi,' he said. 'I could do with a coffee.'

Kylina didn't say a word but merely reached both hands forward and touched the two men. Without even a grunt they both sank, unconscious back in their seats. With one heave, the chief pilot was hoisted out of his seat and Theta replaced him. She reached forward and once again just touched the electronic controls. There was a flash of red lights; a voice warning and the starboard engine cut out. 'We have a problem,' a perfect copy of the captain's voice announced on the intercom. 'One engine is overheating and we have decided to return to base. Relax, the 777 can fly perfectly on one engine.'

*

'My God, she's done it,' Ira Pope grunted from the control tower two minutes later as the radar showed the 777 had altered course and swung south east directly towards Adelaide.

'Lost radio contact, Sir,' the Air controller reported. 'Shall I report an emergency?'

'Don't worry, lad,' Pope said. 'I'm sure Adelaide Control will be talking to that Qantas flight right now.' He reached for the phone and rung downstairs. 'Hello, Major Wikstrom,' he said when Val answered. 'Pope here. You'll be pleased to know the Qantas 777 has diverted to Adelaide.'

'Has it, Sir?' Val answered in an innocent voice.

'My God Val,' the colonel retorted. 'I should have you court martialed. Do you think I don't know what goes on at my own base?'

'I don't understand, Sir,' Val replied but smiled.

*

The 777 flew south out over the ocean for an hour, jettisoned aviation fuel and circled around towards the coast. Only then, did a distress call go out asking for a priority emergency landing at Adelaide's international airport.

Inside, Kylina took off her oxygen mask and walked back through the cabin. The sophisticated craft was on full automatic now and could land without human assistance. She was quite impressed with the plane that, considering its primitive design, operated efficiently.

'Good,' she said to herself when she checked the passengers. They were all unconscious but would suffer no more than a headache when they awoke about ten minutes after the aircraft's arrival time in Adelaide. The drug sucked through the air supply was extremely precise.

'Thanks Theta,' she concluded.

*

Fire engines, crash machines and ambulances howled along the runway as the 777 came in but it was a perfect landing. The captain awoke to find himself sitting on the floor and the aircraft stationery at the end of a runway.

'I'd taxi up behind that vehicle with the flashing light if I was you, Captain,' Kylina said in a soft voice from behind. 'You're in Adelaide, not Nevada.' Her voice turned hard. 'I would advise you to do no more than that. Understand!'

The pilot nodded and glared out at all the emergency vehicles on the runway then at the airhostess. 'You're the woman from the space shuttle aren't you?' he spluttered.

'No,' Kylina said. 'I'm a Qantas airhostess returning to her home base. When we stop, you will remain in your seat for at least five minutes. Otherwise there will be an explosion and you'll be responsible for the deaths of all the marines on board; not to mention your crew.' She nodded at the unconscious copilot. 'The airhostess is in the toilet. Tell her I'm sorry to have had to borrow her attire.'

She walked to the door and tossed her head back. 'Don't worry captain,' she said, 'After five minutes this aircraft will be completely safe.' There was no explosive aboard but Kylina didn't think the air force officer would risk calling her bluff.

When the loading ramp was wheeled up to the door, still dressed as an airhostess, she immediately ran down the ramp.

'Run!' she screamed and tore away towards the surrounding boundary fence. 'It's going to blow!'

In one frantic move, she was behind a fire engine where she quickly checked to see if anyone was watching but all eyes were on the 777. She wriggled out of the uniform, and in her own clothes still underneath, mixed in with the rescue crew.

'What's happening?' she asked a serious looking individual in yellow protective clothing. 'I'm from the press.'

The man glared at her. 'How'd you get here?' he growled and signaled to a driver of an airport authority control vehicle. 'Tom, get this woman out of here, will you!'

'Sure, ' the man replied and glanced at Kylina. 'Come on Madam,' he said in a pleasant enough voice. 'This is a restricted area. I'll take you back to the terminal.'

'If you must,' she glowered but climbed aboard and was driven away.

Twenty minutes later, she took a handful of Australian money Val had given her out of the pocket of her blouse and boarded a shuttle bus for the city center.

'Epsilon gave me Pazz's address,' Theta communicated. 'Have you a city map?'

'Yes,' said Kylina. 'I bought one in the terminal building. She lives about half an hour's drive out. We can catch what is called a train to a station near her place. ' She looked out at the sunshine. 'It's a lovely day and not too hot, here. I think I'll walk from the station.'

*

It was mid afternoon and Lynn was hanging clothes on the line in the back yard when she glanced up and someone Pazz standing in the driveway.

'Hi Pazz,' she called and continued pegging the clothes up. 'Why are you home so early?' She said. 'That pastel fawn colored blouse looks lovely on you.'

'You must be Lynn,' the woman said. Lynn frowned, stepped forward and studied the visitor closer.

'Oh my God!' she exclaimed. The person standing there was identical to Pazz but her hair was slightly longer, face minutely slimmer and perhaps a little younger looking. 'You aren't Pazz!'

'Do I look like her? ' Kylina replied.' I haven't seen her for a while.'

'Identical,' Lynn gasped. 'Are you her twin?' she frowned and shook her head. 'But that's impossible!'

'I'm her sister but not her twin,' Kylina replied.

'But how?' gasped Lynn and dropped the clothes she was carrying on the lawn and continued to size up her visitor.

'I would be ten years younger than Pazz,' Kylina explained. 'The reason we look alike is that I'm her cloned sister. It's done quite a lot from where we come from.'

*

Kylina was fascinated with Baby Jason and also Lynn's car as they drove at a hectic pace back to the center of town and the university. 'Pazz has been working there for two weeks now,' Lynn explained. 'She's got a boyfriend. I hope you don't mind.'

'Why should I?' the other girl said.

Lynn shrugged. 'Pazz said there were hardly any males on your planet.'

'True but I spent the last decade on another planet where there were plenty of men so I'm used to them.' She shrugged. 'I had one special male friend.'

Lynn waited but when Kylina didn't volunteer any more information she didn't press the issue. She watched her companion flick a hand to toss a strand of hair back. My God, their mannerisms were even the same. They drove on; Lynn switched to a neutral topic and described various interesting scenic attractions they were passing. Ten minutes later they reached the university, spent ages finding a park and walked back to the mathematics building. On the way they walked near Duncan's block and Lynn grinned mischievously.

'Like to meet Duncan? It's on our way' she asked. Kylina nodded as she stared fascinated at the campus and everything around her.

'It's so different,' she gasped as she followed Lynn through a sliding glass door and into a lift. On the fifth floor, the door slid open and they walked along a corridor and Lynn knocked on Duncan's office door.

The associate professor answered, grinned, immediately stepped forward tucked his arms around Kylina and kissed her quite passionately on the lips then frowned for the woman did not respond.

'You're in trouble, now,' Lynn laughed. 'You wait until Pazz finds out.'

Duncan stared at Lynn, at Kylina then looked again. Like Lynn, on closer inspection he noticed the very slight differences and had the grace to flush bright red.

'I am so sorry,' he apologized and stepped back. He noticed Lynn's face and grinned. 'You did this on purpose, didn't you?' he accused before switching his attention back to the other woman. 'You can only be Pazz's sister,' he said, held a hand to his forehead and smiled. 'Kyle... no that's not it; Kylina.'

'And you're Duncan,' Kylina said and shook Duncan's extended hand.

'But you aren't twelve!' Duncan gasped.

'No.' The young woman beamed. 'Twenty-two. I had a break on the way to Earth.'

Lynn heard a footfall, glanced up, saw Pazz approach along the corridor and dug Duncan in the ribs.

'Big sister's here,' she whispered.

'Hi Lynn!' Pazz had not really looked at Kylina who was facing the other way. 'How's Jason?'

'Fine,' replied her friend as Pazz gave Duncan a kiss and swung around to speak to the stranger.

She stopped; her eyes grew wide and a hand reached up to cover her mouth.

'Pazz!' Kylina whispered. 'No wonder Lynn and Duncan got us muddled.' She bit on her lip and suddenly without warning, tears flooded into her eyes. 'Do you know me, Pazz?'

The older sister just stood with her face drained of all color and hands trembled. 'It can't be!' she stuttered.

'It is. I'm Kylina but I'm not that skinny little twelve year old that kissed you goodbye home on Delta.' She tried to brush the tears away. 'Well, aren't you going to welcome your little sister to Earth?'

'Oh my God, Kylina!' Pazz found she was also in tears as she grabbed her sister and hugged her so tightly. 'How can you be here?' she sobbed. 'I thought you had died hundreds of years ago.'

Duncan placed his arms around their shoulders and guided the two sobbing sisters back into his office. Lynn, with Jason in her arms followed, shut the door and managed to find chairs for everyone.

'I was on Omega, too,' Kylina explained. 'The computers didn't awaken me until after you'd left the ship. Oh Pazz, I thought I'd never see you again.' She tried to smile but only succeeded in crying.

'But how?' Pazz sniffed. 'My God. My little sister...' Once more, though, she was overwhelmed with emotion and just hugged Kylina who was shuddering with huge tears plopping to the floor.

*

Duncan watched, fascinated. They were identical. Without different clothes and slightly different haircut, he could not tell them apart but he'd been told Pazz's sister was only twelve years old. He frowned. How could this be?

'I'll explain,' Pazz said a few moments later when the two young women had sobbed all the tears out. 'Bearers on our world were either fertilized artificially but at times cloning of DNA cells made the new child like a twin of the person the cells came from. My cells were cloned and later placed in my mother's womb. Kylina grew like any fetus from then on. You'd call us clone sisters in English. The government encouraged it in preference to using male sperm.' She took Duncan's hands and her eyes searched his. 'Our world was a lot different, Dear. Try not to be judgmental.'

Duncan held her close. 'I'm not,' he said and turned to Kylina. 'I am so pleased you found us, Kylina. Sorry I kissed you earlier. I really thought you were Pazz.'

'You what!' Pazz accused and caught Lynn's eye. 'Oh I see,' she said and put her chin out. 'I think somebody else has some explaining to do.'

'Come on.' Duncan interrupted before things became complicated. 'I think this calls for an early day home. I'm sure there is plenty to talk about.'

Together the four adults and the toddler wandered out into the afternoon sunshine with Pazz and Kylina slipping into a different language in their excitement. Duncan walked behind and listened.

'Watch it!' he said in the long dead Aegean language. 'I can understand a little of your conversation.'

'How!' gasped Kylina in the same language.

'Oh he's just showing off,' Pazz said and slipped her hand into Duncan's. 'That's how he found me.'

*

Unknown to the humans walking and chatting together, there was a huge data flow being transmitted between the two armlet computers. 'You could have warned Pazz,' scolded Theta.

'And if Kylina didn't survive, how would Pazz have felt? Anyhow, Alpha directed me not to, as she did with Lunol.' Epsilon replied.

'Figures,' the other computer almost retorted.

*

CHAPTER NINE

It was well after midnight and the two sisters were still catching up with their news, Duncan had dozed off on the couch and Lynn had gone to bed.

Kylina gazed at Pazz, 'I still can't believe I'm here with you,' she added. 'Funny though, you always seemed so tall and old to me, almost like a second mother instead of a sister and now we're the same size and a mirror image of myself. It takes some getting used to.'

'At least you knew about me,' Pazz replied. She folded her legs and reached across for a mug of coffee they had just prepared. 'When I saw you this afternoon I thought you were a hologram and Duncan had set up an elaborate trick then I realized they haven't got the technology to do this on Earth.'

'Yeah, he's a real hulk and great kisser, isn't he?' the younger sister teased

'Kylina!' Pazz frowned and glared. 'If you...' she broke into a smile and gave her clone a playful slap on the back. 'Okay, so, as a twelve year old you were awakened by Alpha and spent a decade on this primitive planet. This explains the reason why you're an adult now but you did not tell me how you came to be on Omega in the first place.'

'I twisted Great Grandmother around my finger a little and it just went on from there,' Kylina replied. Some of the laws of Delta became quite useful.'

'Tell me about it,' Pazz sat forward in the couch and fixed her sister with an intense gaze.

'It seems a lifetime ago,' Kylina began...

*

'Can't we go any faster?' the tall slim twelve year old screamed. She gripped the edge of her safety harness and glared out the window of the hovercar as they traveled at a sedate twenty units along the magnetic highway.

'For another ten credits I can move into the forty unit lane,' the computerized voice replied.

'Do it!' Kylina ordered and held her palm over the fee interface.' My great grandmother Matron Mippard First Flower will guarantee the fare. You can read her approval.'

'Fare approved,' the voice replied.

The hovercar rose five meters straight up, signaled electronically and moved right into the faster lane. It dropped, sensors connected to the magnetic pad and switched back to automatic. Every other hovercar in the lane behind let them in and Kylina had the satisfaction of watching as they passed the slower traffic.

'We shall reach the spaceport in five decaminutes,' the computer reported.

Kylina bit on her fingernails in nervousness. It had taken so long to persuade Great Grandma to sponsor her, it could be too late. 'Go to Level 4, Gate 56,' she ordered.

'Priority clearance is needed for that access route.'

Kylina sighed and ran her palm over the interface again. 'I have proxy approval from my great grandmother,' she retorted.

'Proxy approval cleared. Arrival time at Level 4, Gate 56 is 3.5 decaminutes.'

'Thank you,' Kylina replied sarcastically and lapsed into silence. The sixteen lanes, four level magnetic highways had every hovercar and the larger hover transporters spaced out exactly three meters between bumpers. As they neared the thirty-storied terminal the speeds of all vehicles slowed as many dropped down or rose up to other highway levels. Kylina's hovercar made three vertical and five horizontal changes before slipping into her destination.

She slipped on a small backpack from the back seat and jumped out onto the platform and ran along the passageway. It was faster than the rolling sidewalk. The terminal itself was crowded but Kylina's magnetic ticket flashed yellow then blue as she neared the correct entrance gate.

Finally, she stood in a line of thirty or more women, fuming. More delays! Her ticket flashed red. Damn! In five deciminutes the gate would close and her frantic trip would have been in vain.

Two deciminutes later she reached the counter, presented the ticket and stared into the eye pupil recognition examiner. 'A minor needs authority,' the woman behind the counter stated in a bored voice.

'I have my great grandmother's proxy,' Kylina gulped. Perhaps her mother had already found out and cancelled the approval. It only took one brief videophone call or electronic zap.

The woman smiled and scanned the ticket. 'It's fine,' she said. 'Have a pleasant trip.'

Kylina nodded and stepped over to the entrance gate where a rolling pavement carried her out to the orbiter, a three hundred seat spacecraft that lifted passengers from Delta's surface into orbit to rendezvous with the deep space vehicles tied up to Space Station 5. At the moment,

Lambda, Xi, Upsilon and of course Omega were docked.

Their orbiter, named simply Orbiter 56, was on a sponsored visit to Space Station 5 with most of the passengers spending a couple of days aboard, having a guided tour of one of the deep space vehicles and returning home. Kylina was one of these. She knew Pazz would be on Omega and was probably already in suspended animation ready for the three year journey to Planet 456.7; this really stood for the seventh planet orbiting solar system 456, a Delta like planet with a humanoid population but no space capabilities.

Pazz's community service sentence, Kylina knew, was to land on the planet and kidnap a quota of thirty seeders. They would be drugged, taken to Omega and have sperm removed from them to replenish the almost depleted Delta sperm banks Afterwards, the seeders would be returned to their planet and released. Modern technology meant that these seeders would have no knowledge of their experience.

This one trip, if successful, would ultimately lead to almost half a million bearers being fertilized. It sounded easy but was really quite difficult, as every seeder had to go through a rigid examination and be free of any diseases or genetic flaws. Often, Kylina knew from her school studies, only one in ten seeder was suitable. She shuddered at the though of poor Pazz having to capture close to three hundred of these violent creatures.

Of course, the sperm banks weren't quite so important now that cloning was becoming more popular. Cloned sisters were held in high regard by society as only the top intellectuals were allowed to be cloned from and Kylina was proud to be Pazz's clone sister.

Her mind switched back to Pazz's punishment. It wasn't fair! All her sister did was ask for more individual freedom for Delta's citizens. Kylina couldn't understand why her sister had also sort more freedom for seeders on Delta and guessed that was why the sentence was so severe. But seven years away from home was too much. That was why she was determined to go and help Pazz. After all, even though Pazz was twenty years older than herself they were clone sisters.

'Excuse me, Miss' said a voice and Kylina's thoughts jumped back to the present. 'Would you like me to show you your seat?'

They had reached Orbiter 56. The space hostess led her through the passengers' compartment and explained how to attach the G-Force suit.

'Thank you,' Kylina said and clipped the suit around her torso. It felt tight but she could still move her limbs and head.

'Don't leave it on,' said the space hostess. 'You'll be told when it needs to be worn. We aren't leaving for five deciminutes. You're welcome to go up to the observation deck and have a meal or drink,' she said. 'No mind beverages are allowed to minors, of course.'

'Of course,' Kylina replied. 'She hated the taste of mind beverages anyhow and knew Pazz hardly ever drank them.

She unclipped the suit and stared at everything around, the holograph, music and smell channels and contact ports. There was a sliding cabinet in front to place her backpack in and an electronic book for every passenger.

Kylina loved reading and her stomach was too twitchy for her to eat so she opened the book, picked a fantasy topic and selected a story from the two hundred titles offered. Words flashed onto the page and the youngster sat down to read. Before she realized it, the engines started and they were off. The first fifteen minutes consisted of an atmosphere flight out across the ocean before everyone was asked to clamp their G-Force suits on.

'Anti-matter motors will start up in one minute.' the space hostess warned. 'Could all food, drinks and loose objects be placed in the vacuum cylinders in front of your seats, please. Bearers with a baby, please ensure that your daughter has her G-Force container in the closed position so the blue light is flashing. We should escape Delta's gravitational pull in approximately nine deciminutes. Just relax and enjoy the flight on Orbiter 56.'

Even though Kylina had read about it many times, when it came, the acceleration and pressures made her feel as if the skin was being pushed off her bones; her body was thrust backwards and even her eyes felt like hard rocks. She was, though, determined not to black out as she gritted her teeth and held on.

All sound seemed to disappear and the pressure pushed her so hard she was sure her body would be driven out the back of the seat. She blinked and held her breath then saw Delta out the window, the curve of the planet and turquoise sky. It was so beautiful!

Suddenly the pressure stopped and she felt free and light.

'We're in space, Ladies,' the space hostess announced. 'You are weightless. Feel free to unclamp your G-Suits and float around. There are handles on the walls and ceilings to help you move but be careful at first. Staff will help anyone who has difficulty. Thank you.'

Kylina unclamped the G-Suit and pushed. 'Yowl!' she gasped as she shot to the ceiling, hit the soft padding there and rolled over in a backward somersault. She seemed to be okay but everyone else on board were hanging from the ceiling. Even the seats were upside down.'

'I'll help you, Kylina,' said a voice and the girl felt herself being rolled over so she was floating above her seat. It was a strange experience.

'Thanks,' she said. 'I didn't realize I'd move so quickly.'

'Hardly any effort is needed,' said the smiling space hostess. 'Think of it as swimming; push off lightly and reach for a handhold.'

Kylina grinned and found it was quite easy except when another woman bumped into her and they both shot off in different directions. Passengers were now everywhere in all sorts of weird positions. One old lady was even sitting sideways against a wall reading an electronic book while another bounced herself around like a balloon.

Kylina floated up to the observation deck and stared, fascinated at the space station on the distant horizon above Delta. The starships were like huge black or silver balls around it. The one twice the size of the others must be Omega. Everyone was chatting and a couple of girls only a little older than herself pointed out items of interest on the space station or Delta below.

'We dock in half an hour,' a voice announced ten deciminutes later.

'Could all passengers return to their seats, please. Note that the space station has artificial gravity so when we dock, this will be transferred to us. You will feel disorientated for a few microminutes as your weight returns. After docking, you will be able to walk in an ordinary way. Thank you for joining us on Orbiter 56 and we hope you will fly with Orbiter Spaceways on your trip back to our planet.'

*

Kylina had practiced everything she was going to do several times back home but now she was in the starship it seemed to be an impossible task. The guide showing the tourists through Omega droned on incessantly and security guards stood everywhere, silent but alert with stun guns in their belts. Kylina hung back until everyone disappeared around a corridor corner, saw a guard's eyes following the party and acted. With two quick steps she retreated behind a bulkhead, turned and slipped into to the master control room the group had just come out from.

She breathed a sigh of relief. The room was silent and empty. Shadowless lights lit the whole area and one wall was filled with row upon row of white squares that lit up in random patterns. Five large G-Force couches were arranged in sitting positions in front of a semi-circular console and a row of three-dimensional monitors. Only three were on line and showed views of tourists wandering around.

'Well, here goes,' she whispered to herself as the automatic door slid shut behind. She walked over and sat in one of the couches. 'I am Kylina 4th Flower, clone sister of Pazz 4th Flower.'

She stared around but nothing happened. Kylina bit on her lip and continued. 'I wish to invoke Law 7839, Clause 16, Sub clause 9.8 which gives a clone sister the right to serve half the sentence imposed on a guilty woman.'

'That is not possible,' a quiet voice replied.

Kylina jumped in fright and stared around. She could not tell where the voice came from. It seemed to be everywhere at once.

'Why?' she blustered.

'You cannot split a journey through the galaxy in half. That is impossible.'

'But the time served on Planet 456.7 can be,' Kylina argued. 'I am prepared to capture half my clone sister's quota of seeders so the time she spends on the planet can be halved.'

'You are a minor,' the voice replied.

'I have my great grandmother's proxy,' Kylina continued and hoped the computer did not notice the nervousness in her voice. This was where the plan flawed. Great Grandmother Mippard had been persuaded to let her visit the space station to watch Omega depart but no more.

'Place your palms on the interface, please,' the computer stated in a neutral tone.

Kylina gulped, reached forward and clasped the glowing interface ball.

'That is in order,' replied the computer. 'There are difficulties with your main request, though. I will have to consult with my sister computers. Please wait.'

Kylina found her hands and brow covered with perspiration as she waited. She trembled and gazed in apprehension around the room. Microminutes changed into minutes and onto deciminutes. Computers were usually so fast any reply was instant. What could be wrong?

She shrugged and tried to console herself. She was doing nothing wrong. Even if the worst happened and a guard walked in and found her she would only be sent back home. But perhaps she had broken the law. She was stretching great grandmother's permission and being dishonest. That would earn at least five demerits and perhaps prevent her from attending grammar school. But it was too late now. She was committed!

The voice came back. 'You accept responsibility as a proxy adult for your own actions?' it stated.

'I do,' Kylina replied.

' Do you realize your clone sister is already prepared for the journey.

You will not be able to consult her or gain her permission for this transaction.'

'Yes.'

'Wait one moment.'

This time the wait was short, a mere half dozen microminutes.

'Request is approved,' the voice said. Before Kylina could even breathe a sigh of relief, a door to her left slid open to reveal a long corridor. 'Proceed to Suspended Animation Room 16 and wait for further instructions.'

*

Pazz listened in fascination. 'So you were prepared to help me serve my sentence, Kylina,' she said quietly. 'I am humbled that you, at twelve made that decision but why did you do it?'

'You were treated unfairly, Pazz.' Kylina glanced down. 'I could not bare thinking of growing up without you. At that time seven years seemed a lifetime.' She smiled faintly. 'As it turned out, I grew up without you, anyway.'

Pazz nodded. 'So what happened when you arrived at the planet?'

'Alpha told me where we were and, of course hundreds of years had past so I could not go back. You were still alive but could not be awoken. I even tried a manual over ride but it didn't work, Finally, I agreed to be landed on Planet 38675.6. In return Alpha said she would attempt to override the infinity command keeping you asleep.'

'But you were still a child. How did you cope?'

Kylina smiled. 'The computers became my family and I was given Theta as an armlet.'

*

'Now remember,' said Beta who had taken over Kylina's education. It was two weeks since her awakening and Omega had gone in a stationary orbit above a large land mass in the northern hemisphere.' We have selected the most progressive country on this planet but it is still very primitive. This presented enormous problems to us, as we could not link into electronic equipment, as there are none.'

Kylina sat in her own apartment in the starship and stared at a monitor screen that showed views of the world below.

'So how did you find out everything you've told me?' she asked.

'We sent 647 flybugs to the surface to record data, sent back voice signals, pictures and so forth. We have not found out everything, of course, but enough to help you.'

'Go on,' Kylina said with a pout.

'The planet is inhabited by a fifty percent male population but women are equal in the country we chose. I visited a village called Nkypy and, as a holograph of your mother, Zandra, enrolled you at a boarding school there. "Wasn't that a risk?'

'As long as they didn't try to touch me, it was okay. It is all set and you go tomorrow.'

'So soon,' Kylina gasped.

'Through Theta, we will be in constant touch,' Beta replied. 'Also on holidays and home weekends a landing pod will pick you up and bring you back here. It is not good for you to remain here by yourself.'

'But what about Pazz?'

'If we awaken her we will contact you. This may be several years, I am afraid. You see we have to prove infinity is a concrete number and not just an abstract idea. Once this is done we can use the number infinity to program in the wake up procedures. '

'What about their language? It will be hopeless if I can't talk to anybody.'

'You are speaking and thinking it, Kylina and have been doing so since you woke,' replied Beta. 'It was programmed into your mind while you were still in suspended animation.'

'You think of everything, don't you?' Kylina retorted.

'No,' replied Beta. 'I forgot one thing.'

'You did and what was that?' the twelve-year-old's voice had a triumphant ring to it.

'Your new name. We though it was best if you didn't sound foreign. The countries there are constantly at war and foreigners are regarded with suspicion. You'll be called Kagit Frysyl, which is a literal translation of your real name.'

*

Kylina was landed in the predawn darkness in a field behind a coach way station. She climbed out of the pad and lifted her full-length gown up as she stepped to the ground and found short wet grass beneath her feet.

'I'll never get used to these clothes,' she grumbled.

'You will be fine,' Theta replied. 'They don't have electricity here but there is a tiny lantern in your suitcase. It looks authentic but is really a flashlight. Don't turn it on yet. Just walk straight ahead in the darkness. I'll guide you.'

'Okay.'

Kagit shivered in the cool air and stepped forward like a sleepwalker until she came to a stone wall. She turned and felt quite alone as the landing pod shimmered, became invisible and with a very slight rush of air, headed into the dark sky. She felt her way along to a wooden gate but found her long gown restricted her.

'It's unladylike to climb gates,' Theta warned. 'Find the latch.'

The girl muttered under her breath as she opened the gate and stepped through onto a narrow road. The surface was hard and seemed to consist of smooth stones fitted together. It was pitch dark but after walking for several moments, she came to a curve in the road and saw lights ahead.

My goodness, there was a coach and horses in front of a building. She could see a person, human but somehow different, walking around holding a lantern. Kylina gasped. The lamplight showed the person's face. It was covered in whiskers. This was a seeder, not a woman. A man! The word made her tremble in panic.

'Steady,' Theta's words filled her mind. 'He will not attack you. Go up and speak naturally.'

Kylina felt her face turn cold with fear, and then burn with embarrassment. In her whole life she had never seen a man and now she was expected to talk to one. She gulped, grabbed her heavy suitcase and stepped forward.

'Good morning, Kind Sir,' she said.

The man swung around. 'Kagit Frysyl?' he asked in a deep but kind voice. 'We were waiting for you, lassie. Where is you mother?'

'Mother had to return home to milk the cows,' Kylina replied in a statement she had practiced back on Omega. She had to remember to think of herself as Kagit.

'Aye. Thems cows wait for nobody,' the man muttered. 'Climb inside, lassie. We'll have you at school by mid-mornin' ' He grinned at her, grabbed her suitcase, tossed it to the top of the stagecoach and opened the door.

Kylina stepped into the dark interior and jumped, once again in fright. Someone else was sitting inside. She felt a soft hand touch hers, saw warm eyes and another long gown. It was another girl.

'Hi Kagit, I'm Murik Prawul and this is my first trip away from home. I'm a new pupil at the Nkypy School for Young Ladies, too. God, I'm nervous and so glad you're with me.'

The driver yelled a command, the horses moved forward and the lights from the way station shone in the interior of the stagecoach. Kylina noticed a girl her own age with red hair, wide blue eyes and a smiling freckled face.

*

'My goodness, Murik could talk,' Kylina grinned at Pazz, 'We became good friends. I stayed at the school for four years. They were quite tough and stern days but I was happy. Every holidays I went back to that way station, waited until evening, walked to the field and the landing pod was there waiting to transport me back to Omega. Nobody ever saw us. I guess the computers had some sort of cloaking device in operation.

As time went by, I returned to Omega less often and Custronomus became my home.' She smiled. 'So that's where I grew up, Pazz and now I'm here with you.'

'A beautiful confident woman, not my skinny sister,' Pazz said.

'Watch it,' Kylina added. 'You're talking about yourself, too, you know. We are identical.'

'Yes,' laughed Pazz. She stood up and glanced at the clock. 'My God, it's two thirty. We've been talking for hours. Your room is the one on the left.' She flushed a bright red. 'I sleep with Duncan.'

'Pazz,' Kylina replied and reached for her sister's hands. 'Relax, I grew up on a planet with men, remember. The propaganda they told us about them on Delta was exaggerated wasn't it?'

'Yes,' Pazz replied. 'I was correct in demanding more rights for men on Delta. There are good and bad of both genders.' She had a faraway look in her eyes. 'That was so long ago. I wonder if they ever changed.'

'I guess we'll never know,' the younger sister replied
*

CHAPTER TEN

Research scientists were frustrated with the alien rescue pod, still sealed from the outside atmosphere below the South Australian desert. The small interior where Kylina had lain contained nothing except a mattress made of soft synthetic material similar in composition to nylon. Her air helmet was more interesting but was not a lot different from Earth designed gear. The rest of the pod was sealed without even a trace of a joint. X-rays failed to penetrate the material and diamond cutting gear howled and screamed without making even a scratch on the surface.

It was late at night and a lone scientist remained in the laboratory. After six hours of using electronic equipment to try to discover an opening device, Doctor Tedra Haygrove ran her hand along the hard plastic type dashboard for the umpteenth time. Something, though, did happen. When her gloved fingers touched what appeared to be just the black synthetic surface a small rectangle lit up and began to blink. Tedra touched it, heard a slight swish of air and turned to see a woman standing in the corner of the room.

'Good evening, Doctor Haygrove,' the woman said in perfect American accented English. 'I waited until you were alone and without your male colleagues.' Dressed in ankle length sky blue frock, she looked to be in her late thirties, had short dark hair and wore no makeup or jewelry except for a golden armlet on her bare arm.

Tedra's noticed a faint quiver around the woman and frowned.

'You are correct, Tedra,' the woman continued. 'This is a holograph. If you reached out your hand it would simply go through my image.'

'Did I trigger this?' the scientist asked.

'Only because I wanted you to,' the woman replied with a slight smile. 'I am Computer Beta from the Starship Omega. We originated from the planet we call Delta, the fourth planet orbiting our sun. We needed to gather data about your civilization before further contact was made. Also we were waiting to see if Kylina arrived at her destination. She is safe so we can now move on to the next stage. We have studied your treatment of our human and have given your planet a classification.'

'Interesting,' Tedra commented. 'But please, continue.'

'Your planet was ranked omicron, fifteenth in what you on Earth call the Greek Alphabet but in fact originated in our world. That meant we considered your society was too primitive to help and no further contact would be made with it.'

'But you are making contact!'

'Yes,' said Beta. 'We have been fed information on our other human living in Australia. She is being treated with compassion and is integrating into Australian society well. We picked this society in preference to your own for several reasons that need not be discussed now.' Beta gave a twitch of a smile. 'Service to say, you were high in our list but the clandestine operation by military males to try to kidnap Kylina and transport her to United States did not help your ranking.'

'Colonel Pope and myself tried to prevent that happening, but go on,' Doctor Haygrove placed reading glasses on and peered at the hologram.

'Your commander's empathy was recognized,' Beta said. 'It helped towards an upgraded ranking of lambda, the eleventh level, which means we are prepared to help you with your medical, social and scientific programs except those of a military nature. You are not yet advanced enough to benefit from help in contacting other civilizations in the galaxy. In fact, for your own protection, this solar system remains unknown to all but a few Psi and Omega classified civilizations. These are sufficiently advanced to gain nothing by harming you.' Beta stopped and her lips turned serious. 'There is one condition, though.'

'And that is?'

'Our humans on Earth are to be left in peace, to grow and become part of Earth's society. If they are followed, harassed or imprisoned, all contact will be broken. We shall be observing their integration over the next six months. At that point in time we will give our final decision on whether to help your society or not. You are, shall we say, on probation. I have allowed this vision to be recorded and hope copies will be forwarded to your leaders. That is all.'

There was a shimmer and Beta disappeared. The scientist immediately reached over to her television console and smiled as a video of the whole conversation started up on the screen.

'So if the militants don't blow it we should benefit from this,' she spoke into a microphone and sat at the computer to make contact with her superiors in Washington.

*

Unknown by the alien computers, though, the rectangular light Tedra touched had a thread of fungus attached to it. The slight warming caused the microscopic living cells to grip the scientist's glove. When Doctor Tedra Haygrove left through the airlock, she did everything right, except one thing. She undressed and placed her laboratory clothes in a vacuum unit for sterilization but one glove dropped to the floor and the fungus rubbed off. She picked her glove up, placed it in the unit, showered and changed into new clothes. However, her small toe stepped on the fungus mycelium and it was carried out the second airlock to the living quarters and unintentionally deposited on the woolen carpet.

This particular breed of fungus had been carried to Omega on Kylina's clothing when she left Custronomus and lay dormant for four hundred years in the sub zero temperatures of the spacecraft. By chance, it had survived both Starship Omega's stringent sterilization procedures and those of the station. The natural wool carpet and constant twenty degrees Celsius temperature of the air conditioning was perfect for the fungus to grow.

Two days later, ten marines completed their tour of duty and were replaced by new guards who flew in from California in a United States Air Force military transport. Two of these had a cold and the globules of water they sneezed into the air proved a perfect host for the fungi spawn. It was akin to holding a lit match above an opened can of gasoline.

*

It was a Monday morning; Pazz was at work and Jason asleep in his room. Lynn watched Kylina as the new arrival sat back and gazed at the painting she was working on and dabbed a recently added section with her brush. Though as alike as identical twins, there was a supple difference between Kylina and Pazz. The younger sister had different interests, was talented in art and music and in many ways seemed more confident with people than Pazz. With help from the computers she had taken the surname D'rose and had her birth and other records entered in the government computers. She had, however, refused to have any academic records credited to herself beyond high school level and also refused to have a bank account.

'It is dishonest,' she said bluntly and had her first disagreement with Pazz over the idea. 'Okay, you needed money to get established but I am lucky enough to have you. I'll get a job and earn money like everyone else.'

And she did. It was only shift work in a local supermarket but she mixed with locals and soon found a group of friends her own age. She joined a gym and became a regular customer.

'Well, I grew up in an ancient society,' Kylina said when Lynn mentioned how she was different. 'Sure, I had help from Theta but there were no modern conveniences at all, so much of the time was spent just doing the basic things in life; cooking meals, washing and so forth. I got bored and that's when I began to paint and play music.'

She looked up from the half-finished painting of a woman dressed in seventeenth century clothes standing in front of a massive castle. 'That is a copy of a real scene,' she said in a soft voice. 'That is Gnilyn, my best friend. She never survived the plague. I'll tell you about it one day.'

She glanced up and frowned. 'Lynn,' she asked, 'Am I a nuisance to have around?'

'Of course not,' Lynn protested. 'But why do you ask?'

'Well, with Jason and Pazz, not to mention Duncan who might as well live here, it's getting pretty crowded. It's three weeks now and I'm pretty well sorted out. I could get a flat and...'

'You will not,' Lynn replied. 'Pazz would be devastated if you even considered it.'

'Would she?' Kylina replied. 'She's got Duncan and what about you, Lynn? Are you just being kind to us both?'

Lynn grabbed a chair and sat down. 'If you want to know the truth, here it is,' she said. 'I have never been happier. My marriage was a disaster, I'm not interested in any more relationships at the moment and Jason fills my time. Without Pazz and yourself around, though, it would be a lonely life so don't even consider leaving.' She gazed intently at Kylina. 'I still get the two of you muddled up at times. '

'Yeah,' chuckled Kylina and dabbed some more paint on her canvas. 'They give me heaps at the supermarket when Pazz comes in. The manager started giving her orders last time and turned to see me at the checkout counter. God, he went bright red.'

'Just like Duncan, that day you met,' Lynn chortled.

'Well, I was surprised too, you know. This big bearded hulk of a guy grabs me in a massive hug and plasters me with kisses. I wondered what sort of place Earth was.'

Lynn smiled and reflected on her new life. Everything to do with her husband's estate had been sorted and she'd been able to pay off the mortgage on the house, Jason was growing like a mushroom and the two alien woman living with her seemed anything but from out of the world. Pazz now spent hours at the university and had become a highly respected staff member and Duncan spent at least two nights at 19 Elden Crescent each week. Kylina was a far more of a help than a burden. Yes, she was happy and very contented.

*

Doctor Tedra Haygrove woke up with a throbbing headache, pain shooting across her chest and found she was gasping for breath. Every intake sent spasms of pain through her lungs as they gasped for more oxygen. She switched on the light and staggered across to the bathroom and stared at her image in the mirror. Blood shot eyes and a face covered in red rash gazed back.

'Damn,' she retorted. She had caught some sort of virus and immediately though of the new marines. Two had arrived looking quite under the weather but she'd put it down to jet lag.

Tedra swallowed, gasped for breath and found her heaving stomach was about to react. Her body was burning and the mirror pulsed back and forth in rhythm with her heart. Walls of the room appeared to liquefy. Tedra reached for the edge of the sink, coughed, let out another gasp as pain shot through her body. She took one step and collapsed unconscious to the floor.

Along the corridor, Master Sergeant Colin Fields was completely disorientated as he staggered, gasping and heaving towards the central control room. His vision blurred but he managed to step over two marines squirming in agony on the floor, push the door open and stagger inside. Four men and two women were all slumped over the computer terminals and the stink of vomit and blood filled the room. With almost superhuman effort, Fields dragged his long frame across to a red cabinet, inserted a key and swung the door open. He clasped the ten-centimeter long handle and managed to pull it down before with a groan of agony he too, slid to the floor.

An emergency siren sounded through Magaroona Research Base and the computer warning sounded. 'Attention! Yellow Alert! All Personnel. Please go to your nearest emergency assembly area. Airlocks will be sealed in five minutes and emergency air supply activated. This is not a practice. Attention. Yellow Alert...'

Colonel Ira Pope jerked his eyes awake and knew something was wrong when the console across from his desk flashed a row of red and blue lights. He shut his eyes, gasped for breath and reached for the intercom as the siren sounded again. 'Thank God! ' he muttered when he realized someone had raised the alarm.

'Red Alert!' the bland voice continued. 'Please remain where you are. All sections are isolated. Emergency internal air supply has been activated! Elevators to the surface are off line.'

The base had been built in the 1960s to withstand a direct nuclear attack and could be self-supporting for many weeks. This time though, the concrete and steel panels that slid into predetermined spaces from the surface down through the multitude of levels, kept the unseen enemy in rather than a nuclear fallout at bay.

Inside, fresh air blew through the air ducts to replace the contaminated product. But it was too late. Fungi spawn was everywhere and when breathed into people's lungs, it grew inside and healthy lungs became clogged within hours. Worse though was the toxic liquid the fungus produced which sent the victim into a high rash, hallucinations and, if not treated, death within three hours.

The trouble was this was an alien fungus with no antitoxin on Earth.

In Canberra and Washington military headquarters, emergency alarms flashed on computer screens, data poured in but all contact with Magaroona was one way. Computer Information was pouring out temperature readings, air supply, diagrams showed the closed airlocks and even animated drawings showed where personnel were situated.

There were three hundred and forty one people in the research station when Condition Red was activated but the only reply to demands for an explanation came from a marine sergeant who, with twenty men guarded the airport boundaries. They were safe but had no access to the sealed underground quarters. One other person on the surface was Major Val Wikstrom who had chosen to spend her last night on Australian soil in the small surface bunkroom before flying back home the next day. As senior officer she now had a new task thrust upon her shoulders; that to find out what went wrong dozens of meters beneath them.

*

Within three hours three RAAF Hercules transporters lumbered into Magaroona. Group Captain Rod Davies was the first off the front aircraft followed by a man in civilian clothes.

'This is Stephen Furness from your embassy, Major Wikstrom,' he added after introducing himself. 'Has any progress been made?'

'No Sir,' Val replied in a hushed voice. 'All entrances are sealed, instruments register the air below as toxic and all sounds of human life ceased about half an hour ago. Whatever it is, Sir, I belief everyone down there is dead.'

'Theory. Major?' Furness in spite of his gray suit had the bearing of a military officer.

'I believe the air was poisoned, Mr. Furness but whatever it was did not kill the victims straight away. We monitored voices for the first hour after the station was sealed and moans for another two hours after that.'

'I see. Thank you, Major. Could the packaged returned in the Discovery have caused it?' His eyes fixed onto Val's and she was certain he knew about Kylina.

'The package was delivered to Adelaide, Mr. Furness,' she replied. 'It may have been associated with this emergency but, if so it was by accident.'

Group Captain Rod Davies interrupted. 'You got to know the alien woman quite well, didn't you, Major?' He glowered at Furness. 'We do know what is going on in our own country, Mr. Furness.' he added in a blunt voice.

'She was a refugee, Sir,' Val replied. 'Earth was picked at random because it supported human life. She had no sinister motives.'

The group captain remained quiet for a few seconds as troops assembled near the three aircraft. 'Can men in protective clothing get in safely, Major?' he asked

'Yes, Sir,' There are two emergency elevators, one at each end of the complex. They both lead to airlocks so interior air will not be permitted to escape.' She grimaced. 'They were designed to stop nuclear contamination entering but will work in reverse. Both elevators work independently from the station's computer system.'

'I have the access codes,' Furness added in a clipped voice and Val studied the man. He was not, she was certain, a minor Embassy official, but more likely to be from the CIA or one of the military secret services.

'Right,' the group captain said. 'We'd better get down there.' He fixed his eyes on Val. 'We brought protective clothing for you, Major if you feel up to showing us around down there.'

'I'll come, Sir,' she replied in a quiet voice.

Twelve soldiers plus Val and Furness, all dressed in massive white protective clothing, each with its own air supply, heating, lighting and even interior drinking water accessed by the tongue on a tube. Each suit had a radio and homing device so every crewmember could be tracked by mobile tracking equipment that had been unloaded from the third Hercules.

The rescue team rode to the eastern runway end and Furness walked to a small bunker, another steel door in an artificial hill and flicked down a hinged flap. Inside, a small electronic lock lit up. A seven-digit numeral was punched in, a green light flashed on and Furness turned to Val. 'You have your half of the code, I believe Major,' he said.

Val nodded and entered the digits she'd received in a coded message the previous day. A second light flashed green and the door slid back on silent rollers. Five personnel crowded in the lift for the trip down. When everyone arrived, the whole procedure was repeated to gain access to the airlock that was large enough to hold everyone present.

Lights flashed and a computer voice warned a vacuum was soon to be created so internal air supplies needed to be turned on. There was silence as the air hissed out and replaced by the internal supply. Val gasped. The air coming in was like a fog swirling around all white but filled with minute green particles almost like seeds being blown around a forest track on a windy day.

'Something's there,' muttered the group captain through his radio as the hissing air stopped and gauges showed the air pressure was equivalent to the interior. He nodded to the soldiers and two, holding what looked like flame-throwers stepped forward as the interior airlock doors opened.

In front was a long arch shaped corridor filled with a swirling fog that made the overhead lights just dim lines in the ceiling.

'The air is quite pure, Sir,' another soldier reading an electronic instrument in his hand reported. 'Oxygen level is normal and carbon monoxide is at acceptable levels. Ordinary water droplets cause the fog and the contaminant registers as a type of fungi. The temperature is twenty six degrees, six above normal but still not too hot.'

'Well, they did not suffocate,' Furness's voice came through Val's helmet.

'No noises are evident,' another man reported. 'Not even rattles or scrapes.'

'Carry on Lieutenant,' Davies grunted and turned to Val. 'If you'd go second, Major and help navigate but no heroics; understand?'

'Yes Sir,' Val replied and followed the Lieutenant along the access route. It came out near the living quarters and the first body.

A marine was lying face up just inside their entry door. His dead eyes stared out and the white face showed signs of a body rash. Worse though was his mouth. It looked as though the man was vomiting when he died. Long jelly like mucus that stained his face and shirt had a distinct green tinge to it.

Val swallowed down bile and glanced away.

'Take a sample in a vacuum flask,' Furness said. 'But for God's sake don't rip your protective clothing.'

'Right, Sir,' another soldier replied and bent down with another sophisticated looking piece of equipment.

Val was impressed. Every person there seemed to have a different job to do and knew how to do it.

They continued on but the scene was little different from the first corpse. Everyone was dead and they all showed signs of a rash and many had been vomiting. Val was close to tears as she recognized friends and colleagues, Colonel Ira Pope was slumped over a still lit up console and the continuous warning from the computers could be heard through the protective head gear.

For an hour they searched but found nobody alive, before Group Captain Davies tapped Val's shoulder and said in a quiet voice. 'I think we can go now, Major. These men are professionals and know what needs to be done. What say we both return to the surface.' He stopped Furness who was nearby. 'I think you should return to the surface, too, Mr. Furness,' he said.

Furness nodded and his eyes met Val's, eyes of utter despair and grief. She felt bad enough but those eyes sent a shiver though her. 'Come on, Mr. Furness,' she said in a kind voice. 'As the Group Captain said, we can do nothing for these people.'

'You are right, Major,' the man replied and followed Val back to the airlock.

The journey out was thorough with high-pressure steam cleaning and chemical spraying. The air was sucked out and replenished twice before they were allowed outdoors where mobile dressing rooms and showers waited for them. Val stepped out into the desert heat and just felt ill as shock of the experience tore through her mind. Now she was on the surface the tragedy became almost too much.

The group captain came up to her. 'I think you're right, Major,' he said and his brown eyes showed empathy. 'I doubt if that young woman you rescued caused this.'

'Then what was it, Group Captain?' she replied.

'I would say it was a fungus bacteria which came in with that rescue pod, some microscopic particle that grew and spread.'

'But she could be spreading it?'

'If it's any help, I don't think so,' he replied. 'As far as we know she is still in Adelaide. If she was a carrier there would have been an outbreak there by now.' He shrugged. 'I might have trouble convincing your colleague that, though.'

'Mr. Furness, our CIA man you mean?'

'Exactly,' replied the Royal Australian Air Force Officer and his expression showed his disdain for the man ' I have a small bottle of whisky in the plane. I know it's against regulations but I'm sure nobody will protest if we have a wee dram.'

'I'd like that, thank you, Group Captain.' Val sighed. 'I made a lot of friends in the short time I was here but now…' Her voice quivered. 'Oh hell, no training could prepare a person for this.'

'True,' said the tough Australian. 'It's a tragic day but could have been worse.'

'How,' Val almost snapped.

'Imagine if it had happened up here and was not contained deep below the surface, Major?'

Val nodded. 'Yes, I think I understand now, Sir,' she replied and a shudder passed through her body.

*

In contrast to the day, nighttime became quite cold. Lunol sang an old sea chant he'd sung in during his two years in the King's Navy. Those were tough and cruel times but he had survived. He had survived the plague and he had Kagit, sweet beautiful Kagit. It wasn't until the plague struck that he even knew she was an alien creature from the heavens. Perhaps she was an angel sent to rescue him. No, that was crazy; otherwise she'd be here now. The song disappeared from his lips and he began to count the steps, his mind drifted again, he staggered and stumbled, and began to swing to the right.

'You're off course, Lunol,' Sigma, the ever present Sigma announced. Pretty voice. It's a pity she wasn't real. Bet she'd have a good figure but then of course, Kagit would be jealous. Kagit! It was hard to even picture her face except for the eyes. He'd always remember those twinkling blue eyes. Very few people at home had blue eyes.

'Lunol,' Sigma's volume was higher. 'Concentrate. Go left. Don't let your mind wander. Hear me!'

'Sorry,' muttered the man and stared ahead. The moon was up and he could see a far rise that looked like a water dragon bending over; those monstrous reptiles in the tropical rivers at home.

For five hours the young man, forever encouraged by the voice coming from the stylized koala hanging around his throat, staggered on and on. Dawn broke, a red sky in the east, another cloudless sky, another day in the high thirties or more but still Lunol continued on. He was beyond endurance but the legs still moved out, pushed down and propelled a pain filled body forward.

And it worked! The desert changed. It was cut by a long thin line of red dust that stretched from one vanishing point to another. It was a road, not a major arterial route, a highway or even a country lane but really a track through the relentless desert.

'Now all we need are the King's troopers with the royal coach and eight black horses.' Lunol said as he sat down and reached for the jerrican.

'They have mechanical transport here,' Sigma advised. 'Crude combustion engine vehicles that belch out poisonous gas and travel on wheels.'

'I wouldn't even mind one of those,' Lunol said.

He had to wait but mid-afternoon two days later a land train, a massive tractor unit pulling four trailers behind could be seen as a cloud of red dust, before the rumble of the engine cut through the desert air.

'Get up, Lunol!' Sigma ordered.

He staggered to his feet and waved as the mechanical monster roared closer, there was a screech of brakes, it slowed and stopped.

A window rolled down and a bearded head stared out. 'G'day there, Mate. You're one bloody lucky man. If it weren't for the flooding over the border in the Wales I wouldn't have cut through this track.'

'Can you help me, please,' Lunol croaked in English, reached out, touched the dust caked side of the cab and, with a low moan, collapsed, semi-conscious onto the dust.

'Hang on there, Mate,' the driver exclaimed as he opened his door, let himself down and held a canteen of water to Lunol's lips. 'I'll get on the radio. There's a cattle station two hours down the road. They could have a flying doctor there by then.'

He opened a rear door of his cab and with one mighty grunt, lifted the young man up and deposited him inside. Lunol held on and wriggled forward to collapse again on a bunk like bed. He stared around at the low ceiling. It was like a sailing ship cabin, same size and with a soft narrow mattress.

'Thank you,' he said again in English and hung on as the driver moved an iron handle and the monstrous mechanical beast moved forward.

'Bit of a bloody drongo bein' out here by yaself,' the driver stated. He glanced in his rear vision mirror at Lunol. 'No matter,' he grunted. 'We'll get ya help. Just hang in there, Mate.'

Three hours later the young alien man was flying again, not on a space ship this time but in a twin engine Nomad Flying Doctor Service air ambulance heading for the town of Broken Hill in New South Wales.

'We made it.' He sighed and touched the koala hanging around his neck.

'Yes,' Sigma replied. 'My bloody oath, Mate. You little ripper but you were a bloody drongo bein' out in the desert by yaself.'

'I was.' Lunol laughed. English was a strange language.

*

CHAPTER ELEVEN

The room at the secret location in Canberra was hushed as a dark suited man turned off the video of the Computer Beta's conversation.

'I don't believe a word of it,' the American general retorted. 'My daughter at high school could put on a better performance than that.'

'It was one of your scientists, Doctor Tedra Haygrove, who recorded the message and confirmed it's authenticity, General Jarvis,' Dean Diriwi, the man in the suit replied. 'My government has investigated the reports of Unidentified Flying Objects across West and South Australia over the last few months. There were fifteen sightings and two of these required further investigation.'

The general glanced up. 'That's about normal for a country this size; but continue, Mr. Diriwi.'

The director of the Prime Minister's Office of Special Security, Primoss for short, the government's top-secret agency, fixed the visitor with a glower. The man might be a big power in his own country but in Australia he was a mere advisor from their embassy.

'We interviewed two young Jackaroos, that's farm workers, over in West Australia and they swear they saw a UFO land out in the desert and gave a young woman a ride to the railway. We followed it up and there was a woman who arrived at a motel in the early hours of the morning and took the next Indian Pacific train across to Sydney.

'A tourist or university student. Could be anyone,' retorted the general.

'She came down with the flu on the train and was so ill she had to be taken to hospital in Adelaide. Hospital records show she seemed to have no immunity to a common flu virus. She almost died.'

The General nodded and rubbed his chin. 'Now that is interesting,' he added. 'Where is this woman now?

"She's still there. It seems she was an Australian academic who now works at the University of Adelaide. We checked her out and every record is authentic except for one thing.'

'You're going to tell me, I know,' the general retorted.

'Every file on her is authentic, from birth certificate in Perth to a Ph.D. in the University of Oregon but nobody at any of those places remember her. Sure, they produced her records on the computer but her name or photograph was not included in year books and people we interviewed of her year cannot place her.' He smiled thinly. 'We interviewed over fifty people from her high school, university and a commercial pharmaceutical firm she supposedly worked for.'

'I see,' General Jarvis pouted and leaned forward. 'And the second investigation?'

'Last month a meteorite was seen just over the South Australian border and a few days later a man was picked up in the middle of nowhere by a road train driver. Seems he couldn't talk English very well and kept muttering to himself. He was in a pretty bad way but survived something like three weeks in the desert without water or food. Nobody can last that long.' Diriwi glanced up. 'This fits in with your astronaut's rescue of the alien woman by the Discovery, don't you think, General?'

'It does,' Bradley Jarvis admitted and his earlier bored tone changed to that of interest, 'What about her disappearance in Adelaide. Has she been traced?'

'She was dressed as an air hostess, ran off the Boeing 777, whipped behind a fire engine and changed into civvies. A guard thought she was a reporter and took her to the terminal building. She hasn't been seen since.'

'My God, so there are three of them wandering around Australia,' retorted the general, ' ...that we know of! Who knows how many more there are!'

Another man interrupted. Australia's Prime Minister leaned forward in the chair he was sitting in. 'And your search for that alien vessel circling the globe, General. Omega, I think your astronauts said it was called. Where is it?'

'We have two scenarios,' the general coughed. 'Computers are giving us a minute by minute read out on the projected course it was on when met by Discovery.'

'But you can't find it?'

'Well, no! We think it changed course.'

'And headed where?'

'It could have left the solar system.'

'But you don't think so.'

'No, we think it has gone into a stationary orbit above Australia. Just before Discovery landed, our radio telescopes picked up a minute flutter of star patterns in the region for a few seconds as if something passed in front, something large and relatively close in.'

The Prime minister nodded. 'And now we have this fatal fungi outbreak at Magaroona.' He glanced up. 'Your report Doctor Grandi.'

Doctor Giovanni Grandi stood and handed out a thick document to the dozen people in the room. 'It is all there,' he stated. 'I'll give a quick summary.

The fungus is of an unknown type that breeds in temperatures over twenty degrees and grows in human's lungs blocking them within hours. Furthermore, it secretes a poisonous substance that kills its victim often before they die of suffocation. There is a distant relative in the Brazilian Amazon rain forests where mining crews were dying in a similar fashion. The difference here is the sheer speed in which it multiplied and killed the victims. The mining camp workers died over months, not hours. We are now seeing if the antitoxin developed for that outbreak will work here. In the meantime I recommend the underground station is sealed and the bodies left inside. It would be too dangerous to remove them.'

'And if an outbreak occurred on the surface?' the prime minister asked.

Doctor Grandi turned to the second to last page of his document. 'Computer predictions suggest that without development of an antitoxin and in the same conditions, twenty percent of the population of a city like Adelaide would die in the first month, another fifteen within the next month. After that the death rate would fall.' He glanced up. 'That's the best scenario ladies and gentlemen,' he continued.

'And if that young woman the Discovery crew rescued had the disease when she walked into the Adelaide International Air Terminal?' Dean Diriwi asked.

'That's perhaps the only good news,' the doctor replied and gave a slight twitch of his chin. ' 'It's all on Page 17 of my notes. She could not have had it. If she did, over a hundred thousand Adelaide citizens would be dead by now and we have had no reports of any outbreaks there, or anywhere else in Australia; not one.' He glanced up. 'That young woman does not carry the disease. I can assure you that. '

There was an audible sigh throughout the room and Diriwi stood up. 'Thank you, Doctor,' he said and turned to face the circular table everyone was seated around. 'Ladies and gentlemen, we now have to decide what we are to do next...' He reached for another pile of documents headed in red letters, *Top Secret- Classified Information- Eyes Only.*

*

Three hours later across Canberra in a small room at the rear of the United States Embassy. General Bradley Jarvis sat behind a massive desk and glowered at Stephen Furness. 'I hate it when I have to work with foreigners,' he retorted.

'With all due respects,' Furness replied. 'This is Australia so we're the foreigners here.'

'Yeah, whatever,' Jarvis mumbled. 'Anyway, I'm not waiting around for them to go through all their checks and procedures.' He slapped the pile of documents he'd brought back, on his desk. 'I want action.'

'Like what?' the man in the suit replied.

'Find them, Stephen. Use one of those dart pistols to incapacitate and get them to our rendezvous point. If they're unconscious they cannot divert our plane again. Once in Hawaii they will be under our jurisdiction.'

'There could be major diplomatic repercussions, General. Australia is, after all, one of our most supportive allies. Wouldn't it be better to cooperate? Their plan seems pretty thorough and foolproof.'

Jarvis glared. 'This is not a suggestion, Major General. It is an order.'

'As you wish, General Jarvis,' Stephen Furness replied in a cold tone. 'The order will have to be cleared through my superiors in Washington. My branch of the service is not under your direct command.'

'Oh, the order will be cleared, Major General. It will!'

Furness held the other man's eyes. 'We will not kill them, General,' he said quietly.

'I never asked that, now did I?' Jarvis retorted, his eyebrows heavy with anger.' I want it done this week before the Australians bumble it up.'

'Once your orders are cleared we'll proceed,' Furness stood and walked out without a backward glance.

'Damn the man,' Bradley Jarvis swore and reached for the phone on his desk.

*

'It is so realistic, Kylina,' Pazz complemented as she held the two by one meter frame up to the light and examined the finished painting of a seventeen century man and woman standing in front of a stone breakwater. A sailing ship stood anchored in the background with sails tied but square gun turrets open and ancient cannons protruding.

'It's from a photograph in my mind,' Kylina replied in a soft almost sad voice. 'Except for the facial features which I altered, I am the woman in the painting.'

Pazz stared at her sister. 'This is how it was; I mean those long dresses, the sailing ships and men carrying swords?'

'Yes, that scene is as authentic as if I'd painted one of Delta from memory,' She gave a tiny grin. 'In fact, I'd have more difficulty remembering Delta than Custronomus.'

'And the man with his arm around you. Was he real?'

'He was,' Kylina replied. 'Though Custronomus was a primitive society by ours or even Earth standards, it was advanced in other matters. There was a very high code moral of behavior based on "The Twelve Articles of Civilization", a philosophy of life rather then religion, I guess it was.

Men and woman signed an Article of Loyalty in which they exchanged vows. If they were both committed and faithful to each other after two years it became an Article of Commitment and they were allowed to have children. It was a sort of trial marriage. Lunol and I had signed this vow.'

'And did you, well you know?' Pazz flushed

'Sleep together? ' Kylina said. 'Of course. It was expected. Only children were frowned upon at this stage.'

'And if the woman became pregnant?'

'The vows of loyalty were dissolved, the pair banned from seeing one another and the child put in an orphanage. It was tough but quite a disincentive. It happened to very few couples. Mind you, they had good birth control techniques; every bit as safe as those on Earth.'

'And if, after two years, the couple didn't get along?'

'The Article of Loyalty could be cancelled at any time by either partner. If it was, they went their own way. Sometimes they even entered a second vow with the same partner but usually they met up with someone else,' Kylina explained. 'Women and men were considered partners, with none being superior to the other. In that matter they were more advanced than people here with most women still fighting for equality.'

'Or Delta where women were superior at the expense of men,' Pazz added. 'Tell me, why wasn't I awoken at Custronomus?'

'We tried but the controls had some sort of time lock. I thought you would be left to die in suspended animation but I guess they never realized Omega would continue in space for so long.' She grimaced. 'If it wasn't for the plague I would have stayed in Custronomus. In fact the computers wanted to send Omega on to give you a chance to have a life but I overrode them.'

'Why?' Pazz asked quietly.

'I could not bare thinking of you not being there. Once gone, you might as well be dead. Also, I hoped the computers could override the controls and wake you up.' She gave a little sigh. 'Then the plague came and changed everything. Omega landed and rescued Lunol and myself. The computers told me he had gone when they talked to me before I woke up in Discovery.' She shrugged. 'There was only a fifty-fifty chance, anyhow. We both knew the risk. I was saddened but at least knew you had made it.'

Pazz frowned. 'They said he was gone but not that he was dead. Is that correct?'

'Well you know how computers talk. Death has no meaning to them.'

'I guess not,' Pazz replied but remained deep in thought. She looked back at the painting and smiled at her sister. 'There's a School of Fine Arts at the university,' she said. 'Why don't you enroll? You have a talent, Kylina.'

'It would cost too much,' the younger woman replied.

'I'll pay,' Pazz answered. 'We may look identical but you're still my kid sister, you know.'

Kylina's eyes lit up. 'You would, too, Pazz. Remember that last year we were on Delta? You paid my fees for those music lessons. I'll never forget that. I love playing the piano almost as much as painting.'

'Then let me do it again.'

'Yes, but only the first year. Okay?'

'It's a deal,' Pazz replied. 'I'm pretty sure I can get you in the next semester. I already checked it out for you.'

They were interrupted when Lynn walked in with Jason running along after her. She stared at Pazz holding the painting then at Kylina and retorted. 'Do you both have to wear the same type shorts and tops. Now, I'll never tell you apart.' She turned to Kylina. 'Duncan rang, Pazz and said he'd home be a little late.'

'Thanks Lynn,' Pazz replied. Lynn flushed, leaped around and studied her friend closely.

'Don't do that!' she retorted but her frown turned to a grin. 'I can tell the difference when I look closely, though. You're getting fat, Pazz.'

'Thanks,' her friend muttered. 'Talk about the kettle calling the pot black.'

Kylina raised her eyebrows and Pazz laughed. 'Just another old English saying little sister,' she explained.

*

Lunol spent two days in the hospital before being fit enough to be discharged. He hitched on his backpack, smiled at the nurse who was already dealing with her next patient and walked out the door. The hospital had cool air circulating through it, so the temperature outside hit him like a blast furnace and reminded him of the his sailing boat trips to the tropics at home. It was another hot sultry day with the sun blazing down and, though not yet noon, locals were hugging shady spots under extended verandas. Most buildings were similar to those at home with doors, windows and the interior furniture. Even the shops had a familiar feel about them.

The vehicles around, though were totally different. There were no horses or carriages but cars, as he'd heard the nurse call them, smaller than a carriage back home, that were parked or moving around everywhere. The roads were black and hard so no dust blew up and they even had white and yellow lines painted on them. At crossroads, lights changed colors to tell the cars when to go but Lunol gave up trying to find the person who changed them.

When he was sure there were no pedestrians around, Lunol tucked a hand in his shirt and felt for Sigma. He had discovered that by squeezing it, the computer woke up.

'Well, if you hang me outside your shirt you can hear me easier and I can see what's going on,' Sigma scolded.

'Sorry, I forgot,' Lunol muttered, pulled the leather strap up and flicked the koala out. The eyes, he knew, were more than just glass buttons but some sort of sensing device but he still had not fathomed where the voice came from. The koala's lips were merely a line in the fake wood. 'Anyhow, what do I do, now?'

'You need money,' Sigma advised. 'Look for one of those wall machines like there was in the hospital and I'll watch how they work.'

'Okay,' Lunol grunted.

He wandered along and stared at the unfamiliar words written on signs everywhere as well as the young women around. They had hardly any clothes on! You could see their arms, legs and even, in some cases stomachs and shoulders. It was almost indecent but made him think of Kagit. She had changed into something similar when they arrived on Omega and had giggled when he'd seemed so astonished. Of course, his own shorts and shirt were also different, too and the new sharp razor he'd been given in the hospital to shave with was a wonder. He ran a hand over his smooth face and thought of Kagit again. She never liked the moustaches, long hair and wigs that were in vogue on Custronomus anyway.

'There's one!' interrupted Sigma. 'Stand beside it so I can see what's going on.'

Lunol stood beneath a Westpac sign and watched as several people, men and women walked up, poked a card in a slot, pressed buttons and paper money came out. At least he knew what money was but this was so brightly colored.

'Okay. It seems easy but where do I get a card from to poke in?'

'It's a crude computer and those cards would have magnetic strips on them. ' Sigma explained. 'If we had one I could examine it.'

'But we haven't!'

'Well go in the bank here and tell them you lost yours. Make sure you have me in your hand so I can touch their computer. They'll ask your name and address so we'd better have one made up. If they ask anything else just make up a story.'

Sigma soon overrode the bank woman's terminal and within minutes Lunol walked out with a bankcard, pin number and a thousand-dollar account. 'Why isn't everyone rich?' he asked after he'd withdrawn two hundred dollars.

Sigma almost sighed. 'We ripped them off, Lunol. Normally you have to have money in before you can take any out. I borrowed some from a friend.' Lunol frowned. How could the computer have a friend!

*

Sigma never explained she'd searched the bank records until she found a known name. There was no Kagit but she did come to a Pazz. The surname was unknown but the computer could find no other Pazz so she withdrew the money from this account to create Lunol's one. To a machine programmed to a high moral standard, this seemed a perfect solution. Of course, Pazz was unknown to Lunol and she was programmed not to tell her human about Kagit's sister.

'Now go to a travel agent and buy an airplane ticket to Adelaide. It's too slow by car,' she directed.

An hour later, Lunol boarded an airplane and walked within meters of a man walking in the terminal on a flight from Canberra.

*

When Stephen Furness, dressed in a crisp suit, arrived at the Broken Hill Air Terminal he headed for the cafeteria where he had arranged to meet two local agents in his employment. This guy who'd come out of nowhere in the bush was the easiest one to trace. The abduction from the hospital was already planned and transportation out would be in a United States Air Force Starlifter sitting on the tarmac after an emergency landing the night before. After that, there would be the more difficult job of tracing the women in Adelaide.

*

Doctor Pazz D'rose walked into the lecture theater with some uneasiness. She gazed up at the hundred or more third year undergraduates, mainly twenty year olds who did not lack any self-confidence, but also men and women ranging through to one gray haired gentleman who would be of retirement age. A faint mumble went through the room as she stood behind a small rostrum and waited for the noise to stop.

'Good afternoon, ladies and gentlemen,' she began. 'I am Pazz D'rose and will be taking many of your third year stats. lectures this semester.'

'Oh come off it, girlie,' a youth in the back called out. 'Sit down and wait for the real Doctor D'rose to arrive.' A snigger went through parts of the theatre.

'If you wish,' Pazz answered in a quiet voice and moved three rows back, sat down by an overhead projector and began to write notes on a lecture pad. After fifteen minutes the room was becoming quite noisy as impatient students continued to wait for the lecturer to arrive. Finally Pazz stood, walked to the front and began talking in a low voice. The noise cut off as everyone stared at this young woman, seemingly their own age who watched them with a small smile.

'Now, if Mr. Bradley at the rear there, wishes to question me a second time…'

All eyes turned to the man who'd called out at the beginning. He flushed slightly and said, 'How do you know my name?'

'I made it a point to know every student's name,' Pazz added softly and reached for the computer readout of those taking the course. 'I doubt whether Mr. Bradley will want to waste any more of our precious time so I'll just name a few.' She glanced up and communicated with Epsilon.

'No problem,' the computer replied. 'Most of them have bar coded identification tabs. I'll just read a few for you. It should suitably impress them.

Pazz smiled. 'Welcome Carolyn Anderson, the young lady wearing green sweater in the third row, Diane Appleson, at the back in the black coat…' and so it continued with Epsilon reading the bar. Pazz purposely made a few errors but named twenty-five of the twenty-eight named students correctly.

'But how?' John Bradley asked.

'Mathematical probability,' Pazz replied. 'I studied your photographs, noted features to compare so the probability of putting the correct name to the person was greatly enhanced.' She flicked the overhead projector on. 'As an introduction, Ladies and Gentleman, I have on screen a small problem based on your last semester's work. You have twenty minutes to find a logical conclusion. Work together if you wish.'

The room hushed and calculators appeared. After twenty minutes, five students had correctly answered the problem and another half were well on their way. John Bradley, though had completely floundered. Pazz then gave a detailed but understandable explanation and continued on to show three shortcuts the students could have used to find the required answer. From that moment on, she had no problem with young males who had originally related her youthful looks a lack of ability. At the end of the hour several students made a point of walking up and to thank her for the way she had conducted the lecture.

'You certainly know how to explain the work, Doctor D'rose,' one young woman commented. 'Our lecturers last year, knew it all but had no idea what-so-ever about how to pass their knowledge on to the students. You made complicated work appear easy.'

Pazz smiled with pride but never told her this was the first lecture she had ever taken in her life. 'Why thank you, Valerie,' she replied and, once again used Epsilon to read the bar code on the exercise book carried in the girl's arms.

Valerie grinned. 'And what did you note about me?' she asked.

'Quite easy,' Pazz replied. 'Only five female students have a short haircut like yours, two of those have dark hair and two wear large earrings. That left you.'

'But to remember over a hundred names?'

Pazz smiled. 'All mathematical probability, Valerie,' she said. 'I had a seventy percent chance of getting your name right. The odds weren't too bad.'

*

'How did it go?' Duncan asked back in Pazz's new office on the fourth floor of the mathematics tower block.

She glanced up, smiled and after making sure the door was firmly closed; kissed him quite a passionately. 'I was nervous,' she said and buried her head in Duncan's neck. 'It's another emotion I've had returned to me.'

Duncan glanced over Pazz's shoulder and noticed computer monitor filling up with screen after screen of data. Her armlet was resting innocently on the top of the mouse.

'Research,' Paz said when she realized what Duncan was looking at. 'Epsilon makes sure it is not too advanced.' She grabbed his hand. 'Come on; let's go to the common room. I'm famished.'

'What about Epsilon?' he asked as Pazz walked towards the door.

'No problem,' she replied. 'After five minutes she puts up a force field to bend light waves and becomes invisible. Anyone touching her before that would get a sharp jolt of electricity.'

'And how do you find her later?' Duncan asked.

'I just call her name. She'll respond to yours now, too. If I am away longer than I say, she'll come looking for me.'

'But how?' Duncan began and put his arm out to give Pazz a hug. 'Don't tell me. I don't really want to know.'

'It's good for me, too,' Pazz continued. 'Kylina often takes her computer off and is determined to be an ordinary citizen. She said she rarely wore it in that other world.' She grimaced. 'I guess I haven't got her will power. Epsilon is like an old friend.'

'And why not?' Duncan added. 'I'd say keep her on as much as possible. You never know when she may be needed.'

Pazz smiled. The Earth emotions were overwhelming her again. The feeling towards the man holding her was so intense her body was reacting physically. It was as if it controlled her, not the other way around. Without Epsilon on her arm it was even more powerful.

She flushed, clung onto Duncan and looked up. 'Duncan, I love you,' she said in a hushed voice and turned her face up to kiss him.

*

CHAPTER TWELVE

The trip on the Airbus to Adelaide was almost too much for Lunol to comprehend. Even though it was an almost full flight and people of all different sizes, ages and in a wide range of attire were everywhere, the young air hostesses was patient with his crude attempt to speak English and treated him like the king. The country unfolded below; desert that he knew about but increasingly green areas with lines of roads and, finally the city itself with buildings, roads, the blue ocean and winding river. It was a dream and could not be real!

Sure, he'd seen Earth from Omega and on his descent in the landing pod but that was somehow more remote. Now he was alone in this strange advanced society, all he felt was a sudden pang of homesickness. He thought of the tiny cottage Kagit and himself shared. They were simple, yet happy days; Kagit was a selected leader in Nkypy, their village and had brought benefits unheard of; running water and electricity produced from a windmill; medicines to cure the children and help for anyone who asked for it. They were the envy of the whole county.

He shrugged. Of course that all changed when the plague struck; Kagit revealed she came from another world and their lives could only be saved by leaving Custronomus. So here he was on Earth but without her. He grimaced and held the arm rests with tight, white knuckles and fixed expression as the Airbus landed with hardly more than a slight bump.

If the flight was nerve-racking, the terminal building was beyond comprehension. Lunol stepped through the sliding glass doors and just stared. People, thousands of them, were everywhere and he was totally ignored. Not even eyes contacted his as every individual seemed to be going somewhere. Bright lights, moving signs and the smell of food and coffee, accompanied the hushed bubble of voices.

'Just take it slowly,' Sigma spoke when it was obvious nobody would notice her voice nor really care if they did. 'Go to that cafeteria, select a drink of coffee and something to eat and sit down. If we do things logically, it will be okay.'

So Lunol did and found a spare seat in a corner to relax and gather his thoughts. 'Now,' said Sigma. 'We know Kagit is here somewhere and I found out she calls herself Pazz D'rose. That is a start.'

Lunol was too depressed to query how the computer found Kagit's new name but just stared at the people. There were just too many. The task of finding her appeared insurmountable.

'Be patient' Sigma added. 'We are not far from her. My homing signal tells me she is somewhere within six kilometers of us. I'll record the bearing from here then we can journey towards her position and I'll compare bearings. Its called triangulation. Unless she travels a long way during the day we can get closer all the time.'

'How close?' Lunol asked and felt a little better.

'It depends on the place she is but probably to within a hundred square meters, that's about as big as this cafeteria. Now, go and buy a street map of the area and we'll see where she is in comparison with this airport.'

With something definite to do, Lunol felt better and almost enthusiastic. He purchased one of those large maps he could unfold, a pen and ruler and found a seat with a low table where it could be opened out. Seconds later he had a line drawn from the airport that, by reading the symbols wasn't too hard to find. It went to the northeast near the city center and just south of a winding river.

'Hold me up so I can focus on the map,' Sigma asked and waited while Lunol held the koala out in his hand. 'Good, that's better. That's the center of the city and the line goes through those buildings in the park just north. Let's head there and I'll take another bearing.'

By using his map, sign language and limited English, Lunol was directed to a shuttle bus that took them the five kilometers to the center of Adelaide where gigantic buildings surrounded green parkland. If anything, the street he found himself in when he stepped off the bus was more claustrophobic and nerve racking that the airport. He walked through the towering jungle for several blocks until he came to a wide-open space. There was the massive park and fields he'd passed through on the way in, the sun was shining down and now there was space to move about. He crossed a major road packed with thousands of cars and other vehicles, found a little wooden picnic table and sat down.

'Lunol,' Sigma said and the metallic voice almost showed emotion. 'Pazz is less than a kilometer away at either the hospital or university. They are adjacent to each other. I suggest we stay in this park and walk round. The map shows the open grassland goes the whole way.'

'Right,' Lunol said and leaped up. It was mid afternoon so there was still plenty of daylight time left. He grabbed the map, slung Sigma back around his neck and headed north. The weather was hot but he did not care; he was almost there. His fast walk broke into a jog.

*

'Right,' Pazz sighed and placed the empty coffee mug down. 'I have to get down to the laboratory,' She smiled at Duncan. 'You know we've been here for almost an hour.'

Duncan glanced at his watch and grinned. 'Want to go somewhere later?' he asked.

'Sure,' said Pazz and reached across to deposit a small kiss on his lips. 'Your place.'

She stood, put on the white lab coat that had been placed over the chair and walked out with Duncan's eyes following her.

University of Adelaide's newest scientist walked along the corridor, pressed an elevator button and stood back, waiting. The doors slid back and she noticed three men inside. This was not unusual except that their eyes were on her, staring eyes full of surprise but also determination. A bolt of alarm surged through her, she stepped back, turned and realized a second elevator door was open and the interior empty. Without hesitation, Pazz moved sideways away from the first lift and made a sudden bolt into the second, banged the first button her hand reached and stood trembling as the doors began to slide across.

'It's her!' she heard a harsh voice. 'Just like that identikit drawing. Stop her!'

Pazz eyes were wide as time appeared to slow; a hand appeared in the door and, the fail-safe system stopped it shutting. In seconds, Pazz knew, it would begin to slide open again.

It wasn't rational, but she knew in her heart that those men were the enemy. If the door opened she would be overwhelmed and Epsilon was not there to assist. For really the first time since her arrival on Earth, she felt vulnerable. She bit on her lip, did the first thing that came into her mind and kicked out at the hand! Her new dress shoe was of the modern solid type and crashed into the fingers and exposed knuckles. There was a cry of pain and the hand disappeared. The door slid across the five-centimeter gap and clicked shut.

Pazz let out a gasp of relief when the elevator began to move. She was safe for the moment. There was an emergency stop button but would that help? Tiny blue lights flashed to show the floors and she realized she'd hit the ground floor button. That opened into a large foyer so would be as safe as anywhere. With a pounding heart she waited while the lift continued its journey down, shuddered to a stop and the doors slid open.

The foyer, though, was empty. Of course, Pazz realized; it was mid-afternoon and the students would all be at lectures. She could see the main door a few meters away with the park like grounds outside, and made a decision. After one gulp of air, she grabbed her shoes in her hand and just ran. By the time Pazz reached the path outside, the second lift door opened and two men appeared.

*

'It's definitely her,' a man in a suit and white shirt snapped. 'Get her while there's nobody around.

'Right, Mr. Furness,' the other man, dressed more casually in jeans and a suede jacket replied. He brought a handgun, equipped with an infrared sight, up but the red circle only danced across the door and couldn't reach the frantic woman as she moved to the right and ran at full speed across the concrete walkway.

'Damn!' the man muttered and ran to the door, saw Pazz reach the lawn ten meters away and dash behind an ornamental shrub.

The chase began. Without looking back, adrenaline flowing and senses on full alert, Pazz fixed her eyes on an adjacent building and tore towards it. Her heart thumped but she was fit and, if it weren't for a modern weapon aimed at her, would have made it.

'Get her, Tony!' Furness hissed.

The red spot from the infrared light zapped across the grass and lit up on Pazz's suit jacket. Tony squeezed the trigger; a tiny dart, propelled by compressed air, shot out and, just before the frantic woman ran behind another bush, reached its target.

With a sharp yelp of agony, Pazz crashed to her knees, skidded along the dry grass and stopped on all fours for a second. The fast acting drug was enough to render a human unconscious in three seconds but Pazz was not human. Though similar, her metabolism was slightly different from that of earthlings.

Though affected and feeling violently ill, she did not lose consciousness but manage to stand and stagger forward.

'Bloody hell,' Tony muttered. 'There's a enough anesthetic in that shot to bring an elephant down but she's still going.'

'Grab her, you fool!' Furness yelled. He ran forward with his flash brown tie flying out over his shoulder.

Both men reached Pazz together and managed to grab her in a tackle. Pazz screamed and lashed out but the drug was finally affecting her. Try as she might, her eyelids began to close. The deadly shoe kicked out again and connected with Furness's knee. He buckled over in agony. Meanwhile Tony used his superior weight to grab Pazz in a wrestling hold with her arms up behind her back.

'That's enough, Miss,' he panted and twisted her arm higher so Pazz was bent over at a grotesque angle.

*

Furness was about to poke a hypodermic needle into the woman's arm when, with a scream of rage, a young man ran kicking and thrashing straight into the pair.

However, it wasn't kicking and thrashing but using igloteti, a particularly fierce marshal art practiced in Custronomus and it was Lunol who had arrived! Within seconds he had disposed of the two attackers and had gathered Pazz in his arms before the first spectators arrived. Two semi-conscious men lay partly paralyzed on the ground and hugged their stomachs in acute agony while a vicious looking weapon was out of arm reach on the path.

'It's Doctor D'rose,' one male student called out. 'These guys were attempting to drag her away and this guy stopped them.'

By now, half a dozen students were gathered around and a security guard rushed across from the nearby building.

A dozy Pazz lay clutched in Lunol's arms. She knew someone was holding her. It was a man but not one who had attacked her. He was talking in a strange language and holding her in an embrace almost as Duncan would. Her mind tried to focus but it was. Somehow, just as her sixth sense had warned her that the intentions of the men in the elevator were aggressive, she realized the man holding her was a friend.

She forced her eyes open and saw wide almost green ones staring into hers. "Kagit,' the man whispered. 'Kagit!' The rest of his words were in that unknown language but his concern was real.

Pazz tried to recollect her thoughts and managed to call out. 'Will someone find Doctor Bourne, please.'

But Duncan had already been informed and, at that very moment was walking briskly out of the building Pazz had made her frantic exit from only moments earlier.

He edged through the enlarged crowd as two police officers arrived and hauled the attackers to their feet.

'What about the guy holding her?' one policeman asked.

'He's the one that saved her,' the man who spoke earlier added. 'My God, he was like a mad man. It was some sort of kick boxing but he had those guys disarmed and on the ground within seconds.'

Duncan frowned, bent on one knee and placed an arm on Lunol. 'Thank you,' he said quietly as Pazz grunted and staggered to her feet.

'Duncan,' she said in a rasping voice. 'I think I know what's happening. Can you get Kylina down here.'

'Of course!' Duncan replied. 'Why didn't I realize?'

He glanced up at the second police officer. 'Can you get a call to Pazz's sister,' he asked. 'It is quite important.'

'Certainly Doctor Bourne,' she replied. 'Have you a phone number?'

Kylina was contacted at the supermarket and said she'd get to the university as soon as possible. Yes, her boss said it was okay. Duncan hung up and watched as Furness and his henchmen were escorted away to a police van that appeared out of nowhere.

Pazz still looked disheveled but was quite coherent. She glanced at Lunol who stood by looking hurt and glum. 'Thank you,' she said and took his hands. 'If it wasn't for you, they would have abducted me.' She glanced at Duncan. 'Can we go to your office? It's closer than mine.'

'Sure,' Duncan replied and, with the help of a few students, escorted Pazz and a totally confused Lunol across to his tower block office.

After the students were thanked, Pazz assured the police she didn't need medical attention and would make a statement later. The small crowd left and Lunol sat miserably in a chair and tried to talk to Pazz in his language, but to no avail.

'It will be all right,' Pazz said kindly in English. 'Just wait.'

'Hello Pazz, I'm Sigma,' another voice filled the room and Pazz broke into a broad grin. 'Lunol here has made a mistaken identity. Shall I tell him in his language.'

Lunol frowned. 'You're Pazz?' he asked in his broken English.

'Yes, I am,' she replied

' But not Kagit?' he continued in a confused voice.

'Just wait a few minutes and it will be okay,' Pazz answered.

'I've asked someone to meet Kylina and send her straight up,' Duncan interrupted. 'How are you feeling?'

'I have a splitting headache,' she said. 'They hit me in my back with a dart or something.'

'Let me look,' Duncan replied.

Pazz took her suit jacket off and was about to lay it across a chair when a small metal object tinkled onto the floor. Duncan stooped and picked it up.

'This is it,' he said and placed the object on a paper towel he reached for from his desk.' I'm sure the police will be interested in this little piece of evidence.'

Pazz and Lunol both examined the small one-centimeter metal dart that had a small bubble of liquid still stuck to its point.

Pazz shuddered. 'So it wasn't just a random attack, was it?' she said.

'I doubt it,' Duncan replied. 'They were after you, Dear and if it wasn't for our young friend here, would have probably succeeded.' He glanced at their companion. 'I think we should tell Lunol what's happening, don't you?'

'No, wait,' Pazz replied. 'It won't be long.' She spoke to the computer. 'Tell Lunol he is in for a pleasant surprise soon but don't elaborate.'

'Okay, Pazz,' Sigma said. 'I hope it is worth the wait. Poor old Lunol has been through a tough time since we arrived on this planet.'

'It will be,' said Pazz.

Ten minutes later Duncan tapped Pazz and nodded at the window. Below them, a young woman could be seen striding into the building.

'Just wait here, Lunol,' he said and indicated their visitor should stand behind a cabinet so he wouldn't be seen when the door opened.

Lunol frowned but even Sigma didn't help, 'Just be patient,' she scolded in his language. 'It's going to turn out right.'

There was a knock on the door and Kylina burst in with her eyes filled with concern .She slammed the door behind and rushed to Pazz. 'What happened?' she called. 'I was told you were shot.'

'Kylina,' Pazz asked in a quiet serious voice. 'Weren't you called Kagit where you grew up?'

Kylina looked at her, shrugged and sounded annoyed. 'Yes, that was my name on Custronomus but what's that to do with anything?'

'Look around Kylina,' Duncan said, 'There's a friend I want to meet.'

Kylina turned, staggered and placed an arm out to steady herself against Duncan while her mouth hung open when she saw who was standing there.

Lunol stood with his eyes switching between the two identical sisters .

'Kagit?' he gasped.

Kylina gulped and nodded. 'Lunol!' she whispered. 'But how?'

'I woke up and thought you had left Omega but it must have been Pazz,' he replied, 'I followed her to Earth. The computers never told me...'

'Lunol!' Kylina's voice turned to a scream as she flung her arms around his neck, burst into sobs of emotion and plastered him with kisses. He reacted and held her so tightly she lifted her legs off the ground as he swung her around and around in sheer ecstasy. 'Oh Lunol,' she sobbed and just held on. 'I thought you were dead.'

Duncan reached out for Pazz's hand. 'Both sisters are as emotional as each other aren't they?' he commented in a dry voice.

Pazz grinned and was about to reply when an urgent rubbing noise sounded on the door. 'Oh hell, I forgot,' she said and rushed to open it.

There was a faint whiz and a spinning disk flew in, slowed and landed on Duncan's desk. With a slightly embarrassed look, Pazz picked it up and placed it on her arm. Epsilon had come looking for her.

'You're a bit late,' she thought. 'I could have been tied up in an airplane by now.'

'You're running a temperature, Pazz, and I detect drugs in your bloodstream. What happened?' Epsilon answered. 'And who's the strange guy kissing Kylina?'

Kylina turned while still in Lunol's arms and smiled at her. 'This is Lunol,' she said in a quiet voice and sniffed back another tear of emotion. 'He's the one I brought with me on Omega. I guess you'd call him my fiancée in English.'

'Yes,' Pazz said. ' I worked that out not long after Lunol rescued me from those mobsters. Nobody would be that protective with a stranger.' She turned to the young man. 'Thank you, Lunol, from the bottom of my heart.' She winked at Duncan. 'Yes, I know. It's another quaint English saying.'

Lunol probably only followed some of the words but smiled at Pazz and spoke in his own language.

Kylina but translated his words. 'Lunol guessed that his computer was tracing you all the time but he's glad he arrived at that moment.' She flushed and added. 'He said anyone as beautiful as Kagit deserves to be rescued. Lunol was always a bit of a romantic, you know.'

'Yes, I guessed,' Pazz said. 'A good fighter, too. I wouldn't like to be those two thugs at the moment.' She stopped talking when as a feeling of nausea filed her stomach

'Pazz!' Duncan looked at her in alarm.' You look terrible.'

'I thought I was all right,' she replied,' but....' She stood and rushed out the door. Luckily, a woman's toilet was only a few meters away. She rushed in and vomited in the toilet.

She felt slightly better after washing cold water over her face.

'I was sick as a dog,' she uttered when she returned to the office.

'Well, I'm taking you home.' Duncan gazed around. 'Why don't we all go to Pazz and Kylina's place? Lunol looks exhausted, too.'

When they arrived, Lynn, being typically herself, welcomed Lunol the same as she did earlier with Kylina and insisted he stay with them.

'From what Kylina told us earlier you're just about married anyway, more so than Pazz and Duncan, so lucky we bought double beds for

---

every room.' She chuckled. 'I'm the only one who'll get cold feet, won't I?' She next switched her attention to Pazz and insisted she lie down and look after herself.

*

Australia's prime minister was at a cabinet meeting when a mobile phone rang. It was not an ordinary everyday phone, but the high priority "red" phone that was actually colored white.

'Prime Minister's Office,' an aide answered as the room went deadly silent. This phone would only ring if there was an international emergency.

'This is Inter-galatic Spaceship Omega speaking. You have ten seconds to hand this telephone to Mr. Prime Minister,' said a crisp female voice that, though they didn't know it, sounded exactly like Pazz.

The man paled and caught the Prime Minister's eyes. 'The alien craft we were discussing is on line, Sir,' he said. 'The woman will speak to nobody except yourself.'

The prime minister gave a lopsided smile and nodded. 'Good Afternoon, The Prime Minister of Australia speaking.'

'Are you in a secure environment, Mr. Prime Minister?'

'I believe so,' he answered as every eye glued on his face.

There was a slight swish and a woman appeared at the end of the room, a young woman dressed in a modern suit. Immediately a security guard rushed to tackle her and dived clean through the image to land on the floor with a thud.

'Good afternoon, Mr. Prime Minister, gentlemen and I'm pleased to see two ladies present who are not merely secretaries. As your guard has just realized I am not really here. You are seeing a holograph of the image I wish to portray, in this case that of Doctor Pazz D'rose, the human from our world on your planet.'

While the guard, looking somewhat embarrassed, climbed to his feet and stood once again by the door, Australia's cabinet stared transfixed at the image. 'Can I help?' the prime minister stuttered into the phone.

'There is no need to use that primitive instrument, Sir,' the woman said. 'Anyone in this room can hold a conversation with me.' She frowned. 'My name is Gamma and I am the computer based on the spaceship known as Omega, selected to negotiate with yourselves. We are programmed to protect our species in, if possible, a non violent manner.'

Gamma held her hand up as one cabinet member half rose in his chair. 'Hear me out please.' Her eyes bore into him. 'I can see every move and hear every sound made in this room.' She smiled thinly. 'I can also smell those beautiful flowers in that bowl placed in the middle of your circular table, but I digress.'

'Go on, please…err, Gamma,' the Prime Minister said.

Gamma, using Pazz's grimmest facial expression turned slightly so her eyes seemed to be piercing directly at everyone present. 'This afternoon, Pazz D'rose was viciously attacked in the grounds of The University of Adelaide and, if it was not for the fortuitous presence of a young man who shall remain anonymous, would have been kidnapped or even killed. This is the second attack on my charges; no doubt you are aware Kylina D'rose, Pazz's clone sister, was about to be flown out of Australia when we diverted the aircraft to Adelaide.'

The Prime Minister nodded to a man behind him. 'Check on it, Brian,' he snapped.

Everyone waited while Brian spoke on his mobile phone and nodded. 'Both statements are true, Prime Minister. Two men attacked a Doctor D'rose in Adelaide less than an hour ago. They are CIA agents attached to the American Embassy who, at this very moment, are pleading diplomatic immunity with the South Australian Police.'

'Are they, indeed!' the Prime minister replied. He turned back to Gamma and apologized.

'Thank you,' she said. 'I heard who the men were.'

'I shall contact the American Ambassador and…'

'There is no need,' Gamma said. 'I shall talk to your counterpart in Washington. If you want me, Mr. Prime Minister, dial 66342, that's OMEGA on your crude instrument. Try it.'

The vision vanished.

'Well do it,' snapped the prime minister. His aide punched the numbers on a mobile phone and Gamma instantly appeared but dressed in the clothes of a checkout girl.

'You see me as Kylina D'rose who also happens to be living in Adelaide. I shall be back within the hour. Any attempt to contact me before then will be unsuccessful. I hope, for all our sakes, the attack was not by Australian personnel from your secret service, Sir.'

The vision faded again and the Prime Minister snapped. 'I want the men responsible for the attempted kidnapping, here, in Canberra before breakfast. Understand!'

'Yes Sir!' Brian answered.

*

The President of the United States of America was flying thirty thousand feet above Colorado in Air Force One when, without warning, all engines cut out and the Boeing dropped. In the same instant every electronic instrument on the Boeing 747 cut out. It was a little after eleven p.m., local time but only a second after Gamma's visit to Canberra.

For five agonizing seconds this continued before the engines fired and the aircraft behaved normally. All communications, though were still out and a woman was sitting in a comfortable seat opposite the president. Once again security guards found it was, but a vision.

'I am Gamma from the planet Delta,' the image of Pazz stated. Her eyes looked directly into the president's. 'If you believe this contact is a hoax, I shall show you a view from our starship Omega that is in a stationary orbit above Australia. '

The vision of Pazz vanished and a one-meter high, three-dimensional view of Earth appeared in the cabin. Australia could be seen in daylight but United States only showed as millions of pinpricks of light outlining the western seaboard.

'That is our view of you at this moment,' Gamma's voice continued. 'We have a cloaking device, as your television programs call it, so cannot be detected from Earth. We are, though, there and have constant communication with our two daughters on Earth.'

The vision vanished and the young woman reappeared.

'We thank you for rescuing our human called Kylina with your space shuttle Discovery and regret the deaths of your personnel at Magaroona. We are not what Earth people called God, and cannot restore life to the people who died in your Australian Research Station.

That was caused by fungi bacteria from another solar system. It originated in a pre-industrial planet known only as 38675.6 on our inter-galatic maps. This planet was originally picked to settle our daughters but an outbreak of this fungi plague caused us to reconsider. Unfortunately both our quarantine procedures failed to prevent the bacteria from reaching Earth. '

Gamma stopped and glanced around the room. 'This contact though is because of a more personal problem, I guess of small consequence to yourself, Mr. President but of utmost importance to Omega.'

'Go on, Gamma,' the president whispered.

The vision smiled slightly. 'We are an advanced civilization Mr. President, many hundreds of light years from this solar system. Unfortunately we lost contact with our system two centuries ago and believe it does not exist any more. The humans transported here on

Omega may be the last of their species and are under our protection.'

Gamma's eyes turned cold. 'Your countrymen have just attacked one of my charges in Adelaide, Australia, in a futile attempt to bring her to your country. This will not be allowed. Any further attempt to abduct any of our charges will be firmly resisted.

Our daughters are of no threat to Earth, Mr. President. In fact, we can be of considerable benefit to you all but we do not, and will not condone any violence against us. I would suggest you negotiate with Doctor D'rose who is an expert in biochemistry with an advanced knowledge of the subject. Together we'll attempt to kill this fungus from Magaroona before it escapes and devastates your planet.

Your CIA men are, at this moment, being held in an Adelaide Police Station and your ambassador is about to be contacted by Australia's Prime Minister and asked to explain this outrage. My contact number is 66342, that's OMEGA on your crude instrument, Mr. President. This conversation cannot be recorded, I am afraid. Good evening, Sir.'

The vision vanished.

Like his Australian counterpart, an aide punched in the number and Kylina, in her supermarket uniform appeared.

'Yes it works,' she said. 'By the way, your aircraft didn't really lose its engine power. That was an illusion to get your attention.' She smiled and disappeared.

'Get me our Australian ambassador,' the president grunted then grinned. 'I guess he's already talked to our attractive alien girl.'

*

CHAPTER THIRTEEN

It was a hot evening with everyone exhausted but too excited to even think of retiring for the night. Action was on the back patio where everyone, including little Jason, were in swimming attire and dipping in Lynn's tiny backyard pool. The owner of the property grinned to herself from the kitchen. If the tabloids knew she had three aliens in her back yard they'd be having a field day. She cut some sandwiches, made up another jug of lemon drink and headed out the back.

Kylina lay on her stomach on a towel and Lunol squatted beside her applying liberal quantities of insect repellent on her bronzed back while, in the pool, Pazz was holding Jason as he giggled and laughed in the arm water. Duncan was not far away floating on his back with toes out of the water.

'Supper's on,' Lynn called, deposited the goodies on her little deck table and waited while everyone gathered around.

Lynn and her friends munched sandwiches and sat around to hear how Lunol found Pazz. He spoke quietly in his broken English, with an arm around Kylina. At times he reverted to his home language and his fiancée translated for him.

'You paint a wonderful picture of Custronomus,' Pazz said a few moments later. 'I guess the plague caused a hasty evacuation. Can you tell us about it?'

Kylina, still in a modern brief bikini, smiled slightly and leaned her wet hair back into Lunol's arms.

'Well, we wouldn't be dressed like this in public there, for one thing,' she said. 'It was, as I think we said, similar to Earth about three hundred years ago. The steam engine had not been invented and sailing ships plowed through the oceans. On land, horses, identical to those on Earth, were the main means of transport.' She screwed her nose up. 'Gunpowder was in use and armies had crude musket type weapons and cannon shells. Medicine and other social items were quite basic but, in many cases, amazingly effective. Men and women were equal, almost to an extreme. Until the plague arrived it was, in my eyes, a paradise.' Her eyes looked sad. 'Remember, I grew up there so have a particular fondness for Custronomus. I was called Kagit Frysyl there, which really means Kylina Flower in the local language' She grinned. 'I changed Flower to D'rose here, to fit in with Pazz.'

Her voice continued ...

*

The ball held in the Grand Manor on the hill above Nkypy was the social event of the year. Carriage after carriage rolled up to the grandiose entrance and deposited the graduates and their partners on the blue carpet that led in the ornate front door.

Kagit accepted the doorman's hand as she alighted from her carriage and waited for Lunol to walk around and escort her inside. Villages crowded three deep on each side of the path and clapped as the young woman smiled at them. Dressed in an exquisite turquoise full gown held wide by two petticoats and hair curled high under a tiny bonnet, she was as beautiful as any of the Third Age Ladies. Her handsome partner in wig, triangular hat, maroon breeches, stockings and calf length boots, clasped her gloved hand and walked sedately forward to be greeted by Baron and Baroness Qylda, the King's representative in the district.

Since the revolution two decades earlier, the Baron's position was merely ceremonial but the district's leading family was still regarded with pride by the villagers and the Third Age Celebration was one of the few social occasions where everyone who wished, could take part.

Kagit and Lunol bowed their heads slightly and clasped their hosts' forearms in the formal greeting while a doorman announced their presence.

'Ladies and Gentlemen, we now welcome Miss Kagit Frysyl and Mr. Lunol Pendylf to the Third Age Graduation Ball,' announced the aide-de-camp. ' Mr. Pendylf is a well know business man in the district and owner of the Gilded Crown Stables where many of our finest horses have been trained.'

With applause and some cheers ringing in their ears, Kagit and Lunol walked in the foyer and up the grand stairway to the ballroom itself. Already hundreds of couples, dressed in the most eloquent styles, danced to the tune of a twenty-two piece orchestra seated on a balcony above the main floor.

'I like the lights,' Lunol said as a blue spotlight followed them around the dance floor.

The room was festooned with colored lights run by electricity, "discovered" by Kagit almost two hundred years before its time. The computers of Omega had taken a great deal of persuading before allowing the knowledge of electricity to be given to Planet 38675.6. Finally, though, a small generator had been brought to the village and joined up to a windmill originally used for grinding wheat. Since then, engineers had copied the technology and almost a hundred were in use throughout Custronomus.

Kagit's blue eyes gazed into Lunol's as she sighed with happiness and wriggled her body closer into his arms. It was six months since she had told him that she was from another world and electricity was only one of thousands of advanced ideas she knew about. He had accepted everything with hardly a blink and he had never pressed her for more information about her past. The information about Omega Starship or the armlet she nearly always wore therefore remained her secret. She was there, they were together and both were the envy of almost every young person in town. It seemed as if it was enough that the Vows of Loyalty joined them together as lovers and mates.

The evening continued with dance after dance until finally symbols clanged and Baron Qylda waited while everyone retreated from the dance floor and sat in three rows of chairs around the edge of the room.

'For those entering the Third Age; welcome,' he began in a slightly pompous voice. 'As you all know, Age One is the children, at twelve you become a youth but at twenty two, you enter the Third Age; that of maturity and continue on throughout your life to become a Fourth Age Honorable Citizen at Fifty Two.' He coughed. 'I entered that position a short while ago.'

Everyone laughed, as it was well known that the Baron was well in his sixties, and listened as his voice continued on to praise the hundred and ten Third Age Graduates that day.

'I cannot conclude without making a special mention of one honored guest and citizen.' He gave a signal and the spotlight lit up Kagit and Lunol in a far corner of the Grand Ball Room. 'As well as entering her Third Age, Miss Frysyl, as you are aware is the youngest candidate in the history of the Shire of Nkypy to be elected on the Council Of Governors. We welcome Kagit and her Loyal Partner, Mr. Lunol Pendylf and asked them to start the Grand Supper Waltz.'

'Shall we, My Love,' Lunol bowed gracefully and held his arm out for Kagit; the orchestra started and together the pair swept onto the dance floor. For several moments they swung in a spotlight while the audience clapped in time with the music. The lights came on and every Third Age Graduate with their partners joined them on the floor. It was a night to remember.

*

However, it was remembered for an entirely different reason. The Third Age Graduation Ball traditionally stopped at twenty plus two hours, two hours after midnight in their twenty-hour day. It was 1.80 with twenty minutes until the hour when the final waltz was called. Lunol, slightly merry on bread wine, smiled at Kagit and they walked on the floor, lights were dimmed and in semi-darkness couple had their final dance together.

As Kagit neared the orchestra balcony a voice pierced her mind.

'Kylina,' said Computer Theta. 'There is an emergency! Take Lunol and slip out the door beneath the balcony at once. There is a corridor behind. Take the third door to the left and it will lead you to the cellar. Do it now!'

Kagit paled. The code "Do it now" meant there was a dire emergency and she should act without question.'

'Right,' she thought and guided her partner towards the door. 'Lunol,' she said quietly. 'Trust me, please.'

'Of course, I trust you, My Sweet.' Lunol answered with a merry grin on his face.

They were at the door and in dark shadows. Kagit suddenly opened it and pushed Lunol in.

'You wicked little girl,' he burped but suddenly sobered when Kagit latched the door, pulled a cord and a dim light came on. Her eyes were wide and serious. 'Federal Marshals have surrounded the Manor,' she gasped as Theta poured the information into her mind. 'They're after me.'

'But why?' Lunol gasped.

'The fungus plague,' she gasped as she headed along the narrow corridor and found the steps leading down to the cellar.

'But we are over the plague. The medicine you injected in the villager's arms made us all better.'

'That's the trouble,' the girl replied with a grim expression. 'Every other village has an epidemic with hundreds of people dying. They have heard of my injections and have declared it witchcraft. I have been declared a witch.'

'For helping the villagers!' Lunol replied but his voice shook. So called witches were usually given show trials and guillotined in a public square, often within hours of being arrested.

'They have declared electricity the work of a witch, too and banned it throughout the country,' Kagit continued as she grabbed Lunol's hand and continued down the spiral stairs.

'Why?'

'The King's daughter touched a live wire and got electrocuted,' the girl replied. 'Damn!' she cursed when she tripped on her skirt. She fell sideways and would have fallen if Lunol hadn't grabbed her wrist and yanked her back.

'Thanks, My Love,' she whispered and hitched her gown up to her calves.

They reached level ground and Kagit ran one hand along a brick wall in the dark corridor. 'There's a round trapdoor in the floor somewhere. We have to find it and go down into a storm water drain.'

Behind them, the very faint sound of the orchestra stopped. There was silence, a loud explosion of a musket being fired and screams, hundreds of screams; the sound of people in panic. Another gunshot rent the air and was followed by a harsh command. Screams were replaced by quieter sobs and banging on the floor above. Furniture was being shifted.

'Feel around with your feet,' Kagit gasped. 'It's here somewhere.'

'Here,' whispered Lunol. 'I found it.'

Her eyes were useless in the darkness but Kagit could hear a scrape of metal being lifted, Lunol gasping in effort and the smell of putrid air in her face.

'Got it!' he said. 'You go first.'

Kagit turned, felt the edge and sat over the gap. She let her legs down and swore as her ball gown caught the sides of the hole. Above, screams and thumps started again.

She reached down with one leg and her toes found an iron rung. With this to balance on, she poked the material of her clothes through and stepped down until her toes felt another rung, then another. There was a sudden rip as the material of her ball gown caught somewhere but this was no time to worry about modesty. She glanced up and saw Lunol silhouetted in a circle of light.

'Hurry!' he hissed. 'Someone's opened the door at the top of the stairs.'

Kagit listened. There was water beneath; flowing water and it sounded deep. 'Shut the trapdoor, Lunol. I'm going to jump.'

She did and hit the water with a splash just as the light above went out. The water was freezing and her petticoats and gown immediately clung to her like glue and pulled her down; down beneath the surface. For a second Kagit panicked as water surged up her nose. She could not breathe! Her lungs would burst!

She touched bottom and pushed up to find the water, though swift was not above head height. She was cold and terrified but could stand and catch a breath.

'Lunol,' she shivered with her voice echoing into the distance.

'Here, My Sweet,' he replied, so close she jumped in fright. 'You can stand up. Grip onto the side so you won't get swept away. The bricks stick out a little.'

What was worse; the physical conditions with near freezing water and clinging clothes or the sheer terror of the situation. For hours, it seemed, the pair made their way by walking and later floating down with the current. It was pitch dark, the tunnel stunk of damp soil, rubbish and often debris that brushed past them. The tunnel turned and twisted but continued downwards until, at last they rounded a corner and a shaft of dull light reflected in.

They could hear the water tumbling ahead as the current increased speed. Kagit, took a breath, lifted her feet and floated those last few meters. However, she hit something at high speed and gasp in pain. An iron grid blocked the entrance. The water could splash through but they were trapped!

'Lunol!' Kagit screamed. Her fingers were numb but she gripped the bars and peered out into the darkness. They were below the Manor and their drain flowed into a natural stream. The faint outline of trees could be seen opposite and beyond, dull reflected light from the manor. It was the noise, though, that made Kagit's hair begin to rise on the back of her neck. Screams, yells, the crash of muskets, shouts of command and a military trumpet blowing.

'They're sounding the regroup call,' Lunol shouted above the roaring water and other noises. His wig, hat and jacket were all gone, he looked completely drenched and was shivering from the cold but his determined eyes held hers.

'Theta, Help!' commanded Kagit and a strange warmth surged through her body as the computer took over.

Lunol watched in surprise as she grabbed two iron bars and simply pulled them apart, further and further until the left one snapped. She grabbed the next bar further out and pulled again. A second one snapped followed by a third until there was room to fit through.

'You go first, Lunol,' said a metallic voice through Kagit's mouth.

Lunol nodded in the darkness, bent forward and was gone.

Kagit gasped, realized there was a gap in the iron and also floated through. Her gown, already in tatters, caught in the broken bars, the girl's head went down and water poured over her face and down her throat.

'Theta!' her mind called out a second time in as many minutes. 'I'm drowning!'

This time though, the computer wasn't needed. Lunol saw the predicament, grabbed her head and turned it up out of the water while at the same time pulling her out with all his might. There was another terrible ripping sound and she plunged out like a cork from a bottle. Petticoats and half the gown were gone but she was safe in Lunol's arms in the middle of a deep stream.

Once more, time had no meaning. They were carried away from

The Manor and the lights. There was a glimpse of troopers lining men and women up as they were swept around a bend through dark trees and out of sight. After the sound faded they floated ashore, grabbed a branch and pulled themselves up a wet bank of grass.

'Oh Lunol,' sobbed a frozen Kagit as she felt masculine arms hold her in a grip so tight she could not move. 'I'm so sorry.'

'For rescuing me,' he replied and the girl could hear his chattering teeth. ' My Sweet, I thank you but how did you know they were coming to arrest you?'

She smiled in the darkness. 'I'll tell you everything soon, My Love but we are not yet out of danger. I know the King's Troopers have dogs and it won't take long for them to realize we aren't with the dancers.'

'So what do we do? Head out into the forest!'

'No just wait,' Kagit replied in a confident voice. 'Help is on its way.'

*

' And it was,' Kylina wrapped a towel around her shoulders as one foot kicked the swimming pool water. 'A rescue pod landed right by us. By the time the King's Troopers had enough nerve to fire their muskets or approach, we were off.' She sighed. 'My beautiful ball gown was ruined and that was our last day on Planet 38675.6.

We never went back. Omega remained in orbit for a week until the computers reported the village of Nkypy was safe and the King's Troopers, convinced we had drowned, left. It seems they found two bodies in the stream. I suspect Theta arranged it somehow but she would admit nothing.'

'A couple followed you down into the cellar and were in the middle of a mating ritual when the federal marshals ran in,' Theta's thoughts cut in. 'They panicked, followed you into the storm water drain and drowned. At that time, I though you had enough on your mind without feeling guilty about this as well.'

'Thanks, Theta,' Kagit answered with a little nod. She repeated the news to everyone gave Lunol a brief translation.

'Yes,' he said in English. 'When she pulled the bars apart in that storm water drain, I almost thought she was a witch, too.'

'Then what?' Lynn asked. Her eyes showed intense interest.

'We blasted out of orbit and, after spending four days practicing all the emergency procedures, went into suspended animation.' Kylina replied.

'And the whole time I was there but knew nothing about it all,' Pazz added.

'Until we got to Earth,' Kylina concluded. 'You all know the rest of our story.'

'And Pazz found me.' Lynn added. 'I think I was very lucky.'

'It worked both ways,' Pazz said. 'Without you, Lynn, I doubt if I would be where I am now.'

'We are all very fortunate people, the Earthlings and the Aliens,' Duncan said and ducked as Pazz flicked a handful of water over his now dried body.

'Don't call me an Alien,' she snapped. 'To me, you're the Alien.'

'True,' he confessed, grabbed her in his arms and placed a kiss on her lips. 'You talk like a fair dinkum Australian, though, I must admit.'

'And don't you forget it,' Pazz laughed and gave him a push. Duncan toppled and, with a yell, splashed in the pool. He reached up, found an ankle and, seconds later Pazz was in there, too. Lunol broke into a smile, grabbed Kylina in his arms and tossed her in, as well.

'You wait, Lunol,' she screamed and scooped a handful of water over her laughing partner.

*

CHAPTER FOURTEEN

One block behind Lynn's place, an army truck pulled to the curb and thirty men dressed in camouflage uniforms and equipped with sinister weapons slid out the back and closed the road with a portable barricade. Three men manned the site while others ran quickly and silently ahead to the next intersection. Another barricade was erected while soldiers tapped on doors and informed the inhabitants that there was an emergency and they were to be evacuated at once.

Within twenty minutes the area was sealed off and every householder except those 17, 19 and 21 Elden Crescent and a flat immediately behind 19, were assembled in a nearby church hall. Over a hundred, curious, excited, dumbfounded, annoyed and even angry citizens were told there was a civil police alert and they'd be allowed to return home in an hour or so.

Dean Diriwi and his Primoss Force had arrived!

*

Beyond the wooden boundary fence, three soldiers watched the high jinks though a gap in the boards.

'Bloody attractive identical twins,' whispered one.' If they're our spies, I'll volunteer to rough 'em up a little.'

'You couldn't stand the pace,' his companion sniggered. 'Not with two of them'

'Quiet' the sergeant warned. 'It's almost time. When I say, stand up, shine your torches on them and say who we are. If they panic and run, let them. The guys on the other side will stop them.'

'Right, Sarge,' whispered the first man, once again the professional soldier. 'I'm ready.'

A radio blinked green and the sergeant put it to his ear. He frowned, listened for a moment and placed the instrument down.

'The mission is aborted,' he shrugged. 'Orders from the Prime Minister himself. We go home, Lads.'

With a shrug, the men crept out to the back street while, back at the hall, everyone was told there'd been a gas leak that had been repaired and they could all go home. The next day those at 19 Elden Crescent heard the news of the great gas leak and wondered how they were missed.

'We were making enough noise to wake the dead,' Lynn said. 'Yet they completely forgot about us.'

'Could be,' Pazz replied, 'but I think there was more to it than that.'

Lynn frowned. 'I know,' she added. 'It was eerie wasn't it? Whatever it was, I'm glad we're still safe. After Kylina's story I'm prepared to believe anything.'

*

The next month drifted by with only a few domestic changes at 19 Elden Crescent. Kylina and Lunol moved into their own home less than two blocks away and, on Lynn's invitation, Duncan moved in.

'After all,' she said,' You're here every weekend and at least one week night anyhow and, with Kylina and Lunol gone, I'd be lonely if Pazz shifted in with you in that gritty little apartment of yours.'

Kylina had been accepted for The School of Fine Arts and was due to start in the new semester at mid-year. In the meantime she continued her supermarket position and had had her hours increased. Lunol answered an advertisement and found a job as a hand at a local racing stable. The wages were low but he was back with horses that he loved. His enthusiasm and expertise with the animals soon showed through and he did not even mind the five a.m. start and trip across town to begin at the stables by six. His knowledge of English, learnt the natural way, improved daily but he still carried Sigma as a last resort.

Even though Pazz was still learning to drive, Kylina past her driver's license with ease and bought a little car of her own. She was now trying, unsuccessfully, to persuade Lunol to learn. They were busy but happy times with the three newcomers totally assimilated into Australian society.

Summer turned to autumn and Pazz was working in her office one morning when a message came through on her e-mail that the Vice Chancellor wished to see her the next day. Pazz went home quite worried that night but, unusual for him, Duncan was somewhat off handed about her news.

'There is nothing at all to worry about, My Love,' he said. 'Trust me.'

Pazz frowned and sat up in their bed. 'You know something, don't you Duncan?'

Duncan grinned and wrapped his arms around her soft body. He kissed her tenderly on the lips but refused to say more. Instead the kisses became frantic and Pazz had her mind diverted by their passionate lovemaking.

At ten sharp the next morning, Pazz was shown into the Vice Chancellor's office and sat, as nervous as she had ever been since arriving on Earth. Thoughts of doubt flowed through her mind and even Epsilon's steadying thoughts were of no help.

Vice Chancellor Herbert Williamson was a man in his early sixties with white hair and a soft smile, that held, Pazz had been informed, a sharp mind and determined blunt personality.

His eyes bore into her. 'Since your arrival at our university, Doctor D'rose I have had nothing but excellent reports about your work. The student appraisals list you as one of their most helpful lecturers and Doctor Matthew McHardy is enthusiastic about your research work.'

'Thank you, Doctor Williamson,' Pazz replied but bit on her lip in anticipation. She knew there was more to come.

'Your qualifications, Doctor D'Rose, check out in all but one aspect." said the Vice Chancellor,

Pazz's heart thumped wildly and color drained from her face. 'And that is, Doctor Williamson?'

At both universities where you trained, nobody can remember you, Doctor D'rose, there is no mention of your name in graduation lists nor are any of your photographs on file. Can you explain?'

Pazz clinched her lips and stood with her hands shaking. 'I'll have my resignation on your desk by five p.m., Doctor Williamson. Thank you.'

She stood, brushed her suit down and took three steps towards the door before the Vice Chancellor interrupted. 'Was your title and name once Matron Pazz 4th Flower in your own language, Doctor D'rose?' he said in a voice so quiet she only just heard it.

Her face flushed, she turned and stared at the man smiling faintly at her. 'How did you know?' she gasped.

'Sit down, Doctor,' the Vice Chancellor said. 'I have a few items to show you.'

Pazz sat back in the chair she'd just vacated and watched as Williamson took three, highly ornate certificates from his drawer and handed them to Pazz. She stared and her face drained of color. They were her graduation certificates, written in Delta's language. The certificates all had her name on them.

'How?' she gasped. Her hands were shaking so much one certificate dropped to the floor and she had to stoop and pick it up.

'I will reveal that soon,' the Vice Chancellor continued, 'but first could you explain the significance of these three certificates.'

Pazz swallowed and reached for the smallest one. 'No doubt you know about me, Doctor so it is suffice to say I came from a female society so our qualifications reflect this.

This certificate is a Sister's degree. It took three years to complete and is equivalent to your B.Sc.' She slid it to the back and held the second one out. 'This is a Daughter's Degree like an MA here and this largest is an 8 year degree which gave me the title of Matron. It is equivalent to a Ph.D. in Australia.'

'I see and the red ten pointed star on both the later degrees?'

Pazz flushed. 'They meant I was in the top ten percent of my year's graduating class. You'd call them honors here, I guess.'

'The work you're doing with Doctor McHardy?' His eyebrows shot up.

'I learnt it in my second year,' Pazz replied in a quiet voice. 'In my fields of expertise we are many generations ahead of you. I am not, though, by a strict code of ethics I signed back home, allowed to forward any knowledge beyond what we call one generation cycle, that is what your scientists would learn naturally in a lifetime, say eighty years,' She coughed and flushed again. 'Our life expectancy is longer than yours.'

'These certificates are genuine?'

'Yes, but I cannot prove it." Pazz gritted her teeth and stared at the man behind the desk. 'I demand to know how you accessed these, Doctor Williamson,' she said in a firm resolute voice.

The man smiled and pressed a button on his desk. 'Will you ask Doctor Bourne to come in, please, Mary,' he said.

The door opened and Duncan walked in with a grin that contrasted completely with Pazz's look of concern. He sat next to her and explained. 'The government checked you out, My...I mean Pazz.' They found nobody that knew you, nor was your name in old newspaper records of graduates, yet everything on computers verified your degrees. Doctor Williamson knew we were...err romantically involved.'

'Living together sexually as male and female.' Pazz interjected with a bluntness that made the vice-chancellor glance at her with an intense expression.

Duncan flushed. 'That's right. Anyhow, he asked me if there was any way I could verify your qualifications. I asked Epsilon to help and she arranged a print out of your certificates on the university computer by connecting into Omega's records. As you know, I have been studying your language and, except for a few minor variations, your printed language uses the Greek alphabet.' He turned to the Vice Chancellor. 'It originally came from Pazz's homeland and was given to the ancient Greeks.'

'So you told me,' the Vice Chancellor replied as he rubbed his chin.

'Anyhow,' Duncan continued. 'With the ability to read your language, it was not hard to get Epsilon to download all your records and also rank them, more or less, into our hierarchy. We have, therefore, completed proof of your academic background. You don't need faked records any more.'

'However,' the Vice Chancellor interrupted. 'The government has invoked a Secrecy Act injunction on us and we are not allowed to release any of this information. The Professorial Board has voted in a closed session, that in light of this and the fact that your academic qualifications are more than equivalent to a Ph.D., it will remain intact, as shall your position at this university.'

'You mean...' Pazz gasped and smiled for the first time.

'Yes, Doctor D'rose. You are officially entitled to call yourself Doctor and are a welcome employee of this university. Congratulations, Pazz.' He stood up and held out his hand. 'Duncan, here, spent many hours translating your language into English and it was through his efforts, this all became possible.'

Pazz's eyes turned to her partner. 'You said nothing,' she accused.

'I couldn't,' Duncan said. 'Official Secrets Act, you know.'

'Oh Duncan!' Pazz beamed. 'Thank you.' She turned to the Vice Chancellor. 'Thank you, too, Doctor Williamson. I'll do my best to be a credit to this institution.'

'You already are, Doctor,' the Vice Chancellor replied. He handed the certificates on his desk to her. 'I'm sure the Secrecy Act won't prevent you hanging these in your office. After all, Duncan's the only person around here who can read them.'

Pazz gathered the bundle in her arms and walked quietly out of the room. She felt all tingly and excited inside, almost as if it was graduation day all over again.

'You wait until I get Duncan on his own,' she grumbled with Epsilon as she made her way back to her office. 'You too, you cohort.'

'Sorry Pazz,' Epsilon replied. 'They're tough on the secrets act in this country.'

'Yeah, sure,' Pazz replied but she was smiling.

*

CHAPTER FIFTEEN

After the tragedy, the underground installations at Magaroona Research Station were visited by clean up crews in protective clothing. The bodies were taken into a service chamber, identified and after a moving funeral service, cremated in the huge underground furnace similar to those of a commercial crematorium. Once again, after extensive safety procedures were followed, the ashes were removed and flown home to love ones in United States or Australian cities. The deaths were officially recorded as a result of a massive underground explosion and all information about the fungus suppressed by the Australian and United States Governments. Afterwards, the entire underground complex was sealed and contaminated air pumped in to underground receptive cylinders originally designed to hold radioactive material. In place of ordinary air, an inert gas mixture was pumped into the installation at a temperature of minus twenty degrees Celsius in the hope that the fungi bacteria would be killed.

Now the Cold War was over, the need for underground facilities were not considered necessary so within days, prefabricated laboratories and service blocks were flown in. Within a month, new personnel had arrived and the radio telescopes were back in operation. The only sign of the underground installation was the concrete that sealed all entrances and a marble memorial with the names of those who lost their lives, listed in black granite around the base.

Only one small item had been overlooked, or perhaps forgotten. When the installation was designed in the 1950s, engineers had found a subterranean cave and decided to use this to build the base in. Thousands of dollars and pounds could be saved by using this instead of having to excavate a hole in the desert soil and little regard in those times were given to the natural environment nor and social significance of this cave. The protests of the local aborigine tribe had been ignored.

The decades rolled by and the original caves were forgotten except by the local peoples. Part of the cave had been left intact and the underground stream there actually used as a natural drain from the station. This was replaced in later years by a more sophisticated drainage system but there was still a small pipe from the living quarters that hadn't been joined to the new system. The pipe had corroded over the years and had blocked up with debris but water still occasionally soaked through and dripped into the underground cavity. Once again, this would have been harmless except for one man.

Jimmy, a local aborigine tribesman, worked at the Corran Cattle Station a hundred kilometers south of Magaroona, but like many of his tribe, at times wandered through his ancestral lands. Eight years earlier while exploring the caves, he had found a way into the underground station through original drainage tunnels. This was an interesting find that Jimmy kept to himself. He did, though, enter the place on occasions through a door that opened into a disused storage room and helped himself to minor items; food, tools, clothing but nothing really large. On his last visit he sensed that something was wrong.

First there was no hum of air conditioning as he crawled through the pipe and instead of becoming warmer the temperature dropped as he approached. He stopped and shone his flashlight around. Everything looked okay, the air remained fresh so he decided to continue. The access to the storeroom was an ordinary steel door. It was originally locked but Jimmy had picked the lock years earlier and had replaced it with one of his own. As far as he knew, his new lock had never been tampered with so he assumed nobody ever used the door.

He muttered to himself as he extracted the key from his pocket, unlocked the door and pulled it towards himself. A sudden burst of freezing fog tumbled into the tunnel and he found himself unable to breathe. Coughing and with tears streaming from his eyes, Jimmy took one frantic look at the bellowing fog and slammed the door shut. In the piecing beam of his flashlight, he noticed the fog seemed to gather around his feet so he stood up and found he could breathe air at the top of the tunnel. Still spluttering; he took a dirty rag out of his pocket, tied it around his mouth and staggered away. Within moments, he could breath normally and apart from shock, felt normal.

'Bloody nuisance,' he muttered to himself. His free food supply had dried up but he was not about to open the door again. Instead he made his way through the labyrinth of underground chambers and up to the surface two kilometers beyond Magaroona Research Station's security fence.

The following day back at Corran Cattle Station Jimmy began to feel off color. He ached all over and found it was painful to breathe. After trying to hide his symptoms from everyone for several hours, the independent man realized he needed help and approached the house. He staggered to the front veranda and managed to knock on the door before collapsing onto the wooden floorboards.

Marion Lawrie, the station's owner, took one look at him and radioed the Flying Doctor Service but by the time the Nomad touched down Marion and children were all coughing and feeling miserable themselves. Ten year old Deborah complained of chest pains and, while fifteen year old Andrew teased her for being a baby, he did not feel too good himself.

Doctor Lucas Whitley frowned as he examined the aborigine worker who was conscious but shaking with a fever and barely able to breathe. 'Where have you been, Jimmy?' he asked as he listened to the rattling lungs through his stethoscope and took the man's temperature. It was almost forty degrees; the man was burning up.

'Just walk-about, Doc. Nowhere special.' Jimmy spluttered and began a violent coughing fit. His eyes watered as he spluttered up bloodstained, putrid smelling mucus into a paper towel that Lucas had handed him. 'My chest stings like hell, Doc,' he groaned and began rasping for breath.

Lucas frowned and injected a general antibiotic and sedative into Jimmy's arm. He spent another few moments examining his patient before going into the kitchen. 'He's a sick man, Marion,' he said. 'There's a fever and he's in the first stage of pneumonia. I'll need to fly him down to Adelaide.'

'Thanks, Lucas,' the homesteader replied and began coughing herself.

'You don't sound too good, either,' the doctor said.

'I've had a bit of flu, ' the woman said. 'I've a splitting headache. The kids are a bit under the weather, too. As far as I know, they're all healthy down at the reserve.'

'I reckon I'd better check everyone out while I'm here,' the doctor replied. 'A flu booster shot wouldn't do any harm. Can you give me a lift over to the settlement?'

'Sure, Doc,' Marion replied, 'but I'd like a favor in return.'

'Name it,' Lucas replied as he swung his long frame into Marion's Land Rover.

'Well, I was going to fly Andrew back to school in Adelaide but since you're flying Jimmy to hospital there, could you give Andrew a lift? It's a day early but I'm sure he won't mind. Between you and me, I think there's a girl at school he's keen to get back to see.'

'Sure. No problem,' Lucas replied. 'Tell him I'll be off inside the half hour.'

That evening, two events happened in Adelaide. Jimmy went into a coughing fit at the Royal Adelaide Hospital and, despite efforts by house surgeons, lapsed into a coma and was put on an emergency life support system. A few kilometers away, at Southern Cross Grammar School, Andrew felt so ill he missed the boarding school's evening meal and reported to the infirmary instead. The school nurse took one look at his spluttering, perspiring face and heaving chest and reached for the phone.

'It's the hospital for you, young man,' she said. 'I don't like that chest one little bit.'

Andrew coughed green bile into the sink, wiped his mouth with a paper towel, glanced up and tried to make a brave grin. ' It's my mother's entire fault. She had the flu. I guess I got it from her.'

Within a few hours the alien bacteria had traveled hundreds of kilometers but it wasn't only confined to a remote homestead any more but had arrived in a city of more than a million people. Already hospital staff and pupils at one of the largest boarding schools in the city were feeling wheezy and had chest pains when they breathed.

*

'Pazz, wake up!' Epsilon's voice sounded as urgent as a computer could be.

It was Sunday morning and Pazz forced her eyes open. Duncan was snoring quietly with his arm still around her while their night attire was somewhere in the darkness on the carpet. She grinned at the thought of their love making only a few hours previously and rolled over to cuddle into her partner again. Something had awoken her but it was probably a dream.

'Pazz!'

'Oh, Switch off,' Pazz grumbled as she tucked herself in by Duncan and closed her eyes.

However, the switch off command did not work. Instead, Pazz felt her armlet grow hot, so hot it began to burn. She jerked awake again and sat up with a worried expression. This wasn't a dream. Epsilon was declaring an emergency.

'Okay, you have my attention.' She snapped. 'What is it?'

'Get everyone up, including Lynn and Jason. You'll need clothes for at least a week. It is urgent. Do it!'

Pazz ran a tongue over her dry top lip and shook Duncan. 'Sweetheart,' she said. 'Wake up. Epsilon is warning me about an extreme emergency.'

Duncan woke to find the light on and Pazz already getting dressed. The bedside clock said 5.15 and it was still dark outside.

'What is it?' he asked.

'I don't know,' Pazz replied and was interrupted when the telephone rang. 'Hello, Pazz here.'

'Theta just woke me,' gasped Kylina's worried voice. 'She said I had to bring Lunol and get to your place immediately. Are you okay?'

'So far,' Pazz replied. 'I've been awoken, too.' She gulped. 'It must be serious. Epsilon even overrode the switch off command.'

There was silence on the instrument for a full two seconds before Kylina replied. 'I'll be at your place in fifteen minutes,' she responded in a terse voice and the line went dead.

Twenty minutes later, Kylina's car was parked on the front lawn and everyone squeezed into Duncan's large Falcon station wagon. Lynn cuddled a sleeping Jason next to Lunol and Kylina in the back seat while Duncan tossed two backpacks in the back just as Pazz returned.

'Everything's locked and turned off,' she spoke in a crisp voice. 'Epsilon said we have to be at the airport domestic terminal by 6:30 but would say why.' She jumped in the front and slammed the door. 'I think she is communicating with Omega.'

Duncan saw the intense look on her face, nodded and drove through the almost surreal early morning roads. Streetlights were still on and a damp sea fog hung above them while cleaning trucks washed the curbs and an occasional vehicle drove by. Even the traffic lights cooperated with most of them green in the absence of cross traffic. The airport was just beginning to come to life as, Duncan, on Pazz's orders parked the car in the long term security parking; they grabbed their gear and began the long walk to the Domestic Terminal.

'Someone is meeting us near the Qantas check in counter. I've been told nothing else,' Pazz panted. She had just taken Jason into her arms to relieve Lynn while Lunol grabbed an abandoned trolley and tossed their bags on it. He said little but his eyes showed a haunting fear. It was 6:25!

The terminal was just waking up for a new commercial day as five adults and one child came to a stop at their destination. Everything was completely normal with a few early flight customers lining up, ladies sweeping the floor and most stores still closed with security gratings pulled down. Breakfast was being sold in the cafeteria.

'Relax,' Epsilon and Theta both said simultaneously to their hosts. 'Go and have a good meal. You could need it.'

Pazz and Kylina also spoke together. 'We have to get breakfast...' Their eyes meet and, in spite of the serious situation they grinned.

'I think we're being manipulated,' Pazz grunted.

The breakfast was expensive, as airports tend to be, but quite wholesome. Everyone munched in silence except Jason who sat in a high chair with jam all over his face. He was beginning to talk and his favor his words seemed to be 'Why, Mummy!'

'What now?' Duncan asked but Pazz just looked glum and shrugged.

'I'll get some more toast,' she said and walked towards the counter.

A tall slim woman dressed in a neat suit slipped in the line immediately behind her and gave a wee cough. Pazz swung around, saw the face without noticing different clothes and spoke. 'What would you like, Kylina?' she asked.

'I am not, Kylina,' the woman replied in a somewhat annoyed tone. Blue eyes stared directly at Pazz. 'You know I'm Hycerta. Can you lead me to the people we have to meet? '

'What!' gasped Pazz and stared. The woman was another identical image of herself; only her hairstyle was different. The conversation, though, was confusing.

'There is little time,' the woman continued in an abrupt voice. 'Are the Delta families here, Kappa?'

'Kappa?' Pazz frowned. That was another home language letter, a "K" in the English alphabet. 'Who's Kappa?' she asked.

'Omega 17's computer.' Hycerta replied with a slight frown. Almost on impulse, the new arrival grabbed Pazz's hands and squeezed them so tightly it almost hurt while her eyes looked wide with shock. 'Oh Hell!' she uttered in a tiny voice. 'You're real!'

'Yes, of course I am. What did you expect?' Pazz replied while she tried to comprehend what was happening. Another clone of herself was standing right by her. How could this be?

The other woman's face drained white and lips quivered.' I thought you were Kappa in holograph form, here to point out the families I have to rescue.'

'I see,' Pazz replied. She was beginning to realize was happening. This Hycerta was a clone sister just like Kylina; that was obvious. What wasn't so clear, though, was her reaction to their meeting. 'You'd better come and meet my sister and our families,' she said in a kind voice. 'I guess you saw where we're sitting.'

'Not really,' Hycerta replied. 'When I walked in here I saw you in that queue and assumed... ' Her voice trailed off.

Pazz nodded and escorted her double, or was it treble, back to their breakfast table.

'Duncan,' she said in a quiet but awestricken voice. 'Remember when you first met Kylina?'

Duncan, together with everyone else, glanced up and saw the new woman standing beside her. Pazz shifted her eyes and saw a bewildered Kylina sitting opposite him. Duncan swallowed, stood up, extended his hand to the familiar looking stranger and smiled.

'Pazz's new sister, I assume,' he said and gripped the soft hand in his.

'Hycerta is my... our...' Pazz's embarrassed eyes turned to Kylina, 'clone.' She turned to the newcomer. 'This is Duncan, my partner; Kylina, I guess you realize is my clone sister ...' She continued on to introduce the others.

Hycerta stared at Kylina, Pazz and back to Kylina. 'It's all true!' she gasped but did not elaborate. She was polite to the others and her eyes showed interest when Lunol was introduced. 'Lunol from Custronomus?' she asked when his hand gripped hers.

'Yes,' he replied in a curious voice. 'Do you know the place?'

'Only from our history lessons,' Hycerta replied, accepted the chair Duncan found and sat down. 'This is as big a shock for me as you but please listen and ask questions later.'

The newcomer folded her legs over exactly the way Pazz herself did and spoke in a quiet voice. 'I was told I had to rescue long lost citizens from here and Kappa hinted there would be no trouble in recognizing you. When you arrived I watched and...' She shrugged. 'I thought Pazz was a holograph sent by Kappa to show me who to go to but you seemed just too real. That's why I reached out and touched you.'

'I'll explain,' Epsilon's voice pierced Pazz's mind. 'Kylina and Hycerta are hearing this too. You can tell the others in a moment. It seems your mother Zandra was quite distressed after you two left forever in Omega and was advised to have another child. This, she did in the natural way. Your natural sister, Cruly is Hycerta's grandmother. Apparently, Pazz, you became a bit of a martyr for the new freedom that swept the planet after Omega's departure and Cruly's daughter, Dlynar used your DNA, still on file to have a cloned pregnancy. Hycerta, you are Pazz's cloned grandniece, I guess you'd call it. When you left Delta, it was eighty years after Pazz's departure.'

'That's right,' Hycerta continued after Pazz passed on Epsilon's information to Lynn and the men. 'Five years after your departure, males were given equal rights and births were not genetically altered to produce only females. Our population is now over thirty percent male and with people aged under twenty it is almost; fifty-fifty the same as on this world, I guess. We have families now and males are gradually being elected for government posts and going into business.' She frowned.' Of course, it's not all-perfect. Older women are resisting the change and teenage males don't help with their aggressive stance. Oh yes,' she whispered,' all females are now bearers and artificially suppressing emotions for either gender is strictly banned.'

She coughed and continued. 'But that is not why I'm here. To put it bluntly, the fungus from Lunol's planet has escaped from Magaroona Research Station and is spreading. If you are not evacuated you'll all, except perhaps Lunol, die. We can do nothing for Earthlings but I'm under orders to evacuate you all.' She looked around. 'You will either volunteer or be removed by force. I have only to say one word and Kappa will seal off this terminal within seconds and everyone, except myself will go into a deep one-hour sleep. That will give me time to shift you all to my aircraft.'

Pazz stared angrily at Hycerta. 'I am no coward. If this fungus is spreading, I shall remain and try to stop it.'

'I'm sorry, Pazz. I'm under orders,' Hycerta's voice had changed to that slightly metallic tone. 'You come or we take you. It is as simple as that.'

Kylina was the one who replied. 'Pazz, let's do it. I'm sure we can help from a starship. Staying here and dying won't help. Being carted out while the terminal is sealed will only cause a panic when everyone at the airport wakes up. That wouldn't help anyone.'

'I agree with Kylina,' Duncan supported. 'It's not Hycerta doing this but the computer. Imagine how more advanced they must be after another eighty years?'

'This is my world now,' Pazz answered. Her eyes flashed with anger. 'I will not just abandon it!'

Lynn reached across and took Pazz's arm. 'Pazz,' she said with tears welling in her eyes. 'I have never been so happy since I met you but I don't want Jason to die!' She held the toddler to her breast. 'I don't believe you do either.'

Pazz's eyes switched to Jason.

'Why are you sad, Auntie Pazz?' Jason asked

'Oh Jason,' Pazz replied and reached out for him. 'I just love you, that's all.' She kissed the little boy and turned to Hycerta. 'Tell that bloody computer we'll come but are not about to be run by a bunch of electronic cells.'

'You're living up to your reputation Doctor Pazz D'rose,' Hycerta's metallic voice said. 'I would have been disappointed if you'd acted any other way. Rest assured, we'll do everything we can to save Earthlings from this plague. We do not intend to just leave Earth to its fate.'

'I bloody hope not,' Paz retorted and stood up. 'Well if we're going, let's do it.'

She nodded at Hycerta who led them out a door beyond the Qantas counter until they came to Gate 36 with the sign *Independent Airlines* above the door. Outside dawn had arrived and Pazz could see a small twin engine commuter jet squeezed between the bigger Boeings and Airbuses. In spite of her concern she had to grin. The tiny white jet had "Omega Shuttle" written above the windows.

'It looks like a Learjet, a business airplane,' Hycerta explained. 'In reality, it is a landing pod. We thought this was easier than landing in the desert somewhere in our usual craft.'

'I like the name,' Pazz grunted. 'At least someone has a sense of humor.'

'Thank you, Pazz,' Hycerta replied. 'That was my idea.'

Ground crew loaded their luggage in a small fuselage compartment and they climbed aboard to find two rows of single seats separated by a narrow passageway. The door shut, Hycerta gave a curt command in Delta's home language, the engines started and they began to taxi out.

'We have dummies in the cockpit,' she said. 'We though a seemingly pilotless aircraft moving along would defeat the value of our disguise.'

Within moments they were in the air flying east.

*

The Learjet was one of last aircraft to leave Adelaide that Sunday morning. By seven thirty the fog had dropped over the city like a blanket and all aircraft were grounded. Passengers arriving for morning flights milled in the terminal building and waited for the fog to lift. Nobody noticed an attendant collecting up rubbish in the men's toilet. The elderly man grumbled and shook his head as he emptied a rubbish bin into a polythene bag on his cleaning trolley. As he did so, a few paper towels and a sodden handkerchief fell out. The man picked them up in his fingers to toss in the bag then sniffed and, without thinking ran a grubby finger over his nose. He was not to know that the handkerchief had been dropped in the rubbish bin the evening before when Andrew Lawrie had slipped into the rest room. The man wandered out and zigzagged his way through the shoulder-to-shoulder crowd. During his trip across the room he sneezed three times and a hundred or more unsuspecting passengers breathed in tiny molecules of water. Bacteria thrived in a crowded room.

Forty minutes later, the fog lifted and aircraft began to lift off the ground for destinations all over Australia. It was only a minor inconvenience but one that would have major consequences.

Five kilometers away at the Royal Adelaide Hospital, Jimmy lost his battle for life and was pronounced dead. It was only six days since he'd broken into Magaroona Research Station.

*

After leaving Adelaide Airport, the Learjet flew east for fifteen minutes before changing direction south and the land below slipped away so only the blue ocean was beneath them. A blue light flashed and, following Hycerta's lead, everyone clamped on seat belts and Jason was held secure in a child's safety chair provided.

The Learjet's wings slipped into the fuselage and it became a space ship. There was a shudder; they turned vertical and accelerated. G-Forces thrust them back but within minutes they were weightless and gazing at the curvature of world below. Again within minutes, they felt rather than heard a rocket fire, the craft decelerated and moved towards a black sphere orbiting like a gigantic weather balloon above the blue and white Earth. A door near the center of the starship-slid open and their landing pod floated inside. Huge mechanical arms reached out and gripped it and, behind, the door slid shut.

The passengers found their stomachs churned a little as the starship began to spin and gravity returned to their weightless bodies. For several minutes they waited until Hycerta announced the reception hanger had been pressurized and they could disembark into Omega 17.

The rescue was a success.

*

CHAPTER SIXTEEN

'Welcome to Omega 17,' Hycerta said in a quiet voice. 'I'm only sad it wasn't under better circumstances. You will be able to breathe and walk exactly the same as on Earth. The temperature is twenty-two degrees and we are operating on Australian Central Standard Time. There is artificial light and darkness to reflect this.' She grinned. 'Otherwise we'd change from day to night every ninety minutes.'

She pushed the door open and they all walked out into a well-lit hanger that towered above them. A gigantic screen on one wall showed a view of Earth below but already Australia had disappeared over the western horizon so, except for a white Antarctica, only clouds and ocean showed.

Hycerta walked through an airlock that turned out to be an elevator that carried them upward at a phenomenal speed. The doors opened to a room that could have been a hotel foyer on Earth. Likewise, the next room they entered that could easily have been an office at the university. She offered everyone a seat around a large oval shaped table and produced a light meal and drinks from seemly nowhere. There was even food for Jason. However, everyone only nibbled at the food. There were too many questions to ask; too much to find out.

*

'Were you alone on board?' Kylina began and her clone nodded.

'Yes, but your thousand year journey took only two months.'

'But how?' Pazz asked.

'We broke the speed of light barrier fifty years back,' Hycerta replied. 'We select our destination and the computers do the rest. When we hit light speed we are in suspended animation in protection pods. Apparently our physical bodies sort of disappear and then reassemble when we reach sub light speed. One of the early scientists attempted to stay awake during post light speed flight but he came out completely insane, babbling like an idiot. Nobody's tried it since.'

'But how come you are not thousands of years younger than us, not just eighty years,' Duncan asked.

'The speed of light affects time,' Pazz's clone replied. 'To keep civilization intact we have systems in place so we return to our own time. In fact, even though my journey took two months, a thousand years have past at home. My return journey will take two months but go back those years so I'll arrive home about five months after I left.'

'Could you arrive back before you left?' Duncan added.

'No, it is impossible to go back beyond your natural time. It could appear as if one's return was instant after say a journey to Earth and back to Delta but it is not allowed. We have very strict light travel rules. Once again, at first many test pilots went insane. Even though they were prepared for it, their minds could not cope.' She smiled, 'I guess that what keeps us human.'

'So we could return home to our time,' Pazz said.

'Yes but I couldn't,' replied Hycerta. 'It is before my natural time and the journey would kill me. You could, of course accompany me to my time but you'd find Delta eighty years ahead of when you left.'

'So this makes our Omega a museum piece,' Kylina commented.

'Yes, technology has moved on but Omega 1 will always remain in a stationary orbit above Earth as long as you need her. We have already upgraded the onboard computers, repaired the damaged hull and replenished the air supply. You can return to it any time you wish' Hycerta replied.

'That's all very well but what about our immediate problem? ' Pazz added, 'We're safe but Duncan and Lynn have families in Australia. I don't want to just sit here watching life on Earth slowly expire.'

'Surely something has been learnt about this Fungus,' Kylina added. 'We had it almost beaten back in Nkypy. If the bacteria didn't keep coming in from other parts of the country, I'm sure we would have.'

Hycerta frowned. 'That was an early strain. Later ones became immune to any antibiotic.' She glanced across at Lunol. 'I'm afraid your planet was devastated, Lunol. Only ten percent of the population survived and even now, eighty years later, the population is only beginning to increase.'

'And the fungi, there?' Duncan added.

'There seems to be a limit to its growth. It is a parasite and cannot live outside human tissue for more than a few weeks. After about ten years it died out on Planet 38675.6 as quickly as it came but by then the damage had been done.' Hycerta sighed. 'I'm a biochemist like you, Pazz and have studied this fungi in detail.' She frowned and glanced at Kylina. 'What did you do in that village to protect them?'

'Epsilon developed a dead strain and I inoculated the locals. Their antibodies attacked the live bacteria before it could get a hold. It worked for about three-quarters of our population. Many would not be inoculated so we still had an increasing victim rate,' Kylina replied with a shrug. 'I think that's when I got a reputation for being a witch.'

'You and Lunol were inoculated?'

'Yes, but it did not work with my body, I guess our metabolism is slightly different. I know, Theta wanted to evacuate me earlier but I refused to go.' She gazed around at the others. 'Remember Custronomus was my home. I could not bare the thought of leaving.'

'It worked for me, though,' Lunol added. 'I remember I was quite scared when Kylina took a tube of blood from my arm.'

'He had the antibodies in his bloodstream,' Kylina added. 'It was ironical really. He was safe from the disease but I wasn't.' She reached over and took her partner's hand. 'I never told you that, Dear.'

'No,' he replied, 'but I guessed.'

'So we have somewhere to start,' Pazz added. 'Lunol will still have the antibodies in his bloodstream, the fungus on Earth could only be that early strain. Surely, the computers aboard could breed this antibody?'

'We can try,' a voice filled the room. It was Kappa. 'Time is against us. Already the fungus has reached your city of Adelaide. That fog you drove through this morning contained the fungi spores. Within a few days, thousands of your citizens will be dead. That is why we gave the order to evacuate.'

'Good,' retorted Pazz. 'Where is your laboratory, Hycerta? We'll need a litre of Lunol's blood.'

Lunol paled slightly but nodded. 'My contribution to our new world,' he muttered and followed the others along the corridor to a massive laboratory that, once again could have easily have been in a university or hospital on Earth. Within minutes he'd donated his blood and watched as samples were placed in dozens of tiny test tubes by mechanical arms.

'Go outside and relax,' Kappa said. 'We'll set every available computer onto it.'

'Go outside?' Duncan frowned. 'That could be a bit hard.'

'Follow me,' Hycerta grinned and led them to a different door, opened it and ushered every one through.

'Oh My God!' Lynn gasped. They found themselves in a park with real grass, trees, shrubs and even a tiny stream bubbling over stones. Overhead was a blue sky.

'Look, Mummy,' said Jason and pointed at a bright yellow and blue butterfly that flew by.

Pazz just stood and stared. They appeared to be in a valley that curled up on each side and disappeared above the trees. It was warm and a sweet smelling breeze blew on their faces.

'Some technology,' Duncan added in a dry voice.

'Except for the blue sky, and sprinklers of water to create rain, it is all natural,' Hycerta explained with pride in her voice.

'But how?' Pazz asked.

'Follow me,' Hycerta said and began to walk along the path that was shaded by overhanging trees.

Pazz found Duncan's hand in hers and smiled up at him as they strolled along. Lynn hoisted Jason on her hip but did not object when Hycerta offered to carry the little boy. Suddenly a tiny squirrel like animal rushed up to them and Jason giggled.

'They're tame,' Hycerta said and took a brown pellet out of her pocket. The squirrel took the food in its forepaws and ran away.

They walked on and found the first difference from Earth. The path was level but they always appeared to be at the bottom of a valley and had no sensation of walking up hill.

'We're walking around the interior of the Omega 17's equator,' explained Hycerta. 'If you could see us from out in space it would look as if we're upside down. Where we stand always appears level.' She laughed. 'Stay here and watch me.'

She ran ahead and appeared to be going further and further up hill until she was almost out of sight. She waved them forward but when they followed, the path was level. They reached her without going uphill even a step. All the time the vegetation changed, the shrubs became ferns and the trees became a different variety. The stream bubbled out of rocks at one point but the path continued on to another stream that entered the park via a beautiful waterfall towering above their heads.

'It's all one stream,' Hycerta said.

They continued on for about fifteen minutes before they came to another door. Hycerta opened it and they found themselves back in the laboratory. 'You walked right around the inside and we're back to where we started. 'It's a bit like flying around the world only it is on the inside.'

'I'm impressed,' Duncan said.

'It is, of course a natural source of oxygen as well as being a recreational area,' Hycerta explained. 'We have bigger Starships that can carry two hundred or more passengers. The park is very popular when the ships are in orbit. Companies extracting minerals on a bleak planet or moon use these ships as living quarters and minor towns are set up with even the worker's families being on board.' She said. 'Males are handy to do heavier physical work like mining.'

'Nice to know they have some uses,' Pazz retorted and gave a wee yelp as Duncan pinched her arm. She turned and grinned. 'Sorry, Dear. I forgot you were listening.'

'Come on,' Hycerta said and led them back into the main corridor. 'I'll show you to your apartment. Your luggage should already be there.'

*

At the Southern Cross Grammar School boarding establishment over half the students were ill. Fifteen boys and eleven girls had been transferred to hospital and the Board of Governors had an emergency meeting to decide whether to close the hostel and send pupils home until the particularly bad flu epidemic was over.

They were about to take a vote when the telephone rang. Principal, John Fowler listened for several moments before switching the receiver off. His face was ashen as he faced the nine other people in the room.

'I'm sorry, Ladies and Gentlemen.' he said. 'That was the Royal Adelaide Hospital. I have just received sad news. Andrew Lawrie died earlier this evening. Mary McLean is on life support but is not expected to survive the night and two more of our pupils have moved from serious to critically ill status.' He sat down and stared around the silent room. 'I believe, for the sake of our pupils we should close the boarding house immediately.'

*

At the airport, there was another crisis. Two airport controllers were absent through illness and a replacement operator collapsed without warning in front of his radar screen. It was sheer luck that a supervisor took over just in time to divert an incoming passenger 737 from landing in the path of 747 taking off.

Every hospital in town was filled with people arriving in various stages of distress. Asthmatics were flocking in, many in acute pain and gasping for breath and five more deaths directly related to the mysterious bacteria were reported.

The next morning dawned unusually cold as the fog turned from white to a smudgy brown like the notorious smog of London in the 1960s. But this was Adelaide, a city with a Mediterranean climate. The airport was closed until ten in the morning and every highway in the city was blocked by fog bound traffic or accidents caused by impatient motorists refusing to slow down in the conditions.

Schools reported up to a third of their pupils absent and every industry in town had serious staff shortages. Biochemists and pathologists worked in laboratories through out the city and found the cause of the outbreak. A completely unknown strain of fungi bacteria was attacking the victims' lungs and suffocating them. Worse still though, was that the fungi excreted a poisonous substance which attacked the body's immune system.

It appeared the fungus was spread, like flu, through water vapor and bodily contact. There was no known cure except to quarantine victims and hope the spread could be contained.

*

'You are safe and that has been our primary concern,' Kappa's voice filled the apartment's lounge on Omega 17 where everyone had gathered. 'My advice is to relax and we will have a report for you tomorrow.'

Duncan nodded and glanced at the others. 'That's good advice,' he added. 'I, for one, feel physically exhausted. There is little we can do at the moment, anyhow.'

'I guess,' Pazz replied. She did feel tired and noticed Kylina with dark rings under her eyes. It was fifteen hours since their arrival on Omega 7 and with the starship programmed to Adelaide time, their apartment's windows overlooking the park showed darkness, just as it would be on Earth.

Duncan had gone to have a shower and the others had slipped off to bed. Only Pazz and Hycerta sat together with a cup of wine in their hands. The new arrival smiled across at Pazz and their eyes met.

'I'm glad my mother decided to have me as your clone, Pazz,' she said in an earnest voice. 'I never realized how much until today.'

'It sort of makes one immortal, doesn't it?' Pazz replied.

'Yes,' Hycerta replied. 'But I'm still me, aren't I?'

'You are. Kylina's herself, too. We are individuals who share the same genes.' She grinned. 'I always reckoned my nose was too long. It's a pity we couldn't place an order for good looks.'

'I have a feeling Duncan is quite satisfied,' Hycerta answered with a smile, stood up and placed her empty glass on a low table. 'I'll be across the corridor if you need me. Try to get some sleep. Worrying won't change anything.'

'Night,' Pazz replied softly. 'Thank you for everything. It was appreciated, you know.'

'I know,' Hycerta replied. She squeezed Pazz's shoulder affectionately and walked out of the room.

*

'Kylina, wake up,' Lunol said in an urgent voice. 'There's something wrong.'

Kylina rubbed her eyes in the darkness and took a few seconds to remember where they were. Lunol was in the double bed beside her but the hand that gripped hers was shaking.

'Turn the light on,' he whispered.

Lylina did so and gasped. Lunol was staring at her but his normally clean-shaven face was covered in a lush black beard.

'Your hair's grown, too,' he whispered. 'I think we've been tricked.'

Kylina nodded and sprung out of bed. There were clothes waiting for her but they were crisp and new then she realized she had nothing on. She stopped. Last night she wore shortie pajamas. She remembered because Lunol always commented on them.

'I know,' whispered Lunol. 'I was the same.' His eyes looked serious. ' Everyone else is missing. I've been awake half an hour or so.'

'Show me!' Kylina hissed, grabbed a dressing gown and dashed through to the adjoining bedroom where Pazz and Duncan were. It was empty! Lynn's room was, too. Both rooms were made up as neat as a motel on arrival and clothes, once again all crisp and new were folded in drawers or hanging in wardrobes.

Kylina's face drained of blood. She rushed out into the corridor and across to Hycerta's room. It was empty, too. Kylina swore and glanced at her watch. It said 7:30 a.m. and the starship gave the appearance of early morning. For a moment, the young woman stared at her partner and his beard again then tore over to a mirror and saw her own reflection.

Lunol was right. Her hair had grown five or six centimeters.

'Oh my God!' she gasped and her eyes went back to her watch. 'Look!' she whispered and held her arm out for Lunol to see. 'Look at the date, Lunol.'

Lunol grimaced and kept her hand in his, after seeing the watch. Over two months had gone by!

'Theta,' Kylina gasped. 'Help us, please.'

'You're back home, Kylina,' Theta answered, 'Well, your adopted home.'

'What do you mean?' the young woman snapped.

'Go into the control room,' another voice filled the room. It was Kappa.

Still holding hands, the two humans walked up the short corridor and into the control room where a monitor showed the view outside. A planet hovered in the star studded black sky.

'Oh my God!' Kylina gasped as Lunol reached his arms around her shoulder.

They were not above Australia on planet Earth but Custronomus on Planet 38675.6.

'Earth was doomed so I brought you home,' Kappa announced. 'It is eighty years since you left but the fungi plague has been cleared from this planet.'

What!' screamed Kylina. 'Who gave you permission? Was it Hycerta?'

'No. Our directive is always to protect our humans. We decided this was best. You can go home to Nkypy. It is save there now.'

'And the others?' Lunol asked in a quiet voice.

'They shall be taken to Delta.'

No!' Kylina's voice was raised and her face twisted in fury. 'You had no right to assume what was best for us. None what-so-ever.'

'We were programmed to help our humans.'

'But not this way,' Kylina retorted. 'You said you were going to help rid Earth of the plague.'

'We tried but could not help in time so voted to bring you home?'

Kylina slumped into a seat and sighed. 'Thanks,' she replied sarcastically.

'Why do you sat "we",' Lunol added.

'The computers' collective. Omega 17 has five independent computers but they all speak through myself. I am, I guess the spokesperson for the collective. Your transport to the surface leaves in one hour. Everything is prepared. You will find you have money and positions waiting for you...'

'Damn you!' Kylina shouted and jutted her chin out. 'We are not leaving!'

'But why?' answered the computer. 'It is safe and healthy. Both of you are even remembered with great affection.'

'No!' Kylina cried out as tears washed through her eyes.

There was silence for two seconds before the computer replied. 'Very well. What do you want us to do for you?'

'Where are the others?' Lunol asked in a calm voice.

'Safe but in suspended animation. We did not choose to awaken them.'

'In the same way the computers chose not to tell us about each other when we arrived above Earth in the old Omega,' Kylina retorted.

'We are disappointed you do not approve with our decision,' Kappa replied. 'Our aim...'

'I know,' Kylina sighed. 'I want the others brought out of suspended animation.'

'Very well but it will take seventy two Earth hours to complete the procedures.'

'Do it!' Kylina ordered and stared at Lunol. 'I thought they were dead,' she shuddered.

'I know,' he replied tenderly, pulled Kylina into his arms and kissed her, 'Don't blame the computers, though. They were only trying to protect us. I guess they cannot understand our emotions.'

Kylina gave a tiny smile and kissed him back. 'Your beard tickles but I like it.,' she said.

'I don't.' Lunol muttered. 'It itches.'

*

For three days, Kylina and Lunol watched visions of their old country. Flybugs had been sent to Nkypy and the three-dimensional sound visions were so real it felt as if they could walk into the monitor screens.

In eighty years, the planet had made almost two hundred years of progress. Box shaped automobiles could be seen travelling along sealed roads while power and telephone poles were everywhere. Parks and recreation areas could be seen and painted houses sat in neat gardens and lawns. Steamships were tied up at the wharf and several steam locomotives chuffed their way along railway lines.

'The rapid change in progress was because you, Kylina, introduced electricity. Once that gained a footing, no laws could hold it back.' Kappa explained. 'Planet 38675.6 is like your Earth in the 1920s now, except they did not have any World War. They have motor vehicles; radio and crude aircraft but television, computers or nuclear energy have not been discovered.

Like Earth at the time you both lived on it, there are several government types with Custronomus being a liberal democratic government. Men, women and different races are all equal, equivalent to Western governments on Earth in the 1990s. There has not been an outbreak of the fungi bacteria for fifty years. That was why we chose to bring you back here,' the computer added almost as an excuse.

'After eighty years, we'd be strangers anyway,' Kylina added. She tucked into Lunol on the couch. 'I'm so glad they survived and are progressing well now,' she sighed as they watched a screen of Nkypy's main street. 'Look, Lunol,' she sat up and grabbed his hand. 'That building!'

Between the three and four story wooden buildings was a smaller single story shop with a wide verandah at the front and a faded sign which read, "Huril's General Merchandise and Groceries" in the local language.

'That's where I used to go and get my supplies,' Kylina gasped. 'It hasn't changed.'

Lunol nodded. 'That building, My Love, is where we met. Remember?'

'Of course,' she replied. 'I had bought a load of groceries and you offered to carry them out to my carriage. You tripped up, they went everywhere and I called you a clumsy oaf.'

'You wore that beautiful long yellow frock and tiny white cardigan,' Lunol sighed with a glazed thoughtful expression.

'Did I?' said Kylina and, on impulse reached up and kissed her companion. 'I can't remember.'

'I do,' Lunol replied and kissed her back. 'I think I loved you from that very first moment.'

'It took you three months to ask me out,' Kylina said. 'My God, the things I did to attract your attention.' She sighed. 'I loved it there, My Love.'

'If you change your mind we can still arrange for your transportation to the surface.' Kappa interrupted.

'No,' Kylina answered in a determined voice. 'We are not going to be separated from my sisters and our friends. We'll go if they want to accompany us.'

Though nothing was said, Lunol and herself were afraid of being stranded on the planet while Omega 17 continued the journey to Delta without them.

*

Pazz woke and immediately realized it was more than one night's sleep. Anger surged through her mind but was replaced by relief when she felt strong arms gripping her and a scraggly beard rubbing on her cheek.

She turned and grabbed Duncan and, for a moment, they both held each other. What ever had happened, at least they were together.

'Mummy!' called a tiny voice and there was an immediate reply from Lynn.

'I'm here, Sweetheart,' she said and Pazz saw her friend walking, fully dressed across the room.

'We're awake, Lynn,' she called.

Lynn swung around and gave a small gasp. 'Pazz. I thought you'd never wake up. We're in a different room, all together except for Kylina and Lunol.' She screwed her nose up. 'I assume that's Hycerta and not Kylina still asleep at the end, there. I placed a blanket over her. We were all in the nude. Even poor little Jason.'

'I think we've been in suspended animation,' Pazz said. 'Epsilon, can you help?'

'Yes,' replied the computer. 'You are safe and in orbit above Planet 38675.6, Lunol's homeland.'

'Jason!' gasped Lynn before Pazz or Duncan had time to react to Epsilon's statement. 'You've grown.'

It was true. As well as having longer hair, Jason had grown a centimeter or more and his face had lost baby fat.

'Okay,' Pazz demanded. 'I want an explanation.'

Kappa's voice immediately filled the room and brought them up to date. 'Kylina and Lunol are in the console room viewing Custronomus. Hycerta should be awake within thirty Earth minutes. You are all healthy and were awoken on Kylina's request.'

Pazz frowned. 'Okay. No doubt you had your reasons for making this journey but I'd like a full report later.'

'It will be made available,' Kappa replied and went silent.

*

An hour later after everyone greeted each other and the emotion of finding themselves across the galaxy had been discussed, not once but many times, the fugitives sat around the console room while Kappa showed them visions of Earth. They stared at the monitors as data after data flowed in. It was all bad! At eleven a.m. on the morning they were evacuated, Adelaide was still covered in a thick fog impregnated with the fungi spores and a civil emergency was about to be called. As well smaller outbreaks were recorded in Sydney, Melbourne, Perth, Brisbane and the Gold Coast.

'What's happening on Earth, now?' Pazz asked in a quiet but deadly serious voice.

'Earth is out of communication range at the moment. The following information was transmitted a month after we left the planet,' Kappa droned on and the monitors changed to show central Adelaide.

A thick green fog clung to overhead streetlights but it was the scene below that everyone focused their attention onto. All traffic was halted; buildings were alight with bellowing smoke adding to the fog. The air was filled with screams as hundreds of people were fighting and rioting. People were attacking buildings and anyone in their way. While they watched, three girls were attacked by a group of stick welding youths in the middle of the street, dragged screaming and bloody into a van and driven away. Gunshots sounded and five semi-track gun carriers arrived to seal off the street. Dozens of soldiers fanned out, holding plastic shields and semi-automatic weapons.

But this did not stop the enraged crowd. Flaming canisters of gasoline were thrown at the soldiers, an order was given and weapons fired...'

'But ours was not a violent society,' Lynn gasped, her face lined with tears.

"Humans always react when their security is threatened,' Kappa added. 'Suppressed violence inherited in the genes takes over. The fungi multiplied at a phenomenal rate and spread to every country on your planet.

The scene, sickening and abhorrent switched to other cities. London, England showed smoke bellowing from the Houses of Parliament and millions of people rioting throughout the city. Police on horseback charged rioters in Tokyo while New York was strangely quite as green fog swirled between skyscrapers and bodies lay everywhere amongst stalled traffic.'

'I think we've seen enough,' Duncan interrupted.

The scene on the monitors disappeared to be replaced by the blue and white planet they were orbiting.

'That was the last information we received before Omega 17 went into post light speed,' Kappa added.

The five adults stared at each other in utter horror as the computer's voice continued.

'Two other planets we know of were affected in a similar way. One is now a dead planet with no animal life at all. It has been declared a quarantined planet but is monitored by our remote equipment. Once the fungi there dies out we will repopulate it with settlers. That should be in two decades.

'And we can do nothing!' Kylina added in a hushed voice.

'The bacteria would have taken its natural course. The fungus usually retreats after three or so months but returns in a new generation a few months later. The second generation is worse than the first. We considered staying in orbit and using Lunol's antitoxin to inoculate the survivors to prevent the second stage but it was mathematically impossible to reach everyone. '

'And who will be left?' Pazz asked.

' We have no information documented but evidence from outbreaks in other planets showed a twenty percent survival rate after the initial plague. Of those, ninety percent did not survive the second generation. Earth would have been a dead planet within three years. .'

Pazz stared at the view of the planet below looking so peaceful and serene. 'Stop speaking in the past tense' she snapped. 'I do not believe we are the only survivors from Earth. Surely we could have done something instead of just leaving.'

'Suggestions please,' Kappa replied.

Pazz stared around but it was Hycerta who replied. 'I may be able to help, Pazz,' she whispered. Her face was as white as a ghost but her chin stuck out in determination as she walked across to the console and pressed her palm on the glowing interface recognition sphere.

She spoke in her home language that only her clones, Duncan and the ship's computers could understand. 'This is a direct order from the Commander of Intergalactic Starship, Omega 17. In reference to intergalactic space travel rule 18.7, my authority is absolute.' She grimaced, bit on her lower lip just as Pazz did when nervous and continued.

'I invoke Law 893 and declare Omega 17 together with Omega 1 now in orbit around Earth, an independent civilization with the adult humans in this room the emergency government. The official language of the government shall be English. This government will have the power to make and change any laws inherited by us from the Greater Delta Galactic Constitution. All new laws will be past by a simple majority vote except in an emergency of Strength 7 or above. In that case, the decision of any of the five governors will be sufficient. Dated this day, 4th Day of Month Fourteen in the Year 6794, Delta Standard Calendar, Time Zone 3006. '

She stopped and fixed her deadly serious eyes on Pazz. 'Will you tell the others what I said, please? They have to place the palm of their left hand on the interface and swear allegiance to the new independent government of Omega 17 and 1.'

Pazz nodded and translated the statement as close as she could remember.

Kylina interrupted to explain. 'Hycerta is taking over command of the computers,' she said. 'It's a little like the captain being replaced in a warship by her crew. If it is proven she invoked this law without sound reason she could be tried for treachery if she ever returned to Delta. Theta just explained it to me.'

She glanced around at her friends and walked up to the interface, placed her left hand on the instrument and read in English from an electronic notepad Hycerta handed to her. 'In relation to Law 893, I, Kylina D'rose, recognize the emergency government of Omega 17. I swear to uphold the laws of the new government and will vote for the good of humanity above personal preferences, if and when new laws are formatted. This oath was made on, 4th Day of Month Fourteen in the Year 6794, Delta Standard Calendar, Time Zone 3006.'

She handed the notepad to Pazz who, followed by Lynn, Duncan and Lunol repeated the oath.

'Law 893 is invoked and duly entered on Omega 17's log. The new government of Omega 17 and Omega 1 is recognized,' the computer announced in English.

CHAPTER SEVENTEEN

With a pallid face, Hycerta turned to face the others 'With your agreement, I'd like to make our first new law,' she said. 'I'll explain later.'

Pazz saw Duncan's nod as well as everyone else's serious but slightly more optimistic expressions.

'Go ahead, Hycerta,' she replied. 'We are in your hands.'

Hycerta gave the briefest of nods and placed her hand on the interface ball. 'Under Emergency Condition 9, the threatened life of a human species, I order you to prepare this ship to travel back to Planet Earth in the Solar System of the Sun, Planet 40982.3 on our galactic records, so we arrive at a time simultaneous to Omega 1's first orbit above Earth. Once there, I order that all humans are awakened together with all memories of events lost due to inter-time zone travel, retained.'

'Programming will take a minimum of fifteen Earth hours and twenty three minutes.'

'Do it!' Hycerta commanded.

The screen immediately went blank and the young woman turned to Lynn and took her hand. 'I'm sorry, Lynn. This will affect you most but it is the only way.'

'How?' whispered Lynn with quivering lips.

'We are going back in time but because we're here, we don't change.'

'So!' whispered Lynn.

'Even though the time on Earth will be back to when you first met Pazz; what was it, almost a year ago…?'

Lynn nodded.

'Jason will stay the same as he is now. You will be back in time but he will not revert to being a tiny baby. Everything that happened since that time will not have taken place and will have to be all relived.'

'So Lynn's husband will be alive?' Pazz added.

'Yes, and all your work as Doctor D'rose won't exist. You'll have to do it all again.'

'But, unless we make the same mistakes, the fungi will not reach Earth, the people at Magaroona Research Station and everyone else killed by the plague will still be alive?' Pazz added.

'Yes,' Hycerta replied. 'It will be as if the events did not happen.'

'Except for being older, Jason will be safe?' Lynn added.

'Perfectly,' Hycerta replied. 'We can alter any Earth records to register his birth at an earlier date.

'Like my academic records and bank account?' Pazz said.

'They will all have to be reprogrammed,' Hycerta continued. 'If we go back in time they never happened.'

'Why wasn't this done for Custronomus?' Lunol butted in with a slightly hurt tone.

'We never had the technology then,' Hycerta explained, 'Also laws forbid going back and changing your planet. It is too long a time span. That's why I declared us independent. By simple majority we can make any law we wish at the moment.'

'And it will save Earth/' Duncan said.

'The time Pazz, Kylina and Lunol were on your planet will not have existed.'

'What about our memories?' Kylina asked.

'We will remember everything.'

Pazz reached over and hugged her clone. 'Thank you,' she said. 'I think we all realize the personal sacrifice you have made to help those who are really strangers to you.'

Hycerta's response was immediate. 'You're a clone sister Pazz. We could never be strangers. I'm part of you and Kylina. We are family.'

'Yes we are,' Kylina added and also grasped Hycerta in her arms. 'Family,' she stared at the others. 'Everyone here is family including you Lunol, Duncan, Lynn and little Jason. We are all family and our destiny is tied together.'

'And I don't care if Jason is older,' Lynn said. 'I'd hate to go through all that napkin changing, anyhow. As long as he will be safe and healthy. That's all I want.'

'He'll be fine,' Hycerta said. 'We'll all be.'

'And Earth too,' Duncan replied.

'Yes,' Pazz repeated. 'Earth, too.'

*

'If you want to go to the surface, I'd advise going straight away,' Hycerta added a few moments later. 'A record of our declaration will be on it's way to Delta and we're much closer here than from Earth. I don't want to be here to receive any incoming commands or be intercepted by another starship.' She sucked on her lip. 'I'd say it would take four days for an order to get back here so I want to be gone by then.'

Lunol nodded and held Kylina's waist. 'Would you like to be Kagit Frysyl one last time, My Dear?'

'Only if everyone else comes,' she replied.

'But what about our looks?' Pazz asked.

'Well, ' Kylina laughed. 'They do have triplets down there. Why not identical ones?'

*

Within two hours, early morning Custronomus time, the women were all dressed in long ankle length gowns and the men in wide trousers, jackets, hats and ties Kappa had designed and made up for them.

'The women look beautiful but I feel like a stuffed bird,' Duncan said. 'It's worse than the suits I wear on Earth.'

The four women stood in a line and Lynn grinned. Every clone had her hair cut exactly the same way and wore identical gowns. They even had armlets on; something Hycerta didn't normally wear.

'Which one is Pazz, Duncan?' she said.

Duncan rubbed a hand under his chin, grinned at Lunol and walked along the line. My God they were identical. They all even wore Pazz's tiny round earrings and her shade of lipstick. After studying them for a full minute, he walked to the middle clone and reached for her, smiled broadly and swung to grab the one on the right. In one second he had her in his arms and kissed her passionately on the lips.

'How did you know?' Pazz gasped when she surfaced from his embrace.

'The eyes,' Duncan laughed. 'Hycerta at the other end looked quite nervous so it was down to two. When I walked to Kylina your eyes showed disappointment so I knew it was you.'

'And I knew you, Kylina,' Lunol interjected.

'How?' the middle clone retorted.

'That wee bruise on your neck, My Love,' Lunol replied and also grabbed her to kiss fondly. 'Remember last night?'

Kylina flushed a bright red. 'Oh yes,' she giggled. 'I forgot.'

'You did better than me,' Lynn added. 'I had no idea at all.'

'The landing pod departs in five minutes,' Kappa interrupted. 'Please make your way to the departure hanger.'

'Come on Sweetheart,' Lynn picked Jason up. 'We're going for another ride in an airplane.'

'Why, Mummy?' Jason asked.

'To see Auntie Kylina and Uncle Lunol's old town, Sweetheart. Won't that be nice?'

'Ice cream, Mommy?'

'Yes,' laughed Kylina. 'I'm sure we can find an ice cream for you,

Jason but only if you're good.'

*

Memories of school days flooded into Kylina's mind as the cloaked landing pod landed in a field near the highway and she got her shoes covered with wet grass. A railway station replaced the way station and several locals were waiting for a train.

Lunol took charge and walked up to the tiny ticket office, took out some coins; Kappa had manufactured and bought tickets.

'Excuse me, Sir,' the man behind the counter asked, 'but those women you're escorting...'

'My Loyal Partner, her identical sisters and a friend,' Lunol stated proudly.

'I guessed that,' the man retorted. 'However, they seem familiar somehow.' He broke into a grin and stamped the tickets. 'The train will be here shortly. Lucky for you it's running late or you would have missed it.'

With a hiss of steam and smoke, the train arrived and they climbed aboard. Passengers pretended to ignore the three sisters but sideways glances kept eyeing them, so much so that Pazz felt uncomfortable.

'Don't worry, ' said Duncan. 'Consider it a complement.'

Town felt like home on Earth, a little old fashioned maybe, but certainly closer to Earth cities than the old town Lunol and Kylina remembered. For hours they toured around and found several old haunts. The school Kylina went to was twice as large but the original building still stood, several other buildings and parks were recognized but the shock came in the front of a modern building built back from the road.

'It's a museum,' Lunol explained. 'Lets go and have a look.'

In the foyer of the building was a bronze statue of a woman holding a small bedside lamp.

'Oh my God!' gasped Kylina.

The statue was of her. There was no doubt about it. Underneath was an inscription.

'Read it,' gasped Pazz.

Kylina stared at the language and read it out loud. 'It says "In memory of Kagit Frysyl, inventor of electric light and youngest member of the Nkypy Council Of Governors ever to be elected. Tragically drowned in the arms of her loyal partner Lunol Pendylf on the night of the Third Age Graduation in the Year 3429 uprising, before the Great Plague stuck our country. She will be remembered as a symbol of hope in those dark days."

'Aye,' said a voice behind them and the five friends swung around to see an elderly man standing there. 'If I didn't know Miss Frysyl had no children, I'd swear you young ladies were related to her.' He shrugged. 'I guess one of you posed for the sculptor, though the sculptor swore he used only his memory to create the statue.'

He grinned and held out a hand to Kylina. 'Forgive me. I am Etran Jojyr, Curator of the Nkypy Memorial Museum and one of the survivors of the Great Plague.' He glanced at the triplets. 'If you have a free half hour, I'd be delighted to entertain you all for a wee spot of afternoon tea.'

'It will be a pleasure,' Kylina replied and when out of earshot, translated for Pazz and the others.

In the following half-hour, Mr. Jojyr spent so much time talking he did not even notice most of his guests did not understand the language. He even produced an enormous ice cream for Jason and gave a long account of the plague, the riots and the recovery.

'They were sad times,' he said in a faraway voice. 'Only two hundred and twenty of us in Nkypy survived but do the young ones care, now? No, they're too busy roaring around in those crazy automobiles and listening to ruckus music on the radio.' He smiled. 'I'm sorry,' he said. 'I guess you young folk like the radio yourselves.'

'Not as much as listening to you,' Kylina who quite expertly changed positions so it appeared all of them were talking to him. 'We thank you ever so much.'

'And which one modeled the sculpture?' the old man grinned as he escorted them to the door of the museum cafeteria,'

'We took turns,' Kylina said with an almost cheeky grin. 'That's why the sculptor picked us. One person would have got bored just standing there for hours while he chipped away.'

'Perfectly sensible, too,' the old man replied. 'Though I doubt if the real Kagit Frysyl was quite as attractive as you young ladies.'

'Why thank you, Kind Sir,' Kylina replied, this time pretending to be Hycerta.

'He was a character, wasn't he?' Lynn laughed after Kylina translated a few minutes later.

'Dirty old man, I'd say,' Lunol grumbled. 'My God, he couldn't keep his eyes off you lot.'

'Yes, but he gave us a great history of the last eighty years. It's a pity we didn't record it,' Kylina added. 'I'm sure there were bits I've forgotten to translate.'

'Oh I did,' Hycerta replied and took a small black cylinder, no bigger than a thumbnail out of her dress pocket. 'It has even converted his words to English and back on Omega, will print it all out in ebook form.' She said. 'Including your comments Lunol.'

The time went quickly and before they realized it was time to be back on the train. Kylina sat with Lunol and took his hand. 'Would you like to stay, My Love,' she whispered as the train chugged along.

Their eyes met. 'Not really. It's not the same but I'm glad we came back. ' He sighed. 'Did you see that massive list of plague victims in the museum?' Kylina nodded. 'My parents, brother and two sisters' names were on the list.' He stared out the window at the green fields. 'My whole family was wiped out, Kagit. There's nobody here now.' He sounded sad then squeezed her hand and broke into a small smile. 'Mind you, I guess they would have died of old age by now, anyway. That museum curator would have been only a little boy when we were here.'

'I know,' Kylina answered. 'We are the same but everything else has changed. I hope Earth hasn't jumped a hundred years when we return.'

'I hope so, too,' Lunol replied. 'But if Hycerta is correct, it should be okay. I never knew I had such a famous partner though,' he said. 'Inventor of the electric light, I tell you.'

'Well,' Kylina said. 'I must admit Theta did help just a little with that one.'

The train chugged around a corner and the station came into view. They clamored off and just about bumped into the ticket man from the morning. 'I know who you are,' he said with a smirk on his face. 'You're film stars in that latest movie down at The Regent, the one about the two twins. One was a real nasty one who tried to steal her sister's inheritance.'

'That's right.' Kylina beamed and even signed her name in the autograph book shoved under her nose.

They walked up the road chatting together, waited until two cars and a truck roared by, slipped through a gate and behind a hedge. As they walked across the field the five people and little toddler just sort of vanished. Moments later, the grass was flattened as a whirlpool of wind tossed it around and dirt blew through the air. But there were no locals present to witness. The visitors from space had left.

*

Pazz woke and reached out to find a sighing Duncan by her. Within minutes everyone was gathered in the console room watching the monitor flash on. Earth appeared, blue and white and Kappa had even piped in an Adelaide radio station.

'We did it!' gasped Lynn as the day and date came over the air. It was two days before Pazz originally landed on Earth.

175

'And look at that,' gasped Kylina.

Just floating into view was Omega 1 only a hundred meters away.

'Are we on board there, too,' Lunol asked Hycerta. 'I mean are there two of us?'

'No,' she replied. 'Even with time travel you cannot be two people. In this case our presence here supersedes the original happening. Omega 1 is empty.'

'That's a relief,' he replied. 'Otherwise the whole thing could happened again and we would have gained nothing.'

'The fungus could still be onboard Omega 1, though, ' Hycerta cautioned. 'I would not advise visiting it. When our robots mended the hull over there we did not bring them back, just in case the fungus contaminated them.'

Kappa's voice filled the air again. 'We are in a stationary orbit over Australia but will go into a lower orbit on the day Pazz originally landed. In the meantime we can access the bank accounts etcetera to get Pazz, Kylina and Lunol established. I hope you don't mind but we already did a couple of things while you were all coming out of suspended animation.'

'And that was?' said Pazz suspiciously.

'Relax Pazz,' Epsilon communicated. 'Kappa's working for us now.'

'Your jobs are sorted out. Your position as Doctor Pazz D'rose is confirmed with the university. A holograph of you had an interview with a Doctor Matthew McHardy yesterday. You start work in two weeks. Kylina, your application at the supermarket was accepted and Lynn, your offer for the house at 19 Elden Crescent has also been accepted and paid for from your Perth bank account. You won't find your new furniture there, though. It will be like when you first arrived.'

'And the men.' said Duncan.

'You just walk back to your job Duncan but will have to redo your research on Pazz's language. Of course, we have copies here for you to use but Lunol, that job at the racing stables hasn't come up yet so we couldn't get it for you.'

'Thank you,' Pazz said. 'I think that just about covers everything. ' She grinned at the others but her eye caught Hycerta who was standing there in silence. Pazz walked across to her. 'We haven't forgotten you, Hycerta,' she said tenderly. 'Come back to Earth with us.'

'The last thing you need down there is another cloned sister,' Hycerta replied. 'Sure there can be identical twins but three! You saw how everyone gazed at us in Custronomus!'

'But we don't go around together,' Kylina argued. 'Lunol and I hardly see Pazz except in the weekend so the times when all three of us are together won't be great.'

'I know,' Hycerta said doubtfully,' but I need to go home.'

'Why?' asked Duncan.

Hycerta gave a shrug. ' I visited Earth to complete my research for my Matron's thesis,' she said. 'I can do that now.'

'What was the topic?' Pazz asked.

'My ancestors,' Hycerta replied. 'You two wonderful cloned sisters of mine. I researched your trial, Kylina's disappearance as a twelve-year-old and the affects of coning on people. I've discovered the myth was true and how! ' she said.

'The myth?'

'The rumor was that you two ended up on a strange planet on the edge of the known world, but the filed reports were that Omega 1 perished and you'd both been killed in it.' She frowned. 'There's also the other matter.'

'The taking over of Omega 17, you mean?' Duncan said.

Hycerta nodded. 'Yes,' she said. 'We saved Earth from the fungi but, if it didn't happen how can it be proved?'

'The computer's memory banks,' Duncan said. 'You instructed Kappa to leave our memories intact. Won't that mean the computers will have everything on memory, too.'

'I don't know,' Hycerta replied. 'Something like this has never been done before. We've only used time travel to shorten journeys not to cancel out time in a world. It's against all the laws.'

'But we made our own laws,' Duncan said. 'It was done in good faith and it worked.'

'For Earth maybe but compared with something like ten thousand humanoid occupied planets it becomes quite insignificant. The laws prohibit altering the natural progress, or otherwise, of a planet.'

'But,' argued Pazz. 'This wasn't natural. We brought the fungus here in Omega. If I had not come the fungus would not have arrived either.'

'That is a point,' Hycerta answered doubtfully. 'They might not see it that way.'

'Would it help if we returned to Delta to back you up?' Kylina said. 'I'll be prepared to do that?'

'I'm sure we all would,' Pazz added. 'After all with time travel we can be back here before we're even missed.'

'I would be prepared to go too,' Duncan said. 'As a representative from Earth that might help.'

'You'd do that for me?' Hycerta asked and smiled in appreciation.

'We're family,' Duncan said. 'You'll be my sister-in-law one day.'

'Will she?' Pazz suddenly grinned. 'And how do you work that one out?'

'Well,' Duncan coughed. 'If you aren't interested, Hycerta here is unattached'

Pazz glowered. 'I'd keep quiet if I was you, Duncan, before you say something you might regret later.'

'Yes,' laughed Kylina. 'Pazz does get possessive at times, you know. Jealous, too.'

'Oh, shut up!' Pazz replied but she did grab Duncan's arm tightly. 'I'm learning having clones has some disadvantages.'

'Anyhow, the offers there Hycerta,' Duncan continued. 'We will not abandon you; not after everything you've done for us. Okay!'

'Yes,' said Hycerta. 'Thank you. I've been churning it over in my mind but feel a little better now. What say we check Kappa's memory banks.'

'It has been done,' the computer's voice filled the room. 'Everything to do with the fungus bacteria on Earth is on record. I am itemizing the data and will have a visual summary ready whenever it is needed. In our opinion, what you did was the only possible course of action. We could not have returned here at this time if you had not overridden the Delta laws. We were directed to return to Delta after leaving Kylina and Lunol behind at Custronomus on Planet 38675.6.

'I knew it,' whispered Kylina and pouted at Lunol. 'We both knew it.'

'It's called intuition,' said Lunol. 'Something else human's have.'

*

In natural time, as Pazz preferred to think of it, a year slipped by and the calendar on Earth crept back through the months lost in the time travel, with life more or less a repeat of their first run through.

Pazz was well respected in her position, Kylina in the first semester at The School of Fine Arts and Lunol had a job working with horses. Jason, now two was a bundle of energy who ran Lynn and everyone else at 19 Elden Crescent, off their feet. After being persuaded to accompany the others, Hycerta had also integrated well and worked with a large computer firm in the city. It was inevitable, though, that one event was doomed to be repeated.

*

It was the same day and date, a hot and sultry Friday afternoon. However, the difference was that both Duncan and Lunol were in the house and a year too old Jason was on an extended walk with Pazz, Kylina and Hycerta. Lynn's husband, James Kilmore walked into the kitchen.

Even though his arrival was half expected, Lynn still gave a gasp of fright when she heard a sound behind her and saw him standing there with a tight frown across his eyebrows.

'Hello Lynn,' he said in a quite, almost over controlled voice. 'Nice place you have here.'

'I don't want to talk to you, James,' she replied with her face drained of color. The sight of seeing him standing there alive was more nerve-racking than any fear of attack. 'I have a restraining order out against you. Just leave, please.'

'You little bitch!' his face contorted into anger and his right hand curled into a fist. 'So you thought you could take Jason and just fade away with your lover boy and have a bit of paper to protect you.'

He stepped forward and a knife appeared in his clenched hand. 'Your pretty boy won't like it by the time I've finished, you slut,' he snarled.

Lynn screamed and flung her arms up in an attempt to ward off the attack. My God, she was going to be stabbed like the first time.

But it never happened! The man found himself in a grip of iron from behind. His knife arm was thrust up his back and a tanned face muttered in his ear. 'You were not thinking of anything nasty, now were you, my friend?' Lunol growled.

Though shorter than Lynn's husband, Lunol was wiry and sheer muscle. Physical work all day gave him an advantage so the other man found himself completely overpowered. Lunol pulled the knife out from his hand and tossed it away across the kitchen floor.

'Who are you?' James gasped as he felt himself propelled towards the door. His arm was twisted up in a grotesque angle and he stifled a scream 'For Christ's sake, mate. I was only kidding.'

'I'm the pretty boy you just mentioned,' Lunol hissed in his ear and gave James a shove down the two steps of the back door. The man landed heavily on the concrete but was over the initial surprise. He jumped to his feet with fists clenched and eyes red with fury.

'You bastard! 'he spluttered and launched himself at Lunol who shifted slightly to the left, put a foot out and sent James sprawling across the veranda to hit his head against the wall .

'You wait...' James Kilmore started but his eyes changed from anger to terror and sort of rolled up. Saliva ran down a quivering face; in fact the whole body was quivering as he continued to shake, the face turned white then gray. A gurgle came from the throat and he slumped onto the veranda floor.

'Oh my God, he's having a heart attack,' Lynn gasped from the back door. 'Just like last time.'

Her husband's eyes tried to focus on her but could not. A tongue protruded from a gray face and perspiration rolled down his neck as he groaned in agony. Lunol stood back in horror and it was Duncan who appeared and lifted the semi-conscious man inside and laid him on the living room couch.

Lynn walked to the telephone and dialed the emergency number. 'Hello,' she spoke in a calm voice. 'My husband has just collapsed. I think he had a heart attack. Could an ambulance come straight away.' She turned and looked at Lunol who appeared to be in a state of shock. 'Don't feel guilty, Lunol,' she said softly, 'It must have been his time. I have a strange feeling he would have had a heart attack on this day whether he'd visited us or not.'

Lunol shrugged but still looked shaken. 'Yes,' he replied. 'At least you weren't hurt this time.'

'And I didn't have ten kilos of ugly fat removed either,' Lynn replied.

'You don't need it removed,' Duncan replied in a compassionate voice. 'I don't think you ever put it back on.'

Once again Duncan did nearly all the administrative work for James Kilmore's funeral and the body was returned to Perth. This time, though, Lynn left Jason behind with her friends; having a toddler instead of an infant would be somewhat difficult to explain to relations.

*

The days slipped by and everything returned to be almost too normal. Hycerta enjoyed her new life on Earth but the memory of Delta kept returning her mind. She couldn't just forget her home planet and was determined to return home one day to explain the reasons for her actions on Omega 17.

This opportunity came in a very unusual way. A letter arrived addressed to Commander Hycerta D'rose, 19 Elden Crescent, Adelaide, Australia where she was still staying with Lynn, Pazz and Duncan. It looked all official and subpoenaed her to appear before a tribunal on the Planet 21974.3 to give evidence.

Please note, the letter, written in English concluded. *You are still a member of the Delta Intergalactic Peace Keeping Force and are subject to military law.*

Failure to attend the hearing is in defiance of Military Law 7864.8.

'They have no authority here,' retorted Pazz when she read the letter. 'I think it is a damn right cheek.' She stared at the signature. 'Who signed it anyway?'

Hycerta glanced up. 'Marshall Xabne Dargerepa, the highest ranking military officer on the planet,' she replied in a hushed voice. 'It's true that I am still a commander in the Peace Keeping Force. I signed on for three years. It was the only way I could get a starship to travel to Earth in. If I don't go and give evidence, I can never return. I would be, what do you call it, blacklisted and arrested if I ever entered Delta space.'

'But that doesn't include Earth?' Duncan asked.

'No,' Hycerta replied with a thin smile. 'We're too far away and too primitive to be considered.'

'Well,' Pazz said. 'If you go, we go. We told you that when we arrived back on Earth.'

'I know you offered,' Hycerta replied. 'I had hoped, after almost a year nothing would happen but...' She bit on her lip. 'I don't want you to feel obliged. I was the one who made the decision for my actions and I will accept the responsibility for them.'

'But a little help from Earth won't do any harm, now will it?' Duncan replied with a mysterious tone.

'Duncan!' Pazz frowned. 'What are you thinking?'

'Nothing really,' Duncan answered and glanced back at Hycerta. 'By using Omega 17, we can leave any time and get there before the hearing. Is that right?'

'Yes!' she nodded. 'One week, a year or ten years makes no difference. Why?'

'We go prepared,' Duncan said. 'And we can take as long as it is necessary to prepare our defense, so to speak.' He gazed intently at Hycerta. 'You will not be alone,' he said. 'We're in this together.'

*

CHAPTER EIGHTEEN

When Omega 17 arrived in orbit above Planet 21974.3, Hycerta's apprehension was partly relieved when her clones, Duncan and Lunol were welcomed with the utmost respect, transported to the surface in a landing pod and given accommodation in a dormitory overlooking a white sandy beach with rolling breakers.

Duncan read the written material given to them, all in the Delta home language, with relish. He filled the others in with details they had not already learnt from the computers.

'This planet is similar in size and composition to Earth; being the third planet in a solar system orbiting a sun,' he said as he held a colorful pamphlet up. 'It has though, no intelligent species beyond wild horse-like herbivores and feline mammals that can be dangerous if approached. After initial exploring it will be considered for settlement by humans from crowded planets closer to Delta.

Except for twenty or so scientific and military outposts around the planet, this military installation with a population of five thousand, is the only place of human habitation. We're in the temperate zone on one of four large continents. About eighty percent of the planet is covered in ocean.'

'My God, Duncan,' Pazz took the pamphlet from her partner and gazed at the three-dimensional colored photographs. 'You can read the home language better than I can. I am already beginning to forget it after being immersed in English.'

'Well,' said Duncan modestly, 'It is my field of study. When it comes to math or biochemistry, I'm hopeless.'

Kylina interrupted, 'It's a beautiful place but I think poor Hycerta is extremely worried,' she said in a concerned voice. 'I know she vomited in the toilet a few moments ago.'

Pazz nodded and stood up from the couch she had been sitting on. 'I'll go and talk to her. She takes everything so much to heart. It's so unfair. She should be hailed as a hero not ridiculed.'

Duncan nodded. 'I agree but that's what we're here for. I'm sure our evidence will be sufficient to vindicate her actions.'

'On Earth maybe,' Pazz added with a worried frown. 'But the whole Delta justice system is so different from the one practiced in Australia. In some ways it is quite archaic.'

*

The fifth day of the tribunal hearing, as it was called, began as the five women proctors dressed in pale cream flowing gowns and blue military type jackets walked sedately in behind the semicircular bench.

'This Tribunal Hearing is in Order,' announced the clerk, also a woman. 'You may all be seated.'

Duncan stared around. In the whole room there were only two male officials and these appeared to be only minor assistants.

The Grand Proctor, sitting in the center of her colleagues, looked directly at him. 'Doctor Duncan Bourne, you are I believe from the city of Adelaide, Australia, Planet Earth and wish to make a factual statement to this Tribunal. Do you need a computerize translator so we can communicate?'

'No, Grand Proctor' he replied in Delta's language. 'I can converse in your home language.'

She nodded, quite impressed. 'Very well, Doctor Bourne and may I congratulate you on your accentless presentation. Ours is an ancient and quite difficult language to learn.' She gave a thin smile. 'I would find it difficult to speak with any confidence in English. You may begin Doctor.'

Duncan began, "I have used computer records from Omega 17 and material filmed on Earth to show this tribunal what happened on my planet during the eleven Earth months, that is equivalent to fourteen Delta months, that were eliminated by the time travel.'

He waved a hand over a small interface ball and two scenes appeared on the white wall opposite the Proctor's bench; both showing Earth as seen from Omega 17; a blue and white sphere with the Australian continent mainly a light brown. White clouds covered much of South Australia and Victoria states. Each scene had the similar date in the bottom left hand corner.

'These views show Earth the day before Doctor Pazz D'rose left Omega 1 to land in Western Australia,' Duncan began. 'The date is written in two ways, the Earth calendar with local time and the more familiar Inter-galatical Delta Calendar equivalent.' He coughed and gazed around but every eye was on the projected images. 'I have prepared a two-hour vision. The left-hand view will show the Earth in the original time as the fungus became established; the right hand view, Ladies of the Tribunal, will show exactly the same time scene on Earth after the time alteration. Naturally, some scenes will not be in exactly the same place but we have edited them to be as close as possible.'

He stopped again and caught Pazz's smile of encouragement. 'For every day, I have more detailed comparisons so you may, if you wish, stop me at any time and I'll present a more detailed extract.

Remember that the two scenes will always illustrate the exact time, before and after the time journey. If there is no exact time compatibility to within two Earth hours, one screen will blank out.' Duncan paused for a moment before continuing. 'We begin with Doctor D'rose's arrival in the desert...'

The image on the left switched to Earth to show Pazz's view as she climbed out of the landing pod and was offered the ride in the Landcruiser 4x4 while the right hand one showed the Learjet carrying, Hycerta, Pazz and the others towards Adelaide International Airport.

Pazz's voice in English or Home language, depending on who was listening, filled the courtroom from the left-hand screen.

'I know you're there,' she called. 'So you might as well come out.'

A flashlight flicked on and she bathed the area in light. Two rough Earth seeders stood up, one held with an ancient weapon held ready to fire.

'That rifle is hardly needed,' Pazz said, 'I need a ride to the railway. Can you help?'

One of the men grinned but the look in his eye made several women in the courtroom gasp in sympathy with Pazz's predicament.

'Put the rifle away, Stan,' snapped the other seeder. 'Come on. The poor girl needs a ride. That's why she landed near us. Let's go.' He glanced at his companion and made a signal with a facial expression. 'You drive. Okay!'

The sound switched to the second view of the people in the Learjet. Pazz was also talking. 'It's about this time I landed,' her voice said with a slight quiver. 'My God I was terrified. I knew nothing about males and thought they would attack me for sure.'

The scene continued to show the train journey, Pazz's illness, and Lynn helping and later, Kylina's rescue by Discovery and the first appearance of the fungus.

At times, the proctors just watched while at other times, the views were frozen while Duncan, Pazz, Kylina, Lunol or Hycerta were asked questions or asked to comment on the presentation.

During one such interruption when Kylina was being asked about making the 777 change course to Adelaide Airport, Duncan compared this trial with an Earth one. There were no prosecuting or defense lawyers at all. Everything was controlled by the proctors who asked anyone in the room, anything at anytime. Nobody, except guards, secretaries, the proctors and witnesses were allowed in the courtroom. It seemed quite haphazard and informal but was, in reality, deadly serious.

Duncan's two-hour presentation took five hours; there were no meal breaks and even stops to visit a toilet were frowned upon. But it was worthwhile. The final scenes showing rioting and anarchy with corpses everywhere compared with a peaceful scene of Pazz lecturing her students; had some in the room weeping.

'Thank you, Doctor Bourne,' The Grand Proctor said when Duncan switched the visions off. 'That will conclude today's session. You may give your opinion tomorrow. I thank you for your thoroughness.'

That was something else different from back home, Duncan thought. The case was divided into two distinct parts. Witnesses and Hycerta herself were given a chance to present factual evidence and later asked for their opinion of that evidence. Both parts appeared to be given equal validity.

Along with the other people in the room, he stood as the five proctors filed out. Pazz gripped Duncan's hands kissed him and was immediately followed by Hycerta who cuddled him in a tight embrace and kissed his cheek

'Thank you, Duncan' she said in a quiet voice and turned to Pazz. 'You don't mind, Pazz?'

'No,' said her clone. 'I think we can all be proud of Duncan. I knew he was doing this but never realized how much effort he put into the presentation.'

Kylina stood by almost in tears. 'My God, Pazz, those early scenes had me terrified, especially when you were ill. I remember how I felt when I first arrived.' She hesitated. 'Wasn't Lynn a friend?'

'Yes,' Pazz replied. 'Without her and Duncan, I don't know if I could have survived. Those damn computers should have awoken us all at the same time.'

'Well,' said Duncan and hugged her close. 'At least they did the second time.' He yawned. 'I'm hungry and exhausted. Let's go and have a meal.'

With Lunol beside him and the three sisters in front, Duncan walked out of the courtroom with a satisfied smile on his face. The outcome was still uncertain but he was more optimistic now than on any of the previous, somewhat damning days.

*

The dormitory shared by everyone without any allowance made for gender became a little home for the five and the atmosphere was far more comforting than on the previous evenings. Duncan, though, sat on his single bed writing copious notes in a thick notebook he'd brought from Earth. Finally, after almost three hours he looked up to find nobody in the dormitory. He was so busy writing his speech for the next day he hadn't even heard the others leave.

There was a note left taped to the door.

We've gone for a swim at the beach. It's a lovely evening outside. I love you, Pazz, it stated *Me too,* continued different writing underneath. *Don't tell Pazz.*

Duncan grinned but wasn't sure who wrote the second bit. He changed and walked out and down the few meters to the beach where dozens of people, ninety-percent female, were swimming and diving in rows of curly waves. He heard a voice and saw one of the clones waving at him from out in the waves but which one, he, once again had no idea.

'Come in?' she shouted and he recognized Pazz's voice. 'Relax a little!'

The water was lukewarm and salty just like a beach at home as Duncan bounded into where Lunol and the three clones grinned at him. Even Hycerta looked relaxed and for the first time in weeks, the dark rings beneath her eyes were gone.

'It was pink,' she said when Duncan got within earshot.

He frowned and screwed his nose up. 'I don't understand,' he said. 'Pink what?'

Hycerta's eyes twinkled. 'Wait until tomorrow,' she said and dived away under a massive breaker that almost swept Duncan off his feet.

*

At four the next morning, ten a.m. in equivalent Earth time, the formalities were over and Duncan was invited to give his opinion about his presentation of the day before. He stood and noticed something new. The wall above the five proctor's bench was colored pink. He was certain it had been painted white before.

'Grand Proctor, Assistant Proctors, Ladies of the Court; in my opinion, Hycerta Sixth Flower, now called Hycerta D'rose on Earth, showed great courage in making her declaration of independence on board Omega 17. If it was not for her, the visions we saw yesterday would have only shown the original views. Earth, at this time would be in its second phase of the fungus epidemic with ninety five percent of the population dead.' He stopped and turned a page of his notebook. 'I further believe…'

For another ten minutes Duncan continued but was less than quarter way through his prepared speech when the Grand Proctor interrupted with a polite, 'Excuse me, Doctor Bourne.'

Duncan stopped mid-sentence and noticed the pink wall was decidedly darker; almost red while a thin line along the join with the ceiling was a definite red.

The Grand Proctor was not looking at Duncan, though, but at Hycerta. 'Miss Hycerta Sixth Flower, do you wish this tribunal to continue?' she asked.

Hycerta stood behind her little desk and Duncan could see her hands trembling. 'No, Grand Proctor,' she said in a very formal voice. 'I wish this tribunal hearing to conclude.'

'Very well,' the woman replied. 'Please file your claim for full expenses and military salary for the time you were on Earth, with our office. That is all.'

Duncan watched, flabbergasted as the five proctors stood and filed out of the room. 'What's happening?' he asked Pazz who was by his elbow.

'Hycerta's been found innocent of all charges against her,' Pazz said.

The two others came up and it was all hugs and congratulations, tears of joy flowed and Duncan stared at his notes.

'Beats me,' said Lunol who had also come up. 'One minute you were talking and the next, it's all over. I've never seen anything like it.'

Duncan shrugged,' Hycerta mentioned something being pink last night and look at that wall!' he said.

Lunol swung around. The wall was now colored a dark red.

'We won!' Hycerta rushed up and grabbed Duncan's hands then turned to hug Pazz and afterwards, Kylina. 'We won! We won!'

'How?' Duncan and Lunol both asked. Both men were totally mystified by the events.

Pazz saw their confused faces and explained. 'Throughout the hearing the computers are ranking the outcome which is color-coded. White means they're neutral, cream being swayed towards guilt, light pink towards innocence. If the cream turns to green you're in trouble and blue means they are about to pronounce you guilty. If pink turns to red they're about to pronounce you innocent of all charges.

If red or blue shows on the decision panel; that's what it's called, the person being charged has the immediate right to stop the trial and accept that verdict. That was why you were stopped in the middle of your elegant speech, My Love. The board began to turn red so Hycerta was given the opportunity to accept the innocent verdict, which she did.

'And if she didn't want to accept it?' Lunol asked as he scratched his hair in wonder.

'She could have let the trial continue and have the proctors make a majority decision at the end. It is very rare that this is different from the electronic verdict.' She shrugged. 'It does happen in close cases or if the computers never move out of the white neutral stance.'

'Right at the end yesterday afternoon the panel changed to pink, a deep pink,' Hycerta interrupted in an excited voice. For the first time I knew I had a chance. The day before I was expecting it to turn cream at any moment. Your fantastic double visions did it, Duncan. '

'Can the verdict swing the other way?' Duncan asked.

'Oh yes!' Hycerta replied. 'I've seen a pink panel change back to white as new evidence is brought forward, but unless it becomes red or blue, the trial must continue. If I had let the trial continue there could have been more witnesses who may have changed it back to white or even onto green.' She caught Duncan with her serious blue eyes. 'I know they had two military experts who were about to testify on the legality of my taking over Omega 17. I'm sure it would have swung the trial back to white. That was why I stopped it when I was asked.'

*

After a celebration lunch, provided free by the military, the five went down to the beach for the afternoon. Pazz wanted to get an even tan and absentmindedly slipped her armlet off and placed it in her clothes drawer in the dormitory when she changed into her newly bought navy blue and white bikini.

'My Dear,' Duncan said when he saw her. 'I love the swimsuit. You look so fabulous.'

'Thanks,' Pazz said and gave him a kiss. 'You don't look so bad either. I was told you could get a brilliant tan here without worrying about being over exposed.'

'Yes, but I still wouldn't risk getting sunburned if I was you,' Duncan said and gave her a playful slap on the bottom.

It was hovering close to thirty degrees in Earth Celsius temperature and the waves were pounding in. Everyone swam and body surfed for over an hour before Kylina and Hycerta went ashore and sunbathed beneath a huge sun umbrella behind a small sand dune while Pazz continued to swim with Lunol and Duncan. It was after four, Earth time, when the three staggered out of the water, weary but happy.

'There's a little pavilion along the beach. I'm sure I saw some girls licking something that looked like ice creams. I'll go and see what they are,' Duncan said.

'I'll come with you,' Lunol added. 'Coming Pazz.'

'No,' she laughed as she shook her wet hair. 'I'll go and find the two lazy ones. See you later.' She watched the men walk away and made her way in the opposite direction to where she could see the top of the umbrella they'd hired. As she reached the sand dune Kylina and Hycerta's voices filtered through the air. She could tell the difference, by the slight way Hycerta clipped the words in English.

'What are you going to do now?' Kylina asked.

'I have to go back to Delta,' Hycerta replied. 'I want to complete my Matron's degree and,' her voice sounded sad. 'There's a personal reason, too.'

Pazz was about to walk over the sand dune but hesitated. She was sure the other two had not heard her arrive.

'What's that?' Kylina asked.

'Duncan,' Hycerta replied. 'What do you think of him?'

'Great guy,' Kylina replied. 'We couldn't have a better friend.'

'I mean as a male,' Hycerta replied so softly Pazz hardly heard. She stopped and turned red in anger and jealousy as her clone continued to speak.

Kylina's voice sounded surprised, too. 'I have Lunol,' she whispered. 'I like Duncan but love Lunol. We are mates in the physical way all the time. Quite frankly, I've never thought of Duncan that way and would advise you not to either.'

'That's the trouble,' Hycerta replied and her voice broke. 'I would never do anything to hurt Pazz but all I want is Duncan to take me in his arms and love me.'

'The little bitch,' Pazz hissed under her breath. She dropped to her knees, crawled up the sand dune and peeped over.

Hycerta was facing Kylina whose head hid Pazz from view. Before she ducked back down again Pazz noticed Hycerta. There were tears in the girl's eyes.

'I even hoped Duncan might think I was Pazz sometimes. When he is near me I go all tingly inside,' the girl continued.

'Hycerta!' Kylina warned. 'You had better stop thinking that way.'

'I don't want to but I can't help it.,' Hycerta cried. 'I know we joke about us being the same but I love him, Kylina.' She stopped for a second and bit on her lip. 'That's why I'm going back to Delta. If I stay with you all, I know I'll do something terribly wrong. I've never even had a boyfriend back home. It never worried me. I had my studies but…' She gave a tiny sniff, found a handkerchief and blew her nose. 'Don't tell Pazz. She'd hate me and I couldn't bare that.'

Pazz lay those few meters away and found tears in her own eyes.

Her feelings were in turmoil. She wanted to jump out and scream at her clone, to slap her face and call her a slut but also she felt empathy towards her. After all, Hycerta had not done anything. She was just confessing her feelings to Kylina. Perhaps clones were too much alike. Pazz did not know.

'Why tell me?' Kylina's voice interrupted her thoughts.

'I had to tell you why I've made my mind up to return to Delta with the proctors. They're going back tomorrow.' She sniffed and blew her nose again. 'Look, I'll get over it, find myself another man; they're everywhere on Delta now and then return to see you all…' She stopped and stared out over the rolling ocean. 'It's so lovely here, I imagine what it would be like to have a little cottage here with Duncan…'

'Well, bloody snap out of it,' Kylina retorted. 'I can't help you if you carry on like that.'

'I'm sorry,' Hycerta sobbed. 'Please don't be angry with me.'

She leaped to her feet and ran away, so quickly she slipped and toppled onto the sand before rising to her feet and running into the surf along the beach. Kylina jumped up and was prepared to dash after her but in the process ran over the dune straight into Pazz with an almighty thud.

'Pazz!' Kylina gasped with her eyes wide with fright. 'You heard!'

'Yes,' Pazz replied sarcastically 'Everything! That love confession, the lovely little cottage bit. Everything!'

'Oh Pazz,' Kylina responded. 'I'm sorry. I wish you hadn't heard, but she never actually did anything. She's as distressed as you are.'

'I know,' Pazz replied in a more sober voice. 'That's what makes it so hard. I don't want to hurt Hycerta but I can't…' She stopped and stared at Kylina. 'I'll go and talk to her.'

'No Pazz!' Kylina yelled but it was too late. Pazz was already running up the beach.

Ten minutes later, Pazz caught up with Hycerta beyond the crashing surf; ten minutes of frantic thinking and churning thoughts over and also calming down. She arrived beside Hycerta and their eyes met. The water was deep and she had to tread water.

'You're Pazz,' the other woman cried. 'Go away. You're going to hate me.'

'When I was in Delta eighty years ago there were no men,' Pazz began. 'We were drugged so we had no romantic feelings. ' She moved her arms so she could keep her head above water. 'If we were lucky we could apply to become bearers and later be artificially fertilized. I protested against this treatment and was banished from the planet for my efforts. Delta is a better place now and women can be women. We're allowed to have feelings but sometimes they control us. That's what being a human is.'

'Pazz,' Hycerta replied with her voice almost in tears. 'I have to tell you something.'

'I overheard,' Pazz replied. 'I was angry, annoyed and jealous then I thought about it. You did nothing wrong, Hycerta.' She gave a tiny grin. 'Now if you'd actually seduced Duncan…'

'I'd never do that, Pazz. I told Kylina that.'

'And I believe you, Hycerta,'

'That's why I'm going home to Delta, Pazz.' Hycerta's face dipped below the water as a wave surged by and she came up with water streaming off her face. 'Please don't tell Duncan!'

'I'm not that stupid,' Pazz replied in a determined voice then broke into a grin. 'He couldn't stand the pace, anyhow.'

'Oh Pazz,' the other woman replied. 'So much has happened and with Duncan always around. I shouldn't have told Kylina.'

'No, it was better you did. It's too difficult to bottle things inside yourself,' Pazz replied. 'Come on. Let's swim in.'

She flicked a scoop of water at her clone and dived away through the surf. Her mind was still in turmoil but she was proud of the way she had handled, what could have been an awful situation.

Kylina ran up the beach to meet them as they waded ashore. She handed them both an ice cream, amazingly similar to those on Earth, and looked from one clone to the other.

'It's okay,' Hycerta said quietly. 'We didn't scratch each other's eyes out.'

'But we keep it to ourselves. Okay!' Pazz added. 'Don't even tell Lunol?'

'About you getting sunburned?' Kylina replied with an innocent look. 'That's all I know about.'

'Oh that!' Pazz replied offhandedly. 'I hope the ozone layer here is better than the one on Earth.'

'With no humans to ruin the atmosphere, it should be,' Kylina glanced up. 'But hush up. Here come the men.'

The three clones stood with frothy surf tugging around their legs as Duncan and Lunol came running up the beach. Duncan jumped a line of froth, grabbed Pazz and plastered a salty kiss on her lips.

'How did you know me?' she gasped and kissed him back.

'The eyes, My Love. It's all in the eyes.' he laughed, grabbed the ice cream out of her hand, handed it to Kylina, slung an arm under her knees, lifted her up and tossed her into a wave mounting up behind them.

Pazz spluttered under the green and white water and held her breath as the wave carried her towards the beach. She broke the surface to find Hycerta's eyes searching her but the other girl was smiling. There was thankfulness in those eyes and love! Pazz felt empathy towards her clone and love, too. It was different from her feelings for Duncan but still a deep affinity.

'Everything will be fine, Hycerta,' she whispered. 'I know it will.'

CHAPTER NINETEEN

The last day on Planet 21974.3 was subdued as Hycerta prepared herself for the trip home to Delta and everyone else; Earth. Duncan protested her decision and seemed somewhat surprised when nobody really supported him. It was Lunol who took him aside and fixed him with an intense gaze.

'Do you have to be hit in the face with a fence post before you come to your senses, Duncan?' he muttered.

'What do you mean?' Duncan frowned.

'Have you seen the three girls all last night and this morning?'

'Sure. Why?'

'Really studied them?'

'Hycerta looked a bit weepy but when I told her she should come back to Earth but nobody supported me.'

'She's fallen for you, Duncan and is going home to avoid any confrontation.'

Duncan frowned. 'That's rubbish!' he retorted.

'Think about it,' Lunol replied.

Duncan did. There were lots of little incidents; that bit written on the note, things said in jest, the way Hycerta looked at him. He frowned. 'Did Kylina tell you something?' he asked.

'No,' Lunol replied. 'That's what made me suspicious. Something happened on the beach yesterday. I'd say Hycerta confessed or perhaps Kylina and Pazz found out when they tried to get her to return to Earth.'

'But I never encouraged her.'

'They're clones, Duncan. Couldn't their attractions be the same?'

'I guess, but Kylina was never like that or Pazz with you, for that matter.'

'Kylina grew up on Custronomus and met me years ago and you met Pazz before you knew Kylina, but what would have happened if you'd met the three of them at the same time? Would you have fallen in love with one and not the others? They're identical. Sometimes I still muddle them up.'

'A good point,' Duncan admitted and ran a hand over his beard. 'So what do I do?'

'Nothing. The decision's been made so don't protest too much or Pazz may think you have the hots for Hycerta, too.'

'Okay,' Duncan replied with his eyes deep in thought. He clasped

Lunol's shoulder in a firm grip. 'And I thought everything was turning out so well.'

He walked away along the path to be by himself for a while. However, after a few moments, footfalls came up behind him and a soft hand gripped his. Blue eyes gazed up. He studied the woman as she walked beside him without saying a word.

'I love you, Pazz,' he said and, hoping he had the correct sister slipped his arm around her shoulders. 'When we return home what say we get married?'

'You know about Hycerta?' Pazz replied as they continued to walk together.

Duncan nodded. 'Lunol worked it out but I asked you a question. Did you hear it?'

Pazz stopped, turned and slipped her arms around Duncan's waist. Her intense blue eyes gazed into his and she smiled. 'Of course, Duncan. The sooner the better.'

She reached up and placed a tiny kiss on his lips. 'We can celebrate later in a more private place,' she retorted and stepped out but her hand remained gripped in his.

On a small rise a few meters behind, more intense blue eyes followed their every move. Tears welled in Hycerta's eyes as she turned and walked away. She too, heard footsteps and found Kylina walking beside her. Nothing was said but the smile between them meant more than any words.

*

At the tiny space terminal three hours later, Hycerta hugged her clones and stretched a hand out formally to Lunol and finally, Duncan. Her eyes held his for a second.

'Everything will be fine,' he said in a hoarse voice. 'You'll get your Matron's degree and have a wonderful life.' He grinned. 'I'm not that good a catch anyway; a bit of a loaner really.'

He pulled her into his arms and they hugged each other closely for a moment.

'Bye Duncan,' Hycerta said in a soft voice. She kissed his cheek and was gone.

Duncan turned, walked to the second landing pod on the tarmac where the others were waiting and climbed aboard. The journey home was about to begin.

*

Three Delta Inter-galatical Peace Keeping Force members accompanied them back to Earth in Omega 17 while another starship, Omega 23 followed so, briefly, three Delta starships orbited Earth; all cloaked and unobserved by even the most sophisticated equipment below.

On that last afternoon before they left, the proctors who seemed to have the authority to speak for the Delta government as well as their judicial responsibilities agreed to leave Omega 17 as an independent starship and not over-rule any of Hycerta's commands. Omega 23 had the responsibility of towing Omega 1 back to Delta at post light speed. The eighty-year-old craft was destined to a thorough quarantine and electronic cleaning to rid it of any traces of the fungus and finally have a resting-place in a museum on the home planet.

Attached to Omega 17 were two Learjets that could be called to Earth through Epsilon or Theta. Both computers had been upgraded with modern Delta technology without losing their original memories and 'personality', though tiny gold rings replaced the armlets. Duncan and Lunol were both given remote feeds to their partner's computers.

'They can be engagement rings,' laughed Pazz and dug Kylina in the ribs. 'If I'm about to follow that old Earth custom and get married, you can too.'

'Well that's up to Lunol,' Kylina replied.

Lunol grinned. 'Why not?' he answered. 'Why not a double celebration? You know two identical twins being married together. Imagine how the women's magazines would like it?'

*

The Learjet with "Omega Shuttle" painted on the fuselage, once again attracted no attention as it taxied into the domestic terminal at Adelaide Airport and four weary travelers disembarked. The crowded terminal building seemed so much like home and was even more so when a tiny voice called out. 'Auntie Pazz, Auntie Kylina! Where's Auntie Hycerta?'

'Jason!' Pazz laughed and picked the little boy up in her arms. She glanced at a grinning Lynn. 'How does he tell us apart?'

'Beats me but where is Hycerta, anyway?'

'She was cleared of all charges and went home to Delta,' Duncan interrupted. 'And how's life here?'

'Nothing's happened. After all, it is only a week,' Lynn laughed. 'I guess you've been romping around the universe for a couple of years.'

'Not quite,' Pazz replied. We're certainly glad to be home, though. Oh yes, we're having a double wedding soon.'

'Oh yeah!' said Lynn. 'Between whom?'

'Well,' Pazz said with a twinkle in her eye. 'There was a big change. We all agreed to swap around. Duncan likes younger woman and Lunol goes for experience.'

'You didn't!' gasped Lynn in all seriousness until she saw the grins on four faces. 'Okay,' she retorted, 'Joke's on me.'

They reached Duncan's Falcon, still in the long-term car park car, loaded the luggage and squeezed in.

'Oh, there is one thing,' Lynn said as Duncan drove out. She reached in her purse and took out a long slim envelope, commonly used in North America, and handed it to Kylina 'A letter has arrived from United States for you. It looks like a personal one.'

Kylina gazed briefly at the unfamiliar stamp and handwritten writing, slit it open and read the two page letter with pursed lips.

'Well?' Pazz asked. 'Don't keep us in suspense.'

Kylina handed Pazz the letter. 'It's from Major Val Wikstrom, that woman astronaut who rescued me. She wants to come to Adelaide.'

'But how?' Pazz replied. 'She should not know you. All that was wiped out in the time travel.'

'I know but look at the last paragraph.'

"Do we know each other, Kylina?" the letter read. ' You may or may not be aware that last month I went into orbit aboard The Space Shuttle Discovery. It was a perfectly normal research trip but while up there I had a strange premonition or dream that I'd been in orbit before and we rescued you from something. I definitely remember your name; it was so unusual. It played on my mind and when I found you were a real person living in Adelaide I found your address, hence this letter.

I'll be visiting Magaroona Research Station in South Australia next month and would like to visit you...'

'How would she know the name D'rose?' Pazz frowned as she read the envelope. 'You didn't have that surname when you were rescued.'

'I used my Earth surname in a thank you letter I wrote to her,' Kylina replied. 'That shouldn't exist now, either.'

'Perhaps lots of people remember the old time,' Duncan said.

'But that would be millions of people throughout the whole Earth. It's not possible,' Pazz added. 'The place would be a riot.'

'She was an astronaut. Perhaps being in space made a difference,' Lunol suggested.

'Well, she's coming here,' Kylina added as she folded the letter and slipped it back in the envelope. 'I can't just ignore her.'

'No, her memory could range from a vague recall of your name to full knowledge of everything that happened on Earth when the fungus attacked,' Duncan replied. 'I'd say we will need to be very careful when we talk to her, that's all.' He stared out at the traffic and shrugged.' I wouldn't worry too much about it, though. If it was a major discovery of Omega we'd have the government down on us, not just a personal letter.'

'Could be,' Kylina replied but, if not worried, she was certainly curious.

*

Less than a week had gone by and Pazz was home after a day at work telling Lynn about her busy day when a faint knock sounded on the door. She walked over and opened it to see Hycerta standing there. In spite of herself Pazz felt a surge of jealousy and pouted.

'My God, Hycerta!' she a gasped. 'Why didn't you go home to Delta?'

'I did, Pazz,' Hycerta said in a nervous voice. ' Don't worry, I'm over Duncan now and have a partner actually.'

Pazz frowned and studied her clone. Hycerta looked different. Sure the clothes had changed but also the hairstyle. It was, though, even more than that. Hycerta didn't look Kylina's age any more. A few lines radiated out from the eyes and the facial skin had lost that fresh, almost teenage look. That was it! Hycerta looked older.

'It's ten years since I went home,' explained Hycerta 'I guess my natural age has crept beyond yours. It is very important I talk to you.'

'Well, come on in, Hycerta,' Pazz said and relaxed. 'If you don't mind me saying you look quite exhausted. 'Lynn,' she called. 'We have a visitor.'

'I came from Omega 31' Hycerta started after she sat on the edge of the couch in the living room. 'Have you been recognized by anyone who shouldn't know you? This is important.' Her apprehensive eyes gazed at Pazz.

'Kylina got a letter from a woman astronaut who shouldn't know us. She wants to visit.'

'But hasn't yet?'

'No, she said she'd come sometime this month so I guess that'll be soon.'

'So it's not too late,' replied Hycerta. 'I want you to remove your computer rings immediately. I suspect our computers are being monitored. That's why I came personally and we never contacted you through them.' Her lips gave a slight quiver.

'Don't listen to her,' Epsilon's words entered Pazz's mind. 'She could be a fake.'

'Can you tell me anything you said to me. Something nobody else would know, Hycerta,' Pazz said in a cautious voice.

'You never had your armlet on during that last swim on the planet where the tribunal was held?' Hycerta asked.

Pazz frowned. 'No, I believe I took it off so I'd get an even sun tan. I put it back on again afterwards, though.'

'I can tell you everything we talked about.'

'Don't listen to her,' Epsilon repeated.

Pazz frowned and made a decision. In spite of Epsilon's warning she was certain this was Hycerta. She slipped the computer ring off, placed it on the mantelpiece and reached for her mobile phone.

'I'm phoning Duncan, Kylina and Lunol,' she said.

'She pressed a memorized number and waited until the call was answered. 'Duncan,' she said. 'Can you remove your computer ring and get home straight away? There's an emergency.' she listened for a few seconds before talking again. 'I'm calling Kylina to tell her to do the same.'

Pazz turned back to her visitor. 'Tell me what you said that day,' she said in a serious voice.

'I had just confessed to Kylina I loved Duncan and...' Hycerta flushed slightly and repeated, almost to the word what was said and what happened, even down to the ice creams and Duncan tossing Pazz in the waves. 'I have never written or recorded the conversation or told a sole about it.'

'Okay,' Pazz replied and stepped forward to hug her clone. 'Welcome home Hycerta. Forgive my abruptness. I'm thrilled to see you and I know the others will be, too.' She said. 'Mind you, it has only been a week since you left.'

*

It was dark before Duncan and the others had arrived to gather in the living room. Lynn played the perfect host and rushed around with drinks and sandwiches while Hycerta gave everyone a brief summary of her life over the last decade.

'I graduated with my Matron's degree,' she said. 'I have a partner. Broden and I have been together for five years.' She smiled at Duncan. 'I was like a stupid teenager with a crush, wasn't I? I do apologize. The last thing I really wanted was to come between you two and to destroy the friendship we had built up.'

'It's all forgotten,' Duncan replied and grinned at Pazz, who nodded.

'Anyhow,' Hycerta continued. 'I'd better tell you why I'm here. It started when someone at the Magaroona Research Base accessed the computer Kappa on Omega 17,' she began. 'We don't know how it was done but guess it was just a random selection through the radio telescope. This was always a remote possibility. They downloaded those visions you used at the trial, Duncan, so found everything that happened with the fungi epidemic.'

'I see,' he muttered.

'It seems they had this information but didn't know where it came from so you were visited and your computers accessed. Once they had direct access to Kappa they discovered Omega 17 was in a stationary orbit over Australia. A secret international organization consisting of Americans and Russians sent a Space Shuttle up and took it over.' Hycerta grimaced. 'It took them several years to discover how to operate it and bypass the commands I had programmed in.

We have to undo a great wrong done on Earth a second time. I was refused permission to come due to time-space laws that are even more stringent than a decade ago. There were several quite disastrous errors made throughout the known universe for the three years after my return to Delta. Time travel is only allowed now to shorten space travel journeys, never to alter a place's future.' She grimaced. 'I can never go back as I broke this law by being here.'

'So it is extremely important. Go on,' Pazz said.

'It took this group five years to learned how to operate Omega 17 and they set off in a top secret operation to explore the universe. Their intentions were honorable, I guess, but due to their lack of knowledge, several blunders were made. ' She stopped again. 'It would be like giving one of Earth's jet aircraft to someone on Custronomus in those sailing ship days, you two, Lunol and Kylina, grew up in.

'So what happened?' Pazz added

'They brought the fungus back from a planet we had quarantined. This though, was a new generation that spread even more rapidly in the Earth's conditions. When I left, Earth was declared another quarantined planet. The new mutation fungi can grow and sustain itself by smothering out vegetation as well as killing humans and animal life. On last report, only two percent of human and animal life had survived and forests and grasslands in temperate and tropical zones of the world became desert wasteland. Only the colder climates such as Canada and Siberia can support life, as we know it. '

She stared around the tiny living room. 'It happened on Planet 21974.3 where the trial took place as well,' Hycerta continued. 'The only way to stop this fungus was to destroy the planet. Scientists altered the orbit so the planet swung into its sun and burned up.'

'That was a beautiful planet,' Pazz added in a shocked whisper.

'When I left, the Delta authorities were about to do the same to Earth. It is feared that if this fungus kept developing at its present rate it could wipe out the known universe of humanoid and also mammal life within a century. We have had no visits from humans in our future so fear this could have already happened.'

'And if Omega 17 is not taken over?' Duncan asked.

'Our computer scenario shows the fungus is isolated in Lunol's world and eliminated before the new mutations can develop.'

'So why didn't the Delta government just come back and destroy Omega 17 before it was discovered from Earth?' Lunol asked.

'That was my argument,' Hycerta replied. 'However, they still would not do it. I was placed under restriction and not permitted near any computers or space port facilities.' She gave a brief smile. 'They didn't take me into account Broden's and my determination.' She sucked on her lip and gave a tiny sigh. 'So here I am.'

'Is Broden with you?' Duncan asked.

'He flew me down in the Learjet and returned to Omega 31. We have, we hope, an untapped communication channel that bypasses the computers. ' She said and fingered an attractive earring dangling down.

'Okay, Hycerta, what should we do?' Pazz asked.

Hycerta took a small box out of her backpack and opened it. Inside were four compartments. 'This is an isolating box,' she said. 'Put your computer rings in here and they can't be electronically accessed. Don't meet this woman astronaut or, if she turns up unexpectedly, trick her in some way. She will be able to recognize you all from Duncan's trial visions. There may be agents with her as well, so be vigilant.

Afterwards, you'll need to access the Research Station and wipe the program of Duncan's evidence.' She shrugged. 'The last may be impossible but will prevent the whole scenario happening again. You're pretty resourceful people.'

'Thanks,' muttered Duncan but was deep in thought. 'So if they don't access our computer rings they won't discover Omega 17. Is that correct, Hycerta?'

'That's what Broden believes.'

Duncan nodded.

'With your rings, they'll gain access,' Hycerta continued. 'You need to hide them somewhere they know nothing about. This house, Kylina's place or the university are no good. They'll have quite sophisticated tracking devices and, even with the isolation box, will be able to find the rings if they come within a dozen meters or so of it.'

'What about the farm?' Lunol suggested. 'They don't know where I work.' He turned to Hycerta and explained. 'I have a different job than my original one. It's a stable that boards ponies and horses for rich city kids. It's quite a large farm really with numerous outbuildings, trees and so forth. There are a hundred places where this box could be hidden.'

'Right,' said Duncan. ' I think we should go out there now, Lunol.'

'We'll all go,' said Pazz.

'No,' Duncan replied. 'Only Lunol and myself. If none of you know where the rings are, the information can't be forced out of you, can it? You may still have some implants they can access.'

Pazz nodded grimly. 'I don't think so but admit it could be possible.'

Duncan and Lunol took the tiny box, placed the rings in them and, after giving their partners a brief hug, slipped out the door.

'Take care,' Duncan called back and was gone.

'Now,' said Lynn quietly. 'We'll make up your old bed for you, Hycerta. You're just about dead on your feet.'

Hycerta smiled. ' I know to you all I've just left but to me it's so long' she said in a quiet voice. 'I'd love to slip into my old bed.'

'Yeah,' Lynn said. 'I haven't even changed the sheets. Perhaps I knew something.'

*

General Bradley Jarvis glowered at Val Wikstrom. 'It's not a question of ethics, Major,' he retorted. 'It's of world importance. Make up a story that you're clairvoyant or something. We know they have an advanced computer in the form of a ring on their fingers. You only need to touch or perhaps even be in its vicinity for our own computers to access their data bank. Once that is done we can trace where the main computer is and go from there. With luck, they may not even realize you have done it.'

'And without luck, General?' Val asked.

'We'll incapacitate them and remove the computer rings. They're aliens, Major; human yes but still aliens. Who knows what their powers or ethics are! To them, Earth could be a minor civilization to experiment with and dispose of.'

'So why haven't they done it already, General?' Dean Diriwi of the Prime Minister's Office of Special Security, stated softly from behind his Canberra desk. 'We have no way of knowing how long Earth has been under their scrutiny. It could be decades or even centuries.'

'I doubt it, Mr. Diriwi,' General Jarvis retorted. 'If those discs are to be believed, everything has happened over the last few months. God damn it, man., this is a once in a lifetime opportunity to reach the stars, once in a century even.'

'And we could be playing God,' Dean continued.

'We only want information at the moment,' the general continued. 'Once the source of the signal is found we can then decide what to do.' He fixed the Australian with a glower. 'Any decision, of course will be made by a higher authority than us, anyway.'

'Those people on that disc are Australian citizens and under our protection, General. Nothing will be done to harm them.'

'Faked records?' General Jarvis barked. 'They're illegal aliens, well and truly.'

'We do not know that, General,' Diriwi retorted. 'At the moment we have received this unsubstantiated video. It could be a sophisticated hoax made up by a bunch of computer hackers.'

'Anything is possible,' Val Wikstrom said in a quite voice. 'I agree that the D'rose women or their partners should not be harmed and the computers accessed, if indeed there are any, without their knowledge. On that condition, I will visit this Kylina D'rose and her sister.'

'Thank you,' Dean Diriwi stood up and extended his hand to the two Americans. 'We can provide security for you.' His eyes flicked over to the general. 'If your CIA men are seen in Adelaide, General Jarvis, they'll be arrested and deported.' He tossed a list of twenty names across his desk. 'We don't want an international incident between two allies, now do we?'

General Bradley Jarvis read the list and glanced up. 'I hope your Security Service does as good a job with the aliens, Mr. Diriwi,' he replied but with a new respect in his voice.

'Oh they will,' Diriwi answered. 'I have every confidence in them.'

*

CHAPTER TWENTY

'Lunol.' Duncan hissed as they drove down the expressway,' Keep an eye on that car two back. I think we're being followed.'

'Right,' his friend replied.

He turned and watched the headlights as Duncan accelerated past a slower vehicle and slid back into the slow lane again. The headlights of the car two back did the same so was now directly behind them. A truck and trailer unit was rumbling along in front with a mass of red taillights so Duncan had to brake and slow down. Behind, the car repeated their actions but took an off ramp and disappeared. Lunol gave a sigh of relief but realized their was another vehicle ambling along behind.

'I think they've swapped cars,' he muttered. 'Try speeding up.'

'Will do,' grunted Duncan. He placed his foot down, changed into the outer lane and accelerated past the truck with the speedometer hovering around one hundred and twenty kilometers an hour.

'It's still behind us,' muttered Lunol.

'Okay hang on,' Duncan retorted and pulled beside two large trucks. With a sudden flash of his indicator, he braked and changed lanes between them. There was a blast of a horn from behind but he had achieved his objective. A pale blue Holden tore by on the outer lane.

'Two men in it,' reported Lunol with a grin. 'One seemed to be looking straight at me. Seemed a bit irate for some reason.'

'Good,' Duncan replied. 'We'll sit here a while.'

They continued on between the two trucks for a few moments until the one in front indicated it was taking an off ramp. Duncan followed and within minutes they were in a dark suburban street, lost but without anyone behind.

'There's a map in the glove box,' Duncan muttered as he turned into a relatively busy road.

Lunol reached in for the map but in doing so his hand brushed the isolation box.

'Lunol,' a voice rushed into his mind. 'This is Theta. We're on your side. Listen to us!'

'But we can be traced through you,' Lunol replied in his mind.

'Not this time,' the computer replied. 'We were tricked, too.'

'Computers tricked!' Lunol retorted out loud and Duncan fixed him with a sideways glance.

After hearing Lunol's explanation, Duncan pulled to the curb and reached across to touch the box so he, too, was in contact. 'We can't risk it,' he said. ' I guess you know what's happened. What if you are being traced at this very moment?'

'I understand,' Epsilon replied. 'This box we're in has disconnected us from Omega so there is no trace. We can help.'

'How?' Duncan replied.

'A super virus,' Epsilon replied. 'Put us through your cell phone circuit and we'll get into Magaroona within seconds and wipe every program about us. It'll take them weeks to recover and the vision will be gone for ever.'

'It would have been copied,' Duncan muttered. His eyes were on Lunol and it was obvious his friend was listening to the conversation, as well.

'No, the original had a self scrambling device.' Epsilon continued. 'Let me talk to Pazz and Kylina.'

'No,' Duncan said, 'I'll talk to Pazz first.'

'Tell her; friends who saved her from infinity won't let her down,' Epsilon cut in just as Duncan signaled to Lunol. They both removed their hands and the voices into their minds stopped.

'I never liked those mind things,' Lunol muttered. 'I'd rather have my old Sigma computer any day.'

'I agree,' Duncan said, started the car and drove along until they came to a large and well-lit shopping mall.

'The best place to hide is in a crowd,' he explained. 'You stay in the car and I'll phone home via a public phone. The computers may be able to intercept a mobile phone call.'

'Okay,' Lunol muttered.

Duncan thought about the computer's last comment as he reached a telephone and rung home. Pazz answered. 'That last part was true,' she said after Duncan repeated his information. 'I think that meeting will be okay. Ask your friend to prove her suggestion.' Her voice sounded somewhat stilted.

'Is someone there?' Duncan asked. 'Talk about work if there is.'

'My Dear,' Pazz replied. 'You know I left my credit cards at work. It's a damn nuisance.'

'Is it that woman astronaut?'

'Yes,' said Pazz. 'It doesn't matter about the dry cleaning. Remember to post the mail, Dear.'

'You mean we should still hide the rings at the stables?'

'Good idea,' Pazz replied. 'See you soon.' The line went dead.

'Pazz says okay but still wants us to hide the rings,' Duncan said to Lunol. He touched the box and repeated everything to the computers.

'Sounds fair,' Epsilon replied. 'Just call up exchange faults on your cell phone and leave me on. Check back in twelve minutes.'

'Well you heard,' Duncan said to Lunol.

Lunol nodded, punched in the fault number and placed the mobile phone in the glove box.

*

At that same moment, the original staff at Magaroona Research Station were studying Duncan's video and Doctor Tedra Haygrove was trying, unsuccessfully, to copy the data onto the base's main computer.

'There is some sort of device that prevents any recording or ongoing transmission of this disc,' she said in a hushed voice. 'It can be played but not copied.'

'We know that,' General Bradley Jarvis, who had flown in an hour earlier, retorted in his usual abrupt style. 'Can you bypass the block, Doctor?'

' In time,' Tedra replied and tapped some keys on her computer. 'It's a matter of finding the program to override it. It's a little like unscrambling a code.' She shrugged. 'It may take a while, though.'

'Even photographing it with a camrecorder produces nothing,' Colonel Ira Pope added as he stood beside his superior and studied the video. On the left side, the scene showed world cities in anarchy and jumped from Adelaide to Sydney on to London and, afterwards, New York while, the other side showed a peaceful lecture theatre scene and basketball game in progress. Writing in English and an unknown language showed along the bottom.

'You will notice the date on both halves are exactly the same, 'Ira commented, 'We have not worked out why this is so. The foreign language is written in the Greek alphabet but is not that language.'

He paused as screams from the left scene filled the air and General Jarvis muttered as another scene of an American city, this time San Francisco, showed another riot and people lying dead in the streets. It looked more like Calcutta than San Francisco. Suddenly, without warning everything froze and an unnatural silence descended across the room.

'What the hell!' Jarvis snapped.

Words started to appear, ribbon style across the screen. *You have activated classified information. Your civilization's ranking of lambda, the eleventh level, is not yet advanced enough to benefit from time repositioning. For your own protection, this vision and contact with other civilizations will cease. Your radio telescope will be off line for ten Earth minutes while we reprogram the data banks. Please do not attempt to contact us.'*

'Shit!' burst out Jarvis as every computer and monitors shut down, lights flicked off and only the pale red emergency ones glowed. Through the gloom they heard the faint rumble of motors.

'All the radio telescopes are being lowered off line, Sir,' a lieutenant with headphones on muttered and glanced at Colonel Pope.

'Condition Yellow Emergency Shut Down,' a recorded voice announced over the public address system. 'All personnel are to go to evacuation stations. Do not use elevators or electronic doors. There is a major power shutdown. All security doors will be sealed in five minutes. Please wear emergency breathing apparatus.' This was followed by a siren wailing throughout the complex.

Jarvis fumed but could only drum his fingers on the console and glare through the red semi-darkness, while all around, military officers filed out to evacuation areas. But they were not needed. In exactly ten minutes, everything came on line exactly as before except the disc just showed static. A ribbon began to show. *Classified information* over and over.

'Everything recorded over the last fifteen months has been wiped from the records, Sir.'

'What!' snapped Jarvis? 'How long?'

'We have nothing from the date that disc began, Sir. All radio telescope settings, every point of reference are gone. The lot! Would you like me to contact California, Sir.'

'Forget it Son,' Bradley sighed. 'They won't have anything either.' He glowered and reached for a high security telephone. 'We still have those D'rose women in Adelaide, though. They have a lot of explaining to do.'

*

Pazz hung up the telephone and smiled at their visitor. 'The men will be home soon. They went down to the mall to get a few supplies.'

Val Wikstrom sipped her coffee and watched Pazz through thoughtful eyes before switching back to Kylina. 'I must say I have never seen triplets so identical,' she said. 'You say you have no recollections of ever meeting me before?'

'Sorry,' Kylina replied. 'I've heard of you, of course, and remember your face from news programs. Perhaps it's the same with us. Pazz has been on the news a few times. She's a well-known lecturer at the University of Adelaide.' She grinned. 'I'm a mere fine arts student myself.'

'Not mere,' Pazz laughed. 'A very talented artist, actually.'

'Are you?' Val replied. 'Have you any drawings handy?'

Before Kylina could protest, Lynn whipped up the corridor and brought back one of Kylina's paintings that she had hanging on the wall. It showed another scene of seventeenth century women standing in a village market.

'It's a period of history I enjoy,' Kylina said modestly as Val admired the work.

'Did you paint while you were on Omega?' she slipped in the conversation.

'I never had time,' Kylina replied then realized her mistake and flushed. She flicked her eyes at Pazz and Hycerta before clamping her mouth shut.

Val fixed her with a frown. 'So you do know Omega,' she whispered. 'Is it still in orbit above the Earth?'

'You tell us,' Pazz replied with her own voice serious. 'You had a routine week in space in Space Shuttle Discovery, yet claim you know us. How is this so?'

'I know only what I saw in a video,' Val confessed. 'It was a highly classified video showing a bacteria virus epidemic spreading though Earth. It shows myself rescuing Kylina from a gigantic spaceship but I have no memories of the scene.' She frowned. 'I do remember your faces on the very periphery of my mind like a dream,' she frowned. 'I believe your intentions are honorable. For that reason...' A sound of a mobile phone ringing from her handbag interrupted the conversation. 'Excuse me,' she replied and walked out the door to the patio.

' I'm sorry, Pazz,' Kylina whispered with shame in her eyes.

'Don't worry,' Pazz replied. 'She knew us from the very moment she arrived. I could tell. Nothing you said made any difference.'

Val came back with a strange expression on her face. 'There's been a blackout at Magaroona Research Station and all information saved over the last year has been wiped, including that video I told you about. Coincidence isn't it?'

'Yes,' Pazz replied in a serious voice. 'Quite a coincidence.'

Val nodded with an expressionless face, took a card from her purse and handed it to Pazz. 'I'm on your side, believe it or not. If you want to contact me that is my private mobile phone number.' She turned to Lynn. 'Please forgive my interruption of your evening, Lynn. I love your home and think Jason is a delight. Good night Hycerta; Kylina'

She shook hands, headed to the door and was gone.

Pazz saw the visitor to the edge of the veranda, turned and was about to speak when she felt a sharp prick in the shoulder blades. She staggered forward and attempted to call out but her tongue felt thick, the door beside her seemed to vibrate and the world blacked out. Inside the kitchen, the three other women and one little boy were experiencing a similar fate as anesthetic darts fired by two Balaclava clad security agents hit them all.

Across the room, Hycerta was having the same feelings as Pazz but managed to use her tongue to push a false tooth forward just as she collapsed to the floor. This small pressure was enough. A signal was transmitted to the orbiting Omega craft where Broden was monitoring a special frequency. He frowned, made a quick decision to trust their computers and sent a coded signal back to the city below. Luck was with them for, at that moment, Lunol was holding the isolation box in the Falcon so the signal reached Epsilon and Theta.

*

'Take the rings from the alien women's fingers,' snapped the security agent. 'We do not know their powers.' He glanced a Lynn and tiny Jason slumped on the couch. 'Lift them into the bedroom. They'll be awake in a while.'

'There are no rings Sergeant,' one of the Balaclava clad agents hissed.

'Damn!' the sergeant swore. 'Get that electronic gear in here. The computer receivers must be in the house somewhere.'

Drawers were emptied, clothes pulled off shelves, pot cupboards opened and ornaments smashed. The search was thorough and ruthless. Every room was trashed and even one piece of wallpaper ripped from the wall. The car shed was ramshackle and three patio floorboards ripped up so searchers could squeeze underneath to shine torches around the bare dirt beneath. A Geiger counter type machine cackled in a monotone but the only sped up when pointed at obvious electronic equipment like the television, computer and microwave controls.

For thirty minutes the search continued before the agents gathered back in the living room.

'We'll take the alien women with us,' snapped the Sergeant.

'That wasn't what we agreed,' Val retorted. 'We were going to take the rings and leave.

'Look Major,' the sergeant replied. 'You're outside your jurisdiction here. My boss wants results and so does yours, actually. This is no time to get all sentimental.'

'I still don't like it,' she muttered. 'You didn't have to wreck the place and I don't condone kidnapping.'

The sergeant shrugged and turned to his men 'Do it! he snapped

Pazz, Kylina and Hycerta were bound, gagged, hoisted over men's shoulders and dumped none too gently in the rear of a black van that had backed up the driveway.

*

Duncan turned off the road into a tree lined lane at the back of the farm and drove slowly in the almost tunnel like view caused by the Falcon's headlights.

'There's a small tool shed about twenty meters in,' Lunol said. 'I have a key and it'll be a perfect place to put the computer box.'

He opened the glove box and reached for it. However when he touched it his mind was blasted with both computers screaming into his mind. He grabbed his friend's arm and the voices filled Duncan's mind, too.

'Our humans have been attacked. Let us out of the box,' the voices vibrated together so the sound ended up like a gigantic echo screaming in their minds. Duncan braked so hard the Falcon stalled and almost drove into trees on the left.

'What is it?' he snapped.

'Pazz, Kylina and Hycerta are unconscious and are being transported across town at a speed which suggests they're in a motor vehicle,' Epsilon communicated.

'Open the box and put your rings on. We can find them!' Theta added. Though similar, Duncan could recognize her different speech, or whatever the thought patterns were called.

He glanced at Lunol, nodded and jumped back in fright. When Lunol opened the lid two spinning hissing rings spun up out of the boxes like tiny helicopters.

'Open a window,' Epsilon ordered.

Lunol did so and the two spinning discs disappeared into the darkness outside.

Duncan stared at Lunol's shaken face. 'Well, we're committed,' he said. 'We might as well put our rings on.'

He reached for his ring.

'Thank you, Duncan,' Epsilon's voice immediately filled his mind. 'We shall intercept this vehicle and attempt to stop it. As well, we'll guide you to us. At the moment we believe the vehicle is on the expressway heading towards the city center. Head that direction.'

'Right,' grunted Duncan.

He reversed the car up the lane, swung around and headed back the direction they had come. It was about six kilometers to the expressway.

'Can you tell us what happened?' Lunol asked.

'Hycerta has an interior transmitter that she set off. We received a call from Omega and told her human is incapacitated and unconscious. We assume Pazz and Kylina are, too. Hycerta's transmitter is the one we're tracing. There is no further information.'

'Where are you?' Duncan spoke orally as he accelerated along the empty city streets.

'We are flying at an altitude of a hundred meters and closing in on the transmitted signal. We believe the vehicle continues to head towards the city center. Have you reached the expressway?'

'It's a couple of blocks,' Duncan retorted and skidded left when his headlights lit up a sign showing the direction to an on ramp. 'We would be about five kilometers behind you.'

'Thank you. We'll stop the vehicle when you are closer. Hurry, please. It may be more difficult in the suburban streets.'

*

Ten minutes later Duncan and Lunol saw the taillights of a van in front of them.

'That must be the vehicle,' Lunol said in a calm voice. 'Can you give us any sign, Theta,' he said.

'Will do,' the computer replied.

Immediately, the lights on the van flickered off and brakes screamed as the frightened driver realized something was wrong. The van swung left, right and almost toppled over before the driver gained control as the lights went back on.

'That's it,' Duncan said.

'Pull up close and get ready to pull our humans out,' Theta replied. 'We'll be stopping soon and will attempt to incapacitate the kidnappers. There are only two aboard.'

*

'Slow down!' barked the sergeant. 'We don't want an accident.'

'The bloody lights went out,' the driver retorted but he was quite shaken and decreased speed. Luckily the expressway was empty and his swerve across two lanes didn't hit anyone traveling by. He gripped the steering wheel and wiped a hand across his perspiring brow. 'It seems okay now,' he muttered. He did not notice the faint humming sound above or hear a tiny clunk as a small metal object attached itself to the roof.

Suddenly, without warning the motor cut out.

'Damn!' snapped the driver. He glided into the curb and turned the key in an unsuccessful attempt to restart the motor.

'Well, get it going!' snapped the sergeant, 'The last thing we want is a patrol car to pull in beside us.'

'I'm trying,' snapped the driver. He turned the key again, it rumbled but nothing fired.

'Bugger!' the man swore and opened his door.

That was all the flying rings needed. One touched the driver's neck; he gave a scream of agony and slumped unconscious on the ground as a charge of electricity surged through his body. The sergeant gasped and was about to reach over when he also jerked up and grunted when a powerful jolt of electricity incapacitated him. Both men were unconscious by the time the Falcon pulled in behind.

'Come on!' Duncan called. He rushed to the van and grabbed the back door handle.

'They're in here,' he hissed. 'Give us a hand.'

The Falcon's headlights lit the interior as the men lifted the three clones, still bound, gagged and unconscious, out of the van. While Lunol shut the van door and ran around to switch the van's lights off, Duncan opened the car's roadside doors.

'Get down!' screamed Lunol. 'A car's coming.'

Lights flashed into them for a second, there was a rush of air and a car roared past. 'Suckers!' someone screamed out a window and they were alone again.

'Give me a hand,' Duncan hissed.

'The driver's half out the door,' Lunol snapped back 'I have to get him in.'

Duncan half-lifted and half dragged the second clone, he thought it was Kylina, into the back seat and heard a door slam shut.

Lunol appeared beside him carrying the third clone in his arms.

'The back!' Duncan snapped and ran and lifted the tailgate of the station wagon.

'Kylina!' Lunol almost sobbed and tenderly placed her in the back space.

'No, I had Kylina,' Duncan almost grinned. 'That was Hycerta.'

'Okay,' grunted Lunol. He ran to the front and slammed all the doors. 'What about the rings?'

'We're here,' said a voice. 'Get going. Another car is coming.'

'On my way,' muttered Duncan and headed out along the express way. 'Can you get them untied?'

'I'll try,' Lunol replied and slid over into the back.

'I'll head back to the farm,' Duncan said a few moments later.

It took a while in the swaying car but Lunol managed to untie and maneuver the three women into as comfortable positions as possible with one in the rear area and two lying across his lap on the back seat.

'Their pulses seem okay.' Lunol reported 'I think that were given some sort of knock out drug but where are Lynn and Jason?' he gasped.

'Try the mobile.'

Lunol nodded, gently lifted the two women off himself, scrambled through to the front seat and reached in the glove box. He punched in Lynn's number and waited as it rang. Six rings, seven!

'Damn!' he said and was about to click off when Lynn's groggy voice answered.

'Lynn, it's Lunol. Are you safe?'

'I think so,' she replied. 'Jason is bawling his head off and I have a splitting headache but Lunol, the place… ' Her voice broke into a sob. 'It's wrecked and the others aren't around.'

'We have them,' Lunol replied. 'Listen Lynn. Keep talking but have a look outside. Is there anyone there?' He could hear the toddler's howls in the background.

'I'm scared Lunol,' Lynn cried. 'My God! Everything's smashed to hell. My clothes are even ripped!'

'You'll be okay, Lynn. Turn off the lights and look out the front window. If anyone is there you'll see them in the street light.'

He waited for a few seconds before Lynn's voice came back, sounding a little stronger. 'Nothing's there,' she reported.

'Good. Find your car keys; gather up Jason and drive to the farm. You know where it is, don't you?'

'Yes!' Lynn answered, 'but don't hang up, Lunol. Let me talk to Pazz.'

'She's unconscious, Lynn. They all are but are safe in the Falcon.'

'Thank God!' gasped Lynn. 'I have to put the phone down to get Jason ready but don't hang up. Please.'

'I won't' Lunol promised.

*

Back home, Lynn stood trembling as she saw the devastation around. 'Come on, Sweetheart,' she cried to her son. 'We're going for a ride

---

212

to see Auntie Pazz.'

'I'm cold, Mummy,' Jason whimpered. 'Why is everything a big mess, Mummy?'

'It's okay, Sweetheart,' Lynn cried. 'Come on. Put your new jacket on.'

'My head hurts, Mommy!'

'I know, Sweetheart but be a brave boy.' Lynn dressed Jason and grabbed the mobile phone again.' Lunol!'

'I'm here, Lynn. We're off the expressway now and heading to the farm. Would you like us to wait for you.'

'No,' said Lynn. 'I'll be okay.'

She turned back and took Jason's hand, found the keys from their usual place and walked outside. The driveway seemed empty. With a trembling hand she switched the lights off and locked the door. The eight meters to the garage was like a trip through hell. Every second she expected a hand to grasp her but it was quiet. She pressed the automatic door button and the door slid up.

Lynn breathed out. So far, so good. 'Come on Sweetheart,' she whispered, 'Crawl in through Mummy's seat.'

They were in the car. Lynn's hands were shaking so hard she could hardly fit the key in. She did though, and swallowed in an attempt to lubricate her dry throat.

'Here goes,' she said into the mobile phone, started the motor, accelerated out and down the drive.

Her car almost hit the side fence but Lynn corrected in time and accelerated down the street. My God there was a car across the road to the left and men weree running towards her!

'Shit!' she screamed and turned to the right, up another no exit road. At the end, though, Lynn remembered there was a walkway.

The tiny car hit the small walkway barrier, designed to stop bicycles; not cars, and drove forward between two wooden fences just as two men almost touched the back of the vehicle. There was another barrier at the other end of the walkway but Lynn was too terrified to even slow. The front bumper hit this barrier and smashed through like matchwood. Lynn braked, turned to the left and accelerated into the night

'I saw two men running after us,' she screamed into the mobile phone. 'But I'm away now.'

'Okay,' Duncan's voice said. 'Zigzag around and stay off the main road. Make your way across town. We'll be at the back entrance to the farm. Do you know where it is.'

'I think so,' Lynn replied. 'I'm okay now. You can hang up. I'll call if

I need help.'

'It's okay,' Lunol was back on the line. 'I can talk. Duncan's doing all the hard work here.'

Twenty minutes later Lynn burst into tears as she saw the Falcon waiting under a streetlight and not one, but four people waving to her. She pulled in and noticed three very white faced sisters standing on the curb. The passenger door opened and one, she thought it was Pazz climbed in and gave Jason a big cuddle.

'Hello Sweetheart,' she said and kissed the little boy who was still sobbing quietly. 'Have you been looking after Mummy for us?' Pazz turned to Lynn. 'We'll go to Lunol's office. Just follow Duncan.'

'Oh Pazz,' sobbed Lynn. 'I've never been so terrified. The mobile phone woke me and all I could see was the house in ruins. The bastards junked our whole house.'

'But you and Jason are safe and they didn't get the rings,' Pazz said in the semi-darkness. She held her hand up and the ring was back on her finger.

*

'How about flying out and back to Omega?' Hycerta said in a quiet voice. 'The Learjet can be in at daybreak.'

Apart from throbbing headaches and sore wrists the three abducted women were in a reasonable condition. They all sat crowded in Lunol's tiny office discussing the next move. Jason had fallen asleep; this time in Kylina's arms and Lunol handed drinks of tea around in beat up tin mugs.

'How?' gasped Pazz. She smiled at Lunol and accepted a drink.

'Broden will fly in if I ask him.'

'Can we risk it?' Duncan asked. 'They're sure to have the airport covered.'

'I'd say if we don't go tomorrow, it'll be too late,' Hycerta added 'The aircraft may be still unknown by the agents but I doubt if it'll take them too long to trace it back to me.'

Early the following morning the Falcon and headed into the airport car park. Five weary adults and an excited little boy walked casually through the Domestic Terminal to a Learjet that had just taxied up the tarmac.

They boarded and the aircraft turned around. Just as the small jet approached the runway, five police cars skidded to a stop in front of the Domestic Terminal and a dozen police and security agents fanned out.

Though dressed in civilian clothes General Jarvis looked every bit a military man as he stared at the small white jet roar along the runway and lift into the sky.

He turned to the man beside him. 'You got a Goddamn air force base in this town?'

Dean Diriwi sighed. 'Three F1-11s are being scrambled now, General but I doubt if they'll do much good.'

'Anyone would think you were on their side, Mr. Diriwi,' the general grunted.

'Sides, General?' Diriwi replied. 'If you're classifying this as some glorified game, I'd say we're losing every play, aren't we? Your men at Elden Crescent would not have been any more successful than mine. It's as if they anticipated every move we made. '

'They aren't a couple of dumb chicks or are there three? I'll give you that much,' Jarvis grumbled. 'Now they walk out to their personal jet and fly away. God, you'd think they owned the country!'

'How were we to know they had a jet sitting on the tarmac waiting for them?' Dean added. 'Only when we discovered that Learjet had filed no flight record, did we realize…'

'That was a slick move, I must admit,' the general relented. 'Everyone's looking for a UFO and they use a perfect, dime a dozen, business jet.'

He broke into a grin. 'I'm beginning to come around to your way of thinking, though, Son. If they wanted to roast us alive, I reckon they'd have done it by now. I wouldn't mind talking to those young women, though.'

'Well, why don't we try a diplomatic approach,' Diriwi advised. 'That might just work where everything else failed.'

The general glared at the other man and shrugged. 'I've never been a bleeding liberal but you could be right,' he sniffed. 'Anyhow, how about some breakfast? I'll shout you in that overpriced terminal of yours.'

Dean Diriwi smiled. 'Okay,' he replied. 'I certainly could do with some toast and coffee.

*

CHAPTER TWENTY-ONE

The three RAAF F1-11 s caught up with the Learjet over the Eyre Peninsular west of Adelaide and slowed down to surround the small innocent looking business plane.

'Red Leader to Red 2,' Broden 6th Castle heard over his earphones and grinned at Hycerta sitting in the co-pilot's seat next to him. 'Maintain position above civilian jet. I'll try to make radio contact.'

'You'd better tell the passengers to clamp their harnesses on. We'll switch in the anti-matter motors soon,' he said. The tall slim man with piercing green eyes and a lazy smile, spoke perfect English just like his female compatriots.

'Right,' Hycerta said, reached across and squeezed his arm before poking her head into the cabin behind. 'Fasten up, Folks' she said. 'The journey is about to begin.'

'What about the RAAF fighters?' Duncan replied. 'They're all around and signaling for us to return to Adelaide.'

'Broden's going to pretend to turn back and when they're further away, we'll switch in the main motors. We don't want to damage them.' Hycerta said.

The Learjet dipped a wing and flew into a slow downward curve while the three F 1-11s, who had difficulty in maintaining a slow speed, moved up and out in wider curves. This was what the Learjet required. Without warning, the wings and tail slid into the fuselage, shutters covered the cabin windows and an exhaust opening appeared where the tail had been. There was a shudder, flames and white bellowing smoke shot out behind the former business jet and it shot forward, through the sound barrier within seconds and arched up towards the stratosphere.

'Holy shit!' the radio cackled as one of the fighter pilots watched the spacecraft accelerate forward and upwards in a vapor trail of white.

Hycerta felt the usual G-Forces pushing her body into the seat but felt relaxed. She knew the computer had everything in control and within moments they'd be weightless and well on their way to Omega 31. She almost felt sorry for the three pilots left behind in their primitive jet fighters.

The newest Omega Inter-galactical Starship was smaller than Omega 17 or 1 but was still spherical shaped with the interior almost a duplicate of the older craft. Once aboard, Hycerta and Broden showed the new arrivals through to spacious quarters and afterwards, to another natural area in the center. This also had the feel of a park on Earth except the pathway on each side seemed even steeper from where they stood, due to the smaller inside circumference of Omega 31.

'Look at me, Mummy!' Jason laughed and ran along the little cobblestone path. To run level but end up looking back at his mother on a hillside behind him. He glanced at the blue sky above and the filtered sunlight, dipped his hand in the tiny forty-centimeter wide stream and ran running back to be swept into Lynn's arms. 'Can I have an ice cream, Auntie Hycerta?' he asked.

'Say please,' scolded Lynn but grinned as Hycerta took the little boy in her arms.

'Come on,' Hycerta said. 'I'm sure Uncle Broden will have something in the kitchen.' She glanced at the other women. 'Much of our food is artificially made but is complimented by fresh produce. That's why I always like to restock from Earth. You can't beat real ice cream and dairy products.' When they reached the kitchen, she took a scoop of ice cream from a container, placed it on a cone and handed it to Jason. 'Don't forget to lick around the edge,' she said.

'I won't, Auntie Hycerta,' he replied and sat at the table. The room could have been overlooking a park in Adelaide.

'I'll make us some lunch,' Broden said and walked through to the tiny pantry on their left. Lynn and Kylina smiled and walked across to help while Duncan and Lunol became engaged in a conversation about something.

Pazz glanced up and found Hycerta's eyes on her. 'I like Broden,' she said in a soft voice. 'He seems so relaxed and easy going.'

'Yes but eyes only. ,' Hycerta said. 'You've got Duncan, remember.'

Pazz chuckled. 'I know,' she replied and thought how the two men were similar. Their physical appearance was different but mannerisms and personality were so similar, it was uncanny.

'No,' said Hycerta as if she read Pazz's mind. 'I didn't purposely pick a partner to be like Duncan; it just worked out that way,' She gave Pazz a warm smile. 'Think about it, Pazz. Lunol is similar in nature too, you know.'

'He is,' Pazz said. 'Our choice of partners is another cloned trait, I guess.' She stopped and sat for a moment, deep in thought before she spoke again. ' I'm so glad you returned even if it took an emergency to do it.'

'I was going to anyhow,' Hycerta replied, 'This crisis just jogged me on and, I must admit, motivated Broden, too. I told him I was coming and wanted him with me and that was it.'

'Bossy, bit,' Pazz teased.

Hycerta stood and gave her clone a wee hug. 'If it wasn't for you,' she said in a whisper. 'I wouldn't be me. You know, they hardly ever clone at home now. It's out of fashion, I guess. With half the younger population males, most women want a natural pregnancy.'

Pazz gazed thoughtfully at Hycerta. 'I didn't realize,' she said.' I do know, though that without Kylina and yourself around I'd be pretty lost and lonely.'

'Not with Duncan, surely,' Hycerta laughed.

'Okay,' said Pazz, 'but thanks for coming back. I felt so wretched when you left for home from Planet 21974.3, I...'

'I know,' Hycerta replied. 'I thought about you all every day for months.' She smiled to herself and stood up. 'Come on, let's see how the meal's getting on.'

*

Artificial night settled over the park of Omega 31, supper was over and the adults had been discussing their problems for over an hour and ended up almost talking in circles.

'As one of two adult Earthlings here may I make a few suggestions?' Duncan grinned at Lynn and continued. 'One, I think we have two civilizations to deal with. It is your decision, of course, but I don't think you, Hycerta and Broden, should risk going home to a trial. I suspect you will not be as lucky this time. We need to somehow persuade the authorities on Delta, Earth is too insignificant to worry about.

Secondly, we need to dissuade Earth governments from trying to capture Omega and also stop them harassing us so we can continue our life in peace.'

'One big order,' Lunol replied.

'Not necessarily,' Lynn interjected. 'Duncan and I were talking about it. For close on fifty years we had peace between the major powers on Earth through mutual fear.'

Hycerta frowned. 'What do you mean?' she asked.

'Everyone was too scared to start a nuclear war because they feared being wiped out in retaliation.'

'So?'

'This is more your line,' Duncan continued. 'Couldn't you use Omega to give a demonstration of power, so fearful that the governments on Earth would be too scared to even try anything against you?'

'I see,' Broden's face creased into a frown. 'Something spectacular to impress the militants like those secret service agents who tried to kidnap

Hycerta, Pazz and Kylina.'

'…And so powerful, they'd even be too intimidated to expose our identities and we can live in peace without having to fear attacks all the time,' Pazz added. She glanced at Hycerta and Broden. 'You're the military people here with eighty years more technology than Kylina and myself. Any ideas?'

'But you don't want people actually killed?' Hycerta replied. 'You want a show of force and an offer of peace if we're left alone?'

'Exactly,' Duncan replied. 'A hundred years ago they used to call it gunboat diplomacy.'

Hycerta looked mischievously at her partner. 'Add a few illusions, a touch of melodrama and…'

'… Peace forever,' Broden said. 'Why not!'

*

The USAF C-141B Starlifter was a veteran freighter that still flew equipment and personnel to remote American military bases throughout the world. This particular one was on it's way from Canberra to Magaroona Research Base with General Bradley Jarvis, Val Wikstrom and Dean Diriwi the only passengers jammed in a small area behind the cockpit.

'We cannot find the alien craft but I have a gut feeling it is still out there in orbit,' the general muttered. 'Perhaps this new electronic tracking equipment we're lugging in will help find it.'

Diriwi nodded. He had his own theories but preferred to keep them to himself and there was also the detailed report of the failed abduction to consider. The two drivers of the van, apart from a bit of pride, were entirely unhurt and the vehicle started on first touch. Nobody had returned to 19 Elden Crescent and he had not been impressed with the ramshackling of the house. He grunted and hoped his orders to clean it up and replace everything damaged had been carried out.

'I don't think we'll ever hear or see them again, General,' Val added as she stared out at the desert below.

'But you are wrong, Major,' a quiet voice stated beside her.

Val leaped in fright and saw one of the D'rose woman standing at the end of the cabin. She was dressed in a dark blue military type uniform with dress skirt and jacket done up to the neck .A small square collar and left pocket with the Omega insignia completed the jacket. As well, she wore black stockings, calf length boots with a side zip and white gloves. The clothing was crisp and would make any military academy proud.

'Don't be concerned,' the woman said. 'I am but a holograph speaking to you from Omega 31, a military starship. I am a commander in the services of the Delta Inter-galatic Peace Keeping Force.'

'Kylina?' Val gasped.

'No,' came the reply. 'Commander Hycerta Sixth Flower. The six stands for the generation of my family. Pazz, in our language is Fourth Flower. She simplified the surname to D'rose here on Earth.'

'You mean you are not triplets?' Dean replied. In spite of himself he trembled at the sudden appearance of this alien woman.

'That is correct,' said Hycerta.' My birth mother was Pazz's sister's granddaughter and I was born eighty years after her. I am her clone. Kylina is her natural sister but back on Delta was twenty years younger than Pazz. We are now more or less the same age due to being in suspended animation on our journeys to Earth.'

She turned slightly to face General Jarvis. 'I came to Earth to rescue my two clone ancestors from a epidemic of fungi that, unfortunately the starship that brought Pazz, Kylina and Lunol here was carrying. Pazz persuaded me, General, to use my ship's powers to reverse time and save your planet.'

'So that video showed a real event?' the general stated in quiet precise words.

'Yes. I broke our laws by doing this and am now a fugitive just because I saved this puny little planet, General; this insignificant little piece of humanity of the outer edge of the known universe. I did it because of my love for my cloned grand aunts, I guess Pazz and Kylina are.' Her voice turned hard. 'I wish to get paid back by a brutal kidnapping and wrecking of my dear friend's house. You think of yourselves as civilized nations on an advanced planet! '

'The agents stepped beyond their orders,' Dean said. 'They shall be disciplined and 19 Elmer Crescent completely restored to its original condition.'

'Of course,' Hycerta's blue eyes switched to the Australian. 'There is always revenge in this society, Mr. Diriwi. Something is wrong so some poor person is answerable. You blame these men, fire them and think that solves the problem. A month later more men, and they are usually males, do exactly the same thing somewhere else. It is a primitive attitude, Sir.'

Dean Diriwi grimaced, flushed slightly but did not reply.

Hycerta sat in a vacant seat and crossed her legs. 'But that is not the reason for this visit, gentlemen and Major Wikstrom. This is!' She reached in her pocket and brought out a tiny dragonfly shaped object.

'What the!' the general snarled as the Starlifter's right wing dropped, the engine sound altered and the giant jet freighter changed course.

'Your journey has been lengthened somewhat, General,' Hycerta said in a calm voice. 'Don't worry for you have enough fuel. Your military very prudently full your aircraft up with aviation fuel in case there is a change of flight orders.'

'Young lady,' snapped the general.

'Commander is my ranking, General,' Hycerta's voice was like ice. 'It is approximately equivalent to your own. The aircraft is under our control. Ask your pilots if you wish.'

She glanced up as a grim looking air force officer opened the door and walked in. The man jumped in alarm at the sight of Hycerta but was disciplined enough to continued on to the general.

'All controls on the aircraft are frozen, Sir!' he reported. 'We have changed course north-west.'

'Towards the nuclear testing grounds the British used forty five years ago to be precise,' the alien woman responded. 'Sit back and relax. We'll be there for the demonstration in fifty two minutes flying time.'

'Demonstration!' the general snapped. His face turned hard, he stood up and reached for Hycerta. However his hand went clean through her arm.

'Remember, I am not here, General Jarvis,' Hycerta said. 'Actually I am sitting at a console in my starship looking at a vision of you. If you'd like to punch me in the face to vent your frustrations, do so. Don't hit the wall, though. It may hurt.'

'Damn you, woman!' Jarvis snarled but sat down.

'In our world, General Jarvis, women have over ninety percent of the responsibilities. In Pazz's time, males were merely used for restocking the sperm banks and consisted of point one percent of the population. I'm beginning to see why our ancestors took this position.'

Val gave a slight grin as the general glowered.

'At the moment a flybug like the one in my hand is approaching the nuclear test site. It shall arrive when we do.'

'What for?' snapped the general.

'A tiny demonstration of our power to show what can happen if you ever try to meddle in out affairs again. Excuse me. I am about to have my morning coffee.' she said and the holograph vanished.

'I think she holds all the cards, General,' Dean Diriwi commented in a dry voice. 'Remember, you did want to see her again.'

'Damn you, too!' Jarvis retorted and glared out the window.

Val looked around. The flybug was sitting on the seat where Hycerta had been. She reached across and touched it. The object was made of a cold substance but it was there! The flybug was not a holograph.

'General Jarvis,' she said and handed it to him.

Jarvis reached out and took the small object in his hand. 'Thank you, Major,' he said and studied it intently. 'It's like a model aircraft,' he commented a few moments later as he held it up in the light.' What harm could this do?'

'I think we are about to find out, General,' Dean Diriwi added philosophically. ' A demonstration of power, I think the commander said it was going to be.'

*

The Starlifter was flying at twelve thousand metres, well above it's normal operating height when Hycerta appeared again, but this time she was dressed in a neat business suit.

'Hi,' she said warmly. 'It's Pazz. Please put your seatbelts on. '

The general glowered but reached across and clipped his into place.

'We are about to drop a microgram of anti-matter above this site,' Pazz said. 'In ten seconds, actually.'

Exactly ten seconds later there was a rumble and the heavy aircraft was tossed sideways like a paper dart. The desert below became a huge cylinder of sheering orange flames that turned to white then brown as sand and debris was sucked skywards for ten thousand metres. For one minute, exact to a second, the explosion continued and fanned out. Millions of tonnes of rocks and soil shot skywards as the rumble arrived like a thousand thunderbolts rolled into one.

The passengers clamped hands over their ears but still the sound rocked their eardrums. The aircraft screamed and shot upwards, straight up six hundred metres. The engines stalled and it plummeted down in an agonizing, terrifying plunge straight towards the desert below.

Outside, the sky disappeared as twirling red and brown dust enveloped the aircraft. Val felt violently ill and her eyes bulged as if someone was pinching them from behind. This was worse than re-entry into the atmosphere after a space shuttle flight. She held on and could only now hear screams, screams of agony and fear. Before she blacked out she realized the screams were her own.

After an unknown time Val felt cold and forced her eyes open. The Starlifter was level and all engines were going. The general and Diwiri were slumped in their seats beside her.

'They'll be okay,' said a voice.

Val looked up. 'Pazz!' she gasped and immediately went into a coughing fit.

'No, I am Kylina,' came the reply. 'When your general comes around, tell him there is a five-kilometer wide crater below. It would be, I guess a hundred meters deep but will probably refill almost back to the surface by the time everything falls back to earth.' She smiled. 'We just wanted him to know our powers are real and not a bluff.

Three other things. Keep an eye on the heavens at 0200 hours local time tomorrow morning. The radio telescope will be on the correct frequency on the day in question. And we would appreciate being left in peace in Adelaide'

'And the third thing,' Val asked in a shaken voice.

'Pazz and myself are having a double wedding,' Kylina beamed. 'You're invited.'

She turned to where General Jarvis and Dean Diriwi both opened their eyes. The general groaned and was violently ill in a paper bag he managed to grasp. 'Poor man,' she said. 'I guess it's about time he retired and began to enjoy life.'

The vision faded and the three passengers were alone. Val gazed around and noticed the flybug had also disappeared. 'I'll love to come to your wedding, Kylina,' she said into the empty air.

'The invitation is in the mail,' Kylina's voice filled the cabin. 'Have a nice day.'

*

At two o'clock the following morning an uncloaked starship appeared in a low orbit across Australia and could even be seen by the naked eye as a long meteorite traveling southeast. However, no sooner did the Magaroona Radio Telescope get a fix on it when the monitors all flashed to an interior view and one of the D'rose clones appeared on screen in full military uniform.

'This is our farewell,' she said in a quiet voice. 'Earth is safe from external bacteria at the moment. One day, perhaps we shall return. Meanwhile, look after our four immigrants from the stars. Their combined knowledge can be of great benefit to mankind,' She stopped and pouted. 'Sexist word, isn't it?'

The picture faded and a vision of the Earth replaced it. Suddenly, there was a slight jerk and the Earth began to diminish in size. Within five minutes it was the size of an orange, two minutes later a golf ball, then a pea.

'We are about to enter light speed so this vision will fade. Look after yourselves.'

'It's gone, Sir,' reported a scientist. 'Last recorded speed was 190 000 kilometers a second.'

'Then it changed into high gear,' said Val Wikstrom.

*

Back at 19 Elden Crescent Pazz turned off Duncan's computer and grinned at Kylina, Hycerta, Lynn and the males gathered around.

'Do you think that will convince them Omega has gone?' she asked.

'Possibly,' Hycerta replied. She sat on the edge of the couch and tucked her arm around Broden. 'Let's hope the information on board convinces the authorities on Delta we are dead and Earth is not worth including on their list of humanoid planets.'

'Meanwhile,' laughed Kylina. 'We still have Omega 17 out there if we ever need her.'

'Not to mention two Learjets at our beckoned call,' added Pazz.

She stood up and tucked her arms around Duncan's waist from behind, pulled him back and placed a kiss on the back of his neck. 'I like these primitive Earth seeders,' she said.

'Almost as good as those from Custonumus,' Kylina replied.

'Or Delta,' Hycerta still dressed in her uniform from the vision they'd made earlier, added.

*

The wedding, three weeks later was larger than planned. Hycerta and Broden had already taken mating vows back on Delta but were persuaded to enter an Earth contract as well. It was going to be a small civil service on the university lawn but attracted far more attention than anticipated. After all, Duncan and Pazz were two highly respected lecturers at the University of Adelaide while Kylina and Lunol both had a circle of friends from the supermarket, racing stables and The School of Fine Arts. The press was interested in three identical triplets being married and one weekly women's magazine had not one, but two photographers present.

In a tradition of both home planets and a practice coming in vogue with many modern Earth couples, Pazz and Kylina both decided to retain the name D'rose after their marriage while Hycerta became Mrs. Castle, Broden's last name with the generation number omitted. This was a break from tradition on Delta where the male was expected to take the woman's name so the generations could be continued.

'They'd have a field day if they really knew where we're from,' Kylina whispered to her clones as they stood together in identical long white wedding gowns, for yet another photograph as dozens of students hovered around.

'Yeah,' Pazz added, 'And the fact I was almost your age when you were born.'

Kylina gasped, 'I guess you were,' she said. 'No wonder you're getting those wrinkles around the eyes.'

'Watch it, Kid Sister,' Pazz retorted.

'Now could we have the grooms standing beside their brides,' a photographer gushed.

At a prearranged signal, Duncan stood beside Kylina, Lunol sidled up to Hycerta and Broden tucked his hand into Pazz's just as the bulbs flashed. Their masquerade though almost became unstuck when another photographer wanted a photo of the grooms kissing their brides. Duncan turned bright red and slipped behind Kylina to gather Pazz in his arms while Lunol managed a deft sideways movement to kiss his new wife.

'I guess you must be Mrs. Castle,' Broden greeted Hycerta, grabbed her in a massive hug and plastered a kiss on her lips. It was something one did not do in public back on Delta. Having men in society was all very well but open fraternization between the sexes was still not done in public places.

There were howls of delight from the audience with cheers and spontaneous clapping at the impromptu performance. Even bridesmaid Lynn was taken by complete surprise as she lifted Jason onto her shoulders so he could see his beautiful aunts being photographed.

'They look pretty, Mummy,' the little boy said. 'Just like you.'

'Why thank you, Sweetheart,' Lynn laughed and tickled his legs.

Six people from three planets became three couples on a sunny Saturday afternoon in a civil ceremony in the grounds of the university. It was a day to remember.

*

General Bradley Jarvis glowered at the senators representing the top secret investigation on whether Earth had been visited by an alien life force .He stood and turned over the first page of a thick document in front of him.

'To summarize, Ladies and Gentlemen of this Senate Inquiry, I have had complete cooperation of our Australian counterparts and in particular,

Mr. Dean Diwiri of Australia's Prime Minister's Office of Special Security. We have evidence showing there was no alien presence in that country what-so-ever. Every lead can be explained by natural occurrences. We do believe, though, a small group of protesters deliberately set out to manufacture a gigantic hoax by using sophisticated equipment to infiltrate the Magaroona Research Station Radio Telescope.' He coughed and took a sip of water from a glass on his desk. 'It is detailed in my report.'

Senator Clarence O'Neil, the chairperson of the committee, turned the pages of his copy of the report. 'This is an about face, General Jarvis,' he said. 'Why only a month ago you told this very committee you had proof that a university research scientist at The University of Adelaide was, in face an alien.'

General Jarvis nodded. 'Doctor Pazz D'rose is a highly respected and talented person, Senator but it appears she was a victim of a smear campaign by hostile colleagues seeking to discredit her recent findings. That, along with the hoax computer feeds into the Research Station had me fooled for quite a while.'

'But being a pragmatic man you decided to find further evidence to prove or disprove these theories?'

'That is correct,' the general replied with a slight smile. 'I think when one would like something to happen they can be blinded to evidence that points the other way.'

Somehow, the towering strength of a man who'd proved himself in Vietnam and The Desert Storm of Kuwait showed his full sixty-one years as he began to read the details of the last report he would officially write. It may have been imagination but his hands seemed to shake slightly as he took another sip of water and gazed around the room when he completed his report.

'We shall study your conclusions and recommendations, General and thank you for the time you devoted to this investigation. Also we wish you well in your upcoming retirement,' the senator concluded. 'That was an unexpected and sudden decision.'

'Well,' Bradley Jarvis grimaced and looked almost embarrassed. 'The good wife got sick of me galloping all over the globe and, after thirty-five years, I finally decided to listen to her. I need to reduce my golf handicap, too.'

*

Pazz sat in the air conditioned apartment in her bikini, sipped a wine and gazed out at the waves breaking twenty floors down and across the golden sands of Surfer's Paradise in Queensland. The honeymoon was almost over and she still had not broken the news to Duncan.

He walked in the door with an armful of food, plunked them on the coffee table, walked over and placed his arms around her.

'Duncan,' Pazz said almost shyly. 'I've got something to share with you.'

Duncan sat on the beach chair and tugged Pazz down so she was on his knees. 'So you found out too, 'he said and kissed her ear.

Pazz frowned. 'What do you mean; too?' she asked.

'Lunol told me,' Duncan said as he reached for a slice of pizza and bit into it. 'Lunol. How does he know?' Pazz retorted.

'Well, Dear. They are married. Why shouldn't a man know when his wife is pregnant? Kylina is about six weeks on,' he confessed.

'Oh My God! I didn't know,' Pazz gasped.

Duncan frowned. 'Wasn't that what you were talking about, Pazz?' he asked.

'No,' she laughed. 'I was talking about us. Me!' Her eyes looked directly into his.

'You don't mean?' Duncan stuttered.

'Yes,' Pazz said. 'About two months actually. '

Duncan just stared and broke into a smile. 'So the aliens are about to reseed our planet,' he chuckled and wrapped his arms around his wife. 'I wonder if we make a great leap forward like the ancient Greeks did.'

'Oh Duncan,' Pazz chuckled. 'I'm sure our daughter will be a perfectly ordinary little girl.'

'Girl?

'Yes,' laughed Pazz. 'Epsilon told me.'

'I could have guessed,' Duncan replied, stood up and lowered Pazz to the floor. 'Coming to tell the other honeymooners?" Duncan said. 'The way you clones operate, we'll probably find Hycerta is in the same condition, too.'

He held a large towel out to wrap her in, grabbed her hand and escorted her to the door. She turned, blue eyes twinkled and her hand reached back to clasp his. Outside, the sun blazed down from a cloudless sky, breakers curled up and crashed on the sand just as they had been doing for hundreds of millennia. In that insignificant little planet on the edge of the known universe, the young woman and her husband were, once again, about to prove the immortality of the human species.

The End

www.ingramcontent.com/pod-product-compliance
Lightning Source LLC
Chambersburg PA
CBHW050735230626
47052CB00002BA/195